THE MANIPULATOR

A Novel By
Mary W. Syreen

To Bill and LaVenia —
Best Wishes
and enjoy!

Mary Syreen

4/4/01

Published by: Lakeside Press
433 Mountain View Lane
Anacortes, WA 98221

This book is a work of fiction and all characters, unless well-known celebrities, are figments of the author's imagination. Names of places are used in a fictitious manner and have no relationship to events that actually happen.

This book may not be reproduced by any means in whole or in part, except for a brief review, without permission. For information contact Lakeside Press, 433 Mountain View Lane, Anacortes, WA 98221.

ACKNOWLEDGMENTS

This book would not have been possible
without the advice and assistance of
Kevin Cox. His proficient contributions
were immeasurable and he deserves
more credit than this short paragraph offers.
I will be eternally grateful.

For Marilyn Cox who chose the title,
thank you. It fits the book perfectly.

To Charlie Raleigh who opened up a new
world to me and gives me time to pursue
my dreams.

For Mike, Jim, Shelley, Ben, Tim, Jennifer,
Stephanie, Makayla, and soon Trevor Michael.

To Linda Keltz for her skilled help.

To my friends who offered encouragement
and to those of you who buy my book, I do
thank all of you very much.

Also by Mary Syreen

CONSEQUENCES

HE THAT HIDETH HATRED WITH LYING LIPS
AND HE THAT UTTERETH A SLANDER, IS
A FOOL

- Proverbs 10:18

CHAPTER ONE

"So why not me? What's wrong with me?" Didi threw her five foot one-inch one-hundred pound body across the still unmade bed and raised her snapping brown eyes defiantly to Richard, as he now wanted to be called.

"There's nothing wrong with you." Richard put the emphasis on the word "wrong," but his voice reflected disgust. "I'm planning a different lifestyle as I've told you a thousand times."

"You liked our lifestyle plenty of times, Ricky." She drawled out the Ricky.

"You keep doing that."

"Doing what?"

"Calling me Ricky. A hundred times I've told you to call me Richard. I'm not the Ricky-type anymore."

He walked to the full-length mirror at the other end of the room and ran his fingers through his ash-blond hair, turning his head this way and that, striking various poses. He was tall, six-foot two and carried one hundred eighty pounds on his hard-as-nails frame. His daily workouts and nutritious diet kept him in top physical condition. For the past six months he had diligently groomed himself to project an affluent personality. Not just physically, but mentally as well. He gave up the Friday night poker games and took bridge lessons. He spent hours in the city library learning about composers and the ballet. He studied the biographies of famous men. He even read American History.

Richard memorized the names of American presidents which he never bothered with before. "How To Increase Your Word Power" from Readers' Digest became his Bible. He purchased compact discs of symphony music and played them constantly, relegating the country and western and reggae tapes to the garbage, in spite of Didi's constant protesting that they were hers. When he wasn't perfecting his pronunciation of so many strange words, he stood in front of the mirror practicing various smiles and looks of interest. He had one down pat - the look of complete love and devotion.

Didi wished it was meant for her. Sometimes when he turned toward her and took her in his arms, she almost believed it was. Until he would laugh and say, "Wow, Babe, I really had you going, didn't I?" She would realize that once again it was just an act. His perfect act.

Richard dressed differently now. Instead of tight jeans and loud tee shirts with suggestive remarks, he wore gray polyester pants or cotton Docker's and light blue shirts that matched his eyes. His socks either matched his pants or they were black. No longer were they bright yellow with palm trees or half-naked girls, or any number of what he once thought were stylish. He now put forth elegance, or what he believed elegance to be.

He frequented the exclusive men's shops to browse among the expensive items. He studied the window models and imitated their outfits which he tried to purchase in thrift shops or a warehouse facility. After all, he wanted to look as if he had worn clothes like that all of his life and was too affluent and independent to bother buying new clothes.

Richard read the obituaries and sometimes called to inquire about estate sales. Though most of the time the telephone would bang in his ears, once in awhile he found bargains. He only called when the sale was in a "wealthy" area and his jewelry box boasted of gold cufflinks, a watch or two, gold chains, and rings which had been worn by someone with excellent taste. He managed to slip most of the items into his pockets. Stealing was something he learned how to do at a very young age.

"Do you think I look more like Robert Redford when I turn my head this way or this way?" asked Richard, as he lifted his chin slightly and turned his head to the left and then to the right.

"Are you kidding?" Didi sat up swinging her legs over the side of the queen-size Murphy bed. "I never said you looked like Robert Redford, only your hair is like his. With those gold streaks though it. You don't look anything like Robert Redford."

Didi reached for her nail enamel and began to paint her fingernails a bright blood-red color. She was wearing a skin-tight tee shirt with the word "yes" printed across the front. She was bra-less and knew the effect her body was having on

Richard. She took deep breaths and gazed up at Richard. He reached down and cupped her breast in his hand, but did not push her on her back as she expected.

"Delicious as you are, Didi, I'm heading in another direction."

As she reached up to stroke his face, her wet fingernail brushed the sleeve of his shirt, leaving a vivid red slash.

"Damn it, Didi, look what you've done." Richard wiped at the polish only smearing it. He pushed Didi in the face knocking her back on the bed.

"You've ruined my shirt," he yelled.

"Oh, how much did you pay for that, fifty cents?" Didi scoffed and glared at him. There were red nail polish marks on the yellow spread now.

Richard slapped Didi on the mouth. "Don't you ever make fun of my clothes again."

"Rick—Richard, that hurt." Her eyes filled with tears as she rubbed her mouth and cheek. "You've changed so much. Ever since you, well the past few months you've been so mean to me."

"I'm trying to better myself. Is that so bad?" Richard walked to the small kitchen window, the only one in the apartment. He slammed his fist on the sill. "I want more out of life than living in this so-called apartment. Look at it. It's a real dump. You leave the bed out all day and never bother to put it back up. Those over-stuffed chairs have the springs poking through the cushion and ugly, both of them so damn ugly it must have been a joke whoever made them. And this carpet, what color is it anyway? Red roses on blue. God, can you believe it?" Richard was wound up and angry.

"The table. Formica went out years ago and not one of the chairs without a tear. And this kitchen. Not even enough room to turn around in. If I want more than a six pack, then something else has to come out of that pitiful fridge. God, Didi, I've had it up to here," he drew his finger across his throat, "and you want this kind of life."

"I want you." Her voice was quiet and she held her arms out to him.

"I've worked too hard to stop now, Didi. I'm going to be rich and my wife will have class." Richard looked at Didi with scorn. "Not someone whose hair changes color each week. What is it now?" He flicked up the ends of her hair.

"Red on red or red with black roots. God, Didi you look cheap."

Her eyes were brimming with tears. "So you're tossing four years away. Rick, Richard, I've supported you these past six months so you could, as you call it, better yourself. I thought that was for us so you could get a steady job and we could get a little house and have a baby and a garden."

She gulped back a sob, but the tears spilled out streaking her makeup. When she wiped the tears away, she left smudges of black mascara and eye liner around her eyes.

"You never told me you were looking for a rich girl," sobbed Didi.

"I never told you I would marry you, either. Never did, you know that. Wise up Didi, I don't want a little house." He sneered at the word little. He walked across the small room, picked up a package of gum, unwrapped two sticks and pushed them into his mouth. Then a thought crossed his mind and he threw the gum away. Habits were hard to break. He was sure a rich man would not push gum into his mouth like that.

"And as far as a kid goes, you must be out of your mind. And a cutesy garden? Come on, get real!" Richard could look meaner than anyone she had ever known. His lips curled into a contemptible snarl. While Didi wasn't exactly afraid of him, she lacked the courage to confront him anymore. She pulled her legs up under her and remained quiet.

"I'm going out." Richard put on a clean yellow turtle neck shirt, fastened the belt of his tan pants, took a brown jacket out of the closet and threw his nail polish-smeared shirt at Didi. He lifted his chin and pushed back his hair as he quickly opened the door. He turned at the last minute, pointed at the shirt and said, "Wash it."

Didi sat curled up on the bed for quite some time, contemplating her life. How had she arrived at such a dead end? Why did she always end up the loser? She was twenty-nine years old, and every man who had ever been in her life had walked all over her or just left. Beginning with her father. He walked out on her mother when Didi was three years old. She didn't remember him. Her mother told her he had dark curly hair, almost black eyes and was a real snappy dresser which drew the ladies to him. He never pushed them away, according to her mother.

Her mother put up with the women and the drinking, trying to make a normal home for their little daughter. Then one day her dad said he had found the love of his life in Stella. Away he went with Stella in her white convertible, her red hair flying and Didi's dad waving a bottle of Vodka in the air.

Didi watched the car until it was out of sight, not really understanding what was going on, only knowing something about that car made her mother cry, her head cradled in her arms. Didi ran to her mother and put her little arms around her. Her mother gathered Didi near and after a few moments, the crying stopped.

"It's just you and me now, Didi," said her mother.

And for awhile it was. Then a series of uncles came to live with them. Didi loved them all and they all loved her. Loved her as a daughter and took her to the circus, the candy store, balloon shops, and brought her cute dresses and shoes. Her mother even said they loved Didi more than they did her. Perhaps she was right. But none of them stayed very long. Didi thought she had been in the way and that's why they left.

Then her mother married again and the small family moved to Ellendale where both her mother and step-father became involved in church activities. It didn't appeal to Didi, so she began her wild years. She was in the seventh grade. Her reminiscing was interrupted by the downstairs buzzer. He came back. She joyously ran to the bathroom to wipe a damp cloth over her face.

"Oh, my God," she moaned, "I look like a raccoon." Quickly she ran lipstick across her mouth, sprayed some Esteé behind her ears. She hurried to the door to buzz Richard in. Then she remembered he told her never to buzz open the door unless she knew who was there. She didn't want to set him off again so she asked, "Yes?"

"Hi Didi, it's me, Vinnie. I got some magazines for Richard."

"Okay, he isn't here, but bring them up." Leaving the door ajar, Didi hurried back to the bathroom to slather moisturizer and blush on her face. Her right cheek felt a little puffy.

"Jeez, Didi, what happen to you?" Vinnie had a habit of not ending words or not pronouncing the last syllable. He was short, no more than five and a half feet tall, chunky, with the black Italian hair and brown eyes. His ruddy complexion emphasized his outdoor lifestyle. He worked on the docks in New York City and was the union boss. He got both jobs when he married Ardella. Her dad had been the union leader for years

10

as well as the man to see for any number of services or merchandise.

Vinnie was a good worker, a good husband, and an especially good friend of Ricky's. The two were boyhood friends, perhaps because they were physically opposite. Ricky tall and blond, Vinnie short and dark. They were always on the same side. Each would take up the other's fight. Growing up in Newark, there were many fights. Especially when the Puerto Ricans began moving into the city. Vinnie was quick with a knife and Ricky had a knockout punch. The combination was reason enough for others to test the friends only once.

Ricky and Vinnie learned to fight, to steal, to harass, but never to study. Both dropped out of high school in their junior year. Vinnie stayed around Newark and soon became known as someone the union bosses and politicians could trust. He could deliver almost anything anyone wanted from drugs to whores to votes. It was just a matter of time until he got the attention of Salvador Vacalli, boss of the docks.

Vacalli groomed Vinnie to walk in his shadow. He was impressed with Vinnie's quickness not only in learning how to execute Vacalli's suggestions, but also how easily he could convince others to follow his lead.

Vacalli was not overjoyed that his only child, Ardella, was impressed with Vinnie's other attributes, but he reasoned she could do worse. Beauty wasn't one of her long suits. Neither was brains and Vacalli knew Vinnie would be a good husband or Vinnie would be dead. So the young couple got Vacalli's blessing for their marriage. After a few years, four grandchildren came along. Vacalli was indeed a happy man. He now had two males to carry on his work and two beautiful granddaughters. Even though they did not carry the Vacalli name, Corsica wasn't too bad, Vacalli was a generous father, father-in-law, and grandfather. He provided his daughter with a lovely home on Long Island, away from the crime-ridden area Vinnie grew up in, and a well-paying job to his son-in-law. He carefully made sure Ardella's home, car, and jewelry remained in her name.

Vinnie, being no fool, made sure Vacalli never had a moments doubt of his loyalty or fidelity. Ardella was a good wife and mother. Vinnie had no complaints.

Ricky wasn't as fortunate. His petty thievery brought him several brushes with the law and not many assets. He bounced from job to job and city to city. He hated Newark and its dirty streets. And he hated the Puerto Ricans with a passion. The Blacks at least respected authority. Oh, not legal authority, but they knew who was boss in certain territories. The Ricans thought they could take over anywhere and for the most part they did.

Ricky's parents had long ago left Newark to live in warmer Florida, only living in their adopted state a few months when both were killed in a head-on automobile crash. This on a flat, straight road.

Ricky inherited the Newark house and lived there a few years until he was sick and tired of watching the Ricans burn out houses to collect insurance and throw sofas or stoves or anything else they didn't want out windows to stay on the littered streets forever, guessed Ricky. When the house next to his was burned, Ricky decided to move out and on. He rented the Newark house to, who else, some Ricans. When the Ricans burned it, and he knew they eventually would, he could, at least, collect the insurance.

He moved to Atlantic city, getting a job as a bouncer at one of the casinos. On his nights off, he drove a taxi, keeping up his proficiency in stealing, by rolling winners as he helped them to their rooms. Most of them too drunk to notice what was going on. Most drinks are free and plentiful in Atlantic City.

However, Ricky lost the cab driving job because even in free-wheeling Atlantic city, tourists are protected. After all, if word got out that they were in jeopardy, then they would get out of the city and who else would bring in that much money? He quit the bouncer job when he got punched out nearly as often as he did the punching. He stayed on the fringes of the casinos, couldn't make any money (who does) and moved across the state pursuing other jobs and interests.

One day, a carnival came to town. Ricky watched the barkers enticing the crowds to play games and win some worthless trinket. See a sideshow that anyone could see was pure fake. He saw a carnival worker deftly pick an unsuspecting patron's pocket. He then knew he had found his next occupation.

Ricky joined the carnival and for two years he traveled the eastern states hawking dolls, balloons, whirligigs, or any number of toys that children pestered their parents to buy. He would have stayed with the carnival forever. Instead, he stayed three years in the Utica prison over the senseless killing of a co-worker in a fight over how to repair a starter on the Ferris wheel.

Ricky knew that was a dumb thing to kill a man over. He didn't need Vinnie to tell him so, but he did need Vinnie to hire a lawyer and make sure the right judge was on the bench. Ricky received only five years for the manslaughter conviction, with two years off for good behavior. He knew he was lucky. Ricky knew, too, it was just a matter of time before he would have killed the man for another reason. They had been testing each other for months. That would have been first-degree murder.

After Ricky got out of prison, he spent time in Mexico fulfilling a couple of promises he had made to fellow inmates. Nothing big, just making sure some pure cocaine found its way across the border. He became trusted with drugs. He couldn't use them, never could. They made him violently ill, never gave him the high they were supposed to, so he left them alone. The dealers knew he wouldn't steal them for his own use. He did, however, pocket some of the money. Once again, Vinnie came to his aid.

Vinnie needed someone he could trust to help unload and deliver special cargo. Everyone knew it was drugs or exotic birds from South America, and Ricky could get by customs easily. They never looked twice at the blond man with hair like Robert Redford, when there were Blacks and Ricans around that everyone knew were smuggling drugs into the country. Ricky had an honest look about him. In a city where eye contact is rare, Ricky looked straight into other's eyes and smiled with honest sincerity. Even Vinnie's father-in-law said so.

Vinnie set Ricky up with a tavern in Union City. Money in New Jersey, like anywhere else, can buy anything. Such as a convicted felon owning a tavern that is protected with a half dozen guns under the counter as well as a .38 carried on his person. The tavern offered more than booze, well, what else is new? Vinnie could get almost anything done and if he couldn't then Vacalli could. They wanted Ricky to look legit and what could be more legit than a tavern named "Ricky's" and owned by an All-American type with hair like Robert Redford!

"Oh, I hit myself with my mirror," Didi answered Vinnie, keeping her eyes on the floor. She could never, ever tell Vinnie that Ricky---Richard had slapped her.

"Does your mirror have fingers on it?" Vinnie asked quietly.

Didi's hand instantly flew to her mouth and her fingers felt the slight puffiness that Richard's hand had left.

"Has he done this before, Didi?" Vinnie put his finger under her chin, forcing her to look up at him.

"No." She paused while she closed the door and moved back into the room. "This is the first time," she lied.

"What happen?" Vinnie pulled a chair away from the table and straddled it, his arms resting on the back.

"It was my fault," Didi sat on the edge of the still unmade bed, "I made fun of the shirt he was wearing. Asked him if he paid fifty cents for it."

"He hit you for that?" Vinnie sounded incredulous.

"Yes," Didi was apologetic, "he's under a lot of pressure. He's trying so hard to be better and I guess he gets frustrated sometimes. I know he does. It's hard to learn so many new things."

Vinnie was not convinced that this made it okay to strike a woman. Never, ever, did he strike Ardella. It just is not done in their circles. Not in Richard's either. Women, wives and girlfriends were to be taken care of, provided for, honored. Men were head of the family, the boss. Sure, what they said goes, no questions asked. Men were to be obeyed immediately, but they didn't have to hit their women. They didn't hit their women, period.

Vinnie was shocked at Richard's actions. Sure there had been fights, but with other men. Sure Richard had killed that one time, but it was a man, not a women. Not a woman he lived with. Didi had her faults, but she wasn't one of them sluts. You might jerk one of them sluts around, squeeze an arm, twist a wrist or once Vinnie had to poke needles under some fingernails of that gal, but he had never struck a woman. He almost did when he caught a bitch stealing money. Money to be used to pay an informant, legit money, but he only broke her fingers. Two on each hand. But he hadn't hit her. He must talk to Richard.

"He told me he's leaving. That he wanted to find a rich woman, maybe marry her." Didi sighed as if to accept any decision Richard made. "He's happy with me, most of the time. I know he is." She pleaded for Vinnie's understanding.

"Why does he want someone else. Money isn't that important, is it?" she asked.

"Only if you don't have it Didi. Only when you don't have it."

"Yes, but we have enough to get by," said Didi.

14

"Getting by isn't good enough for Richard. It never was," Vinnie tried to explain his friend.

"If he got a job. After he sold the tavern, he hasn't done anything. Sometimes he has money. I don't know where he gets it, but then he buys something for himself or season tickets to the symphony, for God's sake. Or some long-hair stuff we don't understand." Didi opened her arms as if to say why. "But he sits and listens and I don't think he likes it either, but he thinks rich people like it and he is making himself into someone else." Didi stopped for breath and looked helplessly at Vinnie for advice.

"How long have you been together?" questioned Vinnie. "Four, five years? Did he ever talk about marriage or wantin' a family?"

"No, but he always came back to me. Even that time when he stayed with Sandy for six months. Six months and four days. He still came back to me."

"But did he ever talk about marrying you or having children?"

"I guess not," Didi was balling a tissue in her hands and though her lower lip was trembling, she kept the tears from spilling.

"Four years? Together four years or more?" Vinnie asked once again.

"Yeah, four years and eight months. Time out for a few of his separations which lasted from a few days 'til the longest with Sandy."

"Actually Didi, and I don't want to hurt you by sayin' this. But you are, were, a convenience for Richard." Vinnie put his arms out, palms up to explain Richard's actions. "I know him. He's my best friend, but he does take advantage. Why do you stay?"

"It's my apartment." She gazed at Vinnie as if to say why do you ask something so stupid. "I pay the rent."

"You can't like this situation." Vinnie sympathized with Didi, but still his loyalty was with Richard. If Didi didn't like Richard's actions, then she is the one to make changes, not his friend. Even after years of calling his friend Ricky, as soon as Ricky wanted to be called Richard, Vinnie agreed and now only thought of him as Richard.

"I really don't understand this situation." Didi emphasized the word "understand." "He has all these cruise brochures." She picked up several travel folders from the lamp table next to the bed. "Now he thinks he can find a rich wife on a cruise. How does he get these ideas?"

"Well, that one probably came from Benny."

"Benny?"

"You met him. Didn't you and Richard go to his and Eileen's wedding?"

"Oh, yeah. He married that old woman."

"Rich old woman, Didi. And he met her when he worked on the cruise ship to St. Thomas."

"So Richard thinks he can do that too. But an old woman?" questioned Didi.

"I repeat, a rich old woman."

"Don't you men care what we look like?" Didi was angry that women seemed to have the burden of a relationship and men liked a pretty girl on their arm. But when it came to giving their name to someone, then a good looking gal got lost in the shuffle. Money is what counted. Not fair, she fumed.

"Ardella is nice looking," said Vinnie.

"Yes, but rich too." Didi glared at Vinnie who only smiled and shrugged his shoulders.

"I just don't have good luck with men," whined Didi.

"Well, you haven't had that much experience. You're young."

"More experience that you realize. I was married once." Her look challenged Vinnie to respond.

"You were? When was that?" Vinnie didn't know she had been married. He wondered if Richard knew. Probably not. They shared confidences, happy times, and sad ones. They were closer than most brothers and there was no way Richard wouldn't have told him about Didi's marriage—if he knew. It mattered not anyway. Past is past. Both men thought and acted for the present and future. They wasted no time on the past unless to get even for an action of one of their adversaries. Then they never forgot.

"Billy Dean and I got married the night I graduated from high school. Ran away, called our parents two days later. Boy, were they were mad. Especially mine." Didi brightened somewhat and began to smile as she remembered the worry and heartache she had caused her mother and step-dad. At that time, age eighteen, she was a real smartass and, as most eighteen-year-olds, knew more than they ever did the rest of their lives.

16

"My step-dad was furious. He hated Billy Dean," she smiled.

"Why, why'd he hate him?" asked Vinnie.

"He didn't think Billy Dean would amount to much. I guess he was right." Didi tapped her fingers on the table top.

"Tell me about it. What happen?"

"We were so crazy in love, or at least I was. Both from Ellendale, North Dakota where, if you counted the chickens and dogs, there may be 1500 bodies. Maybe more now, but when we were young growing up. Everyone knew everybody's business and told it. My step-dad worked at the Bible college. Not a teacher, he just did several different jobs, but he thought the sun rose and set at that college. My mother worked part time in the office. Did you ever live in a small town, Vinnie?"

"No. Newark most of my life. Richard, too."

"Well, let me tell you it's suffocating." She gave a long sigh and gazed at the ceiling.

"Billy Dean was my way out, but I guess I loved him so much I would nave even stayed in Ellendale if he wanted me to. But he didn't. He left before I did. Well kind of left. He played in a rock band, traveling around South Dakota mostly. Ellendale is on the border, so he came home a lot and this made my step-dad livid. Billy Dean would park in front of our house and honk. Out I would run to see him. My step-dad said a gentlemen would come to the door. That wasn't all though, he had long hair and had it in a pony tail." Didi laughed.

"He never finished high school and just drifted around. He hung around me since I was in the seventh grade. Neither one of us could see anyone else. My folks yelled at me for going with him, but there was nothing they could do. No way anyone could stop me."

"So you ran away and got married," remarked Vinnie.

"Yep. We ran away and got married. And I never went back to Ellendale. Never wanted to, still don't."

"The marriage didn't last though, did it?" asked Vinnie.

"For awhile," Didi was pensive. "We went to Nashville. Billy Dean was going to be a big star. We had everything picked out we would buy when we got rich. The kind of car, big house, clothes. We decided we would eat at Red Lobster at least twice a week. So many dreams. We had such fun planning and pouring over magazines choosing just the right things."

Didi paused and got a far-away look in her eyes. "Course he found out real quick he had no talent. Nashville is filled with people who do. We hung around for awhile. He tried. He really tried. Then he got a job. If you can believe this, in security at the airport and then we met another couple and," she paused, "do you remember when people lived in those communes. You know in the sixties, four or five families?"

"I've heard about them. That was the thing to do back then. I didn't know it was still popular." Vinnie was interested in her story. He realized he actually didn't know much about her, even though she had lived with his best friend all these years.

"Well, this couple, Anne and Bruce knew another couple who wanted to rent this big house in Pennsylvania. All of us lived together and shared expenses. By that time, I was pregnant and we were tired of Nashville. This place was out in the country near Towand, a big two-story farm house on about six or seven acres."

"Another small town for you, huh," remarked Vinnie.

"It was exciting and we all had a lot of fun. It was like we were thumbing our noses at society, especially our parents. Mine anyway. We smoked pot, gave up red meat, made our own clothes, had a couple of goats for milk, planted veggies. We tried to act like the Amish, but we were so far from their beliefs. Billy Dean tried to get a band together, but that didn't last long. He got part-time work on some of the farms. Bruce worked in town selling cars. He didn't sell much, but did get us a couple of old clunkers to drive. Anne stayed home and so did I, since the kid was almost due. The other couple, Ken and Jean both worked. She was a practical nurse, so got a job in a nursing home and he worked on a nearby farm. So we all had some kind of income."

"So there were three couples, all married?" asked Vinnie.

"Well, I'm not sure about Bill and Vickie. They came later so there were eight adults and three kids. Two boys belonged to Jean and Ken and an older girl, about ten, was Vickie's cousin or half-sister, or something."

"One big happy family," mused Vinnie. "What about your baby?"

"The kid was born in late November or maybe it was October. Anne was kind of the mother figure, so I got a job at a small grocery store. Gasoline, you know the kind of place you pay ten times too much because there's no place else to shop for miles. Not many women will work those late hours and all alone, so I got the job right away."

"Ever have a problem?" asked Vinnie.

"You mean like a hold-up or something?"

"Yeah, it looks to me like you were a sittin' duck."

"Nah, farming area, friendly, safe. I never worried."

"So, you have a boy or girl?" Vinnie couldn't see Didi in a mother role and she couldn't even remember the month the baby was born. Ardella remembered the exact minute, length of baby, circumference of their heads, everything. Vinnie knew these things as well.

"Oh, a boy."

"What'd you name him?"

"That was easy. Dakota, cause that's where Billy Dean and I came from. We just called him the Kid, though."

It was a ho-hum response and Vinnie was surprised. Children had always been very important in his family. His thoughts flashed once again to Ardella and their four children. Ardella who drove the kids to every possible activity, music lessons, tennis, dancing, swimming. Giving them every opportunity for a well-rounded education. Even Vinnie, who everyone said resembled his father-in-law in crooked deals, put his family first. He couldn't understand a parent having an attitude like Didi's.

"I take it you and Billy Dean didn't especially like being parents."

"You got that right. The Kid really tied us down. Billy Dean would play in a band sometimes and I'd have to stay home. Course Anne took care of him while I worked and sometimes at night. But I had to take care of him sometimes, too."

"Were you ever in contact with your folks?"

"Yeah, oh yeah. My folks came through for us. They came to visit when the Kid was about two and a half, or close to three. Got upset cause he was kind of dirty. Hard to train, so he had a soggy diaper. It was my day off, and I just didn't have time to fool with him. I always shampoo my hair on my day off and do my nails, but to be honest with you, I was potted. Anne was grocery shopping or the Kid would have been clean. She fussed over him, but couldn't get him to stop messing his diaper. God, what a mess."

Didi clearly had been exasperated with motherhood. "Anyway, my folks tried to shame me into getting up to take care of him. Hell, they were there. They could have changed him.

So when Anne came home and the Kid ran to her and called her 'mama' my folks came unglued."

"What'd they do?" Vinnie encouraged Didi to continue.

"Left for awhile. A couple hours later, they came back." Didi was gleeful. "Billy Dean was home then. My step-dad still didn't like him. Anyway they asked what we would think of them taking the Kid. Only they called him Dakota. They wanted to take him back to Ellendale. To give us a break, they said."

"Well, what'd you think of that?" Vinnie guessed he already knew.

"Billy Dean and I looked at each other and could hardly keep the smiles off our faces. Course we couldn't be too eager, so we said yes tentatively and tried to act like we were reluctant and wanted only the best for the Kid." Didi laughed as she told this part or her story. "I almost peed my pants I was so excited. Billy Dean kept calling my step-dad sir and showing respect. It was priceless. God, the highlight of the year, getting rid of the Kid." She smiled remembering. "We celebrated for days. Anne was kind of sad, though."

"Where is he now, your son?" questioned Vinnie.

"Oh," she replied brightly, my folks adopted him. A month or so after they left with him, we got some papers from the court or some lawyer asking us to give up custody of him. We did and did we ever celebrate that. We never liked being parents. We felt like kids again."

"But the marriage didn't last anyway. Why?"

"Oh." Didi gave a long sigh again. "Living like that isn't all it's cracked up to be. It was great at first. Then some problems cropped up. Anne and Bruce decided to go back to Nashville, so there went the two that really kept everything under control. Anne was a great shopper. She planned all the meals. Bruce had found some good buys on cars and could fix them. So after they left, we all sort of drifted. Eating out more. It took more money, so we kind of argued about that."

Didi had quite a story. She continued, "Then Vickie and Ken got pretty friendly. Said they would do the shopping and would be gone for hours almost everyday and would come home with nothing. We got another couple, Leeta and Norrie. They were okay. She was a teacher in Sayra and Norrie became our cook. We all helped, but he was the leader."

Didi went to the refrigerator and got a Diet Coke. "Want a Coke or beer?" she asked.

"A beer, thanks." She handed Vinnie a Bud and went back and sat down on the side of the bed. She brushed her hair back from her face. Vinnie noticed her hair really did need a shampoo. It always did, he recalled. And she worked in a beauty shop!

Taking a closer look, Vinnie noticed her face looked at least thirty-five or more. He knew she was twenty-nine. Too many cigarettes, pot and booze. Hard living in spite of her poor-little-me attitude.

"I really should have seen it coming. All the signs were there." Her voice trailed off, remembering the day Leeta brought her sixteen-year-old sister, Christine, to live with them.

"Do you want a glass for your beer?" asked Didi.

Vinnie involuntarily glanced toward the dirty-dish-filled sink and quickly looked away. "No, this is fine. I prefer beer from a can." She really is a slob, he thought as he took a look around the room. The small kitchen counter area was almost covered with dishes. Some may have been clean, but who could tell. A couple of boxes of cereal, an empty pizza box, a container from Kentucky Fried Chicken, at least a dozen empty beer and soda cans. Part of a loaf of French bread, and several unidentifiable objects. What a mess! No wonder Richard wants out. How had he stayed so long. Why had he?

"So what should you've seen coming?" Vinnie took a couple of swallows of beer and set the can down on a newspaper. It was the only spot he could find that wasn't covered by some kind of debris. It looked as if the newspaper had been used before as a coaster.

"That Billy Dean had a thing for Christine. When she first came we all pampered her. She was so cute and young and bubbly. She brought laughter and joy to us. Fun, always dancing and clowning around. Billy Dean was fascinated by her long blonde hair." Didi paused and took a long drink of her Diet Coke. She had laced it with gin and Vinnie wondered how often she had done that.

"Anyway, I usually got home from work around ten-thirty and there they would be. Billy Dean brushing away." Didi took another drink and wiped her moist hand on the legs of her jeans. "Christine would jump up and go around the room and kiss everyone goodnight. Everyone on the cheek except Billy Dean. This one night, the first time I got this knot in the pit of my stomach, she leaned down and kissed him full on the mouth for about ten or fifteen seconds. I watched and then my eyes

21

locked with Leeta's for just a moment. Then I looked at Billy Dean and he was watching Christine walk to her bedroom."

"Wow!" exclaimed Vinnie.

"I knew then something was going on, but it was a month or two later before - before..." she sighed. "Well, to make a long story short, I came home from work one day, I was sick and shouldn't have gone in at all. When I got to work my boss sent me home. So I got home about an hour after I left and found Billy Dean and Christine in bed." Didi set her Coke down and raised her palms. "So that was it. I said 'What's going on here?'"

"Billy Dean said 'What are you doing here' and I said 'I live here.' I felt like killing them both. He looked at me, then at her, and in that instant decided on her and told me he wouldn't give her up."

Vinnie asked, "Tough. What'd you do?"

"I decided to get out of there right then. Had no idea where I was going. Had about fifty bucks in my pocket, so I took the rent money, eight hundred dollars, from the sugar bowl."

"You're kidding. The sugar bowl?"

"Yeah, really. We kept it in the sugar bowl. Each payday we all put in our share and then on the first of the month, we paid the rent. I took it and walked out. Leeta watched me. I guess everyone knew about Billy Dean and Christine but me. I kept going, and no one said anything about the money. They probably thought I would be back. I got in the car and never looked back."

"Didn't take any clothes or anything?" Vinnie was incredulous.

"Nothing. And that was foolish of me cause I had to spend money for stuff I could have taken. I was fuming though. I did stop at the store and got my pay. My boss hated to lose me cause I was good and we were friends." She laughed.

"More than friends?"

"Oh, a few times. He had an ugly wife and she didn't understand him. You know the story. I made good money." The bitter Didi showed through the laughter.

"So commune life is really sharin'. If you and your boss were makin' out, why did you care about Billy Dean and Christine?"

"They were in my bed, Vinnie. That's what made me so mad." Didi emphasized the words "my bed" and looked at Vinnie as if he had lost his mind for not understanding.

"So you just took off like that. Ever hear from Billy Dean?"

"Nope."

"Have you told Richard any of this?" Vinnie pretty much knew the answer. If Richard had known then, Vinnie would have known as well.

"Almost all of it. I just didn't tell him Billy Dean and I were married or that we had a kid. Still are married far as I know. That's why I couldn't tell Richard. I want to marry him and we couldn't if he knew I might still be married to Billy Dean." Why is Vinnie so dense on this. She thought he was smarter than that.

"Just a couple of minor details, huh. Why didn't you tell him when you first met. You weren't plannin' to marry him then. You both no doubt talked of your earlier days."

"I wanted to impress him on how innocent I was. Then it got too late. He would know I lied to him."

"Go on, where'd you go?"

"First I stopped at Wal-Mart and got some clothes and stuff I needed. Like a toothbrush and deodorant. It was real dumb not to take my things with me. Then I kept on driving."

"Headed for where? You must have had somethin' in mind." Vinnie finished his beer and declined another. He refused the greasy bowl of yesterday's popcorn that Didi offered.

"My goal was New York City. I was sick of small towns and I was on my way to the Big Apple." Didi paused, reflecting on her former life. "I was delayed for awhile. Met a guy, got pregnant, had an abortion. All in six months after leaving Billy Dean. The guy, his name was Boyd. We really didn't have it for each other so early one morning I took his money and my clothes. I remember taking a big red thermos for coffee and away I went. I don't believe he cared, except for his money. There was only about forty dollars."

Vinnie didn't respond, but kept his eyes on Didi. This is such a fascinating story. She was so proud of the stealing, abortion, and her flight. He smiled. She could be a great con artist with no feelings of remorse. A basic requirement of the con game. One problem: she had no loyalty to anyone and could never be trusted.

"When I got to Union City, I was low on money and hey, this was a big city to me. I worked in a few places, in bars mostly. Then heaven came along when I met Richard. You know the rest." Didi sighed and shrugged her shoulders. "He does some con stuff, deals a little in drugs, even takes money from my purse, but I thought we were happy. I was - am, but then he started on this self-improvement kick or so he calls it. Now I guess he will be gone or so he says."

Didi gazed at Vinnie as if some magic words would come from him that she could use to lure Richard into staying with her.

None did.

Then her eyes took on a crafty, scheming look and she moved closer to his chair. She squatted in front of him and asked in a seductive way, "Are you always true to your wife?"

"You sell yourself short, Didi. You're an attractive girl. You don't have to put out to every man you see. And yes, I'm always true to Ardella. Richard's my best friend. I don't want to hurt your feelings, but you aren't my type." Vinnie's eyes flicked around the room. "And any one of those reasons is enough to say no to you." He took her hand and pulled her up to her feet.

"Why don't you go back to your folks, check out your son. You might find a great life there."

"Huhuh."

"If you want me to, I can check on Billy Dean for you. We have a network you wouldn't believe and can find out about anyone in just a few hours."

"Why would I want to know anything about him? He's old news."

"You might want to know if he divorced you and maybe he has been in contact with your son and folks."

"Yes, I might like that." Didi was contrite. "I'm sorry I came on to you. I didn't want to embarrass you, but guys usually take it when it's offered."

"Don't offer it so often." Vinnie got up from his chair and moved to the door. "I have to go. Tell Richard I was here. Have him give me a call will you?"

"Yeah, thanks for listening and don't tell Richard any of what I told you. But when you see him, tell him, well tell him he could do worse than me."

"He has something else in mind. You have to realize that and go in another direction. You're a hair stylist, you can get a job anywhere. Richard gave you that." Vinnie reminded her that Richard got her out of the bars and into a relatively secure profession.

After Didi closed the door, she walked to the kitchen window and stood gazing at the stunted oak tree. The only tree or bush she could see. It was one of the reasons she liked the apartment. The wind had stripped all but one leaf from the tree. The leaf was clinging arduously to a bare branch, but it was only a matter of time before it too, would be blown away by the gusty wind. Didi pondered if she was like the oak leaf. Trying to cling to something that was impossible to keep.

"It won't be long for either of us little leaf," she said aloud, though no one could hear her plaintive remark.

CHAPTER TWO

"This is a wonderful trip. Have you been to Hawaii before?" asked Cindi the travel agent. Cindi, a pert blonde, dressed in a bright red suit with her hair tied back and held with a red velvet bow, asked Richard, the good looking and obviously wealthy man seated across the desk from her. Gold earrings and bracelets, plus a couple of rings with turquoise stones, gave her a look of affluence, which was exactly what the travel agency wanted its agents to signify.

The agency sought wealthy clientele and advertised its tours for those who could afford the best. Expensive, yes, but you get what you pay for. In a tour such as this you have travel-mates who are your peers in income as well as interests. Cindi was a pro. Anyone would like to be on a tour when by chance she might be on the same one. As a matter of fact, she wouldn't be. She couldn't afford it and what in the world could she talk to Wall Street addicts about. She dressed the part and sold the tours and added Richard Snider to the flight to Los Angeles to embark on a voyage to Hawaii.

"Yes, I've been there several times, but never by ship, so I'm looking forward to that." Richard reached for his ticket and tapped it on his hand.

"A ship is an exciting way to travel," gushed Cindi.

"I've sailed to Europe many times, so a ship isn't new to me, but I try to be excited about most ventures. You never know what great experiences one may encounter." Lies came so easily to Richard. He had never been on a cruise ship, although he had been to Hawaii once when he spent time on four of the islands seeking a new source of marijuana to supply the ever increasing desires of college students. He netted around fifty thousand dollars on that trip and made a nice down payment on a four-plex apartment building just outside of Atlantic City.

One of the apartments would be his new home after today. When he moved away from Didi, he never intended to see her again. He did, though intend to pay the rent on her apartment for six months and give her checking account a five thousand dollar boost. He had done quite well on the last job at the docks. Cleared thirty grand and added to the 125 grand he had from the tavern sale, he could easily afford this trip. He planned to meet a rich woman. Benny had and he knew he had much more to offer a woman than Benny.

And everyone in his tour group would be rich. There were sure to be single women. Rich, single women. Yes, he knew, as Cindi explained, not everyone on the ship was part of his tour. Only about two hundred travelers would have the special treatment the extra fifteen thousand bought. But it would be worth it if, no, he changed that to when, he reached his goal.

"I hope you enjoy your trip and let me know if there is anything else I can do for you." Cindi leveled her blue eyes directly into his. Her meaning was clear. Richard ignored it, put his ticket into the pocket of his new gray blazer and went on his way.

On the way to Didi's bank he changed his mind about the five thousand. She was his past, the five grand is for his future. Hey, she has a job. He did though buy her a dozen roses and stopped at Pizza Hut for a large combo for dinner. Maybe she would help him pack his clothes. He wanted to move into his apartment which, of course, Didi knew nothing about. He had one more job to do for Vinnie and the tour began in two weeks.

"You expect a lot from me to help you pack to move out on me." Didi was indignant, especially since the roses had raised her hopes.

"Didi, I want us to stay friends." Richard gave her his after-all-we've-meant-to-each-other look.

"Well, speaking of friends, your best friend Vinnie was here today and made a pass at me."

"Oh, yeah?" Richard put his hand on his hips and turned to face her.

"Yeah, he wanted me to go to bed with him, but I told him I love you and he should be true to Ardella, and that I didn't want to hurt his feelings, but he didn't appeal to me, not my type. What do you think of your friend now?" She glared at him and challenged him to respond.

"You told him all that, huh?" Richard had a half smile and knowing sneer.

"Yes, and he was really disappointed," she continued, staring at Richard with a calculating expression.

"Well my dear, did he have his Erecto-Aid with him?"

"What's that?"

"You know he had a prostate operation and can't get it up without it." Richard smiled at Didi's discomfort, her face blanketed with guilt.

"You don't even know what an Erecto-Aid is, do you?" Richard sneered at her. "You never were a good liar and you pick such dumb things to lie about. I know Vinnie better than that. You made the play and he turned you down, didn't he?" Richard laughed.

"Well, if he hadn't had that operation and needed that whatever it is, he would have wanted to." Didi tried to appear indignant.

"His words though, right?" Richard continued his fun.

"Well, you're going to find some other woman, so why shouldn't I do the same."

"His words?" Richard badgered her.

"What's the difference. Yes his words. He wanted to," answered Didi, a defiant look blazing from her eyes.

"God, you're dumb, Didi. Vinnie never had a prostate operation." Richard laughed at her. "Here, help me with this box." His possessions were all packed and he was ready to go. His car nearly full with a stereo, books he felt were impressive, even if they couldn't hold his interest, videos of several movies, CD's of various operas which couldn't hold his interest either, but impressive he hoped. His apartment had been professionally decorated so he felt sure about it being in good taste.

Oh, a new life. It was exciting to think of the future and try to guess what may lie ahead. He would not be returning to Didi anymore. That he was very sure of. Even on this trip if he didn't meet Miss Right he knew he had grown beyond Didi. Six months, as he had given his culture training, had given him an appreciation of the better things in life. Or at least he convinced himself of that. There were those who would argue that country music sounded just as great as opera, and a fiddle another name for a violin, depending on what came from the bow gliding across the strings. But Richard had watched and learned and now knew people who had money lived a different style and like quality rather than quantity. Oh, sure he knew the country music entertainers had more, their homes elegant, their dishes real china, no not plastic like Didi has. Napkins - real linen and not paper. He saw pictures of their homes in magazines, but still he believed the opera offered more rich patrons. Rich being the key word.

There is a big difference between those with money and those just getting by. He didn't want to just get by anymore. He was forty-two, for God's sake. Time to live in an elegant fashion. He knew how, or so he thought.

He decided at the last moment not to pay Didi's rent for six months and to fly first class to L.A. and buy new clothes at Nordstrom's instead of wearing the garb he had purchased recently at thrift shops or some such place. He got a jump on a tropical tan at the tanning salon. He looked good, more than good. Great! Just a little curl in his blond hair and the highlights were excellent. Flat stomach. Sit ups really did the trick. He had at least six expressions that broadcast his feelings or the look he wanted others to think was genuine. Whether it was disappointment, surprise, pleasure, rapt attention, disinterest, or love. He had them down pat and he had fun using them on strangers and was delighted when he saw how wonderfully they worked.

Hey! Maybe he should be an actor. He imagined a wall covered with Oscars. Nah, too much work. Course it looked as if there were plenty of fringes. If it didn't work out on the cruise, then he guessed he would go into acting. He would find someway to cut the long hours. An academy award for his first film would give control of other films and the hours on the set. Jodie Foster would be his co-star. No, not co-star. Second lead. No co-stars. Jodie had class and could keep up with him intellectually, or almost. Hey, this could work. Always smart to have a contingency plan. Give his lucky-to-be-around-me look and Jodie would fall at his feet. A cute gal, she would appreciate the career boost.

"You'll be back. You always come back," whined Didi. "One of these days I won't be here."

That didn't sound like Jodie's voice. Jodie has such mellow tones. Oh, Didi. She interrupted his thoughts. An expert at doing that. Great timing Didi.

"'Maybe you won't be. Since I have no plans to come back, it won't matter. Find another sucker, Didi. And do it quick while you still have something to offer. Such as it is."

"You bastard," she yelled.

"So long kid, see you in the movies." Richard gave a little salute as he opened the door.

"You're sick," she screamed. "Sick, sick, sick." She slammed the door behind him and he still could hear her yelling "sick" as he closed his car door and drove away. He smiled. Oh, how great to be free of her and that filthy apartment. There was not an inkling of remorse.

CHAPTER THREE

The flight from Newark to LAX was non-stop and first class. First class on the Boeing 747, very comfortable. The food delicious, free drinks, and look at the leg room. Wow! The soft seats. He looked around at the colors, soft pastels and so easy on his eyes. First class is definitely the way to go. Check out the way the gals notice everything. Have another drink in your hand before you realize you want one.

A smooth, relaxing flight, he mused as he pushed the button to recline his seat. He closed his eyes and exhaled a very contented sigh. He dreamed of nothing but blue skies and sunshine for the rest of his life. A lifestyle of the rich, if not the famous. Something he could adjust to very easily.

It seemed his eyes were closed for just a few minutes when the red-headed flight attendant leaned over and asked if he wanted dinner or if he preferred to sleep. If he wanted to sleep, she would bring his dinner at a later time. He chose to eat, rather than sleep. Plus he wanted to savor these hours of complete luxury. The redhead was easy on the eyes, too. He fantasized touching the ivory-colored skin of her face and gazing into her dark blue eyes. Just for a diversion, though. After all, she works and he didn't plan to spend much time with anyone who worked for a living. He did reward her with his how-very-kind-you-are-to-bring-me-dinner smile. Not sure if the smile worked, since she gave the same service and smile to his seat companion, who, when you think about it, didn't deserve such nice treatment. After all, he's a Jap, or he guessed he better think of them as Japanese, now with his new way of living. People were so touchy by what they called racism. Hell. A Jap is a Jap. Oh, well.

The guy seemed friendly enough. Shaking Richard's hand when he sat down and offering to share his New York Times. Richard gave him an oh-waste-time-on-a-newspaper look and took a copy of Business Week from his new eelskin briefcase. While reading an article about a new trade agreement between a computer company in Japan and one in the United States, his seat companion leaned over, pointed to the Japanese man in the photo and said, "Me."

Hmm, thought Richard. A big shot. This brought the man up a station in Richard's eyes, he decided to be more friendly. That was all the contact for a couple of hours since the other man decided to sleep.

Richard glanced around at the other passengers, but noticed no one special. The women seemed to be traveling with a male companion. Besides they were overweight and overdressed. The men were as well. However, Richard did pay special attention to what the men were wearing. His confidence rose because his clothes were just right. A navy blue three-piece suit, lighter blue and white striped shirt, blue tie with small white diamond-shaped figures. Black shoes, black socks. He had learned very well.

"Anyone famous on board?" Richard asked the flight attendant when she brought dinner. The dinner was served on Noritake China. Those in coach would be eating from small plastic trays and the entree would be considerably less appetizing than his steak, baked potato and julienne carrots. His tossed salad had big chunks of bleu cheese. Ah, first class.

"No, only me." She smiled, an invitation clearly in her eyes.

"A beauty queen posing as a flight attendant to see how the poor folk live."

"Are you kidding, poor folk." She smiled. "Big bucks next to you," she whispered in Richard's ear. Nice perfume. Opium, he thought.

"Opium?" he asked.

"Are you talking about my perfume, or...?" She trailed off and raised her eyes in question.

Richard felt a rush of excitement. This could be interesting, indeed. "Are you based in L.A. or have a layover?"

"Based. Interested?" She was kneeling down by his seat and he knew he would always ask for an aisle seat in the future. And to think he had complained when he couldn't get a window seat.

"Maybe. Want to give me your number?" he asked.

"Are you crazy?" Her co-worker, Debi asked when Lori told her about the passenger in 2-B who wanted her phone number. "You can't be sure of anyone you meet like this. He looks too smooth and I noticed earlier he seems to be much too interested in the other passengers."

"Oh, Deb, you're such a pessimist. Relax, this could be fun. And you have to admit, he is cute. Handsome, actually."

"Just be careful. People think we are fair game and our service should extend beyond the flight." Debi continued to caution Lori.

"Richard Snider. A nice name don't you think?" asked Lori.

"Remember what I said. Oh, Mrs. Roberts wants another gin and tonic, I bet." Debi walked up the aisle to answer a light. Her friend Lori was so naive. Debi, a few years older thought she was Lori's caretaker.

Lori hurriedly wrote her telephone number on a small piece of paper ready to give to Richard in a few moments. Right now passengers were busy eating, so she could relax a few minutes. She didn't give her number out often, but Richard appealed to her. Or maybe appealing was his remark about opium. She hoped he meant cocaine. It had been awhile and she loved the euphoric feeling of a snort or two. And Richard would have good stuff. She would bet on that! Not that she was drug dependent or even used them all that much. But sometimes the experience was wonderful and they had kept her happy after her marriage with David ended. She couldn't afford to make them a habit and knew better anyway. But recreational use lifted her spirits and Richard looked like a real find. She grew excited.

The two flight attendants gathered the dishes and announced that drinks would be served for another fifteen minutes. Then the plane would begin its approach to LAX and all containers would be collected. Lori brought Richard another gin and tonic and slipped him the paper with her telephone number on it. She gave him her best anticipation smile and received a quick nod from him.

The smooth landing received a smattering of applause from the passengers. Thanks for flying with us and when you have the occasion to fly again remember us. The captain was relieved that he had competed another flight with satisfied customers.

Debi and Lori slipped their high heel shoes back on and waited at the door to bid passengers good-bye and wish them a happy time in Los Angeles. The captain stood with Debi and Lori smiling his thanks from the well-pleased group.

As Richard approached Lori, he handed her back the paper she had given to him. "Sorry, I just don't have the time or the desire to call you," he said loud enough for everyone to hear. Even those waiting in the coach section could hear his remarks.

Lori's face literally turned white, her mouth gapped open and she reached for the side of the exit door to keep her balance. Her eyes opened wide and she took a quick intake of breath. She felt sick, embarrassed, a feeling of shame washed over her. She wanted to hide, cover her face. She was aware of the pairs of eyes looking at her. A series of emotions swept deep into her very soul. How could he? Why did he? She wanted to die right there. She turned to leave the doorway. Debi held her back and whispered, "Smile, laugh it off. Act as if he was rejected and wanted to get even. Do your job. The louse!"

Somehow Lori got through the next half hour, then sat in one of the seats sobbing.

"I'm so embarrassed I could die," she muttered between sobs.

"What a jerk," said Debi.

"You pegged him. How did you guess he was like that?"

"I didn't exactly, it just seems he wasn't exactly, oh, I don't know, quality. And what he did to you is inexcusable. I could kill him."

"The captain isn't too pleased either. But with me, not with him," remarked Lori. "I should have known better. He wants to talk to me as soon as he is finished up here."

"Oh, God, well, it would have to be Captain Wyatt, too. He's probably jealous that he doesn't have your number," said Debi. Then when Lori winced, "I'm sorry, I didn't mean it that way. It will be okay, just relax."

Lori dabbed her eyes with a tissue taking a wet towel from Debi to wipe the streaked makeup from her face. She hurriedly re-applied moisturizer, blush, lip gloss and mascara. No time for liner or any other makeup. She felt half-finished. Who knows what the captain will say to her. Nothing pleasant to be sure.

"I thought I could judge people better," asserted Lori.

"You can. He was a difficult call. Anyway, don't worry." Debi gave her a quick hug and told her she would wait in the employee's lounge.

"Come home with me. Jack will barbecue steaks for us and we'll just sit around and gab," invited Debi.

"Thanks, give me a rain check. I just want to stand under a hot shower for hours and get this dirty feeling off my body."

"Oh, Lori, it could have happened to anybody. Relax and go on from here."

Richard looked around at his co-travelers expecting a smile or a high-five for putting that little tart in her place. Instead, he was getting looks of disgust and down right anger. What the hell, he thought. The rich always put down the little people. Where was the applause, where were the knowing looks of admiration? He caught up with his Japanese seat mate.

"Maybe we'll see each other again sometime," said Richard, patting the other man on the back.

"I doubt that." His words cold and his expression colder. He pulled away from Richard's touch as one would recoil from a rat or snake. So much for him, Richard sneered. Who cares about Japs anyway? Should have dropped another bomb when Truman had the chance. Wipe their slant eyes off the face of the earth. Who needs their electronics equipment or anything else they make. He remembered his dad saying it used to be when something said "Made in Japan" it was a joke. It would break the first time anyone used it if it wasn't broken before it was even out of the box. Who does this computer wizard think he is anyway! Should be lizard, not wizard. Snake in the grass.

Richard turned to the woman who had sat across the aisle. Turned his you-are-wonderful smile and received a you-are-an-asshole look in return.

What the hell is going on? When the guy in that restaurant a month ago put down that snooty waiter, the people all around smiled. What's the difference? So the flight attendant hadn't been snooty, very friendly, and helpful in fact. But still just a glorified waitress. Why shouldn't he put her in her place. What was the difference between the guy in the restaurant and Richard himself. Sure the waiter had a superior attitude, sure he had corrected the young girl's pronunciation of a menu item, and sure he corrected it with a sneer. What was the difference?

When other passengers gave him the same, did-you-crawl-out-from-under-a-rock look, he decided to hurry from the airport and get on with his business. It was true, he thought. He didn't have time to see Lori, but maybe the rich didn't always put down those who served them. Maybe it did depend on the circumstances. Maybe the waiter deserved it and Lori didn't. Another lesson learned. The rich have to think all the time.

Richard got his rental car and wouldn't you know - a Honda Prelude. Japanese! Well, that jerk on the plane wouldn't know it. And to tell the truth, Richard liked the car. Course he would never admit it. The car, sky-blue, two-door, and did this baby ever respond. He quickly left the Los Angeles International Airport and was on his way to Marina Del Rey. His four-day reservation at the Doubletree Inn would be his home until the ship sailed. Richard was familiar with the area and chose this hotel for its proximity to the beach, across the roadway actually, and for the outdoor restaurant just a few steps away.

His appointment with Dino Verico wasn't until the next morning, so he had the evening to wander around the beach and gaze with expectancy at the beautiful yachts anchored at the marina. One of his purchases he decided, when he married his very rich wife, would be a yacht. He chose, in his mind, that long blue sailing yacht, seventy or eighty feet, he guessed, five sails. Easily the kind of vessel that he and his wife could sail to the south seas. He saw himself at the wheel wearing white pants, a navy blue blazer, captain's hat, blue he thought, with gold braid, and he supposed he would have a pipe. And a tan, oh, such a beautiful tan. He could see people lined up on shore, looks of envy on their faces, as he guided his yacht into a south seas harbor. He would wave a greeting and people would applaud. And they would bow and cheer, feeling lucky that he chose to honor them with his presence.

"Excuse me sir. May I see your pass?" The voice came from behind Richard. It belonged to a Hispanic wearing a brown uniform consisting of knee-length shorts, a short sleeved shirt, brown shoes and knee-high brown socks. A name tag with his photo displayed prominently in a plastic holder pinned to his shirt pocket identified the man as Juan Cinco.

Don't they hire any white people anymore? This was Richard's first thought. Then he thought "pass?"

"Why do I need a pass. I'm thinking of buying one of these yachts. The blue one." Richard did not believe he owed the man an explanation. He was egotistical enough to present a superior attitude.

"Sir, none of these yachts are for sale. The yachts for inspection are on Pier D and viewing hours are daily from 8 a.m. to 6 p.m. On this pier, sir, non-owners are required to have a pass."

"How do you know I'm not an owner? You know everyone?" asked Richard in a not too friendly tone.

"Owners have a color-coded card that is photographed as they cross the walkway, sir. Non-owners must register at the office and then receive a pass to enter the moorage area."

"No one was in the office, so I just walked down. What's the big deal." Richard's response was more statement than question.

"Well, it is private property, sir. And I was in the office. I saw you walk by. Perhaps you didn't see me or see the sign that says all visitors must stop there."

"I didn't see you, the walls brown?" sniped Richard.

"No, sir. The walls are white." Cinco responded his polite demeanor, never faltering. "I must ask you to leave sir."

"You are asking me to leave?" Richard sneered. "I could break you in half."

"I wouldn't sir. You are trespassing and I do have police powers." Cinco's eyes met Richard's and never wavered.

Then Richard noticed the gun and knew that he should have seen it right away. It certainly wasn't concealed. He hesitated a moment and then decided it wasn't worth a confrontation. So he turned and walked back to the parking area and to his hotel. He turned once and lifted his middle finger to Cinco, who only watched Richard go. No expression on his face.

Richard had two drinks in the lounge, saw no one who piqued his interest, picked up a copy of the Los Angeles Times left by someone else and went to his room.

Los Angeles. It never changes, Richard mused. Letting the Hispanics, Blacks, and Japs run the city. And sure to make a big impact are the East Indians. Already he noticed they were running the Circle K convenience store up the street. Much as he loved warm weather and beaches, and for his business (and Vinnie's) this was a ripe area, Los Angeles was not for him. Too many foreigners who thought they were smart, running everything, thinking they were as good as white people. Not even the New York Jews were as obnoxious or pushy - well maybe.

Dino and Vinnie were cousins, yet Richard had never met Dino. Dino had moved to Los Angeles with his parents where his dad, Marko, opened a printing shop and, in the backroom, a slot machine emporium. Dino was only two at that time. When his dad retired, Dino took over the printing business and extended it to include "new papers." Social Security cards, driver's licenses, credit cards, passports were all part of the new family business. Marko never knew. He stayed away. While Marko may have bordered on a dishonest project or two, Dino's major income resulted from contraband goods and paper hangers. He enlarged the slot machine business adjacent to the print shop and installed video games and a number of betting devices, booking agents and a telephone number which could get a prostitute of any age, size, sex, or color in less than an hour. Dino made lots of money.

Richard would receive three new sets of identification. Easy to get money using identification which could not be traced. Each new set of "papers" used Richard's own photograph with a few variations of his looks.

"So Richard, my friend, how do you like yourself with a mustache?" Dino smiled as he held up a credit card showing Richard with a small light growth of hair above his upper lip.

"Eric Johnson. Is there such a person in L.A.?" asked Richard.

"Probably no more than a couple of thousand," answered Dino, bringing out a Social Security card, driver's license, and passport, which bore several stamps showing travel in several foreign countries. "Probably a dozen or more on Pico."

Richard examined the address on Pico Blvd. "How do you get the names and addresses?"

The only response from Dino, "We do our homework." Then added, "Here are the other two." Dino took several cards from a small manila envelope and handed them to Richard. Both men were wearing gloves and only touched the edges of the cards.

Envelope number two showed Richard with thicker and longer hair. Brown instead of blue eyes and fuller cheeks.

"How am I going to look like that when I use the cards?" Richard frowned.

"Easy." Dino opened another manila envelope and showed Richard a hairpiece which could easily be attached to Richard's own hair.

"You need to get several different colored contact lenses. Brown, green, and hazel. Put gum in your cheeks. The computer shows the face on the card and everyone looks a tad different than on the card. Not too much. You notice hardly anyone looks or compares the pictures. A person could have gotten a haircut, lost some weight. But believe me, this works." Dino explained.

"Where am I going to get contacts made at this late date." Richard showed some disgust.

"Here." Dino handed Richard a small slip of paper with the name and address of an optician not far from Dino's business.

"You have an appointment at two this afternoon. The three pair will cost you five hundred dollars and don't worry, they are just colored glass. Won't change your vision, just the color of your eyes. Won't hurt your eyes in any way."

"So, what is my name in this one?" Richard picked another envelope as Dino scooped the cards and hairpiece back in the number one envelope.

"J. Harlow Webster on Eleventh Street." Dino smiled. He clearly enjoyed his work as well as the income it provided. Five thousand for each set of "papers."

"It's okay. I hope I can keep me straight." Richard knew he could. He was thorough when it came to con games.

"Who is my third self?" asked Richard. He examined each set of identification very carefully.

"Names Andrew Anderson."

"Andy Anderson?" Richard raised his eyes to Dino. "Really?"

"Thousands of them. I counted three hundred living in apartment houses in this area."

"Let's see what I look like." Richard picked up the California driver's license.

"Hair combed a little differently and that gum again. Glasses. Nothing that you can't do in a couple of minutes. It changes your looks quite a lot," explained Dino. "And each credit card has a twenty thousand credit line."

"How in the hell did you manage that?" Sixty thousand dollars.

"As I said, homework. The banks are too anxious to give credit cards to anyone. They send them out by the thousands."

"How do you get them?"

Dino thought for a moment. But hey, this is Vinnie's friend. Vinnie recommended him. He is safe. But when he looked into Richard's eyes, he saw a calculating expression which Richard had been too eager to hide.

"Ah, homework," answered Dino. He decided to mention his quick distrust to Vinnie. Give him a call this afternoon, Dino told himself.

"Now, here's something else." Dino handed Richard two additional credit cards. "These are in the name of John Steamer and Jack Watson. Real people who keep fifty grand or more of available credit. What you need to do in the next few days is withdraw cash from an ATM machine. It's best in a shopping mall cause banks have cameras going all the time and you don't look anything like these men. You can easily get enough money to pay all my fees with some left over."

"How so?"

"On the fake credit cards, the bills are sent to us and we make the minimum monthly payment. That's all they want. After a few months of prompt payments, they increase your line of credit. The two real cards aren't much of a problem. The bills go out once a month, these on the twenty-fifth, so you want to make your purchases early in the month. They only work for one month. Then Steamer and Watson will report the cards stolen. The banks will send new cards with a new account number, and we will use those for the next customer. If the two extra cards aren't enough, I can get you more. The sets with the identification are best, though, because the computer shows a good credit standing. You can only use them for three months, unless you pay another five thousand."

"Three months should be plenty of time. I have some great plans."

"So Vinnie told me."

"This sounds too good to be true. I'd love to do this in New York," said Richard.

That look again, mused Dino. That was it, he wants part of the action. Vinnie had told him that Richard is a dreamer. Dino wasn't worried now. Vinnie never sent him anyone who would rat on his operation. His biggest fear was that someone, some cop, an FBI man, would be good enough to fool Vinnie.

Sure they had special words they used. A clue that only the two of them knew and Richard had passed with flying colors. But he had that moment of fear. Perhaps he should give Richard another test.

"That maybe possible," responded Dino. "We may expand there. Tell me about Mama Vacalli. Her sister Minerva still hanging around looking for handouts?"

Minerva. Minerva. That was Mama Vacalli's name, not her sister. Was this a trap? Richard took a deep breath. Was this really Vinnie's cousin? How should he answer? Strange and all of a sudden, distrust reared its ugly head. Wasn't there supposed to be honor among thieves or some such utter nonsense. A thief, a murderer, a con man's next victim could just as easily be his best buddy. Except not Vinnie and Richard. They had absolute trust. Always, since they were youngsters, and Vinnie had sent him to Dino.

"Gosh, Dino, you forgot. Minerva is Mama's name. I don't even know if she has a sister. Ardella never mentioned an aunt. Of course, I guess there was never any reason for her to." Richard decided to be straight with Dino. After all, Dino wouldn't be very smart if he didn't check out every aspect of a transaction. Oh, that study had been so successful. He even thought more intelligently. You bet! On his way to riches.

Dino Laughed, "Yeah, Minerva was Mama's name."

"Is, Dino. Mama is still living." Richard corrected him with a smile.

"So, we are all set. You need to give me the fifteen thousand and you can pick these up day after tomorrow. Except for these two. You can start getting money anytime with these." Dino gave Richard the two cards with Steamer's and Watson's name.

"We have to do some smearing and touching up, but I'm pleased. Lennie did a good job." Dino smiled. He did several sets of "papers' each week, each paying five thousand dollars. His income from this source alone netted over one million a year, all unreported to the IRS. His legitimate income of over three hundred thousand made a confortable lifestyle, even in Los Angeles. It bothered him somewhat that he could not openly spend all of his income. He had to pretend that the pearls he gave to his wife were fake, the diamonds only zirconia, emeralds, just pretty stones. In five years he would have enough money to take Janet and the kids to Tahiti where they would live a life of leisure in the land he believed was all sunshine and blue skies.

Richard visited several shopping malls and collected nearly four thousand dollars before going to the restaurant across from his hotel for dinner. Wonderful seafood. That's one thing the west coast offered that the east did not. Oh, sure Maine had its lobster, but even that couldn't compare with Dungeness crab or the delicious clam chowder.

He thought about looking for some action and decided to just feast his eyes on the yachts at the marina. From a distance. He didn't want to be confronted by Cinco again, perhaps making his image indelible in Cinco's eyes. He realized what a mistake to have challenged Cinco in the first place. What did he gain? Nothing. Those kinds of actions must be eliminated from his life. No more thoughtless remarks.

He had two messages waiting when he got back to his room. Calls to be returned to Vinnie and Dino. Richard walked out onto the street again to use a pay phone. No calls to be traced to his room just in case anyone tried. Both Vinnie and Dino had used pre-arranged code names. Oh, con men were so smart.

Vinnie received the first call. Even though it was late in New York, Vinnie answered on the first ring. A friendly chat, asking about the business with Dino. Never mentioning names or specific activity.

"My cousin do okay by you?" asked Vinnie.

"Yeah, he did real good. A nice man, very thorough," remarked Richard.

"He's very smart. Perceptive, you might say. Can always tell if someone is trying to con him."

"I would never do that to your cousin."

"This I told him. That you are an okay guy. He has to be sure, you know. He could be what you call a sitting duck if someone fouls up," continued Vinnie.

Richard no novice to hearing warnings, knew Vinnie was telling him to be straight with Dino.

"No problem with me. I'd like to open the same business if my current project doesn't pan out."

"Maybe, just do exactly what he tells you to do. Exactly."

"Will do. I appreciate the activity and I'll be in touch." Richard waited until Vinnie hung up before replacing the receiver and then lifting it again to dial Dino's number. This was a local call and only cost a quarter. He had used nearly all of his coins to call Vinnie. Didn't want calls on his phone card and certainly couldn't call collect. Pay phones are private, the best way to call.

Dino wanted to check on how the rest of the day had gone. How much money Richard had collected and the other business Dino had told Richard to do. All of this done in such a way anyone listening would not understand. No one was near enough to hear any part of the conversation anyway.

Richard traveled around the L.A. area for the next two days. He collected money with the two stolen credit cards as well as purchased some new warm weather clothes. This was fun! He had thirty thousand dollars when Steamer was told by the machine that he needed to deposit more funds. Enough from that account and perhaps from Watson's as well. He had enough to pay Dino's expenses and around forty grand left - a bonus he hadn't counted on. What a life!

On the identification day pick up, Dino reminded Richard that the cards could be used for three months only. These are on-going papers and would be issued to someone else. A new twist. Richard wondered what the new Eric, J. Harlan, and Andrew would look like. He knew he would never know.

CHAPTER FOUR

Ah, such a beautiful ship. Richard boarded early to observe other passengers and get familiar with the decks and facilities. Members of his tour were to gather at three p.m. for orientation and a get-acquainted cocktail party. Excited, Richard found himself fantasizing about the new people he would meet. What "looks" he would offer. As the song said, this could be the start of oh, he forgot. No matter, this is a new beginning and he was ready and eager.

Richard's stateroom, one of the smaller ones, was located on Plumeria Deck. One of the best decks, but not the best cabin. Miffed that it was not in a better location, he decided he would tell anyone who might ask that he had booked late and had no choice. This was not exactly a lie. He did book late, and the best single rooms were already taken, as Cindi had told him.

He tried to evaluate fellow passengers as he watched them board. So many old people. And wheelchairs. Weren't ships, planes, trains, and places of business carrying these handicapped facilities a little too far? Half of the handicapped parking spaces were never used. Did these cripples need to be everywhere? He did see a few young couples, honeymooners, he supposed. No time for them. Not even considering that they, perhaps, would have no time for him. A group of older women, probably first time on a cruise, since all had what looked like new luggage and new clothes. Well, his clothes were new, too. But he didn't look like a country bumpkin as this group did. Their polyester suits all similar. Nearly the same color as well. Some shades of beige. God! Oh, hell, a group of Japs. Were they everywhere, too? People were arriving quickly now. Too fast to make accurate observations, so he tried to pick out rich, unattached women. They all looked too much the same and there was no way to tell those with money or those without. He guessed all on board were fairly well-to-do, since the cruise cost quite a lot and he had paid even more to join the special group. Enough of this, he wanted a drink and eased his way through several groups to the lounge.

He sat at the far end of the bar watching other passengers and casually reading a USA Today. His eyes flicked to the bartender. Something strange there. A waitress handed the bartender some bills and several floated to the floor. He moved them under the edge of the bar counter with one quick movement of his foot. Richard, just as quick to spot a scam as to do one, saw opportunity jump out at him. Then the bartender took a bottle, which had possibly six drinks gone, and squirted some water into the bottle. He placed it under the counter.

Well, well, well. So he keeps drink money and waters drinks. Very slick about it, too. The whole operation could only be seen from the exact spot where Richard happened to be sitting. Too bad the young man had not checked that spot before pulling his scam. This information excited Richard. It could be useful in some way. He stored it away in his mind.

The bartender had the name "Nate" written just above the pocket of his white shirt. A crimson red tie, black pants and thongs completed the uniform. Richard smiled at the thongs. Young people like to be comfortable, he mused.

Richard left to check the employee's schedule. He wanted to observe Nate at other times. Maybe the entire crew was on the take. Easy to find the schedule. Passengers were always wandering into places they didn't belong. Once they bought a ticket, they thought they owned the ship. Richard would wander into the crew's lounge area. Work schedules were generally posted there. Ah, yes. Nate's next duty, opening the bar at 9 a.m. tomorrow morning. Richard would be at his hidden spot at 8:30. This could be another bonus, at the very least blackmail, for a few dollars. Maybe, if it looked prosperous, he would take a piece of the action. New ventures always beckoned if one happened to be looking. Richard smiled.

The get-acquainted party offered no clue to anyone's net worth. Why did Richard believe he could spot wealth so easily. He had no problem when he attended the various fund-raisers he found so important. Course anyone attending would be fairly well-to-do or how else could they pay the price. Sometimes as much as a thousand dollars a plate for the privilege of seeing some celebrity or shaking someone's hand.

Oh, well, check out the jewelry. He had become quite proficient in determining what was real or the fakes that people tried to pass off as real. It would be wonderful, he thought, if his rich wife was young and beautiful. A fleeting thought. His goal was to marry a rich old woman. When she died, he would inherit her fortune. He didn't want to be a rich woman's husband. A rich widower filled his mind.

Richard observed the women as they joined the party. He saw a couple of possibilities. The white-haired-green-dress woman now picking up a drink got his attention. She was tall, very thin, kind of a hawk nose, seventy at least. Her diamond ring worth a few thou, and a small pendant. A real diamond above an emerald, complimenting the dress. She carried a small eelskin purse. He walked over.

"Nice get-together." Richard smiled his I'm-so-delighted-to-see-you smile.

"Yes, I told Paul he should come, but he wanted to unpack, even though he promised to leave business at home," she answered.

So much for her. Richard moved away. He wouldn't waste time on a married woman. The lady wore a puzzled expression when he made no additional efforts for conversation, which Richard ignored.

It seemed the chubby woman standing by the tray of miniature pizzas was the only unattached woman here. Of all things she wore a black and white polka-dot dress which emphasized her extra pounds. Her face was round and full like the rest of her body. Her short brown hair, falling in soft waves around her face, being her only redeeming quality. Nice teeth, her own, with a warm smile helped her looks somewhat. Richard wandered over.

"Nice get-together." He smiled the same way he had when he met the white-haired lady.

"Yes, isn't it," she replied while reaching for another pizza. She already had two in her other hand. "I'm so glad we have a good tour director. Sometimes it is so boring."

How would she possibly know whether or not the tour director is good. We all just arrived. "It doesn't look as if this cruise will be boring." Richard gave her his how-could-anything-be-boring-if-I'm-around smile.

Chubby considerably brightened at this remark and accompanying smile.

"I'm Bernice Lawler from Milwaukee. Single, traveling with a friend." She smiled, a sly look as she brought her eyes up to look into Richard's. "A lady friend."

"Richard Snider, New York City, across from Central Park. Near Jackie's place if you are familiar with the Big Apple." Richard knew that was an important address. Bernice's smile grew larger.

"Are you traveling alone?" she asked. Her eyes could not conceal her wishful thinking.

"Yes, I have business in the islands and ," he paused, watching her wait for him to continue, "I don't have a wife or companion, so I'm all alone."

"Not for long." She moved a step closer to him. "Do you want to team with me since we're both alone?" Bernice eagerly asked.

"What about your lady friend?" Richard remarked, he knew the answer of course.

"We have an understanding that if one of us finds someone then the other kind of disappears." She giggled, "That's really the reason we took this trip. So we could find someone. I just didn't think it would happen so quick."

"Is this your first cruise?" asked Richard.

"Yes, and I could only get three weeks off work, but if it works out for us, I could quit my job." She gazed into Richard's eyes, waiting for that look again. It wouldn't be there.

Bernice had said that terminating word - job. A working woman with three week's vacation. Not on your life. A woman with a job would be tolerated, depending on the profession. A US Senator was as low as he would go. Well, an actress if it could be Jodie Foster. Then he hit on it.

"You're so honest. I'll be honest with you, too." Richard gave her his darn-the-bad-luck-it-won't-happen-for-us look. "I'm looking for someone, too. But I haven't found him yet."

"Him?"

"Oh good. You couldn't tell. I'm so relieved." Richard clapped his hands together and moved his head back and forth.

"Him? Are you, are you..." Bernice couldn't quite get the words any further.

"Oh, does it matter to you? Can't we still be friends?" Richard enjoyed seeing her discomfort.

"Uh, yes," she paused, "there's my friend and we promised to stick together." And off she went, waddling across the deck on her spike heels. How dumb, he thought. Wearing heels on a cruise. And how relieved to have found a way out of that situation.

So, now, anyone new coming to the party? No, apparently travel agents had booked this tour as a couple's cruise. Still many had not attended the get-together, so there was still time. After all, this is only day one.

Richard's dinner companions seemed uninteresting. They were chattering about what stocks had gone up, trips they had taken, how successful their children are, how many thousands they paid in income tax. Volleying for the upper hand, the one who could arouse the most envy.

"What line of work are you in?" asked the man who apparently owned four grocery stores, each doing the business of Jewels or Albertson's, if you could believe him.

Richard did his oh-dear-there-are-many-projects-so-much-I-own look. "I dabble in various areas," he answered.

"You seem quite young to be away from the office so to speak," said a fairly pleasant lady Richard would guess in her late sixties or early seventies. She was dressed in a long dark-colored skirt, white long-sleeved blouse with a small green scarf around her neck. A wide wedding ring her only jewelry. She sat next to groceryman. Richard thought she had more class.

"Who's minding the store, you mean?" asked Richard.

"Was I that obvious?" she replied.

"My managers are very efficient," Richard stated, knowing he had scored a few points. "I'm sure most things run better when I'm gone. Or I convince myself of that so I don't feel guilty enjoying traveling."

"What is it that you do?" Couldn't miss that Texas drawl. Richard learned later that Rex Arder was indeed from Texas and had a cattle ranch, now run by his sons.

"I manage money. Mostly other peoples. I have apartment houses, record companies," (could he call those records of Didi's a company?), "like the rest of you, I'm a working man." He shrugged as if to say that was such an over statement.

The classy lady said, "Working man?" They all laughed and Richard won the success contest. He told himself he didn't even lie, except to say apartment houses, instead of apartment. And he certainly had been managing other people's money. Especially Steamer's and Watson's.

Eight were seated at Richard's table. Rex and Anne Arder from Texas, in cattle, Cliff and Zona Ross, grocery store owners from St. Louis, and Gerald and Rose Olson with their sixteen year-old son, Jerry, retail store owners from Denver. Jerry was grossly overweight as were both his parents. He looked as if he would rather be anywhere else.

As Richard greeted his dinner companions, he thought most passengers were overweight and had been eating eight meals a day to get in practice for the abundant meals offered at sea. He decided to spend a great deal of time in the exercise room. The group said how lucky they were to be seated at the same table and all were lying. There would be no life-long friendships formed here.

After the others departed in other directions, Richard and Jerry stayed at the table discussing football teams and players. Both decided Joe Montana was the best to ever play the game. And both agreed professional football should not be called a game. Their conversation friendly and quiet. So it was a surprise when Bernice walked by and whispered to Richard, "Home run already?" Richard was taken back by her implication and her self-satisfied manner as if she knew something no one else did. Then he remembered.

As she teetered away, both Richard and Jerry watched her with disbelief. She had changed from the polka-dot dress into tight white knit stirrup pants and a red polyester blouse that strained the buttons and barely came to the top of the pants. And those high heels. Hadn't she read the cruise brochures at all?

They took a drink of their Irish sodas and then immediately sprayed it out, laughter too intense to hold back any longer.

"Oh, God. What an escape," muttered Richard.

"Who is that?" asked Jerry.

"A gal I met earlier. She thinks we're lovers."

"What?" exclaimed Jerry.

"To get rid of her, I implied I am gay and now," he burst into more laughter.

"I just met you. We just met everybody." Jerry shook his head. "And those clothes. I can't believe it."

"Well, one thing," said Richard, "it makes me determined to work out more." He decided to help this young man. "Want to join me?"

"I didn't bring any gym clothes," answered Jerry.

"After this huge meal, I'm only going to bicycle awhile. Come on, you don't need anything special for that. Then if you want to keep going you can get stuff from the shop." For some reason Richard could not understand, he identified with Jerry. A loner perhaps, or someone on the fringe of success or acceptance. Or had parents who thought they were doing great by him but were not. Or maybe not willing to accept a son who had visions they did not understand. Or maybe Jerry was just a dreamer. Whatever the reason, this was only the second person in Richard's life that he had wanted to help without asking or expecting anything in return. The other person, of course, was Vinnie.

The two men stripped down to their slacks and bicycled for a half-hour or so. Richard putting on three times as many miles as Jerry.

"How do you stay in such good condition?" asked Jerry, with admiration in his voice. "Do you do this every day?" Jerry was puffing while Richard seemed relaxed with no strain from the pedaling.

"I work out on something everyday and believe me, it pays off. You may have seen me eat a big meal tonight, but watch. From now on, I'll take it easy. I like looking trim and I like the way women look at me and guys envy me. You can do it if you want and I'll work with you."

"Yeah." Jerry looked at Richard's trim frame and pictured himself looking like that. "I'd like that. How long will it take?"

This late summer and early fall tour and daily workouts could get him looking pretty good by the time school began the last week in September.

"You could make a big difference in six weeks. It's kind of fun knowing you are in control. Start out by skipping dessert and never take second helpings. There's some great exercise equipment in here, so it could be a lot of fun. Just don't over do. No more than an hour a day and not strenuous. Get the ship's doctor to check you out first and talk to your folks." Richard felt good about helping Jerry.

"No dessert?" asked Jerry.

"Just a little. Remember you are in control.." They were quiet for a few minutes. Then Richard asked, "What is your long term goal?"

"Something with computers, although my parents want me to take over the stores."

"So that's it?" Richard stated.

"What's it?"

50

"The reason you are overweight. Too demanding parents. Hell, don't let them run your life. Stick with computers if you want. Course, maybe you could do both," said Richard.

"That's what I keep telling my dad. But he's old fashioned and thinks whatever he does is the only way."

"He makes a lot of money, doesn't he?"

"Yeah."

"So learn something from him. Take the ball and go for a touchdown."

"I guess." Jerry seems uncertain that he could ever bring his dad around to new thinking.

"I try to pick up on everything I can. Sometimes other ideas can be okay."

"Yeah."

"If your folks see the effort you are making in the weight loss program, maybe they'll listen to you more." Richard didn't know if this would work but he had an uncanny way of ferreting out reasons something could or could not be done. It didn't always work for him, since many times he grew impatient and left things undone.

"Think so?" asked Jerry.

"Can't hurt to try." Richard got off the bike and put on his shirt. "Now that I've done some exercise, I think I'll check out the bar. You're too young, so what are you going to do?"

"I brought some books along to study. I'll show you sometime. I'm really good with computers and have a new game figured out. Something that will appeal to adults as well as kids and just hard enough to be challenging. I've never seen any other game like it."

"Okay, see you." Richard liked Jerry and he felt he could help not only with his weight loss, but with his parents as well. Not that he had that much experience with parents, he just had a feeling about Jerry. He knew he couldn't spend too much time with him. After all, his first priority did not include a teenager.

Hey, look who's on duty again this evening. Richard took the stool behind the large potted plant again so he could observe the bartender and his nice little scam. He watched for a few minutes, then moved to the front of the bar to order a drink.

"Yes, sir?" Nate, friendly and efficient. Twenty-five, tops, Richard thought. Maybe younger. Brownish hair, a nice cut. Hazel eyes, about five-feet eight or nine. All-American look about him with a Norwegian background, Richard guessed.

"I'll have Crown Royal, on the rocks." Richard watched Nate reach for a bottle. The label was turned so Richard couldn't see. It was one of the watered-down bottles.

"No. Not from that one. Pour mine from a straight bottle."

"I beg your pardon, sir. You said Crown Royal. This is Crown Royal. Excuse me sir. I'll be right back. The hostess is signaling me." Nate quickly put the bottle in a row of others, including one marked Crown Royal.

"Oh, it's okay. She doesn't need me." Richard only smiled as Nate picked up the Crown Royal bottle turning it so Richard could see the label. He poured the drink.

"Now Nate, I've been watching you for awhile and though I don't mind a scam, in fact, I appreciate a good one. But you know, kid, I saw this within five minutes after I sat down."

"Saw what, sir?" Nate asked, his face coloring a little and his eyes looking somewhere besides at Richard.

Richard took a slow, long sip of the whiskey, savoring the full flavor. "Let me tell you what." He put the stubby glass down and twirled it around a few times.

"First, you have at least ten bottles of booze that you've watered down with four or more ounces. Four, I would say. Just enough to give you a four drink bonus. That's about twenty bucks a bottle. Or, if my math is correct, two hundred dollars that no one knows about. That's just for starters." Richard looked directly into Nate's eyes and Nate seemed to be holding his breath.

"Now the tip money." Richard pointed to a large ginger jar under the counter. "My guess is that the tips are to be divided among all of you after each shift. Right?" Richard raised his eyes to Nate's.

"Yes, sir." The bar and lounge were the only areas on the ship that cash was used. All other activities and the shops used the ship's credit card.

"But." Richard paused and took another sip of his drink. "Your little foot has been pretty busy."

Nate's face colored again and he became very nervous. His breathing became fast and beads of perspiration began forming on his face.

"Take a glance under the counter and you'll see a couple fives and some ones. The evening is still young. How much do you steal from your co-workers in an evening, Nate?"

"Who are you? Are you with security?" Nate asked, his voice almost an octave higher than before.

"Nope, just another passenger. But I know a scam when I see one."

"This is the first time I've done this. I, I won't do it anymore," stammered Nate.

"Ah, Nate. May I call you Nate? Earlier in the day I saw you." Richard gave him a don't-con-me look.

"How? Where? I'm careful. No one is at the bar when, when..."

"You've got potential, but careful? Well, maybe you should move that plant. You never looked that way even once."

"I moved the stool. No one sits there." Nate's eyes were darting around and blinking fast. He was scared, Richard knew.

"I did. I just moved the stool back and you never even noticed me."

"Are you going to report me? I won't do it anymore." His lips were moist since he kept licking them.

"No. I figure we can work out a deal."

"You can have all the free drinks you want-when I'm on duty. No one else knows about this."

"Free drinks. Well, I'll take those, but I need something else."

"What? Anything." Nate would agree to sell his soul at this point.

"I need to know who on board is somebody. Wealthy, I mean wealthy. I need names, what they do, and you to point them out to me. Only the women." Richard knew this was a long shot, but worth a try. Besides, he had no desire to report Nate. In fact, he would offer him a few pointers on the finer ways of working a bar scam. He knew the moves very well.

"Yes, sir. I'll try my best. The only thing I know right now is there are four large stockholders on board," related Nate.

"Stockholders in what?" asked Richard.

"This shipping line. A couple of them own quite a lot of stock. In fact, the captain briefed us on them so we wouldn't foul up."

"Any special reason why they are here. Or is this a regular practice to check on their stock?"

"There's a board meeting in Honolulu and no, we don't normally have board members with us. I guess people who serve on boards don't have time to cruise," responded Nate.

"Any of them women?"

"One. Mrs. Rogers." Nate, beginning to relax, enjoyed talking with Richard. While filling drink orders in a brisk manner, never once using the watered bottles.

"Is there a Mr. Rogers with her?" asked Richard, then, "Hey Nate, use the other stuff." He motioned to the altered bottles.

"Yeah, okay. They all look pretty much alike, don't you think?" asked Nate, who hoped Richard was his new friend, or at least not his enemy.

"That they do, just stick with four additions and watch that plant," cautioned Richard.

"I will, thanks." Nate was grateful for the advice. "I haven't seen any of the stockholders yet. But I'll get right on it. In fact," he called to an attendant and asked him to contact the purser for him. "Should know in a few minutes if Randall can tell us anything. He keeps pretty good tabs on the important people. They are generally our return customers so they get treated super. I don't mean that the others don't get treated super as well. Only well, some people expect more and Randall knows who they are."

"I'll be back." Richard decided to check out the casino and disco, then thought again about the casino. Doesn't fit his new image. He ambled to the top deck to the disco and the music sounded like heaven. Reggae. And, oh how he loved dancing to that. A five-piece band and loud. Good thing the sound went up or some of those old fogies on the lower decks would flip out if they could hear the music. Richard loved the way these younger women dressed. Tight, tight short dresses. Didi had a red one and did she ever do great things for it. Check out the blonde. Her moves should be forbidden. Her partner just stood and watched her. Why not. Wow! Maybe he would cut in. Then the music stopped and an Elvis impersonator got on stage. His gyrations almost matched the blonde's. The young people howled and stamped their feet, hands waving in the air. Richard had no idea there were this many, in his eyes anyway, kids on board. Fifty at least. The little floor was crowded and they were all having such fun.

He looked closer at the crowd and guessed kids was not the right term. Most were in their mid-twenties and early thirties. What a joy it would be to join them. Hey, that guy is good. When he said hound dog, the crowd screamed. A holiday mood and why not? Everyone is on a holiday. Ship-board friendships rarely lasted, but during the cruise everyone promised life-long associations. Richard longingly gazed at the dancers, but knew he wouldn't find his rich lady here. Best go back to the bar and pick Nate's brain. He should have information by now. On the way, he stopped in the card room. Six tables of bridge. He signed a sheet to announce his interest in playing, glanced casually at other names, saw no Mrs. Rogers, so went on his way.

Nate had a list of six women who he said had piles of money. Marian Rogers, traveling alone, did not book the best deck. Maybe to hide her identity as a board member and large stockholder. Gertrude Larson, traveling with a younger woman. Maybe a caretaker since Gertrude was at least eighty, and they had a suite. Very nice! Eva Conroy, probably seventy or so, quite large, demanding. Wears her wealth for everyone to see. Lorraine Baker, a regular cruise traveler, and with two other women. Her companions may not be rich, but for sure Lorraine had big bucks. Eleanor Argus let everyone know she has money. But, alas she also has a husband. And the last on the list, Patricia Koder. Quiet, unassuming, wore very expensive clothes in very good taste, traveling alone.

Nate had no idea how their wealth had been acquired or their marital status. Richard, delighted with this information, vowed to give both Nate and the purser a large tip. And this time, he assured himself, he would do it. Not like his decision to renege on Didi's rent and checking account. These fellows had really helped him. Didi had just been there.

Richard dismissed Eleanor right away. No time to deal with a husband. He didn't want such an extremely demanding wife, so set Eva aside temporarily. Gertrude, a possibility if her companion didn't interfere. Marian, certainly a catch. He would love to be a stockholder in the cruise line. Lorraine would bear spending time with, if she could shake her lady friends. Patricia, though, got his first nod.

Now to work. Plan his attack. How to meet them and to quickly decide who to pursue and who to eliminate. My God, it's eleven-thirty. Almost time for the midnight buffet. Would any of the six be there? He noted with chagrin that none of the six were among the 200 members of the tour he had spent an additional fifteen grand to join. That Cindi sold him a hell of a lot more travel than he needed. She owed him fifteen thousand. He would get it back someway. Well, he didn't have time to think of that now. Probably not tomorrow either. Which one, which one will it be? He reviewed the list again noting the women's residences.

Gertrude from La Jolla, California. Pretty good, an affluent city. But, God, she is so old. Marian from Chicago. Chicago? Machine gun Chicago! Patricia-San Francisco. So that accounts for her elegance, Richard surmised.

Yes, he would begin with Patricia. Pat, Tricia, Patty. Which goes best with Snider. Koder sounded German. Of course, that could be her husband's name. Women that age weren't in to keeping their maiden names yet. Great, she had or (has) a German husband. That means she already knows the husband is the boss. Makes it easier, Richard mused. That is, if she turns out to be a widow. Or, he guessed husbands can be eliminated. Don't people fall overboard all the time?

On with the residence information. Eleanor Argus and her husband were from Salt Lake City. Lorraine Baker, a southern belle from Dallas. And Eva Conroy hailed from Philadelphia.

None of the six prospects attended the midnight buffet. Richard had arrived early, hoping he wouldn't miss an opportunity to encounter the women.

Ah, an early morning walk brought results. Gertrude, in a wheelchair, was being pushed by her apparent caretaker, a woman around thirty, guessed Richard. The younger woman wore a pant suit, stylish perhaps ten years ago, of heavy blue polyester. A white cotton blouse and low-heeled heavy black oxfords completed the ensemble. What an ugly outfit, went through Richard's mind. Her hair, pulled back and held with a blue ribbon was a non-distinguishing brown color and her lack of makeup only added to her plainness.

Gertrude wore beige colored pants, a very pretty blouse in a peach shade, and a lovely cardigan sweater. Perhaps she didn't want the younger woman to be noticed, thought Richard. It suggested, bet Richard, that she dressed in such an attractive manner to accentuate herself even more. However, he could be wrong since he knew neither of them. He wasn't.

Now, how to approach them. Observing for a few moments, he saw the younger woman push Gertrude around the deck, then stop as the two of them gazed at the water.

"It's fascinating, isn't it?" Richard stood near the women and gave his best aren't-we-lucky-to-be-here-together smile.

"I beg your pardon, are you speaking to me?" Gertrude asked in a voice suggesting how could that be possible, since she had no idea of his identity.

Quick on the take, after all he had been practicing for months, Richard said, "Oh dear, I thought you were, oh, I'm sorry. It's so hard to remember names and I was sure we met yesterday afternoon. I'm Richard Snider from New York City."

"Well, I'm Gertrude Larson from La Jolla." No need to name the state, she implied. She made no offer to introduce her companion.

Richard, an expert at small talk, chatted about the waves, the food, soft breezes, all to no avail. He got very little response from Gertrude and none at all from "silent" as he called her in his mind.

"If you would like to give your companion a break, I would be glad to push your chair or even stay here. I enjoy talking with you," offered Richard.

"No, thank you. Ellen is hired to look after me and she will do just that." Gertrude had no warmth in her voice. Her eyes were as ice blue as Richard's could be. She had heavy lines in her face and her very course white hair was cut straight around her neck in a blunt way. There was no question that she clearly expected to have her words obeyed immediately.

So much for Gertrude. He would bet she had never been called Trudy or even Gertie. No, no nickname for her. She would never allow it. This conversation had gone nowhere. Gertrude's responses, when she bothered, were short and bordered on rudeness. Too bad, mused Richard. It could have been easy to get rid of her. Accidents happen so often to people in wheelchairs. Could she swim? Not if strapped in a chair and the clasp unreachable. Maybe the clasp would be "inconveniently" fastened in the back. Or, perhaps a fire and a locked door. Oh, it would have been so easy. No matter how attentive Richard tried to be, she gave no warmth, nor invitation in her voice. Not even friendliness.

Richard might get back to Gertrude, but now he decided to check out the other five women. Bridge after lunch could offer a break. Perhaps one or more of the women played. Now, though he must find Nate and ask him to point out Patricia. Nate had given Richard a brief description of the women, had in fact, given him a few facts about each one making them easier to recognize. Still, there were so many places on the ship. The women could be anywhere. What a stroke of luck it had been to discover Nate's scam. Richard definitely had Nate in his pocket.

Instead of Patricia, Nate guided Richard to Eva. Hard to miss, she dressed in a bright red pleated skirt and over-blouse of the same shade accented with gold buttons. She drew attention to her size with a bold statement of loud colors and an even louder laugh. She found nearly everything humorous. Richard surmised she knew she had enough money to act and dress any way she pleased. Although he hadn't known who she was at the time, he had noticed when she boarded the ship. She had worn a bright yellow outfit and a huge straw hat in the same color. Her shoes were dyed to match her clothes. Her appearance and actions were obnoxious. To Richard enough money overshadows bad taste anytime.

Eva had picked up a drink and a handful of peanuts from the bar when Richard quickly turned and "accidentally" bumped into her, spilling the drink.

"Oh, my God. I'm sorry," he said while giving her his poor-little-boy look while brushing the liquid from her sleeve with his silk monogrammed handkerchief. Hardly any liquid spilled. Still he made quite an issue of it. Eva had no way of knowing he did this to begin a conversation.

"Here, let me get you another drink." Richard took her glass and put it on the bar. "The same for the lady and one for me. He had no intention of paying for the drinks. He guided Eva to a small table towards the back of the lounge.

Nate brought the drinks along with a bowl of mixed nuts. As he placed the napkins on the table and set the drinks down, he smiled and said, "Now that's a unique way for a man to meet a lady."

Eva burst forth with loud coarse laughter which drew several pair of eyes their way. She gave Richard a flirtatious look and nudged Nate's arm.

How much money does she have, pondered Richard. It will have to be tons, he decided. Tons and tons.

"I'm Richard Snider and I do apologize again for being so careless, but I can't in good faith apologize for it happening." He smiled his otherwise-we-wouldn't-have-met smile and she succumbed to his charm.

She laughed again and her mouth sprayed the drink all over the table. This brought on a tremendous roar.

God, what a pig, thought Richard. He might as well learn all about her right now. He could accept a great deal if she had enough money.

"You are?" He knew, but she didn't know that.

"Eva Conroy." No laughter, which Richard judged must be a small miracle.

"From?" Was this always the second question when travelers met?

"All over." Another guffaw. "But mainly from Philadelphia. I vote in Philly, like in the cream cheese." Somehow this was an extremely humorous statement.

Richard smiled, "Let's exchange facts about each other," again putting on the charm, "since fate may have brought us together."

"Fate. You call spilling my drink fate?" Laughter, loud laughter. "Well, what do you want to know?" This question must have been very funny, mused Richard.

"Tell me about your family. Marital status, mainly that, and your likes and dislikes." He gazed into her eyes. "Everything." Richard could abide the laughter, but not if there were many relatives, mainly kids, around with the same sense of humor.

"I have three daughters and if I do say so myself, they all look like me. Or they will in a few years. On their way anyway." Another funny statement. It must be, thought Richard, since the guffaw nearly rocked the room.

"Lucky girls. Whose watching them while you cruise around, a baby sitter?" Richard asked, even making himself a little nauseous at this obvious flattery.

"Oh, you silly man, they are all married. I'm a grandmother." She gushed, pleased at Richard's remarks and clearly believing him.

"Now, let's be truthful. A mother I can believe, but a grandmother?"

"Yes, yes I am. Really." She stated firmly while stuffing her mouth with a handful of nuts.

"How about your husband?" Let's get on with this. Is she in the running or not?

"Dead. Been dead almost ten years."

"So, you were left with three girls to raise. What kind of work did you do?"

"Work," another enormously funny statement. Very loud laughter! "He left me two million dollars." She looked

59

directly into his eyes waiting for the expression that such a revelation usually brought. Richard's expression did not change. He had practiced much too long. Two million dollars wouldn't cut it. Not with that laugh.

"It's been nice talking to you. And again, I apologize for spilling your drink." He got up to leave.

"Hey! What about you?" She pulled at his sleeve. "You said exchange facts. So far I haven't learned anything about you except your name." No laughter.

"I'm very boring. In fact, there are a couple of things you don't want to know." Richard surveyed the lounge, seeing Jerry on deck. Ah, the Gods have smiled on me. He waved, his fingers making little flutters in the air. Jerry did not see him, Richard did not intend him to, wanting only Eva to see his motions. She spun around trying to see and wondering what that kind of a motion meant.

"I see my friend." Richard said this in a sing-song way, hoping Eva would get the impression he was trying to give. Richard had a few gay friends and not one of them fluttered their fingers like that. He was banking on Eva having the misconception that most people in her generation have, that gays act feminine.

At that moment Jerry saw Richard. He smiled and waved. Eva saw that, and immediately jerked her head back to Richard. Of course Richard did another flutter and giggled.

"Does that bother you?" He asked in a pleading way that he did not mean.

"Well, well," she sputtered, "I never, do you mean...?" She could hardly get the words out of her mouth. "What do you mean?"

"Whatever you are thinking could be right." He waved his hand in the air.

"What about all this talk about wanting to know me better?" No laughter now.

"Did I say that?" sneered Richard. "Exactly that?"

"Well, I thought that's what you meant. You said fate brought us together." Eva was puzzled.

"No. I said fate may have brought us together. You women only hear what you hope is said, not what is actually being spoken."

"But, but..." she stammered.

"Come on, get real." Richard's voice was full of contempt.

"You are despicable. You deliberately led me to believe you were interested in me and all the while you are a fairy," Eva fairly shouted.

"Now really, why would I be interested in a fat, loud woman like you," said Richard, this time in a nasty tone.

Then he realized he couldn't drive away to another part of town. Hell, they are on a ship. She will be around the entire voyage.

"I didn't mean that. I got angry." He had to make amends. She could be a fierce enemy.

"All my life I've had to explain my feelings and I overreacted. I'm sorry." Richard hoped he hadn't gone too far and that she would forgive him.

"Why did you make a play for me if, if, well if..." She trailed off her question.

"I didn't mean for it to appear that way. I just wanted a friend," he explained, his little boy pleading eyes seeking hers.

Eva held his eyes a long moment, "Perhaps I overreacted as well. You're right. Why would you want a fat woman like me." She sighed, "The story of my life." Her face told a sad tale.

Richard slowly exhaled, not realizing he had been holding his breath. What a relief, he whispered to himself. The old bag bought it. Must be more careful with his outbursts, and also how many people he wanted to think he is gay. It worked like a charm with Eva and Bernice. At least they will stay away. But what if they gossip about it? What then? Course his actions will speak for themselves when he meets the right woman. She will immediately know he is not gay.

He noticed Eleanor Argus and her husband strolling on the deck. He affirmed once again-no married women. He will, though, be friends with both of them. Who knows they may be ripe for a scam or two. They already provided him with a couple of magazines he found on the deck chairs they had occupied.

Richard, scheduled to play bridge at one-thirty, had time for lunch and a short talk with Nate, hoping he could lead him to Patricia, Marian, or Lorraine. At Nate's signal, he wandered over to the bar.

"Hey, buddy. Mrs. Baker is sitting out on the deck with her friends." Excited, Nate put his hand out to shake Richard's. "You want me to take a drink out so you can spill it or something?"

Buddy, he is not my buddy. Richard didn't like the sound of that familiarity even if he liked what Nate was doing for him.

"Which one is she?" asked Richard, looking past the lounge to the deck.

"She's wearing white shorts and a greenish top. The one with the tightly permed hair. Right near the end of the deck on the left. See those three women?" Nate craned his neck to see around Richard.

"Yeah, okay." Richard pondered his approach, deciding to pretend he had previously met one of the women.

The three appeared to be in their fifties or early sixties. Probably widows spending their husband's hard-earned money.

Richard walked by, then suddenly turned. "Hey Claire, what are you doing here?" He smiled at the one with the salt and pepper hair seated on the end. Lorraine, his target, was in the middle. The one on the end wore white pants, a red and white candy-striped long sleeved blouse, and white sandals. The other woman, to Lorraine's left, dressed in a similar fashion. Only her top was an oversize yellow sweatshirt. Her hair was on the blonde side, with gray beginning to show. Lorraine's hair was stark white.

The three women looked at him, then at each other, making a game of pointing their fingers at the other.

"Claire?" The women said in unison. Then, "not me." Again, in unison.

"Oh, I see I'm mistaken. I thought you were a friend of a friend." Richard used his you're-not-but-it's-okay smile while waiting for an invitation to join them.

"I guess we can be Claire," said the woman in the candy-striped blouse.

"Sure we can." In unison again.

"What do we have here, The Andrews Sisters?" Richard pulled over a chair even though no one had invited him.

"I guess we can be The Andrews Sisters," giggled Lorraine.

"Why don't you sit down?" asked the gal in the yellow sweatshirt, after he had been sitting for a few minutes. They all laughed.

"Are you really sisters?" This brought more giggles.

"Is my hairpiece on crooked?" Richard made exaggerated motions with his hands pushing at his hair, which of course was completely his own and stayed right in place. "Or are my looks funny? What in the world are you all laughing at?"

"Nothing." They regarded each other and laughed again. "We've been like this since the trip began and none of us knows why. Everything seems funny and we laugh."

At least this laughter is not the same as Eva's Richard joyfully asserted. But only to himself.

The women swallowed a few times, wiping tears from their eyes and got back to what Richard guessed resembled normal behavior.

"None of us is Claire as you know. I'm Lorraine Baker, this is Dorothy West," waving a hand towards the candy-striper. Dorothy gave a salute. "And this is Rita Maren." Lorraine turned toward Rita who gave a small wave of her hand. "All of us are from Big D."

"I'm Richard Snider from the Big Apple." They thought it quite humorous that they all lived somewhere "big."

"Where are your husbands?" Let's get down to business. Enough time spent being funny, already.

"Home," again the three voices said the word at the same time.

"All at the same home?" At least we're having fun, Richard decided. The most fun so far, since he caught Nate and the scam. But not much more.

"Actually, no. They aren't even home. All are together though, we think," said Rita.

"Are you going to tell me about it, or do we have another song?" smiled Richard.

"Her husband," Dorothy pointed to Lorraine, "owns the Fort Worth football team and our husbands are coaches.

"Fort Worthless team, if they don't win more games than they did last year," muttered Lorraine.

"Benny Bean is no quarterback and no one can turn him into one," said Rita, defending her husband.

"You're right, but what can Ryan do? He has another three years on his contract and he isn't about to buy him out," stated Lorraine.

"Someone should, or trade him. Of course, who would want him?" reflected Dorothy on the team's problem.

"So you ladies are football widows. Take trips and so forth while your husbands play football?" asked Richard.

"Oh, no," explained Lorraine. "They don't play football, and we go to all the games. Right now there are two weeks before the regular season and the guys have the team in Costa Rica for training soooo we took a little trip." Big smiles all around. "We go back as soon as we reach Hilo."

Richard tapped his foot. Interesting conversation, but nothing to be gained here. He checked his watch and noted the time. Wished he had a Rolex. Maybe he could steal one. They were much more impressive than the brand he now wore. Course he had stolen it, too.

"I have to make a call," He included all the ladies in his statement. "So I'll see you later."

"That's y'all later," smiled Rita. "You know, we are southern gals."

"Have fun, y'all."

"We will," the three responded.

Richard did make a call---to Vinnie. Why he hadn't thought of this sooner he would never know. Vinnie could check the finances of the women within minutes and save Richard tons of time. He listed the women in alphabetical order and asked him to identify them by initial when he responded. Never know who may be listening to a telephone conversation or who may read a wire or fax. Can't be too careful.

Richard had no qualms about breaking up a marriage if the bounty happened to be high enough. He would even have endured Eva's laugh for a price.

Vinnie dug deep. His network of information, as always, bordered on awesome. He discovered all the ladies listed were wealthy. Some had more money than others but then there were other considerations as well. Such as husbands and loud laughter.

Eleanor Argus, called A, only rich because of her husband and a split of assets didn't leave enough to go through the trouble of a divorce. Vinnie, as well as Richard, crossed A off the list.

Eva as E, had increased the original two million to four million so she became a possibility again. Loud laughter and all. Vinnie related that she would be easy to manage.

Gertrude, as G, had money, but her husband wisely placed it in a trust and no one could get to it. Richard had crossed her off the list earlier and now there was no doubt.

Lorraine, as L, became nixed since she loved her lifestyle. "Firmly entrenched," Vinnie had said. She enjoyed the football perks with a passion, one being the very quarterback she had badmouthed.

Vinnie gave Marian, or M, the highest priority. The fax back to Richard said, "M is seventy-three, a widow, and worth twenty or more million. Go for it, couldn't find anyone better."

Patricia, P, about to be divorced after a nasty hearing still interested Richard.

Vinnie, however, said she was absolutely a no go. Her soon-to-be-ex was appealing the judge's decision to award Patricia half of his extensive estate. It looked as if an agreement could drag on for years.

The information excited Richard. No more wasted time trying to worm conversation out of the women. Now he could get right to work and meet his rich soon-to-be-wife. Marian seemed to be quite elusive. Nate hadn't pointed her out, although he had mentioned the stock she owned. High stockholder in this very ship. Gleefully Richard pondered being a stockholder. He fantasized on the changes he would make. Eliminate the handicapped facilities so those old cripples wouldn't be on board. And keep it American. Let the foreigners get their own ship. Tonight he would make a list of the changes he would demand.

Off to play bridge again. He did enjoy the card game and had become very good. The other players were friendly. Still they took the game seriously and winning became very important. Richard won his share of games and the others treated him as an equal. A new experience for him since being "newly rich" still offered much skill in remembering what to do and how.

Where is Marian? She must not be a bridge player since all the players wore name tags. All the better to become acquainted. Perhaps she likes staying in her cabin. A reader? Sick maybe? Richard needed Nate's help again. He must find her to see if she may be suitable as his wife.

The details weren't complete yet. But the end result was firmly in his mind. He planned to become a rich widower. Whatever it takes. Hire it done, with millions of dollars he could afford the best. Or do it himself. He had many specific abilities not necessarily or, perhaps any, to be proud of. But certainly he could get the job done.

First things first. He must meet Marian, win her confidence, perhaps make her fall in love with him. He, of course, would not love her. That, no way, is part of the plan. But marriage is definitely a part. God, he hoped she wasn't another chubby. Or had horrible laughter and was at least tolerable looking. Maybe if his luck held, she would have a heart problem or diabetes. Then he could give her shots. Perhaps with poor eyesight, she couldn't watch the kind of shot he gave her. Maybe he would really luck out. He was due. He deserved being rich. Life owed him some good luck for a change. Too bad Patricia had such a complicated life. She was so far the most attractive of Nate's six, as Richard called the women on the list. She was the youngest as well. Late forties, Richard guessed. He had glimpsed her at dinner the previous evening. Nate had brought him an unordered drink, especially so he could point her out. Course he hadn't seen Marian either, but he had no illusions about her. A woman with twenty-plus million dollars and unattached must be some kind of a dog. All of a sudden he liked dogs, any kind of a dog if twenty million came when he whistled.

Ah, there is Patricia catching a few rays and all alone. She wore a one-piece black swim suit, cut high on the thigh. She also had a multi-colored beach wrap tossed over her shoulders. Her towel matched the wrap. Sun glasses, with rims the same rose color as in the towel and wrap, accented the total picture. Dark roots were barely distinguishable in her short blonde hair. Very classy lady, nicely coordinated clothes and he would know. Hadn't he spent the past six months learning all about that very thing?

Richard wore tan walking shorts, a lighter tan golf shirt with three buttons open and his Birkenstocks were light brown. His clothes highlighted the golden streaks in his hair. Oh, yes, he had been a quick learner and absolutely knew he looked fantastic.

As Richard approached Patricia, she continued reading, never acknowledging his presence. He stood next to her a few minutes before asking, "May I sit here?" He pulled a lounge chair closer. The deck nearly deserted since not many souls were brave enough to endure today's sharp breezes.

Patricia's glance reflected her uninterested feeling, "Whatever you're selling I don't want any." She turned back to her book dismissing Richard.

Richard did not respond, keeping his face turned towards her. After a few moments she again looked at him, removed her dark glasses, and said not pleasantly, "Why on this big ship, did you happen to choose a chair next to me?" She waved her arm as if to include the entire deck. "As I said, I'm not buying."

"I'm not selling."

"Fine. Good-bye."

"Are you always this unfriendly, or did I forget to comb my hair? I know I brushed my teeth."

She glanced at his hair as he knew she would, then back to her book. Richard continued to keep his eyes on her. What a challenge. This could be fun. On the other hand he completely trusted Vinnie's judgment and he had nixed Patricia. Still, he had nothing to do for an hour or so, until he met Jerry in the gym, so Patricia could be a way to hone his desirability skills.

Patricia closed the book, which Richard noticed was the new Stephen King novel, got up from the lounge chair, gathered her wrap and towel, and told Richard, "Good-bye."

"Hey wait, I'll leave. I only wanted to talk with someone and I chose you. I'm sorry." He rose from the lounge chair. She hesitated. He smiled.

"It isn't you," said Patricia. "Right now I hate all men and I don't even want to talk to any."

"Don't punish me for someone else's mistakes. I wasn't in the game." Richard turned on his I'm-just-glad-to-know-you-and-I-would-never-do-anything-to-hurt-you smile.

"Sorry, it will take me awhile." Sadness showed in her eyes and her lips reverted to a thin tight line.

"Want to talk about it?" Richard prevailed. "I'm a good listener."

"So you can tell your wife how lucky she is to still have a husband." Her eyes reflected the bitterness of her voice.

"I wish I could. I wish I could tell my wife anything. Anything at all. I only wish I could." Richard could put on the sad eyes as well as anyone. Actually sad eyes rated right up there as one of his best expressions. Didi really fell for it.

Patricia raised her eyebrows in question. Richard knew this would happen.

"She was killed four years ago. Automobile accident. Drunken driver. Our son," Richard's voice broke and his eyes filled with tears, "lived for two weeks and then...and then..." Apparently he could say no more. Patricia winced. Richard loved this story. He had used it once before and man did it ever work great. Got the gal in the sack within an hour. He had no idea where he got the idea for the story. Perhaps he read a newspaper account of a similar situation. It certainly had never happened to him. And the tears came so readily. Richard would supposedly wipe his eyes when in reality he would poke

67

his finger or the corner of his handkerchief across an eye, making tears quickly available. Course it hurt, but the results were terrific.

Patricia did not know this and her response had the desired effect for Richard. She put her hand on his arm and eased herself back onto the lounge chair.

And that's all it took. They chatted amiably for awhile, covering such topics as traveling, the stock market, books she read, all of Stephen King's, even though she confessed sometimes they kept her awake, and movies.

"I enjoy talking with you. Still you must understand, and please understand, I don't want to become involved with anyone. Not even on a friendship basis," declared Patricia. "I really want to spend my time alone."

"You contradicted yourself," remarked Richard. "You said you like talking with me, yet you want to spend your time alone". He paused. "Both?"

"Maybe."

"You know, I do understand and I accept it." Richard continued, "But do you think it's good for you to cut yourself off from even casual friendliness?"

"Right now I just hate all men. They take and take and then when they don't want you anymore, you get tossed aside," Patricia bitterly remarked.

"Is that what happened?" Richard sounded concerned, his voice and expression told her that, thought Patricia.

Practice pays off. Richard wanted to shout with joy. Or give someone a high five. Instead he remained the caring friend or at least he projected that feeling.

"Yes, that's what happened. So much for that." Once again, she stood and began to gather her towel, book and wrap. "I really must go and although I'm sure you mean well, I'm not into friendship right now."

"Just thought I'd give it a try. I would enjoy a friendship that I knew was just that-friendship. But, whatever you want. Remember, all of us are not rats as you no doubt think." Richard walked off feeling a little let down. He had enjoyed the conversation and Patricia's looks were certainly pleasant to observe. Very pleasant, yet he decided it may require too much effort to break down her animosity towards men. Besides, Vinnie rejected her, Richard reminded himself again.

Richard joined Jerry in the gym for a short workout and it was indeed a surprise to find Gerald Olson there with his son.

Both of them working out on the bicycle and laughing together. Jerry stopped long enough to bring Richard up-to-date on the computer-in-the-store project which apparently he had talked his dad into doing. Jerry's parents were so pleased to see him make an effort to lose weight and aim for better physical condition that Richard guessed they were agreeable to almost anything. Of course, Richard took all the credit for the Olson's change in attitude and Jerry's weight loss desire. His good deed for the week, never once admitting to himself that his good deeds were few and very far in between.

CHAPTER FIVE

Richard saw Marian standing by the railing of the ship looking out to sea exactly where Nate had said she would be. Good ol' Nate. He would become more useful as the weeks went by. What a find, mused Richard.

The wind ruffled her short brown hair and her smile indicated she enjoyed the soft breeze. She wore dark brown pants, a lighter shade of brown linen jacket and slung over her shoulders was a brown and gold soft leather bag that matched her sandals. A little brown wren, thought Richard. She needs brighter colors or at least something bright around her face. He watched without her knowledge for several minutes. No great beauty, yet not ugly by a long shot. She had a self-assurance look about her as if she had always dressed just right for any occasion. That she knew instantly which fork to use, that she always sat in the best seats at the opera and probably never ever had been inside a tavern or seen a girlie show. He explored the thought of how many companies had her as one of their directors and he questioned if the twenty million included all of her holdings, or if there were other negotiable items that could be quickly turned into cash. Did she have a large or small family? And more important, did she have a heart problem or perhaps diabetes? Could he be so lucky? As he came closer, he detected the faint scent of Joy. Was that an omen that she wore a perfume which made such a profound statement of pure delight?

Joy, and it would be, if he could get her twenty million and get rid of her. The ultimate plan. The idea that had lived with him for months. A rich wife then a rich widower.

He came close to her. "A penny for your thoughts." His voice was soft and low.

Her eyes remained looking at the ocean for a moment, then she turned and smiled at him.

"We are quite insignificant when we see all of that aren't we?" Marian waved her hand indicating the expanse of the water.

"Is that what you were thinking? That you are insignificant? Because if you were, then you are wrong." Richard's eyes held hers until she once again gazed out to sea.

"Thank you, but this is awesome, isn't it?" Her voice was low and pleasing. Richard secretly applauded. No screeching, no obnoxious laughter, no coy expressions. In fact, he felt a great contentment that his search may, at last, be over.

"It is," responded Richard and he gazed at the water as well. Both remained quiet. Richard thought can't rush this lady. Don't make a poor judgment call. Take it slowly and ease into situations. What is that song about doing it right the first time. Whatever it is, that's what he will do. Everything right the first time. Think before speaking. Do not lose your temper or make sneering remarks. This is what you have been working for. Don't blow it!

"Is it every seventh wave that's larger or eleventh?" asked Richard, never taking his eyes from the water.

"I think the seventh, but I'm not sure." Marian laughed. "Just when I think I have it counted right a large one comes up on the third or fourth count and I start all over again."

"You do that, too? I spend hours trying to count right. Water has always fascinated me."

"I can never believe that water covers seventy-five percent of the earth's surface until I get on a ship and see this again."

Richard didn't know that statistic. He had never cared about cruising or being on the water until he decided on this plan. Guess now, though, he better begin to like it or at least learn more about it since it seems to mean so much to Marian.

Marian Snider. How does that sound? Mrs. Richard Snider. Mar, Mar? No he guessed she would have always been Marian. No nickname. Classy lady. This may require more work than he expected, but worth it. Definitely worth it. Since Gertrude and Eva had come on to him so strongly he had assumed these women considered themselves lucky to get attention from him. Not so with Patricia and now Marian appeared more interested in the ocean than in him. Oh, well. Keep that twenty million in mind.

"Are you traveling with your husband?" Richard knew the answer. Also knew her age-seventy three-and several other tidbits that she would tell him if he remembered to ask the right questions. He knew this would pique her interest. Vinnie had given Richard great information. Still he needed to keep the conversation going without Marian knowing or guessing what he knew.

"No." That's all she said. Richard knew the pursuit required finesse.

"After a few moments he asked, "A friend?"

"No." She turned to him and smiled, "Why do you ask?"

"Just need to know who my competition will be," he responded.

"Your competition? In what?" Her eyes remained steady on his face.

"Well, I enjoy talking to you and wondered..." He left the sentence unfinished.

"Even if I had a husband I certainly talk to whomever I please."

"Oh, that one but it's hard to tell from this direction." Richard pointed to a wave seemingly to ignore her remark.

Marian quickly glanced at the water then back at Richard. He accomplished exactly what he intended, curiosity with his personal questions and then a quick change of subject and implied loss of interest in her. He knew it worked. It had been used with great results on previous occasions. He smiled.

Marian pondered on what his interest in her could be. After all there is a good thirty years age difference if she calculated correctly. So it can't be, no she knew it could not be a romantic interest. Then what? Is watching the ocean that fascinating to him?

"Are you traveling with your wife?" she asked.

"No." He raised his eyes challenging her to ask the next question.

She did.

"A friend?"

"No." They both burst out laughing.

"Touché," said Marian.

"Now, let's start all over." Richard used his so-wonderful-to-know-you smile. "I'm Richard Snider. Single, forty-eight years old, likes bridge, music, the ocean, and ladies with short brown hair that the soft wind makes dance around her face. And who has an engaging smile." Richard, forty-two, had added six years to his age. Trying to make the gap in age shorter.

"I'm Marian Rogers, a widow," she hesitated, "sixty-six years old, likes bridge, music, the ocean, and I'm very pleased to meet you." She held out her hand and never blinked an eye. She had just chopped seven years off her age.

Marian had a fleeting moment asking herself why had she done that. Never before had she cared about her age. Sixty-six. What must she be thinking she silently speculated. Richard had no such questions. He knew why she cut out the seven years. He felt elated that Marian had done that. This told him that she, at least, found him interesting enough to pursue a friendship.

He took her outstretched hand and held it a few moments, separated her fingers and when releasing her hand let his fingers slowly slide along hers. They were both silent. Then Richard took a very deep breath and slowly blew the air out of his mouth. An act he had practiced many times which, he hoped, gave the impression his feelings came as a surprise. He bit his lower lip and brought his eyebrows together in a slight frown. He knew Marian observed his every action. He planned it that way.

"Marian," the captain walked towards the couple, "I'm glad I found you."

"Hello Peter," smiled Marian.

Captain Jacobson glanced at Richard and offered a quick hello.

"Peter, this is Richard Snider. Richard you know Captain Jacobson." She made the introductions and the two men shook hands.

"Wanted to tell you I persuaded several members of the Denver Symphony to give a private performance in my quarters this evening. Would you like to come?"

"I would, indeed," answered Marian, as she glanced at Richard, then quickly back to Peter.

"Would you care to join us, Mr. Snider?" Richard knew the invitation came as a duty, since Richard had been talking with Marian. However, it didn't matter. Richard accepted with delight.

What a break, he thought. The captain's quarters, no less. And his pigeon knew the captain personally. How cute. Richard did, though, manage to keep the anticipation from showing in his expression.

"See you both around nine then." The captain gave a little salute and walked away greeting other passengers along his way.

"May I escort you to the music, Marian?" Richard's voice caressing her name.

"You want to go with an old grandmother?"

"No, I want to take a very attractive lady and if she happens to be a grandmother, then that's all right too."

"You are so nice." Marian smiled and she felt a little excitement. What is this, she asked herself. It can only be a nice young man being friendly to an older woman. But the feeling is very nice.

"Just lucky I guess. Lucky I happened to meet you." Richard's eyes held hers.

"Well, call it whatever you want. I say you are nice. Sure, let's go together," said Marian. "What deck are you on? I'm on Coral."

"On Plumeria," he answered. "I'm with a tour group all staying on the same deck but that seems the only thing I have in common with them."

"What tour is that?" asked Marian.

"Sunshine is what the travel agent called it. We stay five days on each of the five main Hawaiian islands and then fly home. Six weeks altogether. How about you, how long will you be in Hawaii?"

"Not long. Two weeks at the most. I have two conferences to attend in Honolulu and then home." Marian sounded reluctant. Even now she wished for a longer stay. "I'll be on the big Island the five days the ship is there and then fly to Honolulu."

"How do you happen to know the captain?"

"An old family friend. Actually he grew up in Chicago and lived next door. He was a little kid when I was in high school." Oh, God, she thought. I have given my age away. Peter must be well into his sixties. "Course anyone younger, even just a few years, is a little kid to anyone in high school." She fumbled her response and hoped Richard didn't catch her slip.

Richard only smiled.

"Since I'm on Coral and you're on Plumeria, why don't I meet you on your deck at the settee by the stairs?"

"No, I'll come to your cabin to get you. A gentleman does not expect a lady to meet him just any place."

"All right, thank you. My cabin is 16."

"A few minutes before nine, then?"

"Yes."

Richard almost jumped for joy. Joy, yes definitely an omen. This is the one. Better than he could have imagined. And it happened without any planning on his part. He happened to be in the right place at the right time, as his mother always told him. That's how success is achieved. Oh, sure, he had arranged to "accidentally" meet her, but the rest, meeting the captain, being invited to the get-together, hum, frosting on the cake. Another of his mother's expressions when an unexpected event especially pleased her.

So, he mused, he has four days at sea and five days on the Big Island to convince her to become Mrs. Snider. No small task he knew. Still she had axed seven years off her age for him and they will attend the captain's function together. What a fantastic idea to come on this cruise. And she isn't all that bad. No horrid laughter, no excess pounds, pleasant enough to talk with, and she seemed to know the right people. Best of all, she is RICH!

Finally, finally life seems to be shaping up. He deserved it. He planned to convince her to stay on the ship and tour the other islands with him. And if he could, and he better, he told himself, convince her to marry him before returning to the mainland. Richard shuddered at that thought. Being married had never been something he had ever wanted. Still he did want her money and knew marriage was the only way to get a crack at it.

One year. Certainly the "accident" could happen within one year. And he knew he couldn't count on Vinnie for that. Vinnie is such a family man. Believed in the sanctity of that holy union. Anything else and old Vinnie is right there.

Doesn't mind hauling the "snow" off the ships, really liked the money the prostitutes brought in, but wives and kids completely off limits. In fact, Richard recalled, Vinnie had Rudy Brossi killed when he found out Rudy sold kiddy porn. Rudy signed his own death warrant when Vinnie's thirteen-year old daughter told him Rudy thought she would make a great model. No, no there is no way Vinnie will help with Marian's "accident". Richard decided this may be the only time the two friends would not share an "activity".

Never mind, Richard needed to do more planning anyway. First things first. Another of his mother's expressions.

Why is he thinking of his mother so much? Could it be that his mother and Marian share the same approximate age? Well, too bad rich young beautiful women were not available. They were either movie stars, like Jodie Foster, or rich because of their husbands. Besides, it is much harder for a young woman to have an accident. This is his plan, so go with it.

Ah, the gift shop. Too soon to give Marian a gift? No, Richard decided, he had to work fast. There could be no wasted hours and certainly no wasted days. What should he give her? Then he saw the scarf. Perfect. Pure silk with the colors of the rainbow. The red, orange, yellow, green, blue, and violet were softly blended in muted tones so the colors seemed to gently flow into each other. Four hundred and twenty-five dollars! Richard could hardly believe the price. He had once bought Didi a red wool scarf that even had fringe on the ends and it cost only fifteen dollars. At the time, Richard had thought that way too much. He reflected that the rainbow scarf constituted an investment and hey, he will get the money back. Then he snapped his fingers as he remembered the money in his wallet came from the cash machines in L.A. using stolen credit cards. Free money. He chuckled as the clerk in the gift shop wrapped the small white box with, can you believe, rainbow-colored ribbon.

"Share the joke?" The pretty sales girl would have liked Richard to linger. In spite of the many inviting brochures showing young people having a great time aboard ship, there were few opportunities to meet young single males, as she had discovered.

"Just a fleeting thought. The package is lovely." And he left a five dollar tip.

The girl smiled, an inviting smile. Richard smiled back. "My lady will love the scarf." Make it clear right from the start. He is not available. Definitely not available.

"For you." Richard gave the package to Marian letting his fingers touch hers.

"What?" She had questions in her eyes as well as on her lips.

"To wear tomorrow morning when we watch the sunrise."

"When we what?"

"Watch the sunrise. I'll be here at exactly five-thirty to get you."

"You will?"

"I will."

"Well, all right. Do I open this now or in the morning?"

"Now." Richard's voice soft and caressing, his you-are-wonderful look, and I-love-you-already smile. Didi melted when he used it on her. Marian emitted a long sigh, began to untie the pretty ribbon and gave a surprised gasp when she saw the scarf.

"It's lovely, but I couldn't, we, you, I couldn't."

"Oh, yes you can," responded Richard. "You are the only woman in the world whose loveliness outshines the scarf's beauty."

"Oh," Marian's face colored with a slight flush. Her heart beat faster. She questioned her emotions. Come on, she told herself, don't be a fool. This means nothing. Sure it's a lovely scarf, but it is, after all, only a scarf. He's just a nice man. He saw the scarf and it reminded him of me because we were looking at the water. The sun casts those colors. It means nothing. Marian tried to convince herself and could not quiet her heart and could not deny the slight wishful surge of hope. She could control her actions, her vocal responses, she could keep her eyes to herself and her hands need not reach out to touch him, but she could not, could not still that flutter in her heart.

Richard took her hand and silently they walked to the elevator, rode up to the Commodore deck and up a short flight of stairs to the captain's quarters. Both were quiet with their own thoughts. Richard knew the scarf had made the desired impression and Marian kept her hand in his, only withdrawing it when they entered the quarters.

"Marian, you look lovely." Sybil Jacobson hugged Marian as they both kissed air by each of their faces. Sybil raised her eyes to Richard as she held out her hand.

"This is my friend, Richard Snider." Marian's face slightly colored and Richard wondered if it was embarrassment because of the age difference, or if it could be excitement. He hoped the latter.

"So glad you joined us. The music will be ready in about fifteen minutes. In the meantime, let me introduce you around. You already know several of the guests, Marian," remarked Sybil.

Richard inspected the inside of the captain's quarters. Lovely furniture, deep cream-colored leather sofa and chairs, small tables with figures of Chinese ladies painted on the black lacquered surface, stools depicting the same paintings, the seats

77

covered with lovely silk embroidered flowers. Never used as foot stools, Richard guessed. Copper and brass containers of various designs accentuated the room which nicely held the two dozen or more guests. A small table held hors-d'oeuvres and in the far corner, and getting a great deal of attention, was the well-stocked bar. Beautiful art work graced the walls and Richard knew he was looking at expensive good taste. This epitomized the way he wanted to live, the way he deserved to live. Marian could make that possible.

He guided her to a seat and sat beside her. Another couple joined them. With the four on the sofa, the shoulders of Richard and Marian touched.

The musicians began with "Gypsy Love Song" played the waltz from "A Night in Venice," "The Last Rose of Summer," "Greensleeves," and when they began "The Maid with the Flaxen Hair," Richard reached for Marian's hand and held it gently in his own. She turned to him and her smile told him his search was over. This will be a piece of cake, he mused. The musicians ended the program with "Summertime," and a short "To You Sweetheart Aloha," in honor of the ship's voyage to Hawaii and passenger's excitement to be on the lovely islands. Richard and Marian exchanged smiles and small talk with other guests as they filled their plates with fresh pineapple, sushi, crab cakes, mini quiches, grapes and thinly sliced kiwi. As they once again found seats next to each other Richard felt, rather than saw, someone staring at him. He turned slightly catching the captain's eyes. Their eyes briefly held before Richard looked away.

Peter was both thoughtful and apprehensive. He had known Marian most of his life. What was she doing holding hands with this younger man? This Richard Snider? Exactly what is going on? Peter meant to find out. No chance this evening. Richard gave Peter a chill. How could he feel distrustful of someone he had only met a few hours ago, Peter chided himself. What is it about Richard that gives Peter such apprehension? Would he feel the same if Richard were holding hands with Dondi, the aerobic's instructor? Probably not. Marian is special, a lifelong friend. She baby-sat when his parents were away, reading to him and his brother Chris. Helped the boys make a snowman, took them to movies. The older sister they never had. And she enjoyed spending time with them. Teaching the boys to build model ships, taking them sailing. Even when she attended a high school function many times she would include Peter and Chris. So much that many people thought they were one family.

Peter especially missed Marian when she went away to college. In the fifth grade, he proudly wore the Harvard sweatshirt she sent to him. She sent another one to Chris. Marian attended Wellesley and dated a Harvard football player. She brought Dale home a few times and he, too, included Peter and Chris in special fun activities.

Marian didn't come around as often during her junior and senior years or perhaps Peter kept busy with his school's events. He began his high school years and grew away from his childhood fantasies that Marian was secretly his sister.

Then suddenly Marian married a much older man and the couple lived for awhile in Kalamazoo, Michigan. Her husband, a chemist, developed some ingredient that was widely used in a cold medicine. They became immensely wealthy and eventually moved back to Chicago just a block or two from her earlier home and once again close to Peter's family. Then, Peter was away attending the Duluth branch of the University of Minnesota where he honed his sailing skills on Lake Superior. Their paths crossed during holidays and vacations, Peter showing Marian's children, David and Nancy, the same friendship she had shown to him.

August Rogers developed several more medications and the family's wealth grew. They built a spectacular home on Lake Forest Drive and later moved to a secluded and even more spectacular home in a gated community occupied by fifty of Chicago's richest and most influential citizens. Marian served on committees promoting education and the arts. Peter recalled, though, she never seemed quite as happy as she had when she had brought Dale home. The sparkle went out when she married August. Peter never knew why or whatever happened to Dale. The rumor was he found another girl. Perhaps.

Tonight Marian's smile reminded Peter of her earlier years. But Richard did not fit the image of a man whose hand she should be holding. Not in Peter's eyes anyway. And what had Peter read in Richard's look that fleeting moment when their eyes locked and held. Self-satisfaction? Yes, that was part of it, but more than that, Peter saw a smug, conceited, conniving man. Peter had felt a chill as if a door suddenly opened and cold icy air came rushing in.

Richard, too, felt a chill when he met the captain's eyes. When he looked away, he had a premonition. A warning, but of what? There was no way the captain could know what he had planned. Richard searched his mind. Had he ever met Peter? Never. So it must be the captain didn't approve of Marian being with him. Well, he expected he would see that. See it often and he knew exactly what to do. Disarm the enemy. The captain couldn't actually be an enemy. They had barely met. He is just a concerned friend, Richard knew that. Get Peter on his side. This will be the first major hurdle to overcome on his way to riches.

Richard casually wandered over to the captain. He smiled his, he hoped, charming I'm-glad-you-are-my-friend smile. "I can't tell how much I've enjoyed this evening. The music was grand."

"Yes, they are very good." No warmth in Peter's voice. Richard certainly made that observation.

"How long have you known Mrs. Rogers?" Peter got right to the point.

This will be fun, Richard chuckled to himself.

"Met her on this cruise. Charming lady, isn't she?"

"Very. Does she remind you of your mother? Is that why you are so solicitous of her?"

Woo. Richard knew then Peter was much more than mildly concerned.

"Not at all," smiled Richard. "Except that they are, or I should say in regard to my mother, were lovely ladies. My mother is deceased."

"I meant age-wise."

Peter must be rich since he is so rude, mused Richard.

"Well, as my lovely mother always said 'Age is a state of mind.'"

"Excuse me." Peter abruptly walked away. Richard watched as Peter spoke to Sybil and she hurried to Marian's side.

Richard joined Marian as well, arriving in time to hear Sybil invite Marian to lunch with her in the captain's quarters.

"She may not have time." Richard broke into the conversation. He put his hand on Marian's shoulder in a proprietary manner. "We're playing bridge at one and our morning is filled."

"It is?" Marian glanced up at him, a smile curling her lips.

"Yes." Their eyes held, both smiling at the other.

"I really need to talk to you, Marian. Perhaps a quick lunch or coffee, say around noon. For only a few minutes," pleaded Sybil.

"Yes, of course. Shall I come here then?" asked Marian.

"Fine, it's important." Sybil then joined her husband.

Not to worry, Richard told himself. He and Marian will see the sunrise together and he had definite plans for that.

Reaching her cabin door, Richard tenderly kissed her hand and said, "I'll be here at five-thirty, sharp. Wear the scarf."

Marian barely finished brushing her teeth when a knock sounded on her door. Who in the world can that be at this time of night? Did Richard come back? She gave a quick hopeful sigh pushing her hair back in place and smoothing her robe.

"Yes?"

"Peter and Sybil. Marian, may we see you for a few minutes?"

"What on earth?" Marian opened the door, apprehensive. "What is wrong?" She glanced expectantly from Peter to Sybil. Did they have bad news? Had something happened to David or Nancy or the grandchildren? She began to shake. And she asked again, "What's wrong?"

"Nothing, please, nothing. We didn't mean to frighten you." Sybil put her arm around Marian guiding her back into the room.

"Then what?"

"Let's sit down please." Peter took Marian's hand and led her to the small bed, sitting down beside her, continuing to hold her hand. Sybil sat on Marian's other side and since the bed was very small, Peter moved to a straight back chair facing the two women.

"This is absolutely none of our business, but you are like family to us and we care about you," said Peter.

"Yes, what is it?" Was she about to be replaced on the board of directors or what?

"Well," Peter hesitated, "there is something." He hesitated again. "How well do you know this Richard person?"

"How well do I know Richard?"

"It's just that we are concerned," added Sybil. "You can't be too careful these days and we just want..."

"My word," Marian laughed. "I am flattered you apparently think something is going on between Richard and

81

me. Goodness, he is a fine young man, very interesting and, my goodness, is that what you are thinking?"

"He seems so, well, so much..."

"Younger, you mean?"

"That and..."

"And I'm so rich and he is after my money?"

"You can't be too careful," repeated Sybil.

"He has no idea I'm rich. We never talk money. I must say I resent this somewhat." Marian seemed miffed. "Peter, you invited him to your party. We both enjoyed it." My God what did they think is going on and did she have to explain all friendships just because she had known Peter and Sybil for years. And maybe because she happened to be the major stock holder in this cruise line. Peter's ship, one of the four of this line. Did she have to explain everything!

"Please understand, we are asking out of concern for you."

"What's the concern? That we went to your party together, that we plan to watch the sunrise together, that we plan to play bridge together. Don't you want people to have a good time on your ship?"

"Of course, only..." Peter dropped the rest of what he began to say.

"Only here is an attractive younger man who happens to enjoy my company. Is that such a surprise? Am I so boring that you are surprised at this?" Marian was more than miffed.

"Please don't be angry. We are out of line and I'm sorry. You definitely are not boring. I'm truly sorry." Peter apologized.

"It's all right. I'm not sure if I should be angry or pleased." Marian opened her hands to Peter and Sybil and all laughed.

"Pleased I guess," said Marian. "Yes, I'm pleased you think Richard is romantically inclined towards me. Wait till he hears this."

"We would rather you didn't mention our concerns to him," remarked Peter.

"Well, don't worry. I'm old enough and wise enough to spot someone after my money. But first, he has to know I have some and Richard definitely does not know."

"Please forgive us for poking our noses in," said Peter, as they rose to leave.

"I do and really I appreciate your concern and I know only good friends would care that much," responded Marian. The three exchanged hugs and air kisses.

Marian felt exhilarated. To think that Peter and Sybil thought...she walked to the small mirror peering closely at her reflection. She smiled, frowned, opened her eyes very wide, puckered her lips, smiled again. She reached into her purse for a hand mirror. Held it so she could see the back of her head, patted her hair and preened in front of the mirror for several minutes with a self-satisfied feeling she never knew she had. She felt so good, happy, eager for the morning to come to judge for herself if Richard found her attractive. She fell asleep with a smile on her lips.

Peter and Sybil would have been dismayed had they realized that their concern, instead of being a warning to Marian, did in effect put thoughts into her head that she never would have dreamed of herself.

CHAPTER SIX

Sunrise over the blue Pacific Ocean just a few miles from the shores of Hawaii, weaves magic in a special way few can ignore. Marian was ready to embrace the magic long before Richard tapped on her cabin door. She wore long white cotton pants, a beige shell and a long-sleeved white cardigan. She tied the rainbow-colored scarf loosely around her neck and sprayed the ends with Joy permeating the air with its richness when she moved.

Richard carried two mugs of hot coffee and two mini cinnamon rolls explaining, "To keep us from starving and until you opened the door, I thought they had the most wonderful aroma in the world." He offered the white Styrofoam container to Marian. "Now I know what truly is the most wonderful scent."

Marian smiled. Could Peter and Sybil be right? Is he interested in me that way? Is this really happening to me?

Richard carried a blanket under one arm. He had plans for the morning. The air could be nippy and two people can be very comfortable and warm huddled under one blanket. He noted her cardigan and smiled. She would need more than that to keep warm. His perfect plan will work!

And it did. He added a little magic of his own as his arm encircled her, ostensibly to keep her warm while they both commented on the ever-changing colors of the sunrise. While the last drops of coffee eased into their mouths, and the taste of cinnamon and sugar delighted their palates, Richard closed his eyes and envisioned hundred dollar bills spilling out of his hands.

"We dock in Hilo late this afternoon," whispered Richard. "I have all three days planned for us."

"You have?"

"All three."

"Like what?"

"We, my dear, are taking a tour of an orchid garden, fifteen acres, ten thousand different kinds of orchids all waiting for you to choose your favorites."

"Really, ten thousand?"

"And," he smiled, "if you want to go ashore tonight, I bet we can find a great place for dinner."

"I don't believe Peter plans any boats going ashore. Not according to the itinerary. Tomorrow morning at ten is the first launch."

"Well then tomorrow it will be."

"Where did you get the cinnamon rolls anyway?"

"I bribed the baker. Told him they were for...for..." Richard hesitated hoping to imply he found it difficult to explain his feelings. He swallowed several times, then said, "Let me tell you what we'll do the rest of the time."

"But, you are on a tour. The ground activities have been planned and of course already paid," said Marian, duly noting his discomfort as he intended.

"Unless you can join the tour, I don't want it." Richard hoped he sounded contrite. He had planned it that way. "I don't want it anyway, I want to spend the time with only you."

"But..."

"I want to," he looked deep into her eyes and saw dollar signs, "unless you don't want to spend the time with me."

"Of course, I want to. Only are you sure?"

"Very sure."

Hilo was overcast, not unusual, still Richard had several matters to attend to, so the cloudy skies went unnoticed.

"Keep busy awhile till I do some business?" Richard needed Marian out of his way a few hours. She agreed and got a new hairdo, manicure and even a pedicure, not wanting to ask herself why.

Richard added to his finances by visiting several banks using the fake credit cards. Easy money. In two hours he had fifteen thousand dollars, a diamond bracelet and black pearl earrings. Bankers are so dumb, he rationalized. They ask to be taken. Name tags right by each cage, so easy. Richard learned long ago how to work a bank. This time he just followed his earlier training.

"Hello Malia. Guess I need more money." Richard smiled his remember-me smile. "And I took your advice and used number 25 sunscreen. This Hawaiian sun is hot."

Malia, of course, had never seen him, but she must have, she guessed. He knew her so well and she must have mentioned the hot sun and sunscreen. She smiled trying to remember. She couldn't possibly remember everybody and yes, he does look vaguely familiar.

"You have the authority to cash this don't you. Or do I have to get the okay from Bill?" Richard had noted the manager's name on the gold plaque. Everyone knows Bill is short for William. And asking Malia if she had authority boosted her ego. Richard, a master at working the odds and working people, enjoyed this exchange.

He got the four thousand dollars, knowing, too, she would never recognize him again. This time he had brown contacts, brown hair and a pencil thin mustache. His hairpiece brought strands of hair over his forehead. No one would ever say this hair looked like Robert Redford's.

Richard repeated the banking scenario several times during the day. The larger better known banks were easier targets. More people in and out and friendliness of the workers must be a condition of employment. Or perhaps it is the aloha spirit. These Hawaiians are gullible. Fifteen thousand dollars.

Richard insisted on paying for the orchids, the leis, a black kukui nut necklace, a coral pin, dinner in a Japanese restaurant, (Richard hated this, but Marian wanted to go) and when Marian admired an oriental wall-hanging that was part of the restaurant's decor, he bought it.

"You've paid plenty for this trip and this is my pleasure," he said, brushing away her protests.

Marian was elated. Finally someone not interested in her money. He implied she had traveled on a tight budget. What a wonderful feeling, she told herself. Her self-esteem began to soar. Not that she hadn't been sure of herself in matters of business, she zealously served on the board of directors of several companies, she bought stock with utmost confidence. But it was her relationships with the opposite sex when her self-confidence floundered. When she lost her college lover to another coed, she never regained confidence in her appearance or attractiveness regarding men. Then when she became a widow, she believed men were only interested in her money. Now, though, here is a man interested in her for herself, a man who didn't even know she was considered wealthy by most standards.

But Richard did know. Knew she had more than Vinnie first mentioned. Vinnie had done an update. Richard learned about it when at last he had a private telephone line.

"More like thirty million, my friend," related Vinnie with undenied enthusiasm.

"Liquid or is it all tied up with kids or...?"

"Or can you get your hands on it?"

"Yeah."

"If you can marry her without a pre-nup you'll be in fat city. Especially if you outlive her and hey, man, you should. She's pretty old, seventy somethin'."

"Yeah, I'll no doubt outlive her."

"Can you talk her into marriage? You can't get her dough without it!"

"I'm gonna try Vinnie, I'm gonna try. And it looks good. I've got her pretty well snowed."

"You know, old buddy, money isn't that important."

"Not to you, but it is to me."

"What I mean is that marriage is great. Look at me and Ardella."

"Yeah, I know and Ardella's great, but she is also a very rich lady. Was when you met her."

"That's not why I married her." Vinnie sounded a little miffed.

"I know, still rich is nice. Hey, there's something else. There's a guy, a bartender on the ship I think could work into your organization real great."

"Tell me about him."

"Pulls a good scam. Looking to better himself and actually likes to cheat."

"All great recommendations," laughed Vinnie. "Check him out and if you think he will work out, send him here."

"Now tell me about the kids." Richard knew Vinnie would have a few good stories about his kids---the real joys in his life.

The conversation went on several minutes and left Richard very happy indeed. Thirty million, he could handle that. In his mind he saw the snazzy red convertible, black leather seats or maybe white. A Caddy, or Lincoln. No, a foreign job, not Japanese. A Rolls or Porsche. Ah, yes, definitely a Lamborghini. Red, yes red. And he would have a perpetual tan and wear white shirts, three or four buttons undone to show off that great tan. Dark glasses, so his eyes couldn't be seen, well--maybe not. People seemed to distrust those glasses and hey, his eyes have such great expressions. Especially those he practices. And he would never, ever, shop at thrift shops again or look at the price of anything. Yes, he could handle the thirty mil, and he would get that marriage certificate. First, he had to get her in the sack and that, as easy as it would be, was not at all appealing. Still she was the kind of broad who believed in honor and she would feel obligated to marry him if she slept with him. Or at least he would make her believe it was the honorable thing to do.

A problem though. Whenever he held her hand, or put his arm around her shoulder, when they were wrapped in the blanket watching the sunrise, he had to conjure up the sight of hundred dollar bills held tightly in his hand or otherwise it was throw-up time. Her wrinkled neck and liver spots on her arms and hands were repulsive to him. God, how he wished Didi had been rich. Then maybe she could have learned to be classy as well.

The three days in Hilo were filled with activities, carefully planned by Richard, to impress Marian. He had never shown this much concern or care for any other woman. His fingers trailed along her face when he placed the orchid lei around her neck. The traditional kiss lingered longer than the usual peck, signalizing the exchange of leis. He bought two bentos, the Hawaiian word for a picnic lunch, and they ate chicken flavored with teriyaki, sticky rice, and a slice of mango. They sat on a bench in a pretty Japanese park with red bridges covering a stream in which yellow and orange carp swam.

They strolled around Hilo which is populated mainly with persons of Japanese heritage. The small shops fascinated Marian and Richard noted she didn't mind the pushiness of the people. Richard did mind the shop owners or salespeople trying to block the exits until some item was purchased. Marian found several trinkets. Richard did not.

He rented a car on the second day and to his dismay---a Japanese Toyota. Jesus, he muttered to himself, why don't we just give this island to them. The drive to Hawaii Volcanoes National Park took two hours and both Richard and Marian were amazed to see the large areas of dry black shiny lava. The melted rock looked like a sheet of coal. In several places the remains of an automobile or piece of wood that was once a home pierced ominously out of the lava causing a chill to slither down the spine of even callous Richard.

A barricade blocked automobile travel so Marian and Richard walked a few hundred feet over the crusty ground. Marian stopped to examine a lone green piece of grass which somehow had managed to push itself through the solid rock mass. She marveled at its tenacity and murmured a plaintive, "Hope you make it little plant." Richard kneeled down to admire the little green blade with its high hopes, as well.

He and Marian exchanged a tender smile and Richard immediately seized the moment to take her hand drawing her to his arms, "Some things will make it through seemingly impossible odds. That's us, Marian. Like this tiny blade of grass. I love you. You must know it by now." He kissed her and drew her closer.

"I never dreamed it would happen to me again. I feel like I've been given a brand new life." She put her head on his shoulder and with her face buried in his chest she could not see Richard's calculating smile. And how could she know that in his mind it was the handful of money he saw?

The highlight in the museum of the national park was a twenty minute video highly informative on volcano formations with special attention to Kilauea, the current active volcano. It came as a surprise to both Marian and Richard that the Big Island also housed one of the tallest mountains in the United States, Mauna Kea. It measures 13,796 feet and offers snow skiing—something not usually thought of in Hawaii, they were told.

Interesting as the museum was—in Marian's mind she only remembered the words "I love you" uttered by Richard during that tender moment near the little green blade of grass.

Richard's mind skipped to the shiny black lava and he conjectured how he could make money from, he supposed, the free material. He put his hand in his pocket and felt the smoothness of the small stone he had placed there earlier. He didn't believe in Pele, the Hawaiian goddess of volcanoes, who, the Hawaiians declared would bring bad luck to anyone who took lava from the ancestral grounds. Even a small stone.

In fact, legend has it, many people who had taken a piece of lava have mailed, or sent it back some way, to stop the bad luck from following them. Richard laughed at their foolishness.

Richard didn't mind that lunch at the Volcano House, in his mind, was over priced and under cooked. He had accomplished more than he thought possible this day. Hooked! He had her hooked. Wouldn't Vinnie be delighted with the good news.

Marian waited in the car while Richard telephoned his best friend. Vinnie admonished Richard to think it through carefully.

"You're very fond of him, aren't you?" remarked Marian as she leaned across the seat to open the driver's door for Richard.

"You bet. Best buddies for most of our life." Then as an after thought he added, "You will like him too and he will absolutely adore you."

Carefully she said, "Is he joining you here in Hawaii?"

"No, you'll see him in New York."

"I will?" If a heart actually could skip a beat, then at that moment, hers did.

"Honey, we've only known each other a few short days, but, it's like," Richard used his surprised-that-it's-happening-but-isn't-it-wonderful look, "I've been gravitating towards you all of my life."

"Yes, me too," elated Marian responded quietly.

"There's so much we don't know about each other, but I have one over-powering desire. Well, maybe more than one," smiled Richard. "I want to take care of you. I want to know what you were like when you were a little girl. What your favorite color is, what foods you like or hate, what songs you like, movies, books. I want to absorb you in my heart and mind. And I want you to know these things about me. I want us to do this together."

"Oh, we will my dear, we will. I want to know all about you as well, only Richard my love, I'm so much older. You should have a younger woman." Marian was scared. Would these words drive him away? "Someone who can give you children. Richard I'm..."

He put his fingers on her lips to quiet her fears. "You are the one I want and I'll try hard to make you want me as much as I want you."

"I do, I do already." And she did. She wanted to learn all about him and tell him about her life, her family, and wouldn't he be surprised when he learns about her money?

"Tonight we're having dinner in the best place in Hilo. There's more I want to say, but first I need about a half hour for something. Can you stay busy again for a little while?"

"Sure, I found a book store. I'll be in there."

Richard got to the bank a few minutes before closing. He had spent ten minutes in the men's room of a service station changing his appearance. He had decided on the brown makeover and to once again visit Malia's bank. She was delighted he needed ten thousand dollars for an engagement ring and since by now she knew him as a welcome customer and since the manager had left for the day she readily approved the check.

He added six thousand to the recently acquired ten thousand and purchased a six-carat baguette diamond rimmed with twenty rubies. An investment, he mused. Interest on thirty million. He tucked it away for now and changed back into his own self. Oh, how he loved this life!

Richard quickly picked up on smiling when he saw Marian begin to smile; frown when he noticed her eyes begin to harden with displeasure; act amused when something made her chuckle. Naturally when she remarked, "We seem to think so much alike," he was very pleased, indeed. Very pleased.

Women are so vulnerable and gullible, thought Richard. Especially old ones. Didn't she have any kind of a clue that someone with Robert Redford hair would never be interested in her? Didn't she think at all? Didi, with her manatee mentality, would have seen through his ruse in a minute. Well, lucky for him Marian believed him.

Unlucky for Marian. He wanted only her money and the way he intended to get it deemed very unlucky for her.

The ship sailed around the tip of the Big Island on it's way to the Kona coast. Marian and Richard giggled at everything. Peter and Sybil gave them long thoughtful looks clearly questioning the couple's constant togetherness. Watching the sunrise and sunset became daily rituals with Richard providing the delicious cinnamon rolls and mugs of hot coffee for the sunrise, while Marian brought iced tea for the evening event. Richard hated the tea, but yum yummed when Marian raved about it. He had learned his lessons very well.

Richard so-whated Marian when she bid four diamonds over his three spades and only took eight tricks. He nonchalantly waved his hand when she bid no trump and had no honors in any suit. He garnered all the warmth he could when she spilled her margarita on his new beige linen trousers. The drink's lime juice sure to make a lasting stain. Richard would have knocked Didi across the room for that. He smiled at Marian, though, through gritted teeth, when she told him to do some small thing for her. Told! Women did not tell him to do anything. True, she had been slightly tipsy at the time, but no matter, after they were married he would show her who the boss would be and in a way she would not soon forget.

Marian became a true believer in his devotion and in most instances, she acted like a little lap dog, ready to embrace his every desire.

As the ship approached Kona passengers celebrated Hawaii night. Richard soon discovered why the big party was on this side of the Big Island and not when it docked at Hilo. Hilo being the big outlet for Hilo Hattie's, the real Hawaiian clothes, as most tourists believed. Passengers had been bused to the popular clothing store and gift shop. And who could resist the bargains? Not many did. Giving passengers time to get their purchases back to the ship and gather other party items, Hawaii night was the event most looked forward to as the real beginning of their Hawaii vacation.

Couples gathered at the buffet table dressed in look-alike shirts and dresses. The most popular (and how many bolts of material had been produced?) was bright blue with yellow plumeria flowers. More than two dozen couples had chosen this pattern. Laughter penetrated the dining room when couples met other dress-alikes. The bright colors and large print brought regales of laughter. Richard heard a loud guffaw. Eva! He turned and met her eyes and her outfit nearly blinded him. Red! The brightest red he had ever seen, with the print of green bread-fruit leaves plastered all over it. It had a little ruffle at the bottom and puffed sleeves. Was this a joke or what? Were dresses like hers serious? She should have purchased a larger size, or maybe this was the only size, like one size fits all. Only Eva filled it like a tightly rolled sausage. Oh, God!

Some of the men wore shirts made with the material pattern wrong side out. Is this another joke? Something to see just how far tourists will go to be like the Hawaiians. For some reason the slender ladies dressed more sedately than the overweight women. Richard had no idea why. He watched as the passengers paraded to the party. Eighty percent wore newly purchased aloha shirts and dresses. He later learned the dresses were called muumuus.

Marian joined him and whispered, "We should have bought a muumuu and shirt alike."

Oh, god. Never in a million years, Richard thought, but said, "We will on Kona. What color do you want?"

"Well, we're in Hawaii. Something bright I guess," Her eyes wandered around the room, "but not too bright. Maybe brown or beige."

"Maybe the color of the water," suggested Richard.

"Yes, that's it."

What a guy won't do for a buck, mused Richard. He was tired of her no-color clothes. Still, he wasn't ready for the flashy aloha wear either. Didn't fit his new image. Although Tom Selleck looks great as Magnum. Yeah, Tom Selleck looked very good in those clothes or maybe Richard only wanted that kind of lifestyle. He definitely liked the car Magnum drove.

Richard quickly became solicitous of Marian, filling her plate with Hawaiian foods. The ever popular teriyaki chicken; potato salad that for some reason included elbow macaroni; rice-sticky-he wondered whatever happened to fluffy rice; some kind of green leafy spinach-like vegetable in, he later learned, coconut milk; chunks of fish someone said was dolphin but really mahimahi; and platters of fresh pineapple, papaya and mango. Authentic Hawaiian food or so the passengers believed. Nate told him the locals actually preferred a Spam sandwich with chili and rice swilled down with a can of Primo.

The evening passed quickly with good natured kidding, women using the same designer, eating Flipper, trying the hula, the ladies looking over the young Hawaiian male dancers and the men ogling the shapely native girls. Everyone in a holiday mood, danced, sang, laughed the night away and anticipated exploring the Kona coast.

"You know Richard, I only planned on Kona by ship. I have two meetings in Honolulu so I'll fly there day after tomorrow." Marian had a reluctant tone to her voice.

"I'll go with you."

"You will?" Marian gave a questioning look, her hopes rising.

"You're not getting more than an arm's length away from me any more," he firmly stated.

"Well, I do have to attend the board meetings. But otherwise it will be heaven to be there with you. But, are you sure? What about the ship?"

"After your meetings we can fly back here and then continue on to Maui and Kauai."

"I've given up my cabin."

"They aren't picking up passengers on Kona. There's room. I'll talk to the purser."

"No, I'll see Peter." Marian began doodling on her napkin. "I'll have to let my family know I'll be arriving home a little later than I first planned."

"Why not call them now. David and Nancy, isn't it?"

"Yes. I guess I could."

"Only why not keep our plans just for us," pleaded Richard. "A few weeks so we can savor every minute."

"Our plans. What exactly are they?" asked Marian. She held her breath. She knew she wanted him, but did he really mean forever, or was this just a shipboard romance. She had heard about those and never would it appeal to her.

"We, my dear, are getting married on Kauai."

"What? Married?" Her heart began beating faster, she held her breath longer this time.

"I've made all the arrangements. Smiths will handle everything. We only need blood tests and we can get those in Honolulu. Then..."

"Wait. Wait. You're taking my breath away. When did you do all this? And you never said anything to me. What if, what if?" Marian wasn't about to complete that sentence. She certainly did not want to put questions in Richard's mind.

"This morning. After last night I knew I had found the woman I wanted to marry. And Marian, this is forever. You aren't getting away."

"Richard, this is very public. Let's go to my cabin to talk about it. I have to tell David and Nancy I'm getting married. I have to."

Richard began his I'm-so-disappointed-look, casting down his eyes and protruding his lower lip.

"We'll talk about it, but..." He deliberately left the sentence hanging.

Marian felt the fear again. What if he changes his mind? Maybe it would be better to tell them after the wedding. I'm an adult, she told herself. She didn't need their permission. Still...

Walking to Marian's cabin, Richard took her hand and said, "We'll tell them together. I understand how you feel and you're right. Just wait a few days, for us?" He pleaded, looking into her eyes and noting with joy the relief they showed.

What a patsy, he thought. Like putty in my hands. This will be easier than taking candy from a baby. Another of his mother's expressions.

The planned two days in Honolulu stretched into three. Richard gave Marian the ring, and made, in his mind, quite a production of it. They were dining at the Colony and he chose the moment when the flaming dessert was served to slip the ring on her finger. Marian never noticed the amused smiles and lifted eyebrows of other diners. Richard did and shot triumphant looks back. For thirty million he could field any kind of amusement on anyone's face. He did wish Marian had kept her tears inside her eyes. God, she must be some lonesome broad. She sat there with tears streaming down her face and touching the ring.

"Let's get out of here," Richard told her. As they made their way back to the Hilton, he knew he could no longer stall making love to her. He knew, too, performance would need someone else in his mind. Didi perhaps or Jodie Foster. Yes, Jodie.

Marian bought a wedding dress in Honolulu. They spent hours at the Ala Moana shopping center before finding the perfect peach-colored muumuu with white lace insets in the sleeves and skirt. The headpiece, called a haku, should be made of fresh flowers, the sales clerk explained, and could be found on Kauai. The clerk knew where along with the leis and other floral arrangements. When Richard told the clerk the wedding would be at Smiths, she said. "Oh, you are all set. They do everything beautifully." Marian smiled.

"The traditional wedding lei is made of maile leaves and all this is included with the wedding package, along with a video," said the sales clerk.

Richard spent a few hours replenishing his cash supply with the fake credit cards and checks. So easy, he chuckled. Why does anyone work for a living?

He doubted Marian contributed anything to the board meetings. She went late and left early, never wanting to be long from his side.

They returned to Kona in time to board the ship for the day's travel to Maui and the five-day stay. Then to Kauai. Passengers would see Honolulu after Kauai and then most would fly back to the mainland.

Marian's ring got the usual oh's and ah's and envious looks from other women. Richard got speculative smiles and high-fives from the men. He got a downright unfriendly, piercing look from Peter and Sybil. And of course loving adulation from Marian.

"Honey," Marian's voice held a note of trepidation. "Peter suggested we make a pre-nuptial agreement. What do you think?"

That bastard! I knew he was trouble. Richard was livid. Be calm, think a few moments. This has to sound right. He took a deep breath, put on his I-can't-believe-you-said-that look.

"What do I think? You mean you talked about our, yours and my personal life with someone without telling me? I'll tell you what I think." He planted his feet firmly in front of Marian, lifted her chin with his finger and peered intently into her eyes. She trembled. Good, he thought, she's scared.

"There's no way in God's wide world will I ever give my money, my apartment buildings, my music contracts, anything, to anyone but you. I'm surprised you will even consider it. Exactly what did Peter say, not that it's any of his business, but I'll get to that later."

"He said," she paused, "that if we do get married, then we should have the..." Marian took a deep breath, swallowed, "agreement."

Richard sauntered to the only chair in Marian's cabin, flung himself down, legs outstretched, an insolent sneering smile, eyes like steel, "If we do get married. That's what he said. If we do?"

He volleyed between playing this scene in an agitated angry way, or should he be calm, gentle and concerned. No, he decided, remain angry. She was quivering. He could mold her to his way of thinking. He knew marriage to this young handsome man was uppermost in her mind. She had probably already planned the parties to show off her trophy. Or so it seemed to Richard.

"Tell me Marian, are we together on what we want our life to be, or does Peter or someone else call the shots?"

"No, just us." Her children flashed in her mind. For some reason she had had no time to call them. She managed only a short note stating that she had met someone and planned a longer stay. The note did not mention the gender of the "someone."

"Peter doesn't have anything to say about it," she continued. "Only we are longtime friends and he only wants what's right for me."

Quietly Richard said, "What's right for you? Is it right that I would leave all my money to someone else? I want to take care of you, but..." He trailed off, leaving Marian to think about the loneliness without him.

"But." Something is wrong, she thought. Surely her death would occur much sooner than Richard's. She is so much older. Even more than he knew.

"No buts. There will be no divorce, Marian. I told you this is forever. Till death do us part. Isn't that in the vows?"

"I'm older..."

"Yes and maybe I'll get hit by a car. Life doesn't make any promises. People make promises. That's what I thought we were doing." He is angry, believed Marian.

"We are."

"But I'll tell you what. If you want to do what Peter says, I'll go along with it. I don't want to lose you." Richard gave her his but-you'll-probably-be-sorry look.

"No. No reason for the agreement. I would want you to have my money as well." Her voice grew quieter with each word.

"Little as we have," remarked Richard triumphant. Let her believe he didn't know. So very gullible. God, he is lucky.

"Yes, a little." Her stomach began to hurt. Not exactly nausea, more like something rough, like sandpaper, inside. She gently rubbed it. Richard smiled.

CHAPTER SEVEN

Richard and Marian joined shipmates for an early morning bus trip to watch the sunrise at Haleakala National Park. Even though they carried blankets from the ship and a thermos of hot coffee, the couple, like everyone else froze at the over ten-thousand foot level of the mountain. Marian, surprised to see frost on the ground, tried to gather enough to drop down Richard's neck. He chased her with frost in his hands and both decided enough of this cold. Get back into the lookout building. The building offered a trifle bit more warmth and the couple laughed and snuggled, trying to keep warm.

Richard and Marian, along with other early morning visitors to the park, gave the expected oh's and ah's when the sun began coloring the sky and the scattering clouds. Richard, happy to get back on the bus, believed others were just as happy to leave this high cold place and back into the warm Hawaiian sun.

As the bus passed fifty or so bicyclists snaking down the narrow roadway, Richard's mind flashed to unchecked brakes, or loose wheel bolts. An out of control bicycle plunging over the mountain side, hurling the rider to her death. Marian! He stored this opportunity in his mind.

The days on Maui were filled with tourist activities and they passed quickly. Richard made Marian laugh, bought her souvenirs, and took her to elegant restaurants. While she read or rested, he replenished his cash at banks ever-ready to honor his Visa Cards, never suspecting that they belonged to someone else. He enjoyed being Eric Johnson, of Pico Road. This time he had a light mustache, combed his red-blond hair piece over his forehead, used green contacts and remembered to remove his dark glasses as he entered the bank so the teller would see those vivid eyes. He knew, too, as Richard, he would not visit these banks. He silently thanked Dino again for providing such skillful disguises. And he congratulated himself for being smart enough to use them effectively.

Peter and Sybil somewhat thawed towards Richard, or so it seemed. How could they not, he mused. Hadn't they noticed Richard promoting Jerry's physical fitness, making Gerald and Rose Olson very happy with the ship's facilities? And didn't they see the interest Richard took in Nate? Peter determined whatever Richard had said, Nate seemed much happier and more pleasant to his co-workers. Of course, Richard placed Marian on a pedestal. He treated her like a princess and she fairly glowed. All of a sudden Richard became a hero. Men asked his advice on the market. Richard only smiled at this as if to say he never gave away his secrets. Women questioned Marian on fashions or whatever. Peter questioned how he himself had lost his touch in judging people. Why did he still have such apprehensive feelings toward Richard when everyone else thought him wonderful?

Even Sybil seemed to be falling under Richard's spell. Especially since Richard asked Peter and Sybil to be attendants at the wedding. Maybe it's because all women seem to love weddings. Sybil became very happy to see Marian so excited. Peter wanted happiness for his friend as well, only...he let his thoughts go on to something other than this apprehension. After all, passengers got a bonus on this trip. The single women saw themselves finding Mr. Right aboard ship and the men easily could see themselves in the limelight such as Richard enjoyed now.

The "Love Boat" promise coming true for Richard and Marian could come true for anyone. Hope and anticipation reflected in expectant eyes. Richard and Marian included the passengers in their plans. At least it appeared so. As always, Richard revealed only the surface of his plans. But he did it with skill.

Bernice, who first thought Richard gay, watched the festivities with brooding eyes. Hadn't he implied he was gay? Did she not hear correctly? He would have been quite a catch.

Gertrude and her ever-present caretaker observed the happy couple and while Ellen felt envious of Marian's good fortune, Gertrude thought the whole affair tacky. My God, he could be Marian's son. Gertrude felt tainted for having even spoken to Richard.

Eva joined the parties and laughed at every possible opportunity. She made sexy remarks and while maybe a few chuckles were heard, it seemed no one believed them to be as uproariously humorous as she did. Richard remembered, though, anything could set off her guffaw. He guided Marian away.

Patricia quietly offered her congratulations and made only token appearances at any of the festivities which seemed to crop up whenever either Richard or Marian made an appearance.

"I hope you found what you were looking for," remarked Patricia.

"Yes, I have. I'm a very lucky man," responded Richard.

"I believe I may be lucky too," she added.

Now, what did she mean by that remark, Richard asked himself. Is she psychic or something? His eyes followed Patricia as she crossed the deck apparently going back to her cabin. Or at least to some other part of the ship to a more quiet place.

Peter observed the exchange between Richard and Patricia and felt a chill. Oh, Marian, he isn't right for you, he wanted to shout. He remained quiet and solemn.

As the harbor pilot brought the ship into Kauai's Nawiliwili harbor, passengers glimpsed mountains with their sharp jagged edges jetting out over the aqua-blue water. Mountain sides that resembled plush green velvet and palm trees rimmed a soft sandy beach in front of Kauai's lush Marriott Hotel. Surfers rode the white-capped waves while closer to shore youngsters on boogie boards shouted their glee at finally mastering the long ride in. A photographer snapped photos of lovely native girls and handsome young men placing leis around passenger's necks giving them the traditional kiss on both cheeks. Later, the photos would be displayed in the ship's lounge and hardly anyone rejected this purchase of the real Hawaii, or so passengers believed.

Hyper with anticipation of being so close to millions of dollars, Richard wasted no time making final arrangements for the wedding. Two more days, he contemplated with gaiety. His happiness belied his true feelings. He kept Marian busy. So busy that her long looks towards a telephone were just that.

Long wistful glances. David and Nancy, still unaware that their mother would return home with a husband. A husband much younger than she and one so physically fit he could work out for hours with no sign of fatigue. Marian puffed while climbing a short flight of stairs.

Richard insisted on treating Marian to a helicopter ride over Waimea Canyon. "A breath-taking unforgettable experience," she remarked. And while Marian noted the beautiful scenery, Richard deliberated on how someone could fall from the chopper and surmised that could not be an option. Too bad, she would not have survived such a fall.

Later that afternoon, they moved into their unit at Plantation Hale. Their cruise completed, they planned to honeymoon a few days on Kauai before flying to Marian's home in Chicago. The Plantation Hale unit, one bedroom with king-size bed, one bath, full kitchen and living room, made the couple feel as if they were playing house. They shopped at the nearby Foodland for groceries, not knowing at the time that most of the food would be left behind with other visitors. After all, one does not cook much on a honeymoon. Besides, both Richard and Marian delighted in trying the local foods. They poured over tourist magazines and clipped the two-for-one dinner coupons like any other couple about to be married and needing to save money.

They laughed and pretended they were poor, the dollar off on the suntan lotion became a joke. They spent that dollar time and time again on ice cream cones, Kona coffee, chocolate covered macadamia nuts, professing those items could never have been purchased without that dollar they had saved with the coupon. Marian had never been happier, she reflected on her good fortune. And in her mind she could see David and Nancy sharing her happiness and she knew Richard was right. It would be more exciting to call them after the wedding. What a great guy she had found!

The big day arrived. A typical sunny day with soft breezes which made palm trees gently sway. The air was permeated with the sweet scents of plumeria, ginger and picaki. Richard's white suit brought out his golden tan and as he stood before the full-length mirror that he used so extensively, he murmured, "God, do I ever look great." Marian did not hear his remark. But if she had, she would have joyously agreed. And, he mused, Marian looked good for an old broad. Her hair had been done by a little Japanese lady in a shop badly in need of repair and not too clean. But she came highly recommended by Laine, who managed the tourist desk at the condo complex. Marian's makeup looked almost professional and he reflected that his soon-to-be wife had spent the majority, if not all of her years, in an affluent lifestyle. She knew how to do all of those things that Didi had never learned. Like if one could see the make-up then it was overdone, someone had told him.

As Richard surveyed Kauai, he noted that most areas were like the beauty shop. Not too clean and in need of repair, unless it happened to be a tourist area. Then the island sparkled. Still, the friendly helpful locals had their own standards and didn't he read somewhere that people in Hawaii lived longer than in any other state? They must do something right.

He agreed that Smiths do everything right, especially for a wedding, he related to Marian. They traveled to the Marina in a limousine, boarded an eighteen-passenger boat to cruise up the Wailua River to the Fern Grotto. The boat exuded the fragrance of the many ever-present floral arrangements. Indeed, flowers were everywhere. At least a dozen leis had been draped around Marian's neck by the three-member crew. She received a kiss with each lei and she radiated joy.

The Fern Grotto was even more beautiful than shown on recently purchased postcards. Red and white ginger, red anthuriums, the popular tropical plant flaring at the top with a heart-shaped spathe, and lush green foliage lined a trail leading from the boat to the grotto. An abundance of luxuriant ferns, some cascading ten feet or more, grew from every crevice of the natural cave that provided a cozy setting for the ceremony. An amphitheater seated the dozen or so guests, several from the ship. Many passengers were eager to attend the ceremony, but how was Richard to know the wedding was such an event. He had booked only the smaller boat.

Peter and Sybil followed Richard and Marian along the trail to the landing where the minister and photographer waited. The Reverend Malikeeno gave the ceremony in both the English and Hawaiian language, never once needing to read any part of it except the scripture. Both Marian and Sybil ruined makeup with tears; Richard put on his I'll-love-you-forever look; Peter's expression reflecting a very solemn pondering. The couple exchanged Hawaiian heirloom rings engraved with Kuuipo (sweetheart) on the bands. More tears from Marian.

A highlight of the ceremony came when two Smith employees sang the Hawaiian Wedding Song. The man and woman, dressed in traditional Hawaiian aloha shirt and muumuu, were accompanied by a third man playing a guitar. The beautiful song echoed through the grotto and Marian knew she would never hear any song more touching.

The ceremony took ten minutes. Ten minutes that changed forever the lives of Richard, Marian, David, Nancy, Peter and Sybil.

Riding back to the marina the crew sang Hawaiian songs, told newly-wed jokes, and related much of Kauai's history.

The entire wedding had cost less than a thousand dollars. A real bargain in Richard's eyes.

Richard watched the river, thinking to himself could someone fall off the boat and drown? Could such an accident happen? Not from this boat, he decided. But perhaps a canoe or kayak could be rented and small crafts are difficult to handle aren't they? So much boat traffic. Another Smith boat going by on its way to the grotto and he saw several smaller crafts pulling water skiers. Skiers seemed to always have an observer in the boat, always looking at the skier or for something in the water. No, the Wailua River will not do.

"What are you thinking about?" asked Marian. "You look like you are a million miles away."

"Not far away. Just thinking how wonderful the future will be." Not a lie, he told himself. Not if his plans came true and why wouldn't they? He planned very carefully. Perhaps her death on their wedding day would raise too many questions. Especially by Peter who, Richard noted, did not offer congratulations. Only a sour "Take care of her." Richard smiled. He intended to do just that!

The staff at Kilohana, an old sugar plantation owner's home, restored to elegant beauty, set the scene for an elaborate wedding dinner. The magnificent building and grounds impressed even Marian who was no stranger to elegance. Both she and Richard remarked, "Wow, this place is beautiful!" And they laughed at still another remark made together. An omen to Marian that yes indeed, this marriage was meant to be.

Others from the ship joined the party and as Richard now knew, everyone in Hawaii loves a party. Waiters sang love songs to the couple, Richard and Marian were coaxed into dancing to the Hawaiian Wedding Song, weaving among the tables and acknowledging good wishes as they made their way back to their table. The evening became a highlight for many of the ship's passengers, giving Peter a positive feeling he knew otherwise he would never have felt for this occasion.

Richard gave Marian a black pearl pendant. The pearl was imbedded in a shiny open shell and outlined in eighteen carat gold. She gave him a Wyland painting of Hanauma Bay, an Oahu water park where the two had wiled away an afternoon, plus Wyland's first book, "The Art of Wyland." The message of the gifts completely lost on Richard who cared little about the ocean's inhabitants and less about their preservation.

Still, to satisfy Marian and to impress others attending the party, he acted pleased. But why did she have to order boneless teriyaki chicken? People choked on chicken bones everyday. Why couldn't she be that accommodating?

The long day finally ended. Richard collapsed on the bed longing for sleep and to get the thought out of his mind that he is now a married man. Not that he intended to remain one very long. Still, it did demand certain responsibilities. Thank God Marian seemed tired as well.

"Get up lazy bones. We have a full day planned." Richard shook Marian's shoulder. She winced when he squeezed extra hard. He smiled. She hasn't felt pain yet.

"I've been to the Market Place already. Look at these." He opened a Styrofoam container, permeating the room with the tantalizing aroma of freshly baked cinnamon rolls.

"They're huge and," she raised herself up on one elbow, "ummm, I smell coffee."

"You got it. Breakfast in bed, Mrs. Snider." He handed her a steaming mug of Kona coffee, made from the packet of goodies supplied by the management of Plantation Hale. He joined her in bed and they sat drinking the hot coffee, savoring the cinnamon rolls and contemplating a life full of sunshine and blue skies. Life is wonderful, Marian dreamed. Life will be wonderful, Richard determined.

"I guess we call the kids," remarked Marian between mouthfuls. "Do you have people to call?"

"Vinnie. But you make your calls first. I'll bring in the phone." He brought the telephone from the living room and plugged it in beside the bed. Marian dialed her daughter's number, a smile never leaving her face.

"You what?" Astounded Nancy could hardly comprehend her mother's words.

"Nancy, you'll love him." Marian smiled at Richard. He leaned over and kissed her cheek.

"I can't believe I could be this happy. Is David joining us on a conference call? So I can talk to you both at once?"

"I'm here, Mother. This took us by complete surprise. Why didn't you tell us?"

"Time just got away from us and...you, I don't know why. Aren't you happy for me?"

"Of course. We're delighted you've found a companion, someone you can travel with. Is this the person you told us about? The reason you stayed there? Tell us about him." Nancy questioned her with a slight tremor in her voice.

"You'll meet him next Tuesday. We'll have dinner at home and you can all get acquainted. He's apprehensive about meeting you as well, but. oh, I'm so happy." Marian blew Richard a kiss. He blew one back to her and glanced at his watch. He shook his wrist and put the watch to his ear. Marian glanced at the clock on the TV. She had talked just a few minutes or so it seemed, but it must have been longer if he is anxious to make his call.

"Shall I call Cora and arrange dinner?" asked Nancy, always the perfect hostess.

"No. I'll call. I don't want anyone to know yet, so keep it to just Kira and Kenneth will you?"

"Of course. But how about Carolyn and Jason. Certainly we can tell them?" asked Nancy.

"Naturally. And bring them to dinner," answered Marian.

"Carolyn may not come. She broke up with her boyfriend and she's still morose about it."

"Oh, my. Stuart is such a nice young man, but whatever." At this point, Marian wanted off the phone and back with Richard. "See you around six on Tuesday."

"Wait, Mother. When do you get home and really isn't there more to tell us about your husband. You haven't even told us his name or anything." Nancy had a sob in her voice. All this from a mother who generally wanted to know and tell each tiny detail of the family's life.

"Late Monday night or to be more exact early Tuesday morning. David, are you still there?"

"Still here and in shock, Mother. Kira and I will be there no doubt about it, but Jason is doubtful. It's play rehearsal and he's very involved in that. The long drive may be more than he can manage."

"Okay, I love you both." Marian seemed to be rushing the conversation, or so both David and Nancy believed.

"We love you too, Mother. But I feel there's so much more to say. The information you have given us seems so inadequate," said Nancy.

"Well, you'll know more on Tuesday and I really must go for now." Marian placed the telephone back into its cradle, turned to Richard, "Whew. I'm glad that's over." She finished her coffee in large gulps.

Richard cupped her chin with her hands. "That wasn't so bad now was it?" he asked. "After all, they want your happiness."

"Calling Vinnie now?" asked Marian while she hurried to the kitchen for more coffee.

"Later. There are some people from the ship to see. Jerry for one to make sure he stays on a physical fitness program and Nate." He didn't tell Marian Nate would be joining Vinnie's organization, the group of men and women who drove drugs and exotic birds from Miami to New York.

"Never break the traffic laws, no speeding, don't follow too closely, no hot dogging. Do not bring attention to yourself and for sure don't run red lights." Vinnie carefully tutored his "boys and girls" and Nate was a natural.

"Then, my dear, we are going to Wailua Falls and after that, snorkeling at Poipu Beach. A luau tonight at Tahiti Nui in Hanalei."

"Tahiti Nui?"

"The gal at the desk said it's the best luau on Kauai or anywhere else and she said to be sure to ask for Louise."

Richard felt knowledgeable about Kauai. Locals were very helpful and truly wanted to share information about their island. Although, they are just as happy to tell visitors good-bye, Richard learned from a mainlander who had chosen to stay and seemed to have made a nice life for himself. It helped the mainlander that he had married a local woman. Local people, for the most part, wanted visitors to come, spend money, don't try to change anything, and go home. Richard recognized the message in most contacts with the locals.

"The falls are beautiful," said Marian, awed by the tumultuous water cascading over jagged rocks into a pool of calmness. She could not take her eyes from the fascinating sight.

"Niagara is more majestic, but this is spectacular. You can get closer to these. In fact..." Richard glanced around observing two other couples ambling towards their cars. Good, he thought, we will be all alone. Unless some other tourists come along. And the sound of approaching automobiles can be easily heard. He smiled.

As the drivers turned their rental cars around in the small area, Richard put his arm around Marian and waved. Don't we look like a happy and loving couple, he implored his thought waves to reach the other couples. They smiled, waved back and rolled three fingers into the palms of their hands, pointing their thumbs and little fingers into the "hang loose" symbol locals were so fond of showing.

"Marian, if you're going to take decent pictures, you have to get closer." Richard guided her close to the barricade along the steep incline. "Here, climb over this so you can get a good shot."

"I don't think we're supposed to climb over that and it's straight down and look at those rocks." Marian trembled.

"Come on. Take my hand." Richard smiled his you-do-trust-me-don't-you smile. Still Marian hesitated.

"I think I can get a good picture from here," she remarked, her eyes fixed on the rushing water and jagged rocks below.

"Don't look down. Take your camera in both hands. I have your arms. Look through the lens. See what a nice picture that will make. We may even have it framed." Richard's voice was soft and cunning.

"Raise your foot, put it here." He guided her slippery black flat shoe to the first rung of the barricade, a fence made of what looked like rotting four by fours. "Now the other one. Put your leg over. There now, that wasn't so hard was it?" His voice was soft.

"Hold my arms tight. These rocks are loose," she pleaded, her eyes trying not to see the danger below. But like most people, she could not take them away from the fascinating peril. She shuffled her feet to dig a deeper foothold in the gravelly soil.

Richard gazed at her, elated. Just one more step, a slight push and down she will go. No one could survive a 400-foot fall on to pointed rocks and then a roll into the water.

"Richard, I'm scared." Marian's eyes were fastened to the river below, her hand reaching to hold him tighter, the other hand holding the strap of the camera.

"And well you should be. Bring her back over da barricade."

Richard whipped around and stared into the eyes of a short fat Hawaiian. Marian grabbed the rail.

"Who the hell are you?" snarled Richard.

"The lady's savior, I'd guess." The stranger took Marian's hand, gently pulling her back over the barricade.

"We lose about a tourist a month doin' what you were doin'. Why'd you think dat barricade is dere?"

"What business is it to you anyway if we want a certain photograph." Richard was livid. His almost fool-proof plan foiled by this turkey.

"I'll tell you. If your mother had fallen down the cliff, my bruddas woulda have to get her. A few have died doin' dat. That's why it's my bidness."

Marian's face turned scarlet at the word "mother." Though she felt a great relief being on the safe side of the barricade.

"In the first place, Kamehameha, or whatever your name is, she is my wife, and in the second place, this is none, I repeat, none of your business." Richard sneered, his voice full of hatred. "Why don't you just buzz off and go tend your pineapples or whatever it is you should be doing, instead of trying to mind someone else's business."

"Richard, he is being concerned." Marian gently rested her hand on Richard's shoulder. "It was foolhardy." Her smile offering an apology to the stranger.

"Let's go." Richard jerked her arm causing her to stumble as he pulled her towards their rental car. He jumped in the driver's side slamming the door, never bothering to open the door for Marian, a deed he had never before neglected.

"Why are you so angry?" asked Marian. "We got some great shots, plenty of them."

"I don't like someone sneaking up behind my back," answered Richard. "He spied on us. Probably half Jap."

"Richard! You don't mean that." His remarks shocked Marian. "He seemed very polite."

Richard glared at her. "All of a sudden, now that we're married, you don't like my words. You liked them plenty before we tied the knot."

"It's just...I have some wonderful Japanese friends and David's Kira is Japanese. She's a lovely girl."

"Oh, hell." Silent for a few moments. Then Richard added, "I didn't mean it. I was scared and angry at myself for putting you in danger. I'm sorry. Forgive me?" His eyes reflected his words. Lessons learned very well. And he had to practice a long time to make an apology sound sincere. Being sorry did not come easy to him.

"Oh, yes. Let's not argue over something so trite." Marian could not quite erase the vision of the jagged rocks down to the water. A fall of four hundred feet stayed in her mind. But why? He really held her tightly, didn't he? He would never let her fall. Still it was so close and her foot had slipped on the loose rocks. If that stranger hadn't come along just then would she? Would she—could Richard have kept her from falling? No, she didn't want to argue but, somehow it still frightened her.

Trite, Richard thought. He was within a foot of reaching his goal. It certainly was not trite to him. More a disaster. And it had been such a golden opportunity. With all the terrific things to do and see on Kauai, it would be difficult to suggest visiting the falls again. Even if they did, it was unlikely they would be alone up there. Well, perhaps her snorkel mask would allow water to get around her face and she would drown. Something. Something will happen to help him get rid of her.

"Done this before?" asked Richard, as he fastened the mask around Marian's eyes and gave her the mouth-piece. The mask fit very well, to his dismay.

"Yes. But not this kind of equipment. I use..."

"No matter. This is easy. If you like this then we will go diving. Just the two of us. We don't need an instructor. After all we are on our honeymoon. Don't need or want all those other people around."

If he had let her complete the sentence, he would have known Marian was an expert diver. In his mind he saw her deep in the water with her air-line cut. Richard, who had never been diving, did not know persons renting equipment are never alone and air tanks are strapped on a person's back unless they are doing the new snorkeling when the tank is kept in a boat.

As he watched Marian quickly move through the water while he stood in one place, not comfortable breathing through the mouth-piece and not liking the tight strap around his head, he knew this scheme would not work either.

The colorful fish delighted Marian and even cynical Richard finally found feeding the fish enjoyable. The frozen peas brought the fish to the surface and they felt the fish nibble at their fingers. This seemed to be a popular pastime for tourists. Dozens were in the water feeding the fish. Even though local people told them peas were not the proper food for fish, no one paid any attention. They had come to Hawaii for fun and entertainment, no matter that they may be destroying the very things they came to see and do.

Before leaving Poipu Beach, Richard and Marian fed crackers to the golden carp, or Koi, adjacent to a cactus garden on the grounds of another old plantation owner's home and now a popular restaurant. A close-by Japanese restaurant did not receive even a glance from Richard.

"We are not eating there," he told Marian when she cast wistful looks in the restaurant's direction.

Richard felt frustrated. Marian's swimming proficiency disappointed him. After snorkeling she had swam several hundred yards out into the azure water. He realized drowning her would be a problem. She could swim circles around him. Actually, he had to admit, he did not swim well at all.

Ah, a real Hawaiian luau. The food, Richard noted, was much the same as the luau on Kona, but it was the atmosphere and the show that made the difference. The Tahiti Nui performers made each guest feel special. And Louise. Louise was indeed special just as the girl at the condo activities desk said. A lovely Tahitian lady, her soft brown eyes and exquisite smile gave a new meaning to graciousness and aloha. She sang two Tahitian songs and gave the blessing for the food in the Tahitian language.

Marian and Richard were spellbound by the stories of old Hawaii. The lovely master of ceremonies, an ex-Miss Hawaii (both Marian and Richard could not understand how she missed being Miss America) told that dancers were not allowed to smile when performing to a particular chant. The dancers, true to their ancestral beliefs, did not smile while Sherman gave an ancient chant. Sherman, the M.C. said, was from a long line of Hawaiian performers and indeed, gave the audience a never to be forgotten look at Hawaiian culture.

The charming dancers brought several members of the audience to the stage to learn the hula amid gales of laughter and applause for a special "star" declared to be the winner.

Birthdays were noted. Then the M.C. asked honeymooners to come on stage. When Marian and Richard joined several other couples, Richard observed the questioning eyes in the audience. Marian seemed never to see those expressions. He grew immune. Thirty million dollars could work wonders.

The evening's show closed with everyone holding hands and singing a lovely farewell in Hawaiian. At least the locals were singing.

Marian believed it one of her happiest evenings and wondered how much happiness a heart could hold. Richard made plans to return to Kauai when Marian's millions were his. He could adjust to this laid-back lifestyle. Especially if it included that pretty singer. A real beauty. What did that fellow call her again? Haunani. Yes, that is it.

Richard and Marian spent Saturday and Sunday sightseeing with other friends from the ship. They joined Sybil and Peter for dinner both evenings. Richard smiling his I'm-so-crazy-for-her smile and catering to Marian's every possible need or desire. This impressed Sybil. Peter reluctantly agreed with her that Richard certainly seemed to worship Marian. They had no way of knowing that he quickly turned his back when they climbed into bed. Her wrinkled body disgusted him and she had a partial denture, for God's sake. She hadn't told him that!

Last minute shopping, for chocolate covered macadamia nuts, Kauai and Kona coffee, a box of fresh pineapple, another of golden papaya, plus many souvenir trinkets. The eventful Kauai vacation came to an end.

CHAPTER EIGHT

The Monday afternoon flight from Honolulu to Chicago seemed uneventful and tiresome to Richard. The usual airline food completely tasteless after the gourmet meals of Kauai. Chicago, the end of stolen or fake credit card use. No longer would he be Eric Johnson, J. Harlan Webster, or Andrew Anderson. John Watson and Jack Streamer only memories from now on. They had served him well. He had taken over one hundred thousand dollars from Hawaiian banks. Not a single employee had asked to see identification. People that gullible deserve to be taken, he rationalized. Richard closed his eyes and fantasized his coming lifestyle. In his mind he planned several scenarios of Marian's death and the millions he would inherit. He played out an arrival scene, meeting David and Nancy, his reaction when he ultimately learned of Marian's wealth. Oh, he had his actions down pat. He couldn't have written a better script. No one could. Marrying Marian had been a nightmare, but getting rid of her would be a dream come true. An accident of course. It had to look like an accident. Unless she developed a disease or maybe cancer. No, that would take too long. He had no desire to hang around a sick person. She made him sick now. What if she were really sick? A nurse. He could hire a nurse. A pretty, shapely one. Blonde. Young. Not a real nurse. They were too devoted to their patients. Unless, of course, she wanted Richard and the money they would share. Except Richard did not share and he did not mention his plans to anyone. He would have to be the devoted care-giver.

Marian's mind depicted scenarios as well. How to tell Richard about her money, how would David and Nancy react? Her friends. Would they be pleased about Richard or jealous? No matter. She loved him and anyone could see that he loved her. They were one. United in the exciting years that lay ahead. David and Nancy wanted her happiness and she anticipated their surprise. Their mother being a sexy bride. She reached for Richard's hand, her heart bursting with happy anticipation.

The newlyweds dreaming of their futures and if each was on opposite ends of the spectrum, then who would know? They both wore a smile of satisfaction.

Richard showed proper surprise when a man, wearing light gray coveralls, greeted Marian at the baggage claim. The man, around five feet ten or so, Richard guessed, and probably sixty-something, had graying hair, blue eyes, and false teeth that were very noticeable.

"Richard, this is Henry. He will drive us home. Henry, this is my husband."

Henry's eyes opened wide and his jaw dropped when Marian said "husband," but to his credit and no doubt training, he quickly recovered from his surprise and took Richard's offered hand.

Richard placed his other hand on Henry's shoulder saying, "Henry, how kind of you to meet us."

Henry's expression questioned Marian. After all he worked for her. He always met her plane and drove her around in her large white Lincoln Town Car.

"We got married in Hawaii. Only David and Nancy know. The kids will join us for dinner tonight so I'll tell Cora when we get home. Nothing fancy, just a simple family dinner." Marian smiled at Richard and by her actions it became clear that Henry was an employee.

Richard continued his confused expression and inwardly smiled. He had handled that very well, he reflected. He believed Henry would always remember how surprised Richard had been when it finally dawned on him Marian had several servants. And certainly Henry would always remember Richard's confusion when the Lincoln came to a stop in front of a large white palatial home in the Barrington section of Chicago. Homes unseen by most, the security gate and tall hedges that enclosed an acre or more of manicured lawn gave the homeowners the desired privacy.

As Richard's feigned confusion continued, Marian and Henry laughed.

"Shall we tell him?" Marian's eyes twinkled and Henry's grin grew wider.

113

"Since I'm not in on the joke, I'll get the bags," Richard properly scowled.

"Chy will do that. I've a huge surprise waiting for you." Marian reached for Richard's hand as they walked to the now open door. Opened by Lin, Chy's wife. And like Chy, a small Korean.

"You have great friends, Marian. Is this a bed and breakfast or what?" asked Richard. "Someone giving us a couple of nights here? Very nice, but I thought we were going to your home. What's the deal?" Richard did not join the other's laughter.

"No. No bed and breakfast. I live here. It's mine, or rather ours." Marian, very happy, made this announcement to Richard. The entrance, large and imposing, with a marble floor and two large paintings on either side, led to a living area as large as most homes. Chy continued up a wide curved stairway with the luggage while the other three servants stood by waiting further instructions. Henry had whispered the wedding news to them.

Marian told Cora about dinner and then said they could be excused for the rest of the night.

Richard gave Marian a long searching (he thought) look. No smile, his lips pursed together.

"Richard," Marian exclaimed, "we are rich. That's my surprise. We can do anything. You never have to work again or, or..."

"You made a complete fool of me, Marian. All the while I tried to save you money, buying you cheap Hawaiian jewelry, insisting on paying for everything because I thought you couldn't afford it. You were laughing behind my back. Oh, what fun you must have had. And our wedding rings, what did they cost? Five hundred dollars. What a joke." Richard did not smile. Instead gave her his how-could-you-do-such-a-thing-to-me look.

"Oh, no. Never that." Marian was contrite. "Never did I laugh at you. I love you. I love my ring. I, you can't imagine how happy I am that you chose me and not my money. Me." She began to sob.

Richard had noticed that the servants had disappeared. He walked across the immense living room and gazed out over the yard which was flooded with soft amber lights, making it seem almost daytime instead of three in the morning. How far should he carry this smoldering anger? Did the servants see enough of it to be thoroughly convinced that he knew nothing of her money?

"Let's talk in the morning. Right now I need sleep. Do we need a guide to find the bedroom?" Ah, this is fun, he mused. And the house more spectacular than he ever imagined it would be. What a find!

Richard slept. Marian's eyes remained open, her tangled thoughts pounding in her head. What is wrong? Didn't he like the house, or her money? He had money as well, so why did it matter that she had it too? Did he perhaps not have as much as she had believed? But, what difference did it make? They were married. They shared. What could she do? A joint account. Then there would be no mine and yours. And add his name to her charge cards. After all the bills were sent to her accountant. She didn't even knew the amount paid for groceries. Yes, that will work. The smiles will come back. Not that he needed or wanted her money. He just needed to be in charge. Like most men, he couldn't accept the fact of a woman having more money, and therefore more clout than he did. Men!

With the decision made, she closed her eyes and drifted into sleep.

Of course Richard protested Marian's offers all the while knowing she had made it much easier for him. Charge cards as well as bank accounts. He knew how to use them very well.

And naturally she could not be expected to move to New Jersey. To his apartment? He had never intended that anyway, but he reluctantly agreed to stay in Chicago. Course, he still had business on the east coast and could not, in good faith, quit working. After all, other people did depend on him, so he needed to travel and of course she could come with him some of the time. Not all, though. Some things he had to do alone and she certainly understood, didn't she? Of course she did. Whenever he had to travel, she would be busy with her obligations. He couldn't be expected to change his life completely all at once. My goodness, she understood perfectly. No question about it. And Marian insisted on paying all the household expenses.

"Well, okay. I know this makes you happy," smiled Richard. She loved his smile. The smile that said you-are-so-wonderful. His eyes could be read so easily, she believed. Such an honest person. Couldn't hide a secret if he tried. What happiness! And he guessed it was okay if she put a hundred thousand in a joint checking account. It made her happy, his eyes told her that. If he did not add to the account, then what difference did it make? He no doubt forgot. Like the plane tickets on Kauai. He told her to pick them up while he parked the rental car. But then the excitement of finding that cute local restaurant and the delicious Portuguese bean soup, obliterated the debt from his mind. He just never thinks of money, she guessed. Like a little child. Marian's heart filled with joy.

The family dinner. An event she looked forward to. Just wait till David and Nancy meet him.

David and Kira arrived first. David had the hurried expression most surgeons wear. Always waiting for his beeper to sound. Not a firm handshake. Don't hurt the fingers, his attitude fairly shouted. Kira, very small, very black hair, very Japanese. Richard winced. A Japanese step-daughter-in-law. Kira's handshake was very firm and her eyes held his. He had harbored thoughts such as these of his life, her eyes should be downcast, she doesn't know her place. Had he kept the sneer out of his voice when he greeted her as introductions were made? As expected, Jason remained at school.

Nancy, Kenneth, and sixteen-year-old Carolyn breezed in with Carolyn flying to her grandmother shouting, "I'm so happy for you!" They hugged, clearly very fond of each other. Kenneth, with a typical absent-minded professor look, gave a non-committal response. And Nancy, well, Richard felt the chill, that Nancy could not hide, in her greeting.

Richard blessed Carolyn for her constant chatter during dinner, making the occasion almost festive. Kira played off Carolyn's humor and both teased Marian in a loving and sometime ridiculous manner. David and Nancy remained quiet and Kenneth's mind seemed far away.

Adjourning to the music room for coffee, Nancy asked to speak to Marian in private.

"Mother, how could you. He is a gigolo. He only wants your money." Nancy was near tears, her voice quavering.

"Nancy, don't say that. He didn't even know I have money until we drove home. You're wrong. Even Henry knows better."

Nancy's eyes opened wide showing a shock and surprised expression. "Anyone can see it. How old is he, mother? How old? Is he at least my age? I'm sick about this." Nancy glared at Marian.

"For your information, he's, he's..." Marian quickly added another ten years to Richard supposedly forty-eight, "fifty-eight and definitely not after my money. He has plenty of his own." And he would when she makes the deposit, mentally deciding to add another hundred thousand to the account, whether or not he needed it or even wanted it.

"I can't accept this, Mother. I just can't. How could you do this to us? Did you at least get a pre-nup?"

"Please keep your voice down." Marian glanced at the closed door. "What can't you accept, Nancy? The fact that someone loves me, that I love someone, or that I may be sharing some of your inheritance or that he is a few years younger than I? What Nancy? Don't you want me to be happy? Because I am, you know." Marian's chin quivered, her eyes full of tears.

"A few years younger. I'll wager he's no fifty-eight." Nancy's eyes were blazing.

"Give him a chance, Nancy. Carolyn seems to like him and David—David is okay." Marian hesitated. David is okay about it isn't he? He hasn't said much.

"Of course Carolyn likes him. She's almost the same age. And David, well he probably feels the same way I do. Sick!" Nancy could not keep her voice down.

"You're being nasty and that doesn't become you."

"Oh, nasty Mother. I'm not being nasty. Just, just, I can't believe it. You led us to believe he was your age, a companion. Now, now, we're going to be the laughing stock of Chicago. Can you just see your bridge club? The women and their snickers. They will see what he's after even if you won't. Mother, I can't go anywhere anymore. Everyone will be laughing."

"You're being too dramatic. Never once did I mislead you. You put the idea in your own head. I didn't. And as for your going out, why does my marriage interfere with your social life? And my bridge club? The women will all be green with envy. Especially when they see I don't have to drag Richard out for cards like they have to their husbands. He loves bridge and can beat the pants off any of them."

"Beat the pants off. You never used to talk that way Mother. Has Richard taught you the younger generation language?"

"All right, Nancy. I'm not discussing this any longer. You are wrong about him and I expect you to treat him with respect. After all, he is your step-father."

"Mother, please not that. Don't ever call him my step-father. And you are blind. Someday you'll see."

"No. You'll see, Nancy. I'm joining my husband now. You should join yours. The subject is closed." And with that, Marian went back into the music room. Nancy followed.

Richard knew in an instant that the conversation between Marian and Nancy had been strained. Marian's lips were drawn tightly together. She briefly glanced at him and took the offered coffee, holding the cup in both hands as if the room was freezing. He could see her working to regain her composure. Quickly he walked to her side, leaning down and whispering, "I love you. Whatever it is we'll work it out together."

She visually relaxed and reached for his hand. Damn, he surmised, he will have to make love to her tonight. Come back Jodie come back to my dreams. And he knew that Nancy could be a formidable enemy. She had kept her head high, cold eyes looking directly at Kenneth. Kira came to Marian's side. "I think Richard is very nice. I'm happy for you."

Maybe the little Jap is okay after all, Richard mused. Maybe she hadn't noticed his sneer when Marian introduced them. He knew of her intelligence. Marian touted her awards and job offers in the scientific field. Kira had been an outstanding student at Stanford where she and David had met. Now she held a high position in the same laboratory where Marian's late husband had made millions by developing several formulas used in the medical field. Kira was well on her way to reach the same heights in a quiet unassuming way. Marian dearly loved her. Kira, not only was very intelligent, she also had very sharp ears and a sense of observation and understanding body language. David had noticed Richard's attitude toward Kira as well.

And Carolyn. She held on to Richard's every word, delighted she had found yet another way to annoy her mother.

Quite a family. Richard began to formulate a plan to get Marian away from Chicago. His ultimate goal could only be accomplished in another place, he determined.

CHAPTER NINE

Richard and Marian spent a week with Vinnie and Ardella. Marian and Ardella, as the saying goes, hit it off. Both had attended Wellesley and strangely enough, one of Marian's professors had also taught Ardella. And both women, along with half the student body, called him "Red Nose" for obvious reasons. Vinnie was very pleased that his friend seemed happy with Marian. Still, he knew Richard and an older, much older, woman did not fit Richard's lifestyle. He didn't believe just having a rich wife would keep Richard content for long.

Vinnie, right on the mark again, still had no idea that Richard planned to become a rich widower. Each day Richard played out a scenario on how that would happen.

Richard asked to borrow Vinnie's cabin at Hampton Beach. In his mind he planned his reaction to an unsuccessful rescue when the small boat capsized, tossing Marian into the frigid Atlantic Ocean. Or, he fantasized his deep depression when his hands could not reach her as she fell from a hotel balcony. She only wanted a breath of fresh air and must have had another dizzy spell, he would tell anyone who asked. So what if Nancy said her mother never had dizzy spells? He could only remember two others he would answer with his you-must-believe-me-I-tried-so-hard-to-save-her look. Sleeping pills maybe? She didn't use them. Well, not yet, anyway.

"Deep in thought, again?" Vinnie held out a glass of gin and tonic to Richard.

"Yeah, we need to get away from Chicago more often. Her house overpowers me and her kids don't care much for me either."

"Do you blame them?" Vinnie sauntered over to a window then turned to face Richard.

"Why, I haven't done anything to them." Richard wanted another drink, but knew Vinnie offered only one before dinner.

"No? Don't you think they know there is no pre-nup. With the age difference, they see big bucks flying out the window."

"I could get hit by a car, too."

"Not likely."

"Think I'll look for something in Florida. You got anything going down there?"

"Yeah, I need someone at Lauderdale. Would she go for that?"

"If I go, she goes. She wants to be wherever I am."

"Nice lady. We really like her. Do you or is it a scam?" asked Vinnie.

"It started out a scam. Now it's more. She makes it very easy for me. And you're right. She is a nice lady and believe it or not, we have a lot of fun." Would Vinnie believe him? They knew each other so well, one or the other often completing a sentence begun by the other.

"Yep. Sometimes a sexy broad is too much of a hassle. Speaking of which, your old gal Didi got married."

"You're kidding." Richard's shocked expression was genuine this time.

"Nope. Married a guy who owns a few dress shops. Old guy."

Well, how in the world did she manage that?"

"The way I hear it, Didi was caught shop lifting some panties and bras. Security took her to the manager and who should be in the office but the owner. The security guy held up the stuff she had stole. Pretty stuff, all lacy, black and red. Anyway, guess she gave them a sob story of only wanting something pretty next to her body and so did the owner. Next thing I hear, they were married." Vinnie laughed.

"Well, what ja know. Little Didi learned her lessons pretty well. I'd like to see her. Bet she still has it for me, though." Richard contemplated Didi's reaction if he suddenly appeared on her doorstep.

"So now you both have what you want. Rich spouses." Vinnie raised his eyes to Richard's.

"Still---how about that Didi. Have to hand it to her, give her a lot of credit, she can really bounce back." Richard was pensive. He hated to give her up completely. He thought she would always wait for him, always be there for him. Anytime! Must see if the old charm still works, he mused, and filed the thought away for another time. Right now he must concentrate on getting a condo in Florida and convincing Marian that will be the place to be.

On the drive south along the Florida coast, they found the perfect place. Deerfield Beach. The three million price tag a piece of cake for Richard, he told Marian.

"I have a deal in escrow now and we can close this the same day mine closes. Thirty days and this will be our very own." He smiled. She smiled. The third floor condo was on a white sugar-sand beach, decorator furnished in traditional Florida pastels and rattan. Perfect for us, Richard told Marian.

Marian would enjoy the Olympic size swimming pool and Richard would enjoy ogling the girls around the pool and along the beach. He secretly thanked whoever designed the thong bikini.

Marian believed Richard when he told her the condo would be a part-time residence. "I couldn't ask you to move from your beloved Chicago and your wonderful family."

He did, though, paint glowing pictures of the warm sun, carefree lifestyle, no heavy coats, or boots, lack of snow, the joy of choosing a home together. A master of deceit and cunning, he soon had Marian counting the days until the final papers were signed. Two trips to Deerfield Beach served to strengthen their desire to taste Florida living. Especially now that fall had arrived in Chicago and nights became chilly.

Vinnie had set up another import business in Miami and Richard's Deerfield Beach location was perfect. Just far enough from Miami that Marian could go along for the ride and far enough for the couple to establish a home base, know the other condo owners, the butcher, the baker, and what went along with that old jump rope rhyme his mother had told him about? Never mind, his ideas were falling into place. A great place.

Richard's specific task involved picking up "material"- mostly jewelry and drugs. Then transporting them to Lauderdale where they would be repacked, and then driven to New York or some other pre-arranged location. Richard's car, a medium priced family automobile, four doors, and a very secure trunk, "so we don't look like we're putting on the dog," when Marian asked why not use her Lincoln or buy a Caddie like so many other Floridian's drive? Putting on the dog? Richard used one of his mother's expressions. Certainly this could never be his own. Besides wasn't that exactly what he had studied so hard to do? Marriage! It took so much thinking.

The fact is, Vinnie insisted on average looking everything. From clothes to cars to restaurants. No one would ever question Richard and Marian visiting Miami often. Marian will have a favorite hairdresser and Richard insisted she go to the same one.

"She brings out the highlights in your hair better than anyone," he told her.

Great idea for Marian to go with him to Miami. But then back at Lauderdale he took her to the condo. He planned the scam very well. She gave him a perfect alibi while he loaded "goods" in the trunk of the car.

A touchy situation had occurred while visiting Vinnie on Long Island. Marian had recognized Nate. While she and Richard gazed out an upstairs window, Nate arrived in a green Taurus, spoke briefly to Vinnie, then drove away.

"Why did he leave the ship?" asked Marian.

"Something to do with the lounge and bar requiring to use the ship's credit card instead of passengers paying in cash. The workers felt they wouldn't get as much in tips," explained Richard.

"All ships do that. We went along for two years until too many passengers complained of the inconvenience," remarked Marian. "How did he happen to get here?"

"He decided to look for another job so I told Vinnie about him and the rest, as they say, is history."

"That was nice of you. Peter liked him I know. Such a clean cut All-American."

"Vinnie's that kind of guy." Richard clicked his tongue and nodded his head. "He will do great here. Although he may work in Miami."

CHAPTER TEN

"Nancy called. She's stopping in this afternoon and wants to have tea with us. Isn't that nice?" Marian had spoken to her daughter several times on the telephone, but this was Nancy's first visit since the "talk" a month ago.

"Wonderful. Does she want me here or should I get lost?"

"She wants you here. I think she's coming around. Seemed excited about our condo."

"What time?" Richard had plans to look again through the garden and yard supplies. There must be rat poison somewhere. Didn't these huge homes have rats in the basements. If he couldn't find any, then he would purchase it. But so much better if it had been purchased by someone else and perhaps forgotten about.

"Around three she said. It's one-thirty now. Think I'll go up and change. I feel so good that she is coming over. I know this has been hard for her and Carolyn doesn't help."

"What's she been doing?"

"Only the usual teenage things. Boys and letting her school work go and she gives Nancy a bad time whenever she can."

"Typical, I guess. Glad it's not our problem."

"Hello Mother. This is my very good friend, Jaki. I convinced her it would be fine to come along to meet you and Richard." Nancy, smiling and very friendly, acted as if she had never questioned the marriage.

Jaki, a tall, slender early twenties blonde, looked from Marian to Richard. The ever present look of disbelief that these two were married, showing in her eyes. Her blue eyes darted back to Nancy and her lips curved into a slight smile. Almost undetected. She was dressed quite simply, it seemed to Richard. A light brown button-down-the-front dress gathered at the waist with a beige colored elastic belt. The dress looked as if it had been worn many times and not the greatest fit which contrasted with Nancy's clothes-always perfectly tailored, according to Marian. An unusual twosome. Richard pondered the friendship.

Cora brought tea and petit fours into the richly decorated music room. Richard's favorite room and apparently Nancy's as well, since that's where she suggested having the tea. The room held the latest system to bring excellent sound throughout the house. A flick of the wrist provided wherever and whatever one wanted. Richard had never seen such a system and he mentally calculated the cost as he had with all the furniture. The grand piano must have cost fifty thou, he guessed. Soft leather occasional chairs were placed in front of a gas fireplace, making the room cozy and cheerful. Although this October day reflected Chicago's finest weather, Marian turned on a low flame "just for effect," she said.

The foursome talked of vacations, cruising as opposed to flying. Marian and Richard opted for cruising while Nancy lamented that she never had time for a long vacation. Jaki guessed any way would be okay with her.

When Jaki said, "How about them Bears?" Nancy quickly glanced at Marian who coughed, took a sip of tea and a deep breath.

Richard smiled and said, "We don't follow sports much."

"Jaki, how did you and Nancy become friends. Are you a musician as well?" asked Marian.

"Well, a, no, we just happened to meet." Jaki gazed at Nancy.

"No third degree, Mother," remarked Nancy. "Tell Jaki about the garden and how you chose the trees. Richard probably already knows." She smiled at Richard.

"For goodness sake. I just purchase a different kind of tree each year to show the lovely colors we have around here. Everyone does that and we call them silly names," replied Marian. "The brilliant red, yellow, brown, and orange leaves contrasting with the green grass could never be duplicated in a painting no matter how proficient the artist," she touted.

Marian brought up the subject of schools. Where had Jaki gone? Nancy changed the subject. Of course Marian had no malicious intent in her quest to find common interests. Still, Richard could see Jaki's embarrassment as well as Nancy's uneasiness. He felt a twinge of sympathy for Jaki. Conversation lagged, both Marian and Nancy searching for discussion topics.

Jaki glanced at Nancy, then at Richard, back to Nancy, to Marian, Nancy again. Clearly nervous, mused Richard. Jaki ate several of the small cakes and fairly gulped her tea. Then Nancy and Jaki exchanged a long look. Marian, looking out the window or fiddling with her napkin, missed the exchange. Richard did not.

"Mother, could I talk to you privately for a moment or two? Family business. Carolyn. Will you two keep each other occupied?"

"Nancy, really." Marian's manners were much better than her daughter's. "We have a guest. Could this wait?"

"That's okay," said Jaki. She brightened and smiled at Richard. He thought what's this all about? Then he knew. He was being set-up. Nancy was not the forgiving little sweet daughter she wanted her mother to believe. Richard knew a set-up when he saw one. Not sure exactly what was going on, he knew he had to be on his guard.

As Nancy and Marian left the room, he sauntered over to the sound system and flipped on the microphone, thus whatever was being said in the music room would be heard in other parts of the house. In a scam, Nancy was a babe in the woods compared to Richard.

Richard turned back from the machine in time to see Jaki unbuttoning her dress. Underneath she wore a skin-tight sheer flesh-colored body suit. It looked like she had nothing on. She untied her hair letting it cascade down to her shoulders.

"It's warm in here," she said in a seductive voice, her eyes holding his, her lips puckered as in a kiss. "She's too old for you. Wouldn't you like a warm, young body?"

"Excuse me?" Richard's eyes remained cool even while appreciating Jaki's almost nude body.

"You heard me," Jaki's voice soft and enticing. She took a step towards Richard. He stepped back. He knew Marian could hear every word of the conversation. What a great opportunity to make Nancy look bad. She did it all herself, except, of course, he had turned on the mic. And he couldn't have planned a better way to up his points in Marian's eyes. Not that he needed to. She thought him wonderful now. But just wait until this episode is over. Marian will grovel at his feet.

"Nancy, what is going on. The mic is on. What are, what..." Marian, near tears, started towards the door. Nancy pulled her back.

"Just a minute, Mother. Just listen a minute." Nancy pushed her mother into a chair and held her shoulders.

"Yes, I heard what you said. I'm surprised a friend of Nancy's would say that." Richard put a small table between himself and Jaki in case Marian came back into the room.

"You are wrong if you believe Marian is too old for me. She is not. I love her dearly and I would do nothing to jeopardize our marriage. In which case, if you are interested, is wonderful." His eyes were telling her I-don't-mean-that-you-are-beautiful-I-want-you.

"I could show you a good time." Jaki persisted, stretching and flaunting her body.

"I'm not interested and, my God, you're a friend of Nancy's," said Richard.

"Not exactly. We only met two days ago." Jaki smiled as if to say what a stroke of luck that had been.

"I see. So Nancy asked you to come on to me, is that it?" How terrific this fell right into my lap, he thought.

"Not asked exactly. Besides, I'm pretty good at what I do. You'll like it." Jaki smiled, her teeth perfect like the rest of her.

"As I said I love my wife. Did Nancy offer to pay you to seduce me?"

"Yeah, but I'll do it anyway. You're cute and we could meet someplace. My place is nice." Jaki worked hard at her job.

"You seem like a nice girl. You don't have to do this sort of thing." Richard made it sound distasteful. However, he had sent plenty of prostitutes out to do the same thing.

Nancy was ashen. She could hardly believe what she heard. She had been so sure. Jaki so very sexy, especially in something other than that colorless dress. Should be irresistible in that body suit. Could she have been so wrong about Richard? And her mother, completely fascinated by the conversation. Nancy knew she had lost her mother's trust and worse, had driven her closer to Richard. Nancy had to get back into the music room somehow, but Marian held tightly to her hand.

"You wanted to listen, Nancy. You planned this, so now take your lumps. At this moment I am thoroughly ashamed of you and I think it will be sometime before you regain your respect from me. If ever."

Nancy, wisely, remained silent.

"Tell Nancy to pay you what she offered and tell her if she doesn't I will tell Marian what she did. How much did she offer anyway?"

"A thousand dollars if you made a date with me and another two thousand if you kept it. A cameraman would have been there to prove you were."

"Where was this to take place?" asked Richard, leading Jaki to reveal incriminating evidence against Nancy.

"My place. But how did you know she arranged it? How did you catch on?"

"It wouldn't have mattered if I, as you say, caught on or not. Marian is the only woman in the world for me and there is no way I would ever hurt her. She's everything to me." Oh, terrific Richard speculated, Marian will love hearing that.

"Well, I don't think Nancy will give me the money. Will you? If they came in right now it would look pretty bad. My clothes are half off. I could always say you attacked me."

"Look, I'm trying to help you. Put your dress back on. Get the money from Nancy and use it to get a decent job. Go to beauty school or something." Richard tossed her dress to her. "Turn your life around. Maybe a model. You're a pretty girl and can do better than something sordid like this."

"This could have been a big payday for me. All I had to do is get you to my place—in my place."

"Tell Nancy if she doesn't pay you, I'll tell Marian. I won't. I would never want her to know what Nancy tried to do."

"What if she says no?" asked Jaki.

"Then you call me and I'll talk to her. I'm sure she doesn't want her mother to know what she has done. I'm very surprised at her."

"You really love your wife. Nancy said you only want her money. I wish someone loved me that much." Jaki's voice plaintive and melancholy.

"Money isn't an issue. It wouldn't matter to either of us if we lived on Social Security. We want only to be together. Now if you will excuse me, I have a couple of calls the to make."

Jaki slipped on the dress, tied her hair back, adjusted reading glasses, and picked up a copy of "Newsweek," a magazine unfamiliar to her. She would have preferred "Star." As she sat near the fireplace, she appeared dowdy. She felt depressed. Then cheerful. Hey, she would tell Nancy that Richard agreed. After all, even if there would be no pictures, she could say he was there. Nancy would believe her. She hated Richard. And he is kind of a nerd. Imagine beauty school. She made great money. He probably judged her by this dress. Picked up at a thrift store yesterday and relegated to the garbage today. She was only sorry she had to wear it home. Oh, well, her blazer covered most of it.

"Well, Nancy, are you proud of yourself? Are you ready to admit Richard is a fine man and that he loves me and wants me to be happy?" Marian walked back into the music room, smiled at Jaki and asked, "Would you care for more tea?"

"We're going, Mother," Nancy coldly said.

Jaki gazed at Marian with new respect. "I guess we're going. Nancy and I have some business to discuss."

"Actually we don't. We heard the whole conversation." Nancy glared at Jaki.

"How could you? He made a pass at me. Tried to rip my clothes off. He's an animal." Jaki glared back at Nancy, "You owe me."

"Dear, we did hear the conversation. I'm not proud of Nancy's part, but Richard made me extremely happy."

"But you were in the other room."

"Yes, but the intercom and mic happened to be on. We could hear everything. I know Nancy hired you to seduce my husband and he rejected you. Nicely, but still he loves only me." Very angry at Nancy, Marian was elated by Richard's words.

Jaki blew her breath through her lips. "What a bummer, Mrs. Snider. You didn't deserve this, but I'll tell you this. Your husband's an all right guy. He didn't want you to know Nancy hired me."

"I know. We heard it all," smiled Marian.

"You owe me, Nancy. He said to make you pay." Jaki wanted the money, at least some of it. She had tried. How could anyone guess he would actually love this old broad? Nice as she seemed to be, she was still too old for Richard.

"I'll call you a cab and here's twenty dollars for fare," Nancy coldly said. "That's all we have to discuss. You can wait for the cab outside." Nancy put the twenty on the table as if she wanted no contact with Jaki. Not even a casual touch.

"She said she could, she could... This whole thing is a mess..." said Nancy, near tears.

"Your making, Nancy. I don't know how you can ever face Richard again. He was so happy that you wanted to see us." Marian's eyes remained cold, her voice held no warmth toward Nancy.

"I think I should have at least five hundred dollars for my time. Nancy, you owe me money." Jaki persisted, glaring at Nancy.

"We had a deal. You didn't perform, so no money. It's that simple."

"Okay, Nancy. But someday you may wish you had paid me the five hundred."

"Oh, now a threat?" Nancy looked at Jaki, her snobbish expression left no doubt she felt superior.

"Not a threat, a promise." Jaki took the twenty dollar bill, turned and left the room. Marian followed her.

"Wait, please. You do deserve something. Nancy would never believe Richard loved me so much if you hadn't been here."

Of course, Jaki waited. Her time was money and the three hundred dollars Marian pressed into her hand was more than she expected. She was firm, though, in her resolve to get even with Nancy. Maybe get Carolyn into—well, no it wasn't Carolyn.

Marian turned off the intercom and mic, wondering again how they happened to be on. Had Nancy done that as well, expecting Richard and Jaki to have a different conversation? Was she so spiteful that Marian's feelings meant nothing to her?

"Well, all alone. Company gone?" Richard breezed in pen and pad in his hand. "We close day after tomorrow, my beloved." He danced her around the room.

In her few moments alone, Marian pondered whether or not to tell Richard she had heard his conversation with Jaki. So very angry at Nancy, she wanted to confide in Richard. Still, it may be better to remain silent.

"Okay, let's have it. Don't you want the condo or what?" Richard looked directly at Marian.

"Yes, yes, I want the condo. More than ever." Marian emitted a long sigh.

"Then what?" Ever the innocent Richard playing another role.

"I guess I better tell you." Marian took a deep breath before continuing. "Somehow the mic was left on and , and, Nancy and I heard you and Jaki." Marian's voice belied her thumping heart.

"Oh, my God. I hoped you would never find out." Contrite, Richard put his arms around her.

"No, I'm glad. It's just that I'm so ashamed of Nancy and angry that she would do such a thing to you."

"And to you." Richard held her and reflected this great opportunity. "Let's try to figure out why and then we'll know how to handle it."

"How could I be so lucky to have you?" Marian lovingly gazed up at him.

"Don't judge her too harshly." God, he hoped this was the right way to promote his idea.

"Oh, Richard. I do judge her harshly and she deserves it. And that poor Jaki. She felt terrible."

Richard remembered Marian had only seen Jaki in the dowdy dress with her hair tied back. Not in the slinky body suit and flowing beautiful hair that he had longed to touch.

"Yeah, poor Jaki. Remember Marian, she agreed to do that for money and for some reason, Nancy believed Jaki could get to me."

"She only agreed to make a date with you. Nancy's the culprit."

"Here's two ways you can handle it." Richard had been thinking of this the minute he had recognized the setup. "First she either dislikes me so much that she would do anything to get me out of your life, or she is afraid she will lose her inheritance and therefore must get rid of me. Now she hasn't known me long enough to dislike me as a person so it must be the money, or here's a thought..." He slapped his forehead as if a new idea just came to him. "Perhaps it's a mother-daughter thing and she can't bear to see you so happy."

"No, it isn't that. We've always had a good relationship." Marian was pensive.

"Well, then that leaves only your money she wants, since it didn't matter to her that you heard what Jaki tried. She was banking on me falling for it and you hearing it, then throwing me out. Not caring how it hurt you. That's what bothers me the most. She didn't consider your feelings." Richard stroked her head and gently rubbed her back. Oh, he could manipulate her so easily.

"I'm torn by her actions and elated by yours."

"You didn't for a moment doubt me did you?" He pushed her away in mock surprise.

"I didn't know what was going on. I'm happy I heard what you said."

"Let's get back to what to do. Is there some particular thing she wants, the piano, jewelry, or something? You could give it to her then she would know there will be more, that you care about her."

"Are you kidding?" Marian's voice slightly louder. "After what she did, I wouldn't give her anything."

"Then," Richard's voice soft and cunning, "she should know that as well and won't try anything like that again." He pulled her close.

They were silent, each pondering future action. Richard knew his desires. He wanted Marian to believe she had made the decisions alone.

'Well, sweetheart. Make out a new will and leave her a small amount of money. You can change it later if you want." Did he convince her?

"You mean leave everything to David?" asked Marian.

"No, that wouldn't work. It has to be to me to make her realize we love each other and we do, don't we love?" Richard's words so tender and loving. Marian could only nod. She did love him so.

"Then after a few months or it might take as long as a year for her to see, you can change everything back. It's mostly your life insurance beneficiary anyway, isn't it?"

'It's quite complicated, and I just had everything, stock, insurance, reviewed a few months ago. Before I left on the trip."

"Not complicated at all. And remember, this is only temporary. We just have your attorney name me as your beneficiary for all of your holdings and you won't have to do all that research again so soon. Otherwise," Richard walked to the window gazing out a few moments, "who knows what she will try next." He sighed.

"Yes, who knows. I'll call and make an appointment for tomorrow," added Marian.

Richard glanced at his watch. "Call now and if he isn't busy, we'll go in. It's only four-thirty and then," he smiled his wait-till-you-see-what-happens-then smile, "we'll go to Rico's for dinner and come home early to bed."

Richard slammed doors, stomped around rooms, surly, gloomy, a very unhappy man. Marian's attorney had been out of town and she had been in the right mood. Almost as bad as missing revamping the will and insurance policies, he had to make love to her last night. God, he had to get out of this situation soon. Marian drove him crazy with her constant fawning. He couldn't stand her. Her wrinkled skin, that partial plate in that container on the bed stand. So what if it had a gold cover? Real gold, 14 carat stamped on it. What a waste of gold. And he hated her legs. Those varicose veins were getting worse ever since she decided to work out to keep in shape. Hell, she was never in shape. And that continual smile. Only three times since they've been home has the smile been gone. The first time, he remembered, when he showed his disappointment over such a large house, faked disappointment to be sure. But, she didn't know that. The second and third time involved Nancy. No matter. He had taken care of Nancy, with her own help. She shot herself in the foot as his mother often said about someone bringing on their own misfortune. Another thing. Marian may change her mind about the beneficiary by the time her shyster attorney gets back. They had no pre-nup to be sure. But it was the other items, stock in the kid's names, some other property held in joint trust for Marian, David, and Nancy. And bonds. He wanted it all in his own name. After all, Marian is not a stupid lady. Richard knew a situation such as yesterday's will not come along again. Not soon, anyway.

Get out of this mood and get on with the condo purchase, he told himself. His mind worked out the details, one of his smarter ones, he mused. A scam always lifted his spirits. The telephone rang. Good old Vinnie, right on time. Marian answered, chatted a few minutes. The weather, Vinnie's kids, Ardella, and then called Richard to the phone.

"Yo, Vinnie, how are you doing, buddy?" asked Richard.

"Got this on speaker or anything?"

"Nope. Go ahead." Richard motioned Marian to stay.

"Seems your property sale flipped." Vinnie repeated Richard's instructions.

"What?" shouted Richard.

"I'm hanging up now, so hope this works out for you." Vinnie got off the line.

"Put Leo on." There was no Leo. Of course Richard pretended to be upset and Marian became alarmed. He again motioned for her to stay and indicated a chair.

"No, I don't understand. It was all set for tomorrow." Richard, silent for a moment or two, apparently listened to Leo.

"Wait a minute, I can't do that. No." Silence. "Absolutely not." Silence. "Marian, will you step in the other room, please. For just a minute." No phone in that room. Not a chance she would pick up the receiver, anyway. Honest Marian. However, she could hear Richard's end of the conversation, the only end since no one else happened to be on the line. He made sure he spoke loudly enough for her to hear while all the time pretending not to let her in on the problem.

"I promised her this would close and we could sign for our condo tomorrow." Silence. "Well, she means the world to me." Pause. "Three months." Richard appeared to listen. "Well, I'm very unhappy with your service. This is pretty late to be telling me all this." Pause. "I'll have to get back to you." Pause. "Three months on the outside?" Silence. "All right, go ahead."

Richard put the phone back in its cradle, slung himself down into a large recliner, held his head in his hands, and he hoped, sent out a large unhappy moan. Of course Marian rushed in. He knew she would. He planned it.

"Richard, what is it?" Her eyes filled with tears. Her lover unhappy, what could she do? Richard waved her away, kept his head down, giving her a few more moments of anguish. She hovered, fawned, then cried.

"Richard, tell me," she pleaded.

Enough, he decided. So he told her his property deal was delayed three months so they couldn't get the condo. Their lovely once-in-a-lifetime opportunity to get something of their own. Something they had never shared with anyone else. Theirs. It was kaput, gone, lost. He managed to drag a finger across his eyes, bringing tears. He had learned this trick from Didi. His eyes stung, worth it though. He knew he had her hooked.

"No, it isn't. I'll call my broker and transfer the three million. I'll buy the condo," beamed Marian.

"That won't work. It has to be in my name because I'm doing a trade. A 1031," he remorsefully replied. "My name has to be on the title. I wanted to provide a home for you," moaned Richard.

"What difference does it make if I pay the money? Your name can still be on the title. That won't change. Then when your deal closes, you can replace the money." Marian playfully tugged at him to dance around the room.

"Come on, this can be done in minutes. Give me the name of the title company again and I'll have the money transferred there."

And Richard, a happy man again, hummed as he danced Marian around the room.

The papers were faxed back and he now owned a three-million dollar Florida condo. Not a bad days work, he reflected. And his plan worked like a charm. And if the three million never got replaced, well, he had heard Marian say often enough, that he "just didn't pay attention to money. That comes with having so much."

They decided to celebrate the purchase by buying new wardrobes, especially for Florida. Marian's purchases amounted to less than a thousand dollars. Richard somehow spent twelve thousand. All on Marian's charge cards, of course. He remembered bills were sent to her accountant and the past month or so the accountant had paid over two hundred thousand dollars of Richard's charges.

CHAPTER ELEVEN

Marian received a call from her accountant several days after the clothing purchases.

"Mrs. Rogers, Snider, Marian. I know this isn't any of my business, but there have been quite a few large expenses approved by Mr. Snider and, well, I know you said to pay whatever comes in. But I wonder..." Tom Bennent left his wonderings unsaid. Concerned about Richard's spending, he felt Marian should know. Marian, exceedingly rich, still spent carefully. Richard had purchased jewelry, diamonds, rubies, and emeralds. All precious gems. A few gold chains, top of the line clothing, and gold bars.

"That's fine. Pay them. There's no concern about money, is there?" Marian knew there would not be. Interest alone amounted to more than her yearly expenses. Recently she had transferred three hundred thousand into the joint checking account.

"No. Not at all. It's just that you are so conservative. I thought you should know."

"Well, I do know. Mr. Snider is my husband and we share jointly. His income as well as mine." Although she couldn't remember any contributions from Richard. Goodness, he is such a baby in matters of money. This amused thought had come to her several times. He even forgets to fill in the checks he writes. Look at him. So careless. But then, she never pays attention to expenses either, she mused. Lucky we have plenty.

"There must be over three hundred thousand in that account. We never come close to spending that. More like twenty thousand a month," explained Marian.

"You will spend that this month, Marian. But, I'll do as you say. I would suggest that you review this month's statement, however." Tom was pushing. He had no right and could lose this account—a good one. He made a hundred grand a year just paying the bills and keeping her account straight. This task taking less than an hour a day. Nancy had asked him to keep an eye on the Snider's expenses and his call to Marian was in response to Nancy's request. Nancy told him Marian's new husband liked to spend money and this month's bills certainly reflected that.

Tom did not report to Nancy as she requested. After all, Marian being the client deserved and received his discreet service. He believed Nancy a nosy daughter. And if Richard's spending did not bother Marian, then it certainly was none of Nancy's nor his business. Concerned, yes. But not enough to jeopardize his hundred grand account. Marian had other accounts and a broker who managed the bulk of her holdings. Marian considered Tom's account household money.

Marian did review the statement that arrived the next day. Tom must be concerned, she mused. The jewelry charges were, as Tom said, enormous. Over two hundred thousand dollars. She knew nothing of the purchases and questioned where the jewelry could be. Did Richard plan a surprise? Put it under her pillow for her birthday? Only bring the jewelry out when he replaced the money? Maybe that? And then with a cold chill, is it for someone else? No! That couldn't be. He used the gold visa and checks. He knew she could review the expenses whenever she chose. So he really couldn't hide anything. Although he knew, too, she rarely looked at statements. Richard knew her accountant did. Richard would never be so foolish as to try to hide purchases made with a credit card. There definitely is an explanation. She would wait. Say nothing and learn all about it in due time.

And she did.

The following afternoon Richard called her into the kitchen. He has a surprise, he said. Henry and Cora were grocery shopping. Chy and Lin away visiting another Korean family. Richard and Marian were alone in the house. He had planned it that way.

Richard smiled his you're-the-most-wonderful-person-in-the-world smile as Marian came into the kitchen. It surprised her that Richard had chosen the kitchen. Neither of them spent much time there. Perhaps making a cup of tea or a snack being the extent of their culinary activities.

"What have we here?" asked Marian, as Richard handed her a glass filled with a thin amber-colored liquid. Then she saw the bracelet in the bottom of the glass. Emeralds and diamonds. The eighteen thousand dollar item on the list.

"Oh, Richard. You are so wonderful." Marian knew her assumption was correct. He did buy the jewelry for her and planned little surprises. Her doubts flew out the window like goose feathers springing from a torn and over-stuffed pillow.

"Drink up and the bracelet is yours." Richard kept his fake loving expression.

"There it is. You never did put it in your pocket." Cora and Henry burst through the door, each racing to the counter where the shopping list lay.

"Oh." Cora stopped, turned and noticed Richard and Marian. They, too, were surprised. Richard stunned. He had carefully planned to have two hours alone with Marian. And now this!

"What are you two doing?" asked Cora. "What do I smell?" She moved close to Marian who held the glass for Cora to see the bracelet.

"I don't know." Marian sniffed the air. "Richard says I get the bracelet when I empty the glass." She laughed.

"Oh, my. Look at that." Cora reached for the glass, but Richard was quicker. He took the glass and poured the contents into the sink, catching the bracelet in his fingers. He rinsed the bracelet, as well as the glass, several times. Then added detergent, scrubbing them both with a brush, then rinsed again. Like a man possessed by cleanliness, he scrubbed the sink, almost frantic in his attempt to remove every possible indication of the drink. Marian, Cora, and Henry watched fascinated. At last he stopped, tossed the bracelet to Marian.

"Spoiled my surprised, Marian. You might as well have it anyway." Then he stomped from the room.

The three watched him go, astounded and amazed by his actions. There was dead silence. Marian held the bracelet and wondered what that was all about. Cora puzzled, walked quietly to the counter and retrieved the shopping list. Henry stared at the door Richard had exited, curious as to why the frantic washing of the glass and bracelet. He walked to the sink, examined it, getting no answers to his unspoken questions.

"Cora, give me the list. You stay here, make Marian a cup of tea and let things settle a bit. I won't be long."

Richard returned, apologetic and contrite.

"I'm sorry for my actions. I had planned for Marian to drink the cider and discover the bracelet in the bottom of the glass. Then we would celebrate by going out to dinner and well, I was so disappointed it backfired."

"It's all right, Richard. We'll still go out. I'll wear the bracelet. It's lovely. Thank you." Marian took his arm, happy once again. She forgot the outrageous cleaning. Probably imagined it anyway, she guessed.

Cider? Henry and Cora did not forget the incident.

CHAPTER TWELVE

"Nancy, I left some test results on my desk. Will you drop them off to me on your way to practice?" Kenneth called his wife between classes. Damn. It wasn't like him to forget and he needed them. Nancy drove within a block or two of the college, so it wasn't an imposition for her. She often stopped and shared coffee with him. It became a highlight of her day, although it happened less often lately. Her music practice and performances took a great deal of time since she had joined the concert band as well as the symphony orchestra. She substituted in a chamber group, as well, which together filled her days with music. Today, she was delighted to once again share special time with Kenneth and visit his class.

He had been busy as well. Tutoring three or four nights a week and the previous weekend had helped a student late Saturday night and again on Sunday. One of the reasons that she loved him. He cared about his students and his courses were not easy. This semester he taught Ancient Greek a course well beyond her comprehension.

If anyone had asked, she would have called their life comfortable. She had "made-up" with her mother and the family enjoyed the Sunday morning brunches-at-the-club routine. To Nancy's amazement, Richard had been instrumental in bringing about the reconciliation. As he had explained to Nancy, both he and Marian expected remarks and negative comments about their marriage. They knew others would question their actions. Richard did not blame Nancy in the least for doubting his devotion to Marian. He would have done the same. Marian fairly glowed when she told Nancy Richard insisted they take the first step in making amends.

Carolyn perhaps presented the biggest challenge in the tranquil life of Nancy and Kenneth. She, the typical teenager, or so others had told Nancy this behavior was typical, questioned Nancy's advice. And more often than not, ignored it. Carolyn wanted her own car and when Nancy pointed that Carolyn had never taken driving lessons, Carolyn pouted for days.

Clothing became another disagreement. While by most teen standards, Carolyn was virtuous (no drugs, no alcohol, no sex) she did delight in annoying and baiting her mother.

A family vacation, that's what we need, speculated Nancy as she drove to Kenneth's school. Perhaps to Florida and a stay in the newly purchased condo. Both Richard and Marian had invited them. Nancy had the plans firmly in her mind as she pulled into the parking lot of Collier University, an expensive private institution. Yes, definitely Florida. Nancy smiled and added a quickness to her step. Kenneth could take a day on both ends of the coming holiday, giving the family five full days in the sunshine state. A bonus the three of them needed. She decided to talk to Kenneth about it over the anticipated coffee break.

She gave a brief rap on the classroom door and then entered. The thirty or so students quieted.

"Thank you, Nancy." Kenneth reached for the manila folder.

Nancy smiled, then glanced around the room. She had been here before and knew many of the students, though expecting Kenneth to introduce her again.

But as her eyes swept the room she froze, her smile faded. If a heart could actually break then hers would have at that moment. For sitting in the back row with a smile bordering a smirk and holding up two fingers making a V was Jaki! Jaki with the long flowing blonde hair. Nancy knew at that very moment that it had indeed been folly to deny payment to her in Nancy's little embarrassing episode with Richard. Nancy knew without question that Jaki was paying her back as she had promised she would do. Jaki was the student Kenneth tutored several times a week. The reason he now wore unbuttoned polo shirts instead of the usual starched white shirts with button-down collars. That "Joop" became his choice of aftershave lotion. That he had professed exhaustion when she reached for him at night.

Nancy tore her eyes away from Jaki's victorious smirk, and gazing back at Kenneth, saw him give Jaki the smile he used to give her. As Nancy looked once again to the back of the room, Jaki had put her index finger to her mouth and flicked her tongue back and forth over it. Kenneth could not tear his eyes away from Jaki. Lust blanketed his entire face. Nancy fled the room. Kenneth did not see her go.

She could barely contain the sob that fought to take control. Her face felt on fire, her head throbbed. She knew. She knew. She drove home not seeing anything, feeling an emptiness she had never known. Somehow she reached her driveway and automatically pressed the button to open the garage door. Still, she sat in the car a few moments trying to breathe. Her chest felt squeezed. Her head felt as if it would burst. She opened the car door and stumbled into the kitchen of her immaculate home. Home. What did it mean now? She grabbed the counter top, trying to steady her buckling legs. She worked her way to the bathroom holding the sink, the refrigerator, stove top, anything she could reach. She tried to vomit, producing only dry retching spasms. Perspiration covered her face and body. Snatching a wash cloth and running cold water over it, she squeezed it out and held it tightly to her face. After a few moments, the lurching of her stomach subsided and she swallowed several times. She sat on the stool and began to sob.

Then her body began to shake. "My God, I'm having a heart attack," she screamed, though no one could hear her. Get control, get control. She forced herself to slowly breathe and began to count, sucking in air and blowing it out through her mouth. Exhausted, she returned to the kitchen and pondered her situation. Then she dialed her mother's number.

"Mother, I need you. I know it's a ninety minute drive. But I must talk to you now and I can't come there. I can't make it there." Nancy's voice surprisingly calm as if there was no emotion left inside her body.

"Oh, my God. What's wrong? What happened? Did something happen to Carolyn?" shouted Marian, very upset.

"No. No, please come," pleaded Nancy.

"Right away, of course. Just me or should I bring Richard?"

"Just you, Mommy."

Nancy hadn't called Marian mommy for years. Not since she was a child. Something terrible had happened. To Kenneth? Nancy couldn't come here. Did that mean Nancy was hurt? Marian scribbled a note to Richard telling where she would be, adding that she would call, this being an emergency.

When Marian arrived at Nancy's, she found the garage door open and the kitchen door unlocked. That in itself was strange. Nancy was very cautious when it came to security. She rushed in and found Nancy huddled on the sofa, her eyes holding a blank stare. Marian held her daughter several moments and then went into the kitchen to make tea, the universal soothing liquid, according to Marian. Returning with the hot tea, Marian simply said, "Tell me, dear."

Nancy related the morning's discovery, all the shocking details. She told of Kenneth's changed behavior, the new shirts, shave lotion, increased tutoring which Nancy now believed a lie. The lame excuses for being gone from home, the lipstick she had found on one of his shirts which at the time she blamed on Carolyn, another of Carolyn's attempts to irritate her. The hangups when she answered the telephone. Now Nancy reflected on the past two weeks.

"I never suspected a thing. I still can't quite believe what I saw." Nancy wiped tears from her eyes.

"Are you sure what you saw was what you think?" asked Marian.

"Yes. There's no doubt. If you could have seen Kenneth's face, he . . . " Nancy paused, took a deep breath to regain her composure, "he couldn't take his eyes away from her. And, and, the students were snickering, and watching him and Jaki, and, and, me. Some of them know me. He didn't even know when I left."

"Oh, honey." Marian's heart broke for her daughter.

"Mother, I just don't know what to do. I'm drained."

"I know. Do you want some advice, or shall I just listen?" Marian's arms held Nancy. "Shall we talk about it?"

"I don't know. I don't know. Advice I guess." Nancy blew her breath through her mouth and emitted a long sigh.

"All right. I want to tell you two things to think about. Three actually." Marian filled the tea cups again.

"First, this happens very often. Especially to men approaching middle age. They see the years going by and they wonder what they may have missed. I'm not excusing infidelity, I'm only telling you the way life is. Now, there are two ways to handle it." Marian's voice was calm, serious. She looked directly into Nancy's eyes.

142

"You can ignore it. Say nothing. Hope it is just infatuation which it generally is. A final fling, so to speak. Wait it out. Or you can tell him that you know and force some kind of action. If he admits it, you can tell him to leave or you can leave. If he denies it, you must also make a decision. Believe him and go on as before or accuse him of lying. That's a very strong statement."

"It sounds as if women don't have much choice," said Nancy. "I don't believe I can ignore it. I'm hurt and furious. That tramp. She was actually gloating. A victory sign." Bitterness creeping into her voice.

"Let me tell you a story," said Marian. "First, zap the tea. We need it hot. Have you eaten anything?"

"I couldn't"

Marian opened the refrigerator, took out cold chicken, lettuce and mayo, and began making sandwiches.

"We can eat these while I talk," remarked Marian.

"A few years ago, quite a few years, I knew a couple who had a situation similar to yours. A family well established in the community, cute young children, the ideal respected couple. The husband, in his forties, became involved with his co-worker. Not a pretty woman. Really plain. Hard for the wife to understand, since she was quite attractive, slim, dinner on the table at seven-thirty every night, a wonderful hostess, a caring mother. But it did happen. The wife found out about the affair. She found notes the woman had written to the husband. Love notes. Love poems."

"What did she do?" asked Nancy.

"She chose to say nothing. To remain a dutiful, faithful, and loving wife. To make her husband so comfortable that home was a happy place to be. His affair didn't end immediately. In fact, it went on for three years."

"My God, how did she stand it?"

"She cried a lot. But she felt he loved the children and their lifestyle too much to divorce her. Plus the wife would have gotten half of everything they had acquired. Or maybe more, since he would have been the one breaking up the marriage by his affair. So she held on. She loved him."

"So he gave up the other woman?"

"Yes, he gave up the other woman. She got tired of waiting for him to choose her. Maybe she gave him up."

"Were you the wife, or the other woman, Mother?"

"The wife." A pause. "Was I that transparent?"

"So my dad was unfaithful to you." It was a statement, rather than a question. "I wouldn't have guessed. You both gave David and me a happy life."

"It was a long time ago and we survived it. I'm glad I chose that way to handle it."

"What happened to the other woman?"

"She resigned and moved. I'm not sure where and to my knowledge, your father never saw her again. There were no letters or cards that I ever saw."

The phone rang.

"Oh, the phone." Nancy stood up, then sat again. "Let the machine get it. I'm not supposed to be home now anyway."

"Hi, know you are at practice. Just wanted to let you know I'm helping a student tonight, so don't hold dinner or wait up. I could be late. Bye." The machine gave the end of message beep.

Nancy and Marian exchanged glances and said, almost in unison, "The bastard."

Nancy chose not to ignore Kenneth's actions and not to accuse him of infidelity. Instead, she confessed a questionable action of her own.

"Kenneth, I must talk to you about something I'm ashamed of and perhaps you can advise me on what to do."

"I'm surprised, Nancy. You're very proper. What on earth did you do?"

"A month or so ago I hired a prostitute to make advances to Richard. I was so sure he was only after Mother's money and that he would succumb to the prostitute's charms. She was very pretty and curvaceous. I offered her a thousand dollars if he made a date with her. However, he didn't so I wouldn't pay her. She got very angry and told me I would be sorry."

"Where did you ever find a prostitute? You shouldn't ever associate with such people. You can't tell what you could pick up, pardon the pun, from them. I hope you didn't touch her. Where did Richard see her?"

"At Mother's. I took her up there and took Mother out of the room and somehow the inter-com was on and we heard every word. He turned her down flat. Mother was delighted. Anyway, the prostitute stomped out of the house. Mother was angry with me for awhile but Richard told her not to be."

"I must say that was very unlike you in the first place."

144

"Should I have paid her anyway?" asked Nancy. "She said she would get even when I refused."

"Of course not. People like that have no morals. They always try to get something for nothing. She deserved nothing. Richard is probably better than we thought. Just forget it."

"The only problem with forgetting it is," Nancy hesitated, making sure Kenneth listened carefully. "I saw the prostitute in your classroom yesterday. Her name is Jaki."

Kenneth's face became stark white. Then turned crimson. He quickly glanced at Nancy, turning away just as quickly. Nancy remained still, her eyes never leaving his face. The crackling fire the only noise in the room. Several minutes went by. The couple remained quiet.

Finally Kenneth said in a slow and emotionless voice, "I still say forget it."

"All right I will." She walked to the chair where he sat, put her right index finger under his chin, forcing him to look at her, "I will."

CHAPTER THIRTEEN

Nancy's story amused Richard. Jaki's stock climbed considerably and he calculated her use in Vinnie's work. Certainly she had shown strong determination to get even with Nancy and had used her profession well. Kenneth never had a chance, smiled Richard. He wished he had met her under different circumstances and in a different place. Jaki was very luscious. She wasted her time in Chicago. Miami needed her. She had all the characteristics to qualify for Vinnie's employment. Richard laughed. Miami, close to Lauderdale. He would see her there. His groin reminded him how she looked in the flesh-colored body suit. Richard was very happy to know she could be back in his life. An unexpected pleasure. He should send roses to Nancy. Just kidding, he mused. He and Marian agreed Nancy should never know they had discussed Kenneth and his weakness.

"She what?" Vinnie fairly shouted. His voice held excitement. "She that good?"

"She's that good. And I see her doing what Denise does. Class. Real class. Only she needs some cultivating, a little enlightenment on the finer things in life."

"Well, a little cultivatin' did you no harm. Look where you are now. Only, we take her on she don't leave to get married. She don't leave till we tell her to."

"I know, Vinnie."

"Make sure she knows that."

"I know, I know. She's a real smart gal." Richard wanted Jaki in Florida, no doubt of that.

"You talk to her. Make sure she understands our rules. No second chances." Vinnie was adamant that he controlled his operations, and there were many. Drugs, exotic birds, unions,

146

prostitution, money laundering, credit cards, and more. All the while serving as a deacon in his church and an elementary school volunteer.

"She will understand completely. What do you think about doing what Denise does?"

"Yeah, that might work out if she can handle the younger kids. Denise is getting antsy to spend time with her grandkids. Maybe I'll let her do that. She earned some consideration, I guess."

"How old's she about would you say?" asked Vinnie.

"About twenty-eight or so and a real looker."

"Okay, send her over. But tell her I don't fraternize with the help. No way would I want Ardella to be unhappy. Know that, right? She don't need to come on to me. No second chances. One mistake and she's gone and she may not like where she goes. What she does with the rest of you guys is okay by me."

"Right!"

"Whatja think of the name of the Miami business? Interior Designs for Discriminating Men and Women."

"Genius. And Jaki will love being an interior decorator."

"Yeah."

"Got an order for a thousand videos of that kid's movie."

"Which one?"

"The little Rican with the two old guys."

"Yeah. The most popular one we got. Gonna raise the price to five hundred. Everyone's fantasy, right?"

"Right!"

"What you told me about Jaki and how she got the professor is just what we need. It takes more than just doing something you have to like doing it. Right?"

"Right." Richard knew exactly what Vinnie meant. To really be a part of his organization you had to like being crooked and outsmarting the honest dude. Have a don't-get-mad-get-even attitude. And Jaki had that. Oh, boy, did she have that.

Richard found it difficult to find Jaki. He waited outside the college three days before deciding she did not attend classes anymore. She never registered anyway, so no one in administration had ever heard of her. He learned later she had never returned after giving Nancy the V sign. She had accomplished what she wanted and no matter that, Kenneth told her he loved her, wanted to leave his wife, or so he said. She had been in that scene before. They never leave their wives.

Course she didn't want him anyway. Just wanted Nancy to know it would have been smarter to pay the five hundred dollars.

A little pressure on Marian and nudging from Marian on Nancy, he learned Jaki was a friend of the woman who managed the clinic where abused women could stay. Nancy served on the board of directors and met Jaki one day as luck would have it. Or perhaps unlucky for Nancy.

Richard easily convinced Jaki that Miami offered all kinds of perks, including himself, and she agreed to leave the cold Chicago winters, to embrace humid Miami. She would embrace more than the climate, but that was her profession anyway and the two hundred dollars a night party call girl became the discriminating assistant manager of high-priced call girls masquerading as interior decorators. Of course, they had been called that for years, in some circles anyway. Jaki's new "shop" offered anyone, any age, any sex, anytime.

Jaki could spot a cop almost as quickly as Richard, which made her more valuable to the business. However, several of Miami's finest were frequent visitors Keeping up on new designs. All for free, of course. Always helped to have friends. Jaki already knew that.

Richard gave Marian several more pieces of jewelry. Half-carat diamond stud earrings, a topaz enhancer on a gold chain, and a baguette diamond cocktail ring. She noted the jewelry had been listed on the statement received from her accountant making her happy that she, indeed, was the intended recipient. The emerald and diamond bracelet, the earlier gift, had a poor clasp. Rather than bother Richard with the problem, Marian decided to take it to the jeweler on her way to her monthly birthday-girl's luncheon. Thirty miles or so out of her way, but so what? Richard had projects of his own to do. No need to mention it to him. She wished he had purchased the jewelry at the nearby mall. So much easier to park and certainly there were plenty of shops. In fact, the mall entry had a jewelry shop at each corner. She knew them well and they were so accommodating. Oh, well, he often shopped downtown. Such a dear. She smiled. What a great life.

"Yes, madam. How may I help you?" The clerk was very courteous and Marian liked him immediately. Great choice for shopping, she silently told Richard.

"My husband bought this bracelet here two weeks ago and I have trouble with the clasp. Could you perhaps put another fastener on it so it doesn't keep falling off?"

"Certainly. May I see it please?" Marian handed him the bracelet while eyeing a man's ring with a large ruby. Richard would love that. Maybe she should buy it for him.

"Oh, Madam. This bracelet was not purchased here. This is not our merchandise. I'm afraid the clasp..."

"Of course it was purchased here. He bought several lovely pieces," insisted Marian.

"Not this one." The clerk unlocked the case and brought out a similar bracelet. "I'm sure you can see the difference."

The emeralds were clear and bold. More brilliant than Marian's bracelet. She compared the two. They were identical, except for the clear green of the shop's bracelet and brilliant diamonds.

"I have the invoice. The, the..." Marian became flustered and uneasy.

"Just a moment, please." The young man put the new bracelet back into the case and took Marian's with him through a door to the back part of the store.

"Mr. Wells, we seem to have a problem out front. A lady claims her husband purchased this bracelet here two weeks ago and it clearly is a fake." The clerk related the incident to the owner of the jewelry store.

"Bring her back here. Do you think it is some kind of a scam?" Wells stopped straightening papers on his desk and gave his full attention to Kyle.

"She doesn't look the type and only wanted the clasp repaired. She seems upset."

"I'll talk to her." Wells nodded his head, dismissing Kyle.

"Good morning, madam. I'm Raymond Wells, owner of Wells' Jewelry. You are?"

"Marian Snider. My husband bought my bracelet here and your clerk says he didn't." Marian blurted her accusation.

"This bracelet?" Wells held Marian's bracelet out to her for her inspection.

"Yes. The clasp doesn't hold and I brought it in to get it repaired. I don't understand this. I saw the invoice. It was put on our Gold Card. Eighteen thousand dollars," explained Marian.

Wells punched a few keys on the computer. Waited a few moments and took a sheet of paper from the printer. He studied it for several seconds.

"Your husband is Richard Snider?"

"Yes."

"Let's see. Richard Snider, October ninth, purchased ninety-four thousand dollars of fine jewelry. One of the pieces an emerald and diamond bracelet for eighteen thousand dollars. But, Madam. This is not the bracelet he purchased."

"It has to be. He gave it to me."

Wells picked up his desk telephone, pushed two buttons, and said, "Kyle, bring the emerald and diamond bracelet in, please."

Kyle place the bracelet on a tray lined with black velvet. Wells added Marian's bracelet along side of it. The three remained very quiet. Marian stared at the two bracelets. The men watched her.

Finally Marian sighed, "He gave me this. It came from here." Doubt began to creep into her voice.

"Mrs. Snider, your husband did buy a bracelet here along with several other lovely pieces." Wells handed Marian the computer printout. "But this is not the bracelet he purchased." Wells spoke quietly and with deep feeling. He remembered the man who had purchased the jewelry. In fact, he had watched the transaction from the security panel. Something about Mr. Richard Snider shot red flags up in Wells' mind. All checked out okay, the Visa charges were approved and nothing unusual happened. Still, Wells watched until Richard Snider left the store.

"The invoice..." Marian began to feel nauseated. What had happened? The store bracelet looked elegant. Sixteen emeralds surrounded by diamonds. Diamonds that sparkled. Emeralds shining on the black velvet so bright they nearly jumped up to her eyes. And the gold. Gold. She looked at the bracelet Richard had given to her. Even to her untrained eyes, she could see the emeralds were not real, neither were the diamonds. And she had to admit, neither was the gold. She perhaps knew what happened. Richard had switched bracelets. Switched the lovely elegant one for a piece of costume jewelry. But what became of the real one? And what about the rest of the jewelry? Fakes as well? No, the store did it. Richard wouldn't. Why would he? After all, he gave her the pieces. Stores were always doing that, weren't they? Think of the profit.

Someone paying ninety-four thousand dollars for items worth two thousand or less. Quite a scam. And she thought Wells' Jewelry a dependable, honest place to purchase fine jewelry. They should be reported.

Her eyes never left the two bracelets. Wells said nothing. Kyle had returned to the showroom. Marian's hand reached out and stroked the bracelet with the genuine stones and then her fingers touched the imitations. She felt emotionally drained. She picked up her bracelet and dropped it in her bag. She rose to leave.

"We will repair the clasp as a courtesy, of course," offered Wells.

"No. No thank you. I'm sorry I bothered you. It was a mistake." Marian's face felt hot. Her hands trembled as she held her bag. The trembling had happened several times lately. She held tightly to the bag. The trembling stopped. She left the store seeing no need to make a report on the dishonesty. A little nagging thought told her perhaps it wasn't the store that had switched bracelets and never knowing maybe best.

Then her mind flicked to the three million dollar condo. Quickly she made her thoughts concentrate on something else. Dinner, gardening, shopping, no not shopping, movies. Oh, the birthday luncheon. Could she face her friends? Could she smile and ignore once again the knowing stares, the thinly veiled remarks about husbands, never saying young but meaning it all the while. She couldn't face them today. Not today. She slowly drove home. A deliberate drive, stopping when the amber light flashed on. At intersections looking left and right, then left again. Glancing in the rear-view mirror every few seconds, at the speedometer, at the automobiles ahead and seeing nothing. Why the depression? So it wasn't the bracelet from Wells'. What difference did it make? She had plenty of bracelets to wear. Still, she felt unsettled.

Richard's car was in its usual place in the garage, which came as a surprise. He had so many business meetings, many out of town. They seldom spent their days together and not many evenings either. She knew he worked long hours making contacts, at what she had no idea. Having him home now made her spirits rise.

"I thought you had your birthday girls' luncheon today." Richard gave her a peck on the cheek.

"I decided to skip it." Ah, he's in a good mood, she smiled.

"You left though. Where did you go?" His eyes seemed to bore into hers.

"Just a short errand. Nothing important."

"Not important enough to tell me, is that it?" His eyes and voice grew cold.

How had that happened? He was so happy when she came in. It seems any little thing can set him off. Marian grew concerned.

"Well, no. I didn't think you would be interested," she explained.

"Where did you go?" Now his voice became menacing.

"I returned something." Marian fiddled with her hands, twisting her wedding ring around her finger.

"What? What did you return, Marian?" Richard asked without any warmth in his voice.

"The clasp was broken on my bracelet, so I took it in to get it repaired."

"I thought you said you returned something. Was this the bracelet I gave to you? Was it?" demanded Richard.

"Yes. I'm..." Marian hesitated, unsure of what to say. "I didn't mean I returned it. I meant I returned to the store to get the clasp..."

"You mean," interrupted Richard, "you took it back to Wells'?"

"Yes." Marian spoke very quietly.

"Well, isn't that just great. I give you something and you take it back."

"No, I didn't take it back..." The trembling began again.

"You just said you took it back to Wells'. Now are you changing your story?" Richard put his hand under her chin forcing her face up to meet his eyes. He squeezed very hard.

"I didn't leave it there. They didn't even repair it." How did this conversation get out of control? He totally mixed up her remarks. She became alarmed.

"Why? Why didn't they fix it?" He kept her chin in his hand, beginning to squeeze it harder. Marian winced.

"I don't know," she lied. The first time she had ever lied to him. She wished she had never taken the bracelet back to the store.

"You don't know?" smirked Richard. No loving looks. No tender touches. "You don't know? Well, it's clear to me you don't like what I give to you. So I'll take it all back." He gave her head a twist.

"Oh, please. It isn't like that at all. It was only the fastener. I love the jewelry," pleaded Marian.

"No. Come on." Richard grabbed her wrist, pulling her toward the stairs. She winced again. Her wrist hurt. He took large strides. Trying to keep up caused Marian to stumble and nearly fall. He jerked harder. Once in their bedroom, Richard shouted for her to open the safe and give him the pieces of jewelry that only days before he had given to her. He watched as she turned the combination knob on the safe. Three times to the left to zero, then right to five, back to twenty-four, then right to ten. Easy to remember, he thought.

Marian took out a small tray which held several pieces of jewelry and handed it to Richard.

"Is this all the jewelry you have in there?" asked Richard.

"Except for a couple of rings and a necklace or two," answered Marian.

"Where is your other jewelry?" Richard looked into the safe which, as he saw, was nearly empty.

"I have another safe behind the chest with more."

"Why in two places?" This surprised Richard. He knew only of this safe behind the painting of a seascape.

"Well, if we were ever robbed, I could open this safe and would lose only part of it. A safety measure my husband, my late husband, wanted," explained Marian, hoping he heard only late husband.

"So you put mine in the safe you would open." He sneered. "You won't have that problem anymore. You can put all your jewelry in this safe." He spat out the words.

"I think it's a good idea to have it in two places," responded Marian.

"You don't listen. I said put it all in here. Right now," shouted Richard.

"Wait. What's wrong here, anyway? I've never seen you like this," asked Marian, concerned.

Richard suddenly realized his anger was unjustified. He did a turnabout, smiled his I'm-only-kidding smile. "Just wanted to see your reaction. Of course it's a good idea to have it in two places. But, sweetheart, if there's a problem with anything I give you, I'll take care of it. Don't you bother with it, okay?"

"I wanted to save you some time." Marian explained once again why she had taken the bracelet to have it repaired.

"I know," Richard patted her head. "Just remember I take care of it."

"Can I keep the jewelry then?" asked Marian.

Richard studied her quite some time, weighing his options. He knew most of it was fake. His friend Ardie, a master at switching gems, made a fortune working for several recommended individuals, as well as several shady jewelry stores. Ardie gave Richard forty percent of the market value, switched the genuine stones to fakes, and then peddled the expensive merchandise to select clientele. Richard gave the fakes to Marian and pocketed sixty grand. Of course, Marian had paid the initial purchase with her credit cards.

Richard pondered whether to give them back to Marian and risk the fakes being discovered as indeed the bracelet had been. Or to return them to Ardie and get the genuine stones. Or at least get better grades of fakes. He gazed thoughtfully at the jewelry. Looks very good. Indeed it would take a jeweler to distinguish the difference. Nearly everyday Ardie switched a perfect diamond for a lesser quality and the owner never knew. He did this for the shady stores when customers left their jewelry to be cleaned or repaired. The suckers!

"I'll let you keep them. They look beautiful on you. Remember what I said, no second chances."

Marian beamed, but her smile turned to fear and a chill ran through her body as Richard's piercing blue eyes met hers. Before he managed to change to a smile, she saw the cold look of loathing come through. She had never seen this look and it frightened her. Frightened her still more as he left and closed the door so silently no sound could be heard. She looked at the door several moments. What is going on, she wondered. Why this reaction to such a small matter? And how could he say in one moment the jewelry looked beautiful on her and in another look at her like that? Almost as if he hated her. He's so changeable. She never knew what to expect anymore. Secretive. Quickly ending a telephone conversation when she walked into the room. She noticed he had a post office box now. She discovered that by accident when she placed freshly laundered shirts in his chest of drawers. She just as quickly took them out and put them on his bed knowing very well opening the drawer would call up another fit of anger. She had, however, seen a letter addressed to him with a PO number. She didn't examine it. Instead, she just closed the drawer and walked to her side of the room. Now she thought about the changes

Richard had gone through in these five months of marriage. Some very puzzling.

"Come down and have a drink with me, Marian. I fixed something special for you." Richard called to her, his voice full of joy and love. His old self back again. Perhaps she imagined the other instances. He's really very thoughtful.

"In a minute, dear. I'm changing my shoes." Marian responded with love in her voice. Such a wonderful life when Richard was happy. She decided to add a little makeup and sprayed Joy around her arms and neck. His favorite scent, she knew.

"Mr. Snider," Henry called from the kitchen, "do you have a moment to check the list of garden supplies?" Richard had made it very clear that he decided what purchases were to be made. Mr. Boss! Even if he knew nothing of gardening, he wanted to okay the acquisitions. He established that the very day he moved in.

"All right." Richard glanced toward the stairs. Marian not yet in sight. He set the tray holding two drinks on the dining room table and joined Henry in the kitchen.

"I don't believe we have a rat problem," said Henry, his eyes scanning the list once again.

"You don't?" remarked Richard. "Well, I do. So get the rat poison as I requested."

"The pest-rid man was here on Monday and he said there was no sign of any. But I'll certainly get a box." Henry prided himself on keeping the home and grounds spotless and never had he seen any indication of rats or mice.

"If you see one rat, there are fifty or so you don't see. And since I've seen two. Well, I would say we have a problem." He, of course, had seen none.

"Don't mention this to Mrs. Snider." Richard smiled his aren't-we-buddies smile. "Women are so squeamish."

Henry did not return the smile.

Nosy old prick, thought Richard. He's on his way out.

Oh, God. Marian has her drink. Did she pick up the right one? Now what should he do? He couldn't chance drinking the other one.

"You didn't wait for me." Richard had placed the drinks side by side on the tray and intended to give her the one on the right. Now since she already had a drink in her hand, there was no way to tell which one had the "special drop."

He lifted the other glass to his lips, pretending to drink and let the glass "accidentally" slip through his fingers, spilling amber liquid on the soft, green carpet.

"Damn," he exclaimed. "Look at that. Get a towel, Marian, and get it off the carpet before it leaves a stain."

Marian obeyed. She always did.

"I'll share my drink with you," offered Marian.

"No. I'll grab a beer. Drink up." There was a fifty-fifty chance she had the right drink, he considered. The one he made special for her. The one that would bring on an excruciating headache that after a few more of the "special" drinks would develop into a permanent sleep. His goal in life! After the fiasco with the earlier drink attempt, Richard decided it best to poison her gradually. The first time he had put a half teaspoonfull in her drink and she, as well as Cora, had noticed the odor. True, she would have been dead by evening. That still was a stupid thing to do. The smell of one drop could not be detected and it would build up in her body. She would get slower, have more headaches, and eventually all the money he deserved would be his. Perhaps three months or so. In three lovely months. Be patient, he cautioned himself.

"We leave for Florida one week from today," gushed Marian. "We better get packed."

"Why pack anything? Whatever we need is there." Oh, boy. Is it ever.

"There are a few things I want to take, besides our new clothes. Not much, only one bag."

"Yeah. You're right. I want to be sure to take that photo of you on the beach at Hanalei. Remember that day?" Richard really planned to make sure there were enough mementos around the condo to show anyone who may ask that he and Marian were indeed a happy couple. A great plan, he needed to be patient so not to arouse anyone's suspicion. Being patient was not something Richard could easily do.

"Of course I remember. I'm taking the one of you on the calendar." She smiled, remembering his surprise and pleasure when she hung the extra-large calendar near her three-way vanity mirror. His reflection could be seen in all parts of the room. He had worn only the brief white bikini trunks that emphasized his sun-bronzed body and hard rippling muscles. Thrills still permeated her body when she gazed at the photo. The cute local gal who took the photo seemed equally impressed.

Richard smiled. The photo really was great. He worked hard to keep his body in terrific condition. And now the Florida sun would help keep his splendid tan.

Life wasn't all that bad with Marian. She gave him unlimited spending power, beautiful places to live, and freedom to come and go as he pleased. It could be worse. Then his mind flashed to what he would have when she died. Far more money, the homes, cars, and more freedom. He could move someone like Jaki in and wouldn't that be a plus? Luscious Jaki. He had seen her twice since she moved to Miami. She did a great job still saying she saved the best for him. He knew better, but hey, he could share. Even Nate had found his way to her door.

Nate drove drugs or whatever, from Miami to various places on a regular basis, taking different routes, different cars. No one ever questioned the all-American-looking young man who drove medium priced automobiles, always obeying the speed limit. Sometimes another young man or woman accompanied him. Students on their way to or from college. Their bags in the back seat, never in the trunk. The trunk, always full, and never opened until he reached his destination. Deliveries were made in various locations. A grocery store parking lot, bank parking (Vinnie liked this one), apartment buildings, near schools. Always out in the open. No one ever noticed. After all, Nate didn't try to hide, did he? The boxes didn't contain anything illegal, did they? Did they? He guessed they did. Not many times did deliveries occur at night-time. Vinnie knew that something done out in the open hardly garnered a second look from law enforcement officers. Thieves sneak. Or so most people believe, even cops. Vinnie's men operated so brazenly no one suspected they may be smugglers, or worse.

One day Nate's job was to drive to an isolated area of Georgia, east of Macon and off Highway 49. He had no idea what he carried in the trunk of his car. But no matter, he had made dozens of deliveries in the few months he had worked for Vinnie. He enjoyed the salary. Five-hundred dollars a trip. Sometimes taking only a couple of hours or so. And the living arrangements weren't hard to take, either. An apartment a block from the warmest white sand beach he had ever seen. He swam in the azure blue water every morning and his skin became the desired golden color of Floridians. What a life. If he wondered about the cargo, then someone else would be making the deliveries and reaping the money. Why shouldn't he?

He glanced at the odometer, one and seven-tenths miles to go until he arrived at the turnoff marked with a small yellow four by four. He had traveled the designated miles on this gravel road since leaving the highway. The wooded area reminded him of the foothills in Washington state, where, as a child, he had visited along with his parents. The tall evergreens cast ominous shadows across the roadways and brought back the childhood memories of suspected giants waiting to pluck him from his parent's automobile and take him to far off lands never to see his parents, nor his sister again. He shivered at the remembered time and then laughed. No giants out here!

Nate nearly missed the turnoff. The faded yellow marker nestled deep in grass that by now, on this winter day, changed from lush green to brown. Several yards along the narrow dirt road a gate had been left open for him. Someone expected him. The timing of the trip was perfect. He had slept in a Valdosta motel. Sometime during the night his car had been driven away by whom he never knew. Then mysteriously returned to the same parking place with the cargo secured in the trunk. All in the plan. Driving the legal speed limit and allowing three half-hour stops along the way, Nate arrived right on target.

He eased his car to a stop, careful not to raise any unnecessary dust that would soil clothing hanging on a makeshift clothesline. A single-wide fifty-foot trailer anchored by cement blocks perched in an area that had been cleared of thick pine trees. The so-called home had only dirt for a yard. On one side fifteen cords of wood were piled high and covered with black plastic. On either side of the trailer door five gallon buckets holding dying marigolds made rather a pitiful sight.

As Nate turned off the ignition, a man opened the door and beckoned him to drive the car around to the back of the trailer. The short, muscular man, dressed in faded jeans and a sleeveless sweatshirt, had tattoos from his wrists to his shoulders. His thinning dark-blonde hair nearly covered a nasty scar along his forehead, almost reaching to his right eye. Nate guessed his age to be around fifty.

The token "Hi" from the man offered no warmth. He pushed a wheelbarrow to an area that to Nate looked as if it was arranged in small garden plots. He noticed dying corn stalks, sunflowers almost gone, and, he assumed, other vegetables neatly in symmetrical oblong raised gardens. Towards the back of the garden some of the plants were dead, while lush greenery covered those closer to the trailer. With a wave of his arm, the man directed Nate to back the car where he waited with the wheelbarrow. Concentrating on his driving, Nate did not see the mound of soil which hid an open hole. When the car stopped, he released the trunk latch and climbed out to help unload the cargo. His mind jumped to the realization that the hole was the size of a grave and whatever was in the trunk of his car would be placed in that hole.

What was in the trunk? His mind shouted the question while his facial expressions remained impassive. Nate was well aware that his deliveries contained illegal traffic, that he could be smuggling drugs, and on at least two occasions, he knew the crates held exotic birds.

But he was unprepared for the shock of this discovery. He knew, deep in his bones, as soon as the trunk lid opened and he saw the two bundles wrapped in black plastic, he had transported a dead body.

Pushing the wheelbarrow closer, the man said, "Here, help me get this in here."

Nate picked up one end of the surprisingly light bundle, while the man took the other. They put the smaller of the two bundles on top of the first one. The man wheeled them to the hole, whipped a four-inch knife from around his waist and cut the nylon rope that held the plastic in place.

"Here," the man quietly said, as he handed Nate an end of the plastic. "Hold tight," the man said and unrolled the bundle, letting a torso drop into the hole. He repeated the action with the second bundle.

This time Nate saw the legs, arms, and head of a dark-skinned man. A Cuban or Mexican, he guessed. Nate swallowed several times, willing himself not to be sick. As he averted his eyes, he saw movement in the window of the trailer. The slight flutter of a curtain. A chill ran down his spine. His eyes focused on the woodpile. The black plastic covering the wood. Had the plastic held bodies at an earlier time? He shivered.

"What are you thinking?" The man stared into Nate's eyes. Very intently.

"Just that you," Nate fiercely hoped his lie would be believed, "have a lot of wood around. A lot of wood for fires."

"Well, you're lying. That's not what you had in your head. I'll let it go this time. Help pull this up." They pulled the plastic from the hole.

Nate then noticed the tattoos across the man's upper arms. They read "Kill the Pigs," and various signs, unfamiliar to Nate, covering the rest of the man's arms. Nate could make out words such as acid power, gun-cotton, and another that looked like Death King. He became frightened.

"Yeah, I been in jail. My arms amuse you?" asked the man.

"Just looking." Nate took his eyes away.

The man gave a soft whistle and an old three-legged yellow-colored mongrel dog came limping from the trailer step where she had been lying since Nate had arrived. With an effort, the dog slowly wagged her tail at her master. She lifted her head and the man reached down and scratched behind the dog's ear.

"Goldie can't hunt anymore. Can't chase off strangers. Can't do anything but eat." The man gazed at his dog. Nate thought, perhaps the man pondered Nate taking the dog with him. Instead, the man said, "Jump in the hole, Goldie." The dog, trained to obey her master instantly, did as the man said.

Nate stood dumbfounded. Did the man plan to let Goldie gnaw on the bodies in the hole? Dogs do like to chew on bones. The dog will have a hard climb to get out. Or could this be a test to see if Nate will make an effort to get the dog out or utter a protest? Nate remained speechless. He couldn't take his eyes away from the dog. The man watched Nate.

Goldie sniffed around the body in the hole but made no attempt to chew on the remains. In fact, the odor emitting from the grave nauseated Nate. Goldie began to whimper and scratch at the sides of the hole trying to get out. The man, with a quick glance at the trailer, climbed upon a rusty tractor holding a scoop full of dirt. He dumped the load into the hole covering Goldie. He scooped up another load, dumping it on top of the first load.

Nate last glimpsed Goldie's sad and pleading eyes looking at her master. It was a sight he would never forget. The man methodically filled the hole, smoothing it out, ready to plant a garden or so it would seem.

He had buried Goldie alive!

Nate backed away and reached for his car door. He felt sick to his stomach.

"Wait," the man shouted over the noise of the tractor. "Carmen made some cupcakes and we'll have some coffee before you go."

"I'm not hungry and I can't be late." Nate wanted out of there. He knew if he didn't leave he would lose it all. Appalled, he opened the car door.

"No." Just one word and Nate obeyed. He was absolutely sure if he didn't the man could just as easily dig a hole for him. He might anyway. Oh, God. What is he into?

They walked together to the trailer and as the man promised, Carmen had coffee and chocolate frosted cupcakes on a table covered with checkered oilcloth. Carmen gave a tentative smile, glancing at both men. Cuban, guessed Nate. Black hair pulled back from her face and held in a ponytail with a rubber band. Small, five feet tall and very pregnant. She wore a man's long sleeve blue shirt over jeans with large rolled up legs. Probably belonged to the man.

The coffee, hot and strong as Cuban coffee usually is, did nothing to quell the gurgling in Nate's stomach which was not caused by hunger. He debated on attempting to eat one of the cupcakes. He pushed Goldie's eyes out of his head and tried to concentrate on the coffee as if his life depended on it. It may have.

"When is the baby due?" Nate asked, looking at Carmen.

Carmen glanced at the man who gave a short nod. "Next month," she replied.

"My sister is expecting her first in about two months," remarked Nate. "Is this your first?"

Carmen again looked at the man before answering.

"Yes," she said.

"My sis has the whole house filled with things she's making. Do you do that, too?" Nate tried to smile. God, she's just a kid. Can't be more than fifteen or sixteen and living with this monster. Maybe a baby will give her something to live for.

"It won't need nuthin," responded Carmen, a sad note creeping into her voice and a furtive glance at the window. The same window where Nate had seen the curtain move and which looked out upon the "garden."

Oh no he wouldn't. He couldn't. Not his own baby. Nate willed his emotions to be still. He made his hand pick up the hot coffee and bring it to his lips. He broke off a piece of the cupcake and placed it in his mouth. He chewed it then swallowed it. He drank more coffee. He finished the cupcake.

He emptied the coffee mug. He said he better leave, that he had another stop to make. He told Carmen the cupcakes were delicious and thanked her for making them. The man walked Nate to his car.

"Whatever you see here, whatever you think, keep it to yourself. I'll know if you don't and I hardly know you. I loved my dog."

And with the man's menacing words ringing in his ears, Nate got back into his Buick LeSabre and very carefully, obeying all traffic laws, drove back to his apartment in Miami, stopping only to sleep a few hours in his car, to purchase gasoline, and to vomit. He would never, ever forget this day and he wished a hundred times that being detected for watering drinks was the only thing he had to worry about. And that same hundred times he wished he had never met Richard Snider.

When he arrived at his apartment, Nate found an envelope containing one thousand dollars on top of his pillow. He froze. Who else had a key to his apartment and could come and go as they pleased? He knew he would never ask. He knew, too, that he would be looking over his shoulder for the rest of his life. Knowing as well, he must be careful or his life would not be very long. And why did he think of it as his life. It would never again be his! His life now belonged to some unknown person that in some unknown way planned his every move. Would he ever get away? Where could he go? Greed. He had been greedy and now he lived in fear.

CHAPTER FOURTEEN

"Mother, whatever happened to your wrist? It's all black and blue. And your thumb is swollen." Nancy had arrived to take several exotic plants to her house while Marian and Richard spent six months in Florida.

"Oh, I bumped it. Silly me." Marian rubbed her wrist. Her hand hurt. Her thumb throbbed with pain. She thought it may be broken.

"You bumped it? On what?" Nancy stared at her mother.

"A chair. You know how I am. If a fly lands on me I bruise." Marian did not make eye contact with her daughter. This fact raised red flags in Nancy's mind.

"A bump on a chair would not do that. I don't believe you, Mother. Did Richard do this?"

"Of course not. How can you think such a thing as that?" Marian gazed out the window. "Let's get the plants ready."

"Tell me what happened. We stay right here until you do," said Nancy adamantly.

"Suit yourself." Marian absently continued to rub her wrist and thumb.

"Have it your way, but if I ever find out Richard hurt you in any way, I'll kill him."

"I hope you do," Richard remarked from the doorway. "But, I did cause the bruises. We were horsing around and I grabbed her arm to go upstairs and she tried to pull the other way. We both let go at the same time and her thumb hit the banister. I'm sick about it." He walked to Marian's side and draped his arm around her shoulder.

163

"It wasn't forceful. It was just plain fun. But the bruises came." He shook his head as if he could not understand how such a thing happened. "We were just having fun."

"Some fun. What about her thumb? Did you have it looked at?"

"Nancy, you're making too much of this. Its all right, truly." Marian still had not met her daughter's eyes.

Nancy observed her mother several moments, then turned her eyes to Richard. He gave her his I'm-sorry-it-happened-but-not-my-fault look, raising his eyebrows and giving a small smile. He continued to keep his arm around Marian.

Nancy shrugged, "Well..." she knew her mother would stand by Richard's explanation right or wrong. She didn't believe for one minute bruises could be that pronounced by horse-play.

Marian felt a chill from Richard's soft voice and oh, so easy lie. It hadn't been horse-play. Not play at all, but a deliberate attempt to bend her to his will. It's happening more frequently now, she thought. It began with a hard squeeze on her shoulder. Then pushing her forehead back until she heard a faint snap. The pain in her neck lasted several days. Now, though, for the first time, bruises clearly showed on her wrists. It was as if he knew she would never tell anyone he deliberately hurt her. Maybe he didn't. Maybe she just imagined he did it on purpose. Nancy didn't believe the explanation. She must smile. She must make Nancy believe Richard and that it was all in fun.

Marian playfully hit Richard's shoulder with a light tap.

"Now if you did that to me, my entire shoulder would be black and blue." Marian smiled at him.

"I have to be more careful." His smile looked sincere.

"Are these the plants you want me to take?" asked Nancy.

"Here, I'll put them in the car for you." Richard carried the box to Nancy's car.

"Mother." Nancy made one more attempt to get the truth. Or as she perceived the truth to be.

"Let it go, Nancy. Enjoy the orchids. We'll see you at dinner Friday."

"One more thing." Nancy tried to catch Marian's eye to no avail. "What ever happened to Chy and Lin? I haven't seen them for weeks."

"They aren't here anymore. Don't forget orchids need sunlight and not much water," Marian nervously answered.

"Mother, come on, where are they?"

"They are with another family. A lovely family, members of their church," said Marian.

"But Mother, you're their sponsor. You brought them to this country. Weren't they supposed to stay here another year?"

"I send money to them and to their host family. I'm still their sponsor. They just don't live here."

"I wonder why," commented Nancy. Marian made no response.

"Do you ask yourself, Mother, why David and Kira haven't visited you lately?"

"I know what you're suggesting, Nancy. I choose not to discuss it. Please let the matter drop," reminded Marian.

"Think about it, Mother. Just think about it," Nancy firmly said, as she turned to add an orchid to another nearly full box.

"These are lovely. I take it Henry and Cora will be gone as well. Will they be with you in Florida?"

"No. Visiting Henry Junior's family in Minneapolis for a month or more. So then they will be here. The plants wouldn't survive a month without attention and you've always liked orchids."

"I do very much. We all do. And I have the perfect place for them."

Marian breathed a sigh of relief. She had handled Nancy's questions and got the emphasis away from Richard and his known racism. Everyone had heard his remarks about Japanese people. Kira cringed and she had been the one person in the family who had welcomed him with the most friendliness and warmth. And Marian hoped no one in the family would learn that Richard had insisted that Chy and Lin leave. Never accepting her explanations of sponsorship. Never once being sensitive to her embarrassment or her emotions in telling these shy, gentle people they could no longer live in her home. The only home they had ever known. In their homeland, they had basically moved from place to place. Camping, finding food wherever they could. Waiting, hoping to find a sponsor to begin a new life in America. Richard couldn't understand her reluctance or her sadness in making them move.

Chy and Lin understood. They were perceptive in regards to Richard. And to Marian's joy, they seemed happy and content in their new home. That she felt disappointed by

Richard's action, was an emotion she kept to herself. And she had had more and more disappointments lately.

Like the burglaries.

No, she knew Richard did not commit the burglaries. She never, ever suspected him. Only he didn't seem too surprised. Although he joined the other neighbors in getting door locks changed immediately.

She pondered the events of the past two weeks. The telephone call telling her four of their close friend's homes had been burglarized. The four couples had been on a ten-day cruise celebrating three birthdays. Marian and Richard had been scheduled to join them, but at the last minute Richard had a pressing business appointment. They canceled. Richard got a refund. Marian had never seen the tickets. He liked making travel arrangements. Lucky, she told him. Or maybe their home would have been hit as well.

"You worry too much," Richard told her.

No one knew exactly which day or days the burglaries had occurred. Since the residents were gone, and the homes empty, it could have been any time. And several other couples knew the victims had given their live-in housekeepers a vacation as well. The vacationers announced this information at the bon voyage party attended by almost fifty close friends. But Marian knew none of the friends mentioned it to anyone. Did they? There had been no sign of forced entry. The burglars were very selective. An original Monet, a Rembrandt etching, one of Ruben's smaller pieces of work, silver, several first editions signed by the author, a coin collection dating back to the 1700's, computers, electronic equipment, stereos, and various expensive collections. Of course, each home had a wall safe with negotiable bonds and stocks kept in it. And of course everyone knew they should have been in the owner's safe deposit box, along with several valuable pieces of jewelry. Altogether, two million dollars in treasures had been taken, as well as several thousand dollars in cash that had been carelessly left around.

After all, wasn't this a safe area? Didn't owners have sophisticated security systems, a locked entry gate that could be opened with a card issued only after a careful background check? Or by punching correct numbers and receiving an answering acceptance? The problem? All the homes had the same type of system and numbers corresponded with resident addresses preceded by code numbers. The first street in the expensive development began with A as in Ash Avenue. So the security system number to open the door was 1001 plus the address. Streets were named for trees, the letter number matching the alphabet number. Simple. For instance, Richard learned when Marian first brought him to her home, Maple's Street code - 130013-160 opened the Snider's door. The address being 160 Maple Street. The system amused Marian.

"It is so simple, but it looks sophisticated," she told him. She had no idea all of the homes had the same system. However, Richard had solved the system the first week they were home.

Detective Walker canvassed the neighborhood seeking clues and trying to pinpoint how the burglars managed to gain entry to such a secure area. No one had admitted a stranger during the ten days. No pizza or any other delivery person, was ever admitted unless arrangements had been made in advance. No one had seen anything suspicious. However, as Detective Walker pointed out, vehicles being driven into the area could not be seen from any of the homes. The very features of the homesites, the distinctive privacy, made observing the unusual impossible.

And what were the residents doing those evenings? Richard and Marian had dinner parties, then bridge, the first three evenings of the cruise. Richard's pressing business appointment canceled for some reason. Those attending the dinners lived adjacent to the very homes that had been burglarized. Strange? Detective Walker asked. Not very, Richard explained. These are regular visitors to the Snider home and none had noticed anything unusual when returning to their homes. And if there had been no unfamiliar automobiles or trucks around, where could the stolen items be? Should the neighborhood be searched, asked Richard? Never! None of us would do such a thing! Someone or a gang entered the safe residential area, not "one of us."

Marian contemplated how this could be. A chill traveled down her spine. She remembered a couple of days before the cruise, opening her wallet for some obscure reason, and noticing her gate card missing. She always, always, kept it in the top plastic pocket. She searched through the other card pockets, then dismissed it from her mind, deciding she had placed it in another bag. Richard usually drove when they went out and used his own card. Henry and Cora knew the correct numbers to punch when they used the gate. Besides, in just a few days,

Richard and Marian will be on their way to their winter home. She certainly did not need her card in Florida.

Marian stayed busy. Packing, calling friends, canceling newspapers, changing addresses for mail and magazines. Still, she found it puzzling when changing the contents of her winter bag into one to use in warm weather, there in her wallet, where she always kept it, was her gate card. How had she missed it? And why now, after all the burglaries, did she have this apprehension? The Sniders had been so busy the first three nights their friends had been on the cruise. And then, no entertaining at all. Those were the same nights her card had been missing.

Marian remained quiet when questions were asked. What could she add? Richard handled Detective Walker's questions very well. Even added suggestions of his own. She felt a little ill.

The burglaries remained unsolved. So far none of the stolen items had been recovered. The shock of their homes being violated never quite left the residents. And as most wealthy people tend to do, they took extra precautions with their holdings. Richard could have easily relieved them of their fears. He knew the homes were safe. Residents still asked themselves how could anyone have gotten into their secure little area, unless someone pressed the right numbers or had a card? Who? And then holiday plans began to form. Residents relaxed and enjoyed the good life, or as they perceived the good life to be.

"A check up? Good idea, Marian. Course Florida has great doctors, you know," said Richard, contemplating Marian's announcement.

"Yes, but I've gone to Steven for years and all my records are here. It's only the yearly visit," remarked Marian.

"If you don't mind, I have several business arrangements to handle, so I need to be gone a couple of days."

"Where are you going?"

"Detroit. For Vinnie. If you weren't so busy packing and getting things done here, you could come with me. But first things first, right?" Richard seemed to have picked up Vinnie's expression of ending each sentence with the word right, thought Marian.

Ah, Richard speculated. Not long now. The warm Florida sun, white sand beaches, gazing at the girls in thong bikinis. And Jaki. He actually wanted Jaki. Forever. Maybe he would marry her. A tall blonde instead of a short dark-haired gal like Didi. Dark hair some of the time. Who knows what it may look like now. And another thing, Henry and Cora always hanging around. One of them in the house at all times, listening, watching. For what? They couldn't know his plans. No one knew, not even Vinnie. Maybe, though, Marian suspected. The glow had gone out of their marriage. Her puzzled expressions lately. Her silence when he twisted her arm. Not even wincing anymore. Always an accident, he told her. Didn't know his own strength. She didn't smile quite as often as she had months ago. Still, she eagerly packed for the extended visit to their winter home. Richard surmised she hoped for a new beginning and looked forward to being away from the pressure of her friend's cutting remarks. More than once the remarks had brought tears to her eyes.

"We expected this," Richard told her. It hurt, though. Some remarks were made by her best friends.

Marian knew Nancy had planted seeds of unhappiness in her mind. Chy and Lin were disappointed at being shuttled to another home. Marian knew this even as she told Nancy of their contentment. Marian wished she had stood up to Richard when he insisted she send them away. And she missed seeing David and Kira. As Nancy had said, they didn't come around anymore. Marian's life had changed lately. Richard away so much and when he was at home, his mind seemed far away. Perhaps, she hoped, he anticipated life in Florida as she did. A new beginning for the two of them. Get back the spark they had in Hawaii. Maybe he thought of new activities, new friends, more togetherness. Perhaps. Their beginning had been so wonderful. Perhaps they will come back. Those wonderful feelings. All marriages have problems. How very well she knew that. Marriage takes nurturing. She vowed to get the spark back.

"Marian, you are doing great. Keeping your weight down nicely and for the most part, I'll give you a ten health-wise. Your blood pressure is a little high, but nothing to worry about. It looks as if you are exercising regularly." Dr. Steven Murray sat on the end of the examining table while he gave Marian the good news.

"Sounds great," responded Marian.

"So, you're joining the snowbird population down there and flying south for the rest of the winter. Marriage seems to agree with you."

"Yes, we're driving, though, and looking forward to Florida and warm weather. These cold Chicago winters can be long and tiresome."

"You've been there before, haven't you?" asked Steven.

"Yes, on the Gulf side. When the children were small, we went a few times to Anna Maria Island. Rented a condo right on the beach. But, only for short periods. August was so busy, he couldn't get away much," answered Marian.

"Well, you're doing fine." Steven slid from the table, preparing to go on to his other patients.

Marian remained seated, her hands twisting a tissue into a small ball.

"Marian, what's on your mind?" Steven gazed at her. "I've known you a long time and I feel you are, shall we say, pondering some situation." He searched her face for answers to his concerns.

"There is something I'd like you to do for me." Marian bit her lower lip and hesitated as if trying to decide whether or not to continue.

"Of course. What is it?" Steven sat down at his desk, eye-level with Marian who sat in an adjacent chair.

Marian withdrew a white paper bag from her purse, opened it and handed Steven a small bottle containing a clear liquid.

"Could you get this tested to see what it is? I would ask Kira to do it at the lab, but, well, could you do it? I'll pay the lab fees."

"It looks like water." Steven put the bottle to his nose and sniffed.

"Where did you get this, Marian?"

"I found it. It's probably nothing and, maybe I should just throw it away," Marian nervously said.

Steven studied Marian several moments, reflecting on her seeming depression.

"You want to leave it with me? I can get it done overnight for you," asked Steven.

"Could I pick it up early in the morning? I should put it back where I found it, I guess. It doesn't belong to me."

"Tell you what. I only need a few drops. Here, I'll put them in here." Steven put three drops in a clean bottle and returned the more than half full container to Marian.

"When should I call about it?"

"Before noon. Around eleven should be fine. And don't worry. This is probably harmless. But if we find it isn't, then bring it back and I'll destroy it for you. Just don't get any of it on you or near your mouth until we know for sure what it is."

"Thank you." Marian rose to leave.

Steven put his hand on her arm and said, "I'm here if you have a problem. Talk to me."

"I will."

Steven remained at his desk quite some time before attending to his next patient. He had detected a slight, very slight, odor of bitter almonds in the bottle. Something else as well. He would have the results immediately. This cannot wait until tomorrow, he determined. He gave the sample to the lab technician and an urgent request for results. Where had his long-time friend, as well as his patient, found this substance, he asked himself.

Marian replaced the bottle in the exact spot she had found it. In the right shoe of a set of brown leather loafers. They were in the third drawer of Richard's dresser under some tee shirts and socks. She had found them when deciding to surprise him by packing a few of the tee shirts he would be taking to Florida. Thinking it was an unusual place for shoes, she removed the pair and examined them. She had never seen them before. When she pulled out the right shoe, she felt something jiggle in the toe section. It was the bottle. She quickly placed the shoes back where she saw them. She decided just as quickly to leave his packing alone as she vividly remembered his reaction when she had placed a few of his monogrammed handkerchiefs in the top drawer where he kept them.

"Don't you ever interfere with the way I keep my clothes," shouted Richard, bending her fingers back for emphasis. Of course, he immediately apologized.

"My mother always went through my things. I hated it," he explained.

"I only wanted to help," said Marian.

"Well, don't."

And she hadn't, until two days prior to her visit with Steven. When she had found the bottle.

"Doctor Murray is on the line for you." Cora entered the living room where Marian sat, thumbing through a magazine and sipping tea. Richard, still in Detroit, had not called during the two days he had been away. Marian hoped the call was from him when she heard the faint ringing of the telephone. Unusual. He generally called every day. Still, she knew how full his days had been with last minute business, especially tying up loose ends before going south. She missed him. Yet she did enjoy a little respite from his demands that now seemed more frequent. Although, she had to admit, he quickly soothed her feelings when tears began to fall. He's so busy, she often remarked to herself. And she always forgave his brusqueness.

"Hello, Steven." Marian took the telephone from Cora. "I wasn't expecting to hear from you so soon. What a nice surprise."

"Marian, I had the drops tested and..."

"Steven," Marian interrupted, "I should tell you I threw it all away. I thought it was something we'd had around for a long time, so it's all gone."

"That's a relief. It was very poisonous. Actually, I have no idea where it could have come from. Maybe something August may have used in an experiment. Around that long?"

"Yes, that's it. What is...was it, anyhow?"

"Have you ever heard of poison dart frogs from South America?"

"Heavens no. What are they?"

"The secretions from the frog's skin used in poison darts. You know long ago, a highly potent poison was put on the tip of an arrow and just a slight amount penetrating the skin caused instant death."

"You mean that is what..." Marina began what was becoming more and more familiar to her: trembling and apprehension.

"Along with a small, almost minute, amount of cyanide."

"My God!" Marian became very alarmed.

"So you can see why I'm relieved you got rid of it."

"What would happen if someone swallowed some?"

"Of course it would cause death. And how quickly would depend on how much got into the body. There is another substance as well. I'm still checking that out. But the two we found are frightening in that form.

"How much would one have to take to cause death?"

"About a teaspoon. There is a very small amount of each in the substance, and almost undetectable by taste and barely by smell. A drop or two could not be detected at all, but would cause quite a reaction."

"Like what?"

"Severe headaches, slowness of breathing. But the worst part is that it never leaves the body. It stays forever and if more is taken, then it continues to build until death occurs," explained Steven. "A teaspoon would cause the legs and arms to become paralyzed, the throat to constrict. Death in one-half hour."

"My God."

"I'm not done with researching it yet, but it seems I read somewhere that it causes a tumor to form in the brain that is also undetectable until too late and inoperable as well."

"Sounds horrid."

"Very. Especially in the wrong hands."

"It looks just like water." Marian could hardly breathe.

"Well, we don't have to worry about it," laughed Steven. "August certainly knew what he was doing. Gave us some great medicine. Check around for other stuff and don't take any chances."

"Yes I will. Please don't worry."

"But who would have guessed August used this in his experiments," remarked Steven.

"Who would, indeed?"

CHAPTER FIFTEEN

Florida. The sunshine state. The retirement dream of so many. And talking to local residents, all the dreams had come true. Didn't anybody go to any of the other so-called retirement states? Did they all come to Florida? Lines in grocery stores were endless. Restaurants offering early-bird specials (between 4 and 6 p.m.) caused traffic jams unheard of even in New York. And impatient drivers. Horns blasting. It became a nightmare for those needing to travel the roadways during that time. Wall-to-wall people. Everywhere. And for some reason, most snowbirds drove Lincolns or Caddys, and drove very slowly. Even Vinnie realized that someone who could afford a three million dollar condo would drive a large luxury automobile. Marian enjoyed having her Lincoln in Florida.

Richard had said many times that snowbirds were the real hazards in the sunshine state. And old. They were so old. How could such old people still get around? He hated the handicapped facilities. His own condo provided the best parking space for the handicapped and marked it with that stupid blue painted wheelchair outline. God, what a waste. What a crock! Marian thought all the attention paid to the old people just dandy. Well, why wouldn't she, Richard remarked one day. She was there herself.

"I didn't mean that, you know. I'm just sick of so many people," he said.

"I know. But the pool isn't crowded and look at that huge beach. Still plenty of room."

Looking and running along the beach continued to be Richard's favorite occupation. And since Marian could not possibly keep up with him, he ran along the beach by himself and out of Marian's sight. He nearly always found a companion.

"It's the crowded road I hate," remarked Richard.

"We have lots of time," she responded.

Not you, baby. Not you. Better enjoy each day while you can. Richard calculated his next move. He found an undetected supply of Digoxin and Quinidine. But since both would affect her heart and that quack doctor friend of hers had given her such a clean bill of health, Richard was apprehensive about using those particular drugs. Could be detected, too, if a question arose and an autopsy performed. Course he would never allow that and certainly as the spouse, he had final rights. He smiled. Change that to Final Rites. He liked that expression.

Richard happily noted that Marian showed more enthusiasm since being in Florida than she had in weeks. She cheerfully found the perfect hairstylist in Miami and made a weekly appointment. A small nearby book store offered hard-to-find or out of print books which delighted her. Suddenly she developed an interest in cooking, an activity she had voluntarily given up years ago when the Rogers' lifestyle became affluent. In fact, she enrolled in French cooking classes and prepared delicious meals which Richard found a welcome change from Cora's standard fare. And Florida's varied and delectable fresh fruit provided another taste treat.

All in all, Richard found living in Florida more rewarding than he imagined it would be. He grew more tolerant of other people. Excusing the honking horns, slow drivers, complaining workers, and indifferent salespersons. Marian's activities left plenty of time for him to develop new interests of his own as well as carry out his tasks for Vinnie. Jaki, of course, promoted his well-being.

He learned that Jaki had grown up in Iowa, one of five children from a blue-collar-worker father and a mother whose goal in life centered on her husband and his needs. Jaki, always the tallest girl in her class, had no idea she had such spectacular looks and body, until she was a sophomore in high school and the chemistry teacher educated her in more than laboratory chemistry. She caught on quickly when he gave her a small amount of money for a few quick touches, so she demanded and got larger amounts for longer and more intimate contact. The life of a prostitute beckoned her from that point and she never looked back. She never talked of college as other girls did. Never, ever, dreamed of marriage and a family. She liked her life and the money she made. Before leaving Iowa for the big city of Chicago, her ultimate goal, she had slept her way around so much she felt like a yo-yo. In Chicago, she charged more for her services and became more select. Always alone, though, she never joined with other hookers or had a pimp. She had regular clientele and that was just fine. The money she made amounted to fifty thousand a year, more than she dreamed possible. Then she met Richard.

"Enough of you slaving away in the kitchen. Tonight, I'm taking you out for a seafood dinner," announced Richard, as he opened the door and danced Marian around the room.

"Wonderful. Where?" beamed Marian.

"You'll see." He smiled. "It won't compare to your cooking, but let's give it a shot. You need a break."

The restaurant, close to Miami, offered seating on two levels overlooking the Atlantic Ocean. The succulent seafood brought customers from afar. Richard had taken Jaki there and he could still see the melted butter dripping from her lips as she consumed the delicious lobster and sucked the last morsel from the crayfish. Her blue eyes sparkled with delight. Jaki made everything seem new to him. She acted like a child still believing in Santa Claus and the Easter Bunny. Her pleasure with the race horse he bought for her was overwhelming. Well, Marian bought. Only Marian did not know about it. Another two hundred thousand dollar check. Marian had fallen back into her old habit of never looking at statements. And if she did show a remote interest, Richard quickly allayed her concerns. He could manipulate her actions and nearly control her thoughts.

The restaurant reminded Richard of Jaki and he liked those feelings. Even with Marian, his mind flicked to Jaki. Marian's conversation, never stimulating enough to keep his mind occupied for long, let him think of other things-Jaki and melted butter.

The drive down from their condo at Deerfield Beach offered great views along the coast. Richard usually drove the freeway, so the change in scenery gave him pleasure, as well as giving Marian a new view of their adopted state. Oh, he could be such a great guy!

"Did I tell you I got a letter from Sybil? They have a two week lay-over in Los Angeles." Marian's voice sounded tentative. "What do you think of inviting them here for a few days? Be fun for them and we enjoy them."

Like hell we do, thought Richard. He remembered Peter's attempts to interfere with his plans for Marian. Failed interference to be sure. Nevertheless, Peter rated very low in Richard's estimation. He hated thinking Peter may be around for even a short period. Sybil, he could tolerate. This would require some very heavy thinking.

"Marian, look at that marina. Let's stop." Richard took the next exit and turned back to enter the driveway of a large boat harbor.

"What lovely yachts," remarked Marian.

"That's what we need, sweetheart. Everyone in Florida needs a boat. Almost everyone has one. You like boating?" Richard's eyes gleamed.

He's excited, Marian reflected to herself. Just like a little boy in a toy store. Wonder what they cost?

"Let's check out some prices, shall we?" Richard urgently said.

Marian, amused that she could read him so well, agreed.

"Let's do."

Richard gravitated towards a seventy-foot motor-yacht. The sleek white 1992 craft, with five staterooms, and impeccably maintained, was priced at just a little over two million dollars.

"It's beautiful." The craft appealed to Marian as well. "Could we handle something this large?"

"Might need a crew, but that's no problem. We can always hire only when we are using it." In Richard's mind he saw elegant parties. He would wear his captain's clothes, of course. Just as he pictured in Los Angeles that day. His dreams were coming true. This is even better than the yacht he had wanted when that Mex kicked him out of the marina. Maybe he and Marian would cruise to L. A. and stay there and just show that know-it-all.

"Shall we get it?" Marian would buy Richard the moon and stars to keep that loving look in his eyes.

"We'll try it first. Tomorrow. Let's make an appointment. And if this isn't exactly what we want, we'll get something else. This looks like a great size for us and the price is workable," remarked Richard. "I have a deal that will just about cover it." He gave her his see-how-much-I-love-you smile.

"Where the money comes from doesn't matter, does it? We are one, remember?" Marian took his hand.

"How could I be so lucky?"

"How could I?"

They smiled at each other and if they each had different thoughts, well, how many people think the same way anyway? Richard thinking Marian may fall off the yacht. Marian reflecting how happy he is.

"Ah, here we are. You'll like it. I'm told the food is terrific."

"You haven't been here before?"

"Not without you, babe."

Butter did not run down Marian's chin. If as much as a drop oozed to the corner of her mouth, she quickly blotted it away. Her napkin placed carefully on her lap was never far from her finger tips. In fact, she wiped her lips after every bite and no sucking on crayfish or any other sound came from her mouth. Very proper. Richard ate the same way, one of his lessons. Jaki, though, had brought glances to the table more than a few times and generally smiles. She thoroughly enjoyed the rich seafood and showed it. Marian, of course, never brought attention to herself. Oh, well, he had both women in his life and between them, they provided everything he could possibly want. He gave a very contented sigh.

"You seem especially happy tonight," remarked Marian, taking small and precise bites of her food.

"I am. I like being here in the warm weather, fresh air. You're happier as well, aren't you?"

"Yes, away from so much pressure, although it didn't seem to be pressure when we were home. It's as if people here mind their own business more." Marian glanced around the room, not meeting smug eyes as she so often did around her friends in Chicago.

"You're more involved with outside activities here. In Chicago you spent so many days inside, sometimes not seeing anyone except me, Henry and Cora.

"Getting back to Peter and Sybil. Shall I invite them?"

Richard, deep in thought contemplated how to say no. "Let me get back to you on that." He bought a few hours at least. Enough time to think of an objection.

"Is something wrong with having them?" Marian at once became apprehensive.

"I'm not sure." Think, think, think. Buy more time. "For now, tonight, let's concentrate on dinner and our new yacht."

"Okay. I'm excited about getting it."

The faint sound of tinkling laughter hummed in Richard's ears. Jaki. Jaki is here. No one else in the world sounds like that. No one can make goose bumps on his arms like that, can make his heart lurch, his face feel flushed. Only Jaki. He tentatively peered around the room, searching for the familiar face. God, he hoped Marian didn't see her. How to explain that! Not down here. She must be upstairs. Who with? This is his and Jaki's spot. The laugh again. She sounds happy. He must know. Is she working? Will she take this unknown, to Richard anyway, back to her place of business? Will she? He willed his mind to stop thinking or seeing what her job entails.

"You look as if you've seen a ghost," Marian playfully remarked, "Come back, come back."

"Sorry, guess I'm thinking of the yacht. Shall we hurry so we can look at it again?"

"I know I eat slowly. But if I hurry too much my stomach gets upset. I could take it home or leave it, but..."

"No, take your time." Perhaps no encounter will be made. After all, Marian has her back to the stairway. He and Jaki agreed if Marian was with him, then Jaki would stay out of sight. The two meeting seemed very unlikely.

"Hey, look who's here," Nate jubilantly said while pulling Jaki towards Richard and Marian.

"Well, hello," Richard, wishing he could disappear, quietly said.

Marian's eyes became glued on Jaki. Jaki, as well, stared at Marian.

Nate, being the only one relaxed, said, "This is a great surprise. Isn't the food great here? This is our favorite place." His eyes darted from Marian to Richard and back. "Hey, you don't know my girl Mrs. Rog...Mrs. Snider. This is Jaki, my love."

Jaki flashed a quick glance at Richard, then held her hand out to Marian as if they had never met.

"Hello," said Jaki, her voice quiet.

Marian calmly remarked, "What a small world. Jaki and I have met before."

Nate then, became the puzzled one. Jaki became uneasy. Marian became suspicious. And Richard? Richard became furious and he had to keep his fury inside.

She is with Nate. That laugh for Nate. She dressed in that clinging white silk for Nate. The dress Richard had chosen for her. Nate had called her his love. This is their favorite place. What in the hell is going on here? And Marian. Gullible maybe, but not dumb. What is she thinking? How will he explain Jaki? And Jaki, embarrassed as hell, how will she explain Nate to Richard? These thoughts rolled around Richard's mind. How will Jaki ever explain Nate calling her "my love."

The four remained in a strained silence.

Finally Nate said, "Jaki and I are going to Hialeah to watch the races. She has a horse she likes to watch." Nate squeezed Jaki's hand, his glance full of love, hers awkward.

Bet she has a horse she likes to watch, Richard fumed to himself. The horse he bought for her.

"Nice of you to stop by. And Nate, I need to see you tomorrow. I'll give you a call around ten."

"Remember the appointment to see the yacht," said Marian.

"I remember," Richard grimly answered. God, what a lousy thing to happen. Of all the seafood restaurants in Miami, of all the time of the day or days of the week, why did the four of them hit it exactly at the same time? His big worry was how to handle Marian.

"So?" Marian questioned as Nate and Jaki left the restaurant.

"I'm in shock. I know this is the most popular place in the world in the wintertime. But can you believe she is here and with Nate?" Richard gave his incredible-this-could-happen look, his eyes wide open as if the situation bordered on disbelief.

"As a matter of fact, I can believe it," Marian quietly said, her eyes trying to look into Richard's. For some reason, he found the wall above her head so interesting.

"I'm ready to go whenever you are," announced Marian.

"There's no rush. Please eat, the food is delicious."

"Then why aren't you eating yours?" she asked, not expecting nor receiving an answer.

The cheerfulness of the earlier evening completely gone, caused by the same person, even if for different reasons. Richard and Marian, for the most part, were silent on the ride back to Deerfield Beach. Each had thoughts about the evening. Thoughts that could not be shared with the other. Richard took the freeway out of Miami, not driving past the yacht. He murmured that they could inspect it the next day and since it's getting late maybe they better head for home.

"As you wish," agreed Marian. She couldn't shake the uneasy feeling that seeing Jaki had given to her even though Nate and Jaki were an obvious couple. Anyone could tell Nate appeared very smitten. Still Marian remained apprehensive and curious. Had Nate known Jaki before Nancy had met her? Had Nate convinced Jaki to move to Florida? Yet to Marian's knowledge, Nate had never been to Chicago. So how could they have met? Marian absolutely knew Richard must have made the connection. She had seen the look pass between Richard and Jaki. And yet, they never spoke a word to each other. Both had an expression of trepidation as if they were uncertain of what to say, if anything, or how to act. Alarmed, yes, that's how Richard and Jaki looked. And why? Both seemed surprised and not pleased to see the other. Perhaps their first, and Marian guessed, only meeting continued to embarrass them. Except, Marian contemplated again the intimate look that passed between them. And while still in Chicago, Richard had asked about Jaki. Almost insisted that Marian quiz Nancy on Jaki's whereabouts. On the other hand, Nate and Jaki are lovers. Quite a dilemma. This will be another fitful, sleepless night, she told herself.

Richard certainly did not feel at ease with the situation. His emotions raged. Jealousy because Nate and Jaki were together and by their actions he knew they were more than casual friends. The jealousy tore at his insides. Gave him a throbbing headache. And, of course, Marian must have guessed he had been instrumental in bringing Jaki to Florida. Did she see the exchange of glances? And if she did, how would she read it? And exactly how did Jaki feel about him? About Nate? Nate will have to go! God, this whole evening is making his head pound. Ransack his brain. First of all, allay Marian's fears because he could see she was brooding over it.

"You know, my dear, I mentioned to Vinnie about Jaki and her pursuit of Kenneth. Only I didn't mention Kenneth by name. And maybe he told Nate or something. Or for all I know, Miami has always been her hangout. Who knows? I'm stumped and shocked." That sounded sincere, didn't it? Richard assured himself. Did she believe him?

She did! She wanted to. It sounded plausible. Certainly a huge coincidence. But don't they (the mysterious they) say that truth is stranger than fiction? And before Nate and Jaki appeared, wasn't hers and Richard's life and love back on track? He hadn't squeezed her arms or bent her fingers since the move south.

"It doesn't concern us anyway. I guess she can come to Florida if she wants. Like anyone else. I hope she's sincere about Nate. He seems like such a nice young man." Marian accepted Richard's explanation. She did so want those smiles back.

And back they came. She could be manipulated so easily. Richard smiled.

CHAPTER SIXTEEN

Richard met with Nate, outlined his next project, which didn't please Nate, but one which Nate could easily handle. Richard had contrived it during the early morning hours. He contemplated asking Vinnie to get rid of Nate, then doubted Vinnie would see the need, unless he knew how Richard felt about Jaki. And for Richard's ultimate goal to succeed, everyone, every single person he and Marian knew, had to believe in his devotion to her.

Marian and Richard bought the yacht. Jointly, or so Marian believed. Richard to add his share in a week or two at the very most. He convinced her that with each of them paying half it would truly be "theirs." Course the entire amount must be paid immediately to get the best price, right? Richard already knew his "deal" would be delayed. Oh, he loved this life.

And he could just see Jaki cruising along with him. When she saw the yacht, Richard knew she would dump Nate. She told Richard Nate was a smoke screen anyway. Got her out of a "job" she couldn't stand and Nate never demanded or even asked anything in return. The "my love" part? Just to keep unwanted people away.

"Nate and I are platonic friends," Jaki told Richard. She emphasized the word platonic and certainly sounded sincere. They all sounded sincere in their explanations to the others. Still, her laughter with Nate bothered Richard. She had laughed like that with him so many times and platonic did not describe their relationship.

"Richard, I know you have something on your mind regarding Peter and Sybil, so could we talk about it?" asked Marian, handing him a gin and tonic, their favorite afternoon drink. Their cocktail hour consisted of a couple of drinks and snacks. Both were putting on a few unwanted pounds. So easy to relax in Florida.

"I hoped, Marian, it could have been taken care of without you knowing," he responded.

"What taken care of?" Marian's eyes opened wide as she stared at him.

"Are you sure you want to know this?" he asked, knowing this is the kind of remark that she, or any woman, could not resist.

"Please tell me. Are they ill? Sybil said nothing about a problem," pleaded Marian.

"No. Well, you might call it that. I would give anything if I didn't have to tell you this, dear," said Richard.

"Whatever it is, tell me."

"Nate didn't leave the ship because of the credit cards and tips."

"What do you mean? Why then?" Marian, full of panic, started to perspire.

"Marian." Richard's voice became low and depressing, or so it seemed to Marian. He clearly did not want her to know the situation, she reasoned. But she must know.

"Please go on," she asked.

"Peter abused Nate. Sexually abused him." Richard dropped his head as if ashamed to say those words. He seemed surrounded by humiliation.

"Oh, no!" Marian literally screamed, tears flooding her eyes as she began to hyperventilate. Richard put his arms around her, trying to stop the shaking.

"There, there, calm down. Take deep breaths, take it easy."

"I, I don't believe it." Now she began to hiccup.

"I'm so terribly sorry you have to hear this. But, I'm afraid there are things you must know and actions you may contemplate." Richard's voice could be so smooth and cunning.

"Action, what action? What things?" She continued to tremble, nearly in shock. Richard thought, had he gone too far? Had he handled it wisely?

"Nate told me sometime ago while we were on the ship. I recognized the symptoms. I used to counsel abused youngsters, so I saw at once what Nate tried very hard to hide." Richard lied once again to Marian.

"It can't be true. I've known Peter all of his life. It's a mistake." Marian was incredulous. She simply could not believe Peter abused Nate. "He wouldn't abuse anyone."

"Abuse isn't a strong enough word, Marian. He raped him. In Nate's own cabin and threatened his life if he told anyone."

"No, I must hear this from Peter. I don't, I can't believe it. Sybil. He and Sybil are very happy." Marian continued to be unwilling to believe this about her friend.

"Nate wasn't the only one. Did you happen to know a young man, Bill, who worked with the purser?" Richard knew Bill had left the ship in Honolulu to work with his brother in construction.

"No, I don't know him. My God, Richard. Tell me you are joking."

"This is no joke, Marian. Nate and Bill want to take this to the newspapers. To save other young men, they said. I talked to Nate and Bill two days straight trying to talk them out of it."

"The newspapers. It will ruin Peter even if it isn't true. And the cruise line." Marian began to weep, huge sobs, gasping breaths she could not stop.

Richard waited. Then, "I believe I have them half-way convinced there's another way."

"What other way?" Marian asked between sobs.

"If Peter was relieved of his duties." Richard quietly said.

"That would kill him. It's his whole life."

"Marian, he is forcing members of his crew to perform sex acts on him. Is that someone you want as a captain in your cruise line?" asked Richard, his voice low, almost a whisper, and his blue eyes staring at Marian.

"I need to question Nate. I need to talk to Peter."

"Talking to Nate is possible, but don't you think you should talk to your other board members and get opinions from them?"

"What if Nate is lying?"

"Ask him. Ask him exactly what Peter demanded. You may not like the answers."

"But, I just can't take his word."

"I've done all I can. If he goes to the newspapers it could be tragic for many people," shrugged Richard. "Better think about it, very hard."

"What can I do?"

Now that's what Richard wanted to hear. Now he could tell her the "right" thing to do.

"I'll get Nate over here and you question him. Bill left for Dallas, but he will do whatever Nate does. If Nate says keep quiet, then Bill will keep quiet. If Nate decides to make it public, then Bill will add what happened to him."

"Do they want money? Is that it?" asked Marian.

"No, they only want Peter away from his captives. There was no place for Nate to go. He couldn't get away. Peter had complete control."

At Marian's mention of money, Richard thought of a few quick thousand, but rejected the idea. He wanted her to believe he is trying so hard to help ease her pain and to help "their" friend, Peter.

"Oh, God." Marian blew her nose and wadded the tissue. Richard gave her a new supply.

"I'll call Nate, get him up here if he's available and we'll both talk to him. I would give anything if this wasn't true, dear. But I know abuse when I see it. I'm trained in that."

"I didn't know that. You never told me."

"No reason to. I don't work in it anymore. I know what I see. There is no way I could ever miss."

"What do you look for?" asked Marian.

"Oh, please, Marian. You don't expect a course in sexual abuse in ten minutes do you?" scoffed Richard.

"No, I guess not. I'm glad you're here with me. I couldn't handle it alone."

"Would you prefer to meet him somewhere else, rather than here?"

"No, I know I'll cry. So I better be here, at home."

Of course Nate could come right over. Richard told him to be available in case Marian wanted to see him. And Richard was sure she would insist on talking to him.

"Nate seemed so happy when we saw him at the restaurant. I thought if someone had been abused. Well I thought it..." Marian faltered.

"Can't ever tell by outward appearances unless you know what to look for. That's where my training comes in. Let me tell you this, he is very happy to be away from Peter." Richard paused, "Shall I make you another drink while we wait for him?"

"Coffee. I want a clear head so I can be sure of everything," remarked Marian. "I'll make it. Give me something to occupy my mind."

Marian puttered around the kitchen, her mind on Peter. The little boy and how she had adored him from the moment she knew his family. Always such a dependable person. When other youngsters wore long, shaggy hair, Peter kept his short, nicely combed. And he always dressed immaculately. Never in dirty jeans with torn knees as most boys did. Top of his class, honor student. No. He did not abuse Nate or anyone. She would never believe it. And Sybil, a wonderful supportive wife. Marian reflected on their wedding. If ever a couple were meant to be together, then Peter and Sybil were. The perfect couple. They complimented each other and it seemed as if they could read each other's mind, sometimes ending a sentence the other had begun. Then laughing as if they had a private joke no other person could understand. They went everywhere together. And wanted it that way. Holding hands as they walked along the street, sitting next to each other at a party or event. Never wanting to be far from the other. Exchanging intimate glances if, by chance, they were across the room from each other. No, Peter did not abuse Nate.

Marian handed Richard a mug of hot steaming coffee and carried hers to a window where she could see the ocean. Water soothed her. Her thoughts reflected on another time, not so very long ago, when she stood watching the ocean. That time it was the Pacific when that young handsome stranger entered her life. Now, on the other side of the country she watched the calm Atlantic Ocean. How her life had changed in these short months. A young husband, a young active husband, and for the first time Marian pondered perhaps too young for her. The excitement of new discoveries about each other gone unless a new and expensive toy came along. Like the yacht that so far she had been on only once — the trip from Miami to Fort Lauderdale where they rented moorage. Richard had taken the yacht out several times, but, always on the spur of the moment when Marian had other plans and was gone from the condo. And, she had seen a canceled check endorsed by Topping Racehorses that she knew nothing about. A two hundred thousand dollar check. When will he mention the race horse, she asked herself.

And she thought of David and Kira pleading too busy for visits. She had seen them only twice since her marriage to

Richard. And Nancy, Nancy still mistrusted Richard and never missed an opportunity to question his actions. The warm feelings between mother and daughter strained at best. Nancy, always watching, always listening, always concerned. Yes, it is concern. She wants the best for her. She always has, Marian admitted. Chy and Lin, another unhappy time. She missed them. And now her good friend Peter accused of sexual abuse of Nate.

How had so much gone wrong? Why had so much gone wrong? She couldn't and didn't blame Richard, although the problems seemed to begin when he came into her life. Still he is her bulwark. He, to coin a phrase, ran interference for her, trying to allay Nancy's suspicion; urging Marian to invite David and Kira once again and hoping they would accept at least one of the many dinner invitations; and now working to convince Nate not to make his accusations public.

Yet, Marian deliberated, would any of this have happened if Richard had not been in her life? When she turned back from the window Richard gazed at her, his eyes full of warmth and sympathy. No, she reflected, Richard caused none of these situations, all coincidences. She needed him in her life. Still.... She left the thought far back into her head.

Richard had been pondering the events of the past few months as well. He smiled when thinking of the millions of dollars he had bilked out of Marian; the rifts he had caused between her and her youngsters; and Kira. No one had heard him tell her that Truman should have dropped a hundred atomic bombs on Japan when he had the chance. Kira had gasped and Richard knew she had too much class to mention his remark to anyone. She and David stayed away. He thought of Nancy. Nancy right on target about him, could have proved to be a difficult match for him since she and Marian had been so close. Instead, she had brought about her own downfall by trying to beat Richard at his own game—a game he had played all his life.

Now it's Peter's turn. Time to get even with Peter for, well, Richard reflected, anything Peter may have wanted to do. Not that Peter had accomplished much. He had tried, though. And Richard reasoned that was just as bad as completing the act. He had tried to convince Marian to get a pre-nup didn't he? He tried to talk her out of the marriage didn't he? But, perhaps his biggest mistake was remaining a close friend to Marian.

Richard could not allow anyone that intelligent to be around Marian. And Peter wanted to visit them in Florida. Oh, sure, Marian is promoting the invitation. But Peter would accept if he got the opportunity. Well, Richard would see that the opportunity did not occur.

As for Nate and Jaki. They are much too friendly. Richard couldn't blame Nate for hanging around Jaki. Richard had never seen a more luscious broad. And Nate. So young and good looking. He might ease Richard out of her life. And what about Jaki?, Is she lying about Nate and the smoke screen premise? Deep in Richard's bones he believed she may be lying. She better not. Richard did not like being lied to. He gets even, always!

And Marian. Much too gullible to have that much money. She didn't deserve it and if he didn't take it, someone else would be Johnny-on-the-spot. Like her jewelry. She never guessed that most of the genuine stones had been replaced by either fakes or poor quality. Once he knew the combination to her safe, it was child's play to replace a few at a time. He chuckled, remembering the day she told him her jewelry didn't seem the same.

"My tennis bracelet doesn't sparkle like it used to," she told him a few days ago.

"The sun is so bright here in Florida that diamonds and, I guess, other gems seem to lose their brilliance."

"Oh."

Now, really, no one should be foolish enough to believe such a statement. Yet, Marian did. She did, didn't she?

As Richard raised his eyes, Marian was looking at him, her expression unreadable. He immediately produced warmth from his eyes and a sympathetic manner. Could he pull this off? He hated Peter!

"Marian, we'll face this together. Whatever it is, and remember, Peter isn't alone. But to be fair, we must know the truth." Richard guided her to the sofa and held her hand as they waited for Nate.

"Yes, the truth. I'll keep an open mind. But I can't help but believe there's been a mistake. A terrible mistake."

The buzzer sounded indicating Nate had arrived. Marian sprang from the sofa, anxious to talk to Nate and put an end to these ridiculous accusations.

"Please come up," said Marian, pushing a button to allow the security door to open.

"Ah, Nate. Thank you for coming." Richard guided Nate into the room and to a chair near the sofa where Richard indicated Marian should return. Richard stood behind the sofa, his hands on Marian's shoulders.

"Nate, Richard tells me you have quite an accusation to make against Peter Jacobson, the captain of the ship where you worked." Marian kept her eyes level on Nate.

Nate glanced at her, then to Richard, back to Marian. He licked his lips, then focused his eyes on the window. He kept his knees together and his feet flat on the floor. His folded hands rested in his lap. Nervous, both Richard and Marian reflected to themselves.

Richard watched Nate. So much hinges on Nate's ability to lie while sounding contrite and truthful. Of course the nervousness helped. Anyone would be nervous when revealing such instances. Even Marian knew that. At least Richard hoped she knew and accepted that Nate would be nervous.

"Mrs. Snider," Nate began, his voice sounded a pitch or so higher than normal, "I didn't want to come here."

Richard cleared his throat. Nate quickly glanced at him. Richard's blue eyes were like ice. Nate's mind jumped to Goldie and the man. Richard's and the man's eyes reflected the same coldness and evil, yes, definitely evil. Nate shivered.

"What I mean is, I know you are such a good friend of the captain and them being at your wedding and all. I'm real sorry..."

"Yes, I'm sorry too. I'd like to hear what you have to say." Marian, in spite of her earlier near breakdown, now seemed to be in complete control.

"Well." Nate again glanced at Richard.

"Tell us what you and Bill told me. That Peter forced you to perform..."

Marian interrupted, "Richard let's leave the coaching out. Nate, tell me exactly how this started and what took place."

"I'm trying to help, Marian, but if that isn't what you want we might as well call United Press right now," sneered Richard.

"Well Nate?" continued Marian.

"He, I don't like saying this, I wish I didn't have to, but, he, well he..." Goldie, Nate remembered. Goldie's eyes begging to be rescued from that grave. "He came to my cabin and told me to... I'm having a problem saying this in front of you Mrs. Snider."

"Would you have a problem saying this in front of Captain Jacobson?" asked Marian.

She's tough, Richard brooded. She keeps her eyes on Nate. Hang in there Nate, Richard sent his thought waves to the young man.

"I have a problem saying this to anyone," stammered Nate.

"Not to Richard, though. You explained it all to Richard. Now explain it all to me," demanded Marian.

"Marian, you're being very hard on someone who came here voluntarily. Since you seem to have made up your mind already, I see no other way than to let the newspapers have the story. Thank you for coming, Nate." Richard walked to the door ostensibly to show Nate out.

"No, wait," Marian quickly responded. "Perhaps I'm being uncharitable. I do want to hear your side, Nate. Please continue. I appreciate you coming."

"Well, it's like Richard said. The captain made certain demands." Nate seemed to get control and communicate to Marian what Richard had drilled into his head.

"What demands, Nate?" asked Marian.

"That he wanted certain things done or else, I guess."

"Or else what?"

"You know."

"Did he threaten your life, Nate?" asked Richard.

"Oh, yeah. He threatened my life," agreed Nate.

"If you did not perform?" questioned Marian.

"Or if you told anyone?" added Richard.

"Yeah, yeah, that's it," continued Nate.

Marian held her eyes on Nate several moments, remaining quiet, studying his body language and facial expressions. At last she concluded that it would, indeed, be difficult for him to tell her about the allegations. He certainly did not show jubilance or an attempt at conceit. In fact, she reasoned, just the opposite. His demeanor reflected embarrassment and genuine sorrow that he had related such painful information to her. He couldn't, or wouldn't meet her eyes, however. She noticed he often glanced at Richard. Perhaps gaining support to describe these shocking experiences. Nate had, after all, talked to Richard about Peter, so it's only natural he would feel more comfortable with him than with her. She noticed Nate did not use explicit words or describe explicit actions on Peter's part. But that must come with the embarrassment that she is a woman.

"Please go on," said Marian.

"There were a whole lot of times and nothing I could do about it," said Nate.

"Were you the only one Peter visited for those reasons?" asked Marian.

Nate glanced at Richard. They hadn't talked about anyone else.

"I already told her about Bill so it's all right to mention him. Bill, Bill Olson." Richard quickly added a last name.

"Oh, yeah, Bill Olson. The captain visited him, too."

Marian picked up on that exchange immediately. Something wrong there. She couldn't let it pass. She couldn't let it pass.

"Nate, do you know what slander is?" asked Marian.

"Sure, saying something about someone that's not true."

"To ruin someone's reputation. Do you know what the penalty is for that?"

Marian's questions miffed Nate. What did she think, that he lied. So what if he did? Either this or join Goldie. He knew that for sure. Richard had made it plain what Nate needed to do and say.

"Mrs. Snider, I'm telling you the truth. And if you think no one will believe me I can always take a lie detector test. Captain Jacobson puts on a real good act. But, I'm not doing this for any other reason than to keep him away from young guys. The ones he likes so much." Nate glanced at Richard who nodded and smiled.

"Richard got me away and found me a job so I owe him a lot. I didn't know what to do. Richard knows I'm telling the truth even if I wish it didn't have to be to you Mrs. Snider."

"Only because I've been trained in this. Otherwise, yes, Peter puts on a great front. Marian, as they say, the ball is in your court."

"How often did Peter come to your cabin?" asked Marian.

"Three or four times a week." Nate began to enjoy the exchange. Hey, she believes him. Then he sobered. The captain and his wife treated him great, like family. Treated all the crew as equals. Asking advice, inquiring about families. A real great guy. Nate loathed what Richard was making him do. Maybe he could leave now. He had said enough. Richard, out of Marian's sight, smiled, took his hands from her shoulders and gave Nate a thumbs up sign.

"All right," said Marian. "And this Bill. Bill what?" She questioned Nate, who had forgotten Bill's last name. Richard, though, much more experienced in the lying game, quickly added Olson.

"Bill Olson will swear to these things as well?"

"He told you that, Marian," snarled Richard.

"Yes, well, thank you Nate for coming. I'll see what I can do. For now, though, it's between us. No newspapers, no talking to anyone else. Okay?" Marian forced a smile and a handshake.

"Yeah." Nate, eager to be gone, quickly walked to the door. The door clicked. Nate had left the building. Marian remained on the sofa deep, in thought.

"Well, what do you think?" asked Richard, sitting beside her and reaching for her hand.

"I'm not sure. I still have questions and I feel I should hear Peter's side as well."

"It's quite a situation and one that needs careful handling. What do you think of sounding out other board members before you talk to Peter? Kind of a what if without mentioning any names."

"I suppose that would be beneficial," agreed Marian.

"From my work with sexually abused persons, all indications confirm that Nate is telling the truth."

"Wish I knew what you see that I don't."

"For one thing, his nervousness."

"Anyone would be nervous. I was nervous just listening," remarked Marian.

"Different kind. Believe me Marian. And his reluctance to tell you details. For me, a trained counselor, that is a definite sign. And there are some other little signs that a lay person would not be aware of but leaves no doubt in my mind."

"I see."

"Does your board have power to hire or fire?"

"To a certain extent. We seven are the major stockholders and we hire the captains. He then hires his department heads and they hire their crew. There are five department heads on each of our four ships."

"But the captain is your domain?"

"Yes, that's true."

"Who owns the line?"

"I own most of the stock, or I should say my grandchildren. When August inherited it from his father he decided to skip a generation and give the stock to the grandchildren. They get full control of it when they become twenty-five. Until then I control it. The seven of us on the board own ninety percent of the stock so you see we pretty much control the whole operation."

"Do all cruise lines work that way?"

"I doubt if any work that way except ours. Ours is a unique situation. The seven families conceived the idea of a cruise line sixty years ago. They began with two ships. All of them were extremely wealthy. It passed on down the line to the children and grandchildren. It couldn't be done in today's time. August put millions of dollars in it. Carolyn and Jason will be very rich."

"Who owns the other ten percent of the stock?"

"An attorney, two attorneys actually, and a bank. They earn about fifty thousand dollars a year. Course the profit from my shares is put into a trust for Carolyn and Jason."

"Well, with this background on the ships, it is much more imperative that you inform the other board members or they should be called owners. You could cause major harm by sitting on this."

"I know you're right." Marian was pensive even though she knew her obligation rested with the cruise line, not a personal friend.

"We meet every three months. Remember when we went to St. Louis a couple of months ago for the meeting?"

"This won't wait until the next meeting."

"No, it won't. I'll arrange a conference call for tomorrow."

"Good girl. That's one of the things I admire about you. Your ability to organize and do the right thing. Just one of the things I admire." Richard gave his you-are-so-wonderful smile.

"Now, we are going out to dinner and will only talk about where you want to go on our yacht. Do you realize you haven't gone cruising on it yet. You stay so busy."

Marian shrugged. Plenty of times she hadn't been too busy if she had only known. Well, she couldn't get distracted from the duty that lie ahead. Very painful duty.

CHAPTER SEVENTEEN

"Jaki, I need to see you. Can you get away for awhile?" Nate had called her soon after leaving Deerfield Beach. He needed to unload his emotions and Jaki listened better than anyone he had ever known.

"I have an appointment at ten and I am scheduled to be on the desk, but I could be with you at about six. That okay?" Her voice had a breathless quality that made her sound as if the person she happened to be talking with was her favorite person in the world. A major asset in her profession.

"Great. can you come to my place?"

"You got it!"

"You seem kind of shook up. Depressed. What's wrong?" asked Jaki, as she entered Nate's apartment.

"We've got to get out of here!" blurted Nate.

"Where do you want to go? Why not just order pizza in. I'd like to relax."

"No, I mean out of here, Miami. I can't take this any longer. All this stuff."

"What stuff?"

"You know. I'm sick of what I'm doing. The money isn't worth it."

"You knew when you came you weren't going to be teaching Sunday school."

"I didn't know it would be like this and I don't want you to be doing what you are either. I want us to have a normal life."

"What's the latest 'stuff' as you call it. You haven't really felt good about yourself since you went to Georgia that time."

"I only feel good about my life when I'm with you, Jaki. You make it all worthwhile. Only we need to be in a different place."

195

"We can't Nate. You know that. And you know the others are just jobs to me. I love you."

"Aren't you sick of it? Don't you want something better?"

"Of course I do. I have days like you are having now. Days when I wish I could begin my life again at sixteen. Take another direction. Days I hate to see who's coming in the door."

"Let's leave. Together," pleaded Nate.

"Are you crazy! With what we know, how far would we get before someone taps us on the shoulder. We can only leave if Vinnie says we can. And he won't."

"I can't stand it anymore." Nate held his head in his hands and moaned.

"What happened to bring this about?" Jaki sat beside him and took his hand in hers.

"If I tell anyone I'm dead," said Nate, his voice flat.

"I'm not anyone. I'm Jaki. I'm the one you can talk to just like you're the one I can talk to."

"Jaki, don't ever, ever, tell anyone this or I'll be killed. I'll be buried alive like Goldie."

"Who's Goldie?"

"I never told you. I couldn't tell anyone. I tried to push the memory away. But, it won't go away. And probably the baby, too. And Peter."

"You aren't making a bit of sense to me."

"It doesn't make sense to me either. Things like that shouldn't happen---to anyone---to anything."

"What did happen? What caused you to be like this?"

"Well, I've been delivering drugs. I knew what I did was against the law, but lots of people are doing it and I liked the money."

"That's not as bad as some of the things I have to do," remarked Jaki.

Nate continued as if she hadn't spoken, "Then this day I went to Georgia. I didn't have drugs or birds. Sometimes I delivered exotic birds, brought up from South America. That day there was a dead body in the trunk. I didn't know until we, the man and I, put it in the hole, the grave. There are lots of graves there, Jaki, dozens. And black plastic covering the woodpile. I saw all those graves. I thought it was a vegetable garden. It's a graveyard."

"Poor Nate. Poor baby. You didn't kill the what, man or woman. You didn't did you?" Jaki opened her eyes wide in question.

"Man. No, I didn't kill him, but that's not the worst part."

"What is. What is the worst part," Jaki quietly asked. Did she really know this man she professed to love?

"He, the man made Goldie, his old yellow dog, jump in the grave and he covered her with dirt. While she was still alive. Her eyes pleading for help." sobbed Nate.

"Oh, Nate. Oh, sweetheart." Jaki put her arm around him trying to help him block out images of that horrible day.

"Then we went in the trailer and the girl, pregnant, said, said, the baby wouldn't need any clothes and I knew the man was going to kill the baby."

"Honey, don't talk about it." She rocked him back and forth patting his back.

"Now Richard made me lie about Captain Jacobson."

"About who?"

"The captain on the ship that I worked on."

"How does Richard know him? Go back aways. I'm lost again."

"I met Richard on the way to Hawaii, on the ship I worked on. I was the bartender. I admit I watered drinks and took tip money from the others. Richard caught on and kind of gave me advice and stuff. He asked if I wanted to work for Vinnie. Better myself. I wanted the big money so I said yes."

"Richard was on the ship?" Jaki questioned Nate as if that was the only remark she heard.

"He wanted to meet rich women and I set him up with a few. That's where he met his wife."

"I see."

"They got married in a hurry. Everyone figured she had money. I knew she was a big stockholder in the cruise line. The captain told us so we wouldn't foul up."

"So, he met his wife on the ship and married her. Where?"

"On Kauai. Some of us went to the party. Fun. Richard never left her side. She positively glowed. They live in her place in Chicago. I saw them once at Vinnie's place on Long Island and then a few times here in Florida. She really is a nice lady."

"What about the captain?"

"Richard wants me to swear he sexually abused me. Get him fired. For some reason Richard hates him."

"Tell him no. Just say you won't do it."

"I had to do it or end up like Goldie."

"He said that?" Jaki was appalled.

"Might as well. He made the meaning clear."

"So you did what?"

"Told Marian, that's Mrs. Snider's name, that the captain came to my cabin for sex and she believes it. Richard can make her believe anything."

"Yes, I'm sure he can," said Jaki, deep in thought. So that's why Nancy was so sure Richard wanted her mother's money. Of course he did.

"She mentioned she had met you before. Do you remember her?" asked Nate.

Jaki related her involvement with the Sniders. "Nancy hired me to pursue Richard. Entice him to make a date so Marian could see what a gigolo she had married. Backfired on Nancy when someone left the intercom on and Mrs. Snider heard the conversation." Now Jaki was sure she knew who manipulated the intercom. She omitted her liaison with Kenneth. A situation she wasn't exactly proud of. It did however, bring Richard into her life that ultimately led her to Miami and Nate.

"I guess the captain will get fired and I hate my part in it. That's why I want us to get out of this place."

"I do want out, but I'm scared. I never told you what goes on over there. They take videos of kids, porn, and sell them. Big business. But the worse thing is what some of those old guys want the kids to do. It's one thing taking videos if it's acting and most of the time it is, cause the camera has to be relocated, take a shot over. It's mostly faking, but not when the guys or sometimes women come in. They want the little kids. Younger the better and I can't stand it. The kids have no choice. Most of the time their parents bring them in or they're street kids. Do anything for a few bucks to buy crack or in some cases maybe buy food to take home to feed the rotten parents that brought them in."

"Jaki, I'm so sorry," murmured Nate.

"One day this Cuban came in ranting and raving to get his son, six-year-old son. The kid's mother had brought him in for twenty-five dollars. Anyway, Orville, our benefactor, as Vinnie calls him, restrained the father. Too hard. His big hands, big and powerful hands, choked the father to death. I was half-way down the stairs to see what all the noise was about, then something made me turn around. Here was the guy's little son standing at the top of the stairs looking down. He saw the whole thing, his dad killed before his eyes. The little boy didn't make a sound, just big tears running down his cheeks. He went into the room he had come out from and, as he walked through the door, he pulled off his tee-shirt. And I wondered what kind of a life the little boy had been subjected to—that he could see his father killed and go on with business as usual." Jaki's eyes were full of tears and she would never, ever, forget that day or the silent tears of the little boy.

"Maybe that was the body I took to Georgia." Nate held Jaki to quiet her sobbing.

"Maybe, but there have been others. I know. There's talk. We aren't working in Disneyland are we?"

"About as opposite as anything can be."

"So, we can't leave. They will never let us go," Jaki solemnly said.

"There must be something we can do. I can't go on like this and you can't either."

"If I didn't have to see it. If I could just make app-ointments like Richard said I would do. Now sometimes I run the camera, tell the kids what to do. I try to tell them it's play-acting. Like television stars. I tell myself that, but, it's ruining their lives. When I began." Jaki took a deep breath and continued. "It was so minor to what goes on now."

"When I'm with you I can put most of it, the evil, out of my mind," said Nate.

"You know, I wonder if Vinnie and Richard know everything that goes on. Vinnie has kids, surely he must have sympathy for these kids."

"You would think so. But tell me, are there ever any little white kids involved? I know Richard hates anyone who isn't white with a passion," remarked Nate.

"You're right, There never are. It makes it worse some-how," said Jaki. "Nate, how did you happen to contact the place where I am. Did Richard send you?"

"Sure, all one big happy family, he said."

"Maybe Richard's wife would help us. She's not in any of this is she?" asked Jaki.

"She isn't, but she hangs on his every word. Today she started out believing I lied about the captain. Got kind of gnarly at first. Then Richard turned the conversation completely around."

"How did he manage that?"

"He kind of snarled at her and she changed her tactic. I think she is so afraid he will leave her, she will do anything he says. She would be so embarrassed if he walked out after all the remarks she must have heard about a young husband. He will make her fire the captain, wait and see. He's quite a manipulator."

"Oh, yes, he is that."

"Call, tell them you can't come in tonight. Stay here with me."

"I can't. After my appointment I'm on the desk. Susie is the only other one in the office and she's afraid of Orville."

"Are you?"

"No, I told him I'm Richard's girlfriend. He's afraid of Richard."

"So am I, are you?"

"Not exactly, but, I'm very careful what I say. He knows or thinks there's something going on with you and I."

"There is."

"Yes, but he can't know that. He wants to control everyone."

"Have you been his girl?" Nate didn't want to know, but had to ask.

"I have to cover all the bases. Just remember it's you I love. Being with Richard sometime protects me from the likes of the Orville's in this world. In fact, it protects me from a lot of things. I just tell them Richard wouldn't like it and they leave me alone."

"What a mess we've made of our lives. The only salvation is that I met you."

"I'll come back after my shift. I stay until three in the morning. Susie leaves then, so it will be okay."

"I'll be here. I'll be doing some heavy thinking of an escape."

"Good luck."

CHAPTER EIGHTEEN

"How old is Carolyn, Marian?" asked Richard as he casually surveyed the beach from the condo deck.

"Sixteen, the age of super intelligence."

"Why don't we have her down to enjoy the warm sun and beach?"

"She could, during a school break, I suppose. There's one in February. Three days and maybe she could take a couple of extra days."

Marian did miss her family. The holidays in Florida had been lonely. Her first Christmas without any of her family or friends. It didn't seem like Christmas without snow, sleigh rides, church services, listening to choirs sing traditional carols, the family gathered around a large evergreen tree with its brilliant lights twinkling and favorite decorations, many made by the children and kept through the years. Richard and Marian had a small artificial tree complete with small attached lights. No work to decorate anymore, the salesman said, just take it out of the box and set it anywhere you please. Fits in with any decor, he said. The trouble was, it didn't fit in with Marian's idea of Christmas.

The Sniders Christmas dinner, at a local seafood restaurant, seemed depressing to Marian. Somehow conch chowder and deep fried grouper didn't quite cut it for Marian as holiday fare. No mashed potatoes and gravy, no turkey with cornbread stuffing, no pumpkin pie, but perhaps the most disappointing---no left over for turkey sandwiches.

So, yes. Having Carolyn for a short visit would be most welcome. Not that other family members had not been invited. They had. Even Richard, wanting to surprise Marian, had called Nancy with an invitation. Nancy had declined, Richard related to Marian. David and Kira were too busy, couldn't get away, Jason so involved in school activities, but, thank you, Mother, maybe some other time. Letters and telephone calls had to suffice.

Richard gazed out the window quite some time contemplating the future. Marian's revelation that Carolyn would inherit half of her cruise line stock garnered his interest. By his calculations at that time, nine years from now, Carolyn's net worth would exceed Marian's. But nine years. Course Carolyn currently had income from the ships—only it went into a trust. There must be some stipulations for using it sooner than nine years, reflected Richard. He knew Carolyn protested that she never had spending money, yet there never seemed to be any lack of expensive merchandise. In a day or two he must work a conversation around with Marian to learn more about the trust and how it is managed and by whom. Carolyn's a cutie, but sixteen. That's trouble. Vinnie hated that kind of trouble. Not that easy to fix anymore. Still in two years she will be eighteen, that wonderful age of consent, but could he stand being with Marian that long just to stay in contact with Carolyn? Perhaps he can develop rapport with Carolyn when she visits. Include Marian to alleviate suspicion. In fact, make it seem as if Marian is promoting the close relationship. Ah, yes, everything is possible if plans are made properly.

"Marian," Richard gave his listen-to-this-great-idea-look, "has Carolyn ever been an exchange student or has she spent all her school days in the same neighborhood?"

"Her school isn't all that bad, it's private and very highly regarded. Spending her school years there is the envy of many girls her age. Why do you ask?"

"Just a fleeting thought at how much fun students seem to have down here. She could stay with us and attend school in the great sunshine. Wouldn't she love it?"

"Wouldn't she though. And you, how would you handle having a teenager around?"

"I would try very hard no not try, I would make her stay enjoyable. You know I always welcome your family, Marian. Our family. So, my dear, if it is your desire to have her here for school, than by all means call and ask."

How did that happen? Marian contemplated Richard's response. Now all of a sudden she is the one who is suggesting that Carolyn attend school here. She dearly loved Carolyn, but everyday for weeks, for months? So she could enjoy the sun and warm weather plus the beach. Is that what he said? Well, there is no need to worry. Carolyn isn't about to leave her boyfriend. Nancy will say no. And if by some chance it is a go from all of them, Marian will nix it. She knew, though, someone will put the kibosh on it long before she has to step in.

"Good idea, but wouldn't it be better if you did the inviting?" Marian asked and smiled as she anticipated Richard's response.

"I would, dear. But you know the family cares more for your desires than mine. The invitation really should come from you."

Almost word for word what Marian guessed he would say. Is she now reading him better than before?

"Okay, I'll speak with Nancy and Kenneth first. If they agree, then I will ask Carolyn."

"Not Carolyn first? She could put pressure on her parents?"

"No, parents first. If we spoke to Carolyn first, we would be undermining Nancy's and Kenneth's authority and we can't do that."

And exactly as Marian believed, Carolyn could visit during the school break, but not attend school in Florida.

"Do you have any idea what we pay in tuition?" Nancy fairly shouted.

"Do you think I would leave all my friends?" Carolyn was aghast at the thought.

"Whatever for? She goes to one of the top schools in the country." Kenneth added to the denial.

Marian only smiled.

CHAPTER NINTEEN

The conference call to the cruise line board offered no solutions to Marian's dilemma. If Marian wouldn't reveal names then it couldn't be taken seriously, members said, after a lengthy discussion of a hypothetical situation. Marian convinced the other five men and one woman that a closer look should be taken to make sure the alleged abuse had received proper and intensive consideration. Robin Barker, a member living in Washington DC and Lewis Maxwell, wintering in Naples, Florida, agreed to meet at Marian's to discuss the situation. Other members consented to approve any decision made by the three. They planned to question Nate, and as Robin and Lewis said, Nate may be more open to revealing explicit acts to men rather than to Marian if indeed there were such acts. Richard and Nate reviewed possible dialogue if and when Nate met with the committee. Of course, Nate pleaded to drop the whole matter. Richard, adamant, said that Nate must continue disclosing the abuse. Richard quietly mentioned results when someone disobeyed Vinnie.

Now, Nate thought to himself, it is Vinnie who wants Captain Jacobson's hide. He guessed correctly that Vinnie and the captain had never met. He also guessed correctly that Richard could be as vicious as Goldie's master. Wisely, Nate agreed to proceed with the deception. Richard would be there every minute. And if by chance a question comes up that they haven't discussed, Richard told Nate to glance at him. A scratch on the nose would mean the answer is yes; no movement means a negative response.

Richard told Marian he would not participate in the discussion. He cited patient privilege (would she believe that?) and not a complete fool, he knew better than to have his "credentials" questioned by anyone. He did, though, convince Marian that he did have a background in counseling. After all, she reasoned, he had to have spent years doing something.

Now she couldn't find her butterfly pin. The one with wings of diamonds, rubies and a topaz. A gift from August on their tenth anniversary when their net worth reached ten million dollars. She treasured it. And she had worn it to a luncheon two days ago. She must be more careful. She seemed to misplace so much lately.

Robin, Lewis and Marian chose to meet in a local restaurant, and as requested, had a private area as not to be overheard by other diners. The lunch crowd seemed small anyway. Most people waiting for the early-bird specials later in the day. Not that anyone in Florida would be interested in a situation that took place on a ship that cruised the west coast and Hawaii. Besides, almost anyone in the sunshine state could match the concern with a story that rivaled the board's. Robin revealed he had met Peter one time years ago when Peter was named captain. Lewis, more familiar with Peter, had taken the Hawaii cruise once, but generally preferred the smaller ship of the line that operated around the Caribbean . Therefore, Marian became the expert on Peter. Her glowing remarks revealing that they had been lifelong friends, made her revelations a trifle clouded.

"I know him so well I'm having a hard time believing this story of Nate's. But I feel we owe it to the ship's future to explore every possibility of its validity," said Marian.

"There is some doubt or you wouldn't have insisted on discussing it. If you were so sure there's no truth to this, why didn't you tell Nate to buzz off?" asked Robin.

"That's just it. I do have some doubts and my husband, whose background is abuse counseling, explained why he believes Nate."

"Will your husband explain those things to us? Banking doesn't exactly prepare one for abuse recognition," asked Robin.

"He feels he shouldn't interfere. But of course, he will be present when we meet at our condo and question Nate."

"Why then?" asked Robin.

"Nate is comfortable with Richard and won't meet with us without him. Richard discovered the 'situation' while on board ship and talked to Nate about it. He was instrumental in finding Nate other employment so Nate thinks of him as a friend and confidant," explained Marian.

"How does Richard feel about Peter. Are they friends as well?" asked Lewis.

"Peter was best man at our wedding. They are very close. Richard is very concerned about this, but agrees Peter should not have the control he does—captive victims—he calls it, and should have intensive counseling."

"I see."

"Our job, as I see it, if this is all true and we should take a counselor's word for it, is to remove Peter as captain or remove him completely from our ships and suggest he have counseling," added Lewis.

"This breaks my heart," remarked Marian. "But I know what you say is right."

"What if the young man is lying?" Robin seemed to be unconvinced of such drastic measures as yet.

"If he were asking for money or some favors, I would question it more I guess, but he isn't. He's very reluctant to talk about it and only wants Peter to stop," explained Marian.

"Are you convinced then?" Lewis asked Marian.

"I just don't know. I've trusted and believed in Peter for such a long time. I can't turn it around that quickly. I know I don't want to believe it, but then again, all evidence points that it is true."

"Well, let's give it a shot by talking with him. He agreed to come to your place again?" Lewis directed his question to Marian.

"Why don't we sit around the table so it doesn't look as if it's us against you, no matter how we stand on the issue." When Marian said "us" she included Nate and as she said "you" she pointed to the window, ostensibly to remain neutral. She wanted to be absolutely fair and not make it seem as if anyone had to chose sides.

"Lewis, will you please be monitor and lead the discussion?" asked Marian.

Marian, Lewis, Robin and Nate sat in the four chairs at the table. Richard chose a stool a few feet away where he could face Nate. The stool was directly in back of Robin.

"Nate, you've made some very serious accusations against Captain Peter Jacobson. We would like to hear your explanations of the situations." Lewis smiling at the young man, was anxious to learn the truth. He hoped his smile would put Nate at ease. Lewis, very well experienced in dealing with personnel, had hired and fired many persons during his tenure as owner of a Fortune 500 manufacturing company. He, was comfortable taking charge.

"I want to say first of all I hate being here. I just wish the whole thing would go away," Nate glanced at Richard whose steely eyes told him he had said the wrong thing.

"Why don't we drop it then?" asked Lewis.

"Well, he did do those things and he shouldn't be allowed to." Nate stumbled over his words.

"What things?" asked Robin.

"Well, I don't," Nate glanced at Marian, "like to say it."

"You haven't said anything yet. We need concrete answers," remarked Robin.

"Nate, don't worry about me. I've heard it all. Please be truthful with us. It's very important," said Marian.

"I am being truthful," Nate blurted. "If you don't believe me I can just go home."

At this point Richard came to Nate's side and patted him on his back. Richard glanced at Marian as if to say "better get control." Marian gave Robin a warning look.

"When did Captain Jacobson first approach you in this regard?" asked Lewis.

"Oh, I worked on the ship two years and he came on to me from the beginning."

"Why didn't you leave when the ship was in port?" asked Robin.

"The money was good and I liked the job. At first he didn't make me do much." Nate glanced at Richard who scratched his nose.

"But later, why did you stay?"

"I needed the job and just getting off somewhere would leave me all alone someplace without money or a job. We only go between Los Angeles and Hawaii. Not much choice." Nate explained.

Lewis observed Nate. He seemed reluctant to talk about the implied abuse. But that in itself did not sway Lewis' opinion either way. He had no idea how victims reacted to sexual abuse. But Marian had related Richard's version of victim's conflict, so Lewis reasoned Nate could have been Peter's puppet.

Robin wished, as Nate did, that the whole thing would go away. A bank merger in Washington DC needed his attention, though he knew he was obligated to this situation as well. This allegation, the first major problem the cruise line had faced, could be lengthy. If Nate wanted money they could chalk it up to blackmail and then it could be solved immediately. But that is not the issue. Perhaps the board should make an offer to test the waters, so to speak.

"Would several thousand dollars make you forget this alleged abuse?" asked Robin.

"I'm not after any money," answered Nate.

Perhaps discharging the captain could be accomplished quickly and that would settle it, mused Robin.

Marian, as well, contemplated what action should be taken. If the stories are true there are serious ramifications whichever decision the board makes. If the stories are true. What is the truth? If Nate does a newspaper interview and later the story is proved to be false, does anyone ever see the correction? And if Peter sued Nate what would that accomplish? Nate has no assets. Send Nate to jail? Not very likely. And if Nate is telling the truth? Peter has two years before he retires. Maybe retiring early is the answer. That's really what Nate wants, isn't it? To keep Peter away from other young men. Still, wherever Peter goes, he will find young men. Is it fair to them to only discharge him without offering treatment? And is she now beginning to accept Nate's story as the truth rather than disbelieve it? When did she begin to lean that way? When did she begin to figure ways for Peter to be away from the ship? Could it be Richard's convincing explanation? Or, as it is in her own life, who knows what goes on when doors close? She rubbed her wrist. Another "accident."

"We need you to tell us exactly what the captain demanded," continued Lewis.

"Can't you guess?" Nate said agitated, wishing again it would all go away.

"Do you think it would be fair to take your word, your vague accusations and dismiss a man who has performed exemplary over twenty years? Not only on our ships but he had very high recommendations when he came to us from another line," added Lewis.

Nate became angry, he needed the board to believe him. Richard made that perfectly clear. "I really don't care if you believe me or not. I'm sure the newspapers will."

"Is that a threat? Absolutely take your word or you make the accusations public?" asked Robin.

"I have a suggestion," said Richard, pushing the stool away and standing at Marian's side. "Why not call Peter and ask him?"

"We decided not to do that until we have proof. Leaves us vulnerable if he suspects we are making some kind of attack," explained Lewis.

"Perhaps if you ask in a way that he would have no cause for alarm." Richard had a plan. Richard always has a plan.

"How?" asked Marian.

"I shouldn't interfere."

"Please. We want to do the right thing. No matter who makes the suggestion," pleaded Marian.

"My suggestion is that Marian call Peter, since she knows him better than the rest of us, and ask him if he ever visited Nate's cabin. If he says yes, then ask if, well, here, I'll write it down. Only, and this is important, ask for generic answers. Never suggest he may have gone there for sex. Make him answer in one word or less."

"But, we should tell him what Nate has told us," said Robin.

"Robin, that's exactly what we don't want. You want a whopping law suit?" remarked Lewis.

"From just a question?" persisted Robin.

"Let's do as Richard suggests. Are you up to this Marian?" Lewis glanced at Marian, who nodded.

"I'll do my best." She took the notepaper from Richard reading the two questions with puzzlement. This is all? she pondered.

Nate remained quiet. He and Richard had gone over this scenario. The purpose of his contrived anger, Richard had explained to him, was to reach the point of calling Peter.

"Do you know where to reach Jacobson now? Is the ship at sea or still in Los Angeles?" asked Lewis. And no one noticed he omitted calling Peter <u>Captain</u>.

"In L.A. for another week. We had planned to have Peter and Sybil visit us here. But now, with this, we certainly will not. Till this is all cleared up, at least" said Marian. "I do have a number where they are staying." She moved to a desk and took an address book from a drawer and returned to the table.

"It's noon there so they may be out for lunch, or if at the pool we can have him paged."

Richard handed her the telephone. "Remember, it's important to ask the questions just as I've written them. No long conversations or explanations."

"Yes, I will." She dialed the Los Angeles number. No answer. Contact the hotel desk. Could he be paged? He could, easily. He and Sybil are having lunch in the dining room.

"Hello, Marian. Sybil and I were just talking about you. How are things?" Peter said, upbeat and confident as usual. Marian felt a pull at her heart.

"Fine, Peter, I have two questions I must ask you and I need short responses. One word if possible and no questions for me."

"This sounds ominous. Shoot."

"Have you ever visited the cabin of Nathan Omstead?"

"Nathan Omstead. You mean Nate our bartender?"

"Yes."

"Sure, many times. Why?"

"When you went to his cabin did you have a specific thing in mind? Please no questions for me."

"Of course I did. Nate always knew my reasons."

"Thank you." Marian pushed the antenna down and handed the telephone back to Richard.

"He admitted it." Marian's eyes filled with tears.

"My God," exclaimed Lewis.

"Who would have thought it," remarked Robin.

The three owners looked from one to another, the disbelief showing in their eyes slowly turning to anger. How could this have happened on our ships their silence shouting the question to each other.

Richard and Nate exchanged a fleeting glance. Nate relieved his part in this deception completed. Richard cherishing this turn of events. Better than he dreamed. Marian did exactly as she was told. Never letting Peter ask questions and never letting him make explanations. Of course he had visited Nate's cabin, and of course it was for a specific purpose. Nate served as steward for the lounge crew and new uniforms were in the planning stages. Peter and Nate discussed colors, materials, even how many and what style of buttons, many, many times. Not always in Nate's cabin but certainly there several times. At least two or three times a week. When Nate related this information to Richard, well then it was just a little manipulating to turn the purpose around. And the board fell for it. Richard smiled.

"I'll call the other owners," stated Lewis. "And we'll get a letter ready for dismissal. Nate, I'd like to offer an apology from the owners and thank you for coming forward with information on this unfortunate situation. It will never happen again on any of our ships and we will see to it that he never again finds employment on any cruise ship."

"We will recommend that he seek counseling shouldn't we Richard?" Marian's eyes sought his for guidance.

"We'll do what we can, Marian."

The telephone rang immediately. Richard took the call in the bedroom. He knew who it would be and was ready with his answers. He spoke cruelly to Peter, explaining that Marian had nothing to say to him and would not be available to come to the phone anytime soon. Please do not call again. While away from the others he made another arrangement. Their new unlisted number was now in effect. The explanation to Marian coming at a later time.

> Dear Mr. Jacobson: (No longer captain and Lewis contemplated the "Dear.")
>
> It is with profound regret that we must ask for your immediate resignation. As an assertion of our generosity, the board of directors of Golden Cruise Line, you know as the owners, are giving you the option of submitting your resignation rather than face the embarrassment of termination.
>
> As you know your contract reads that employment may be terminated by either party with thirty days notice. We are terminating your employment immediately and in good faith will give you three months salary rather than the thirty-day notice. You will be assisted with removing your personal effects from the ship. We must have your resignation in our hands by February 3. All owners are in total agreement of this urgent requirement.
>
> Sincerely,
> Lewis Maxwell
> President, Golden Cruise Line

All owners signed the letter. If Marian shed tears, well, then Richard was there to comfort her and assure her that sometimes duty can be painful.

The new telephone number only given to family and close friends with the promise that it not be revealed to anyone.

"Anyone needing it, has it," Richard explained in the note accompanying the new number. Nancy's pleas that since Peter had called her repeatedly asking for the number, couldn't she at least give it to him, met with negative response.

Marian reluctantly told her no.

Letters from Peter remained unread and were sent back refused. Richard cautioned Marian that she must not let her personal feelings interfere with the owner's decision. And he explained that it was her telephone conversation with Peter that decided the owners to terminate Peter's employment, and that it was her conversation that proved Nate's accusations to be true. Richard manipulated her thoughts to the point where confusion reigned. All the owners had agreed she told herself over and over. Still the picture of the little boy building his toy ships leaped across memories in her mind. Many, many good memories. Smiles came slowly to her lips now and her eyes remained flat with disappointment.

The arrival of Carolyn brightened Marian's days somewhat.

"Nothing like a teenager around to let you know a new language is being spoken," Richard joyously remarked.

He and Carolyn watched popular game shows on TV, a nightly contest on who could guess the color of Vanna's clothes.

"You're pretty enough to do that someday," Richard whispered to Carolyn.

"Of course you are," Marian added when Carolyn relayed his remark. Marian knowing that the remark was only grandparent talk. We seem to be having such fun with Carolyn here. When the discussion about Walt Disney World came up, Marian begged out of the trip.

"You could watch Richard and me do the rides. We won't make you do them," Carolyn pleaded.

"I can't keep up with you young people." Marian laughed, delighted that Richard kept his promise to show Carolyn a good time. And he's such a good sport about it. It can't be too much fun having Carolyn hanging on to him like glue, she mused. Marian pushed her doubtful thoughts about some of his actions far back and out of her head. It's only natural that there are opposing ideas at times. Besides, he really doesn't know how hard he squeezes her wrists. He's always sorry. Carolyn's enthusiasm rubbed off on both of them. We needed this change in our routine.

The day-long outing to Walt Disney World was like money in the bank to Richard. He couldn't have predicted a happier, more responsive Carolyn. She grabbed his hand to pull him along to a new attraction. They feasted on unusual snacks. He played the games of chance, knowing exactly how to win, or so it seemed. Soon Carolyn carried Pluto, Mickey Mouse, and other stuffed animals around with her. They bought tee-shirts—his Mickey Mouse and hers Minnie.

"We'll wear these home," remarked Richard. "We can change in the car." He added a smile of conspiracy.

Carolyn felt a small tug of anticipation. He is so much fun and more her age than her grandmothers. What does he see in her? Nice to her, though. It must be hard for him to be so active and her grandmother not able to keep up. And he has such young ideas and is so strong. His arms held her when she screamed during that ride. And standing in line for the rides, she could feel his breath on her neck and smell his after shave. She liked him and he didn't treat her like a kid. In fact, he told her she acted and looked a lot older than she is. Looks twenty, at least, he said. He smiled at her and told her she was special, that he would rather be with her than anyone else. Did he mean be with her here at Walt Disney World, or be with her? She remembered her grandmother, but only for a moment. Richard took her hand and raised it to his lips and gently kissed it.

"Oh, sorry, I keep forgetting I am your grandfather." He gave her his you-don't-think-that-for-a-moment-do-you smile.

"You aren't my grandfather, far from it. We aren't any relation so that..." Carolyn hesitated.

"Yes doesn't it," said Richard, just as if he could read her mind. He squeezed her hand. "Time for a couple of more rides and then we better head for home."

"Do you have a curfew?" Carolyn asked, her eyes challenging,

"No, but I know better than to stay out late with you. As it is, I..." He deliberately dropped the conversation knowing she would ponder his unspoken words.

After a few moments of silence, both of them thinking of what may come, and Richard knowing full well that the answer better be nothing, he said, "What ride do you want to go on?"

"The scary one again."

He held tightly to her as she had hoped he would, and he knew she felt exactly as he planned she would. Now to promote a closeness for just the two of them. If anyone found out about his intentions then he could kiss off Carolyn's millions.

"Are you hungry?" asked Richard, as they reached the car and she placed her stuffed animals in the backseat.

"A little."

"Well, no more junk food tonight. What do you say I take my girl to a real nice place for dinner?"

"Super." His girl. Carolyn never wanted the day to end.

For the first time in months her boyfriend remained below the surface in her thoughts. He was a like a child anyway. Going out to dinner with him meant pizza. His girl. He called her his girl. That's what Richard said. His girl. The two words pounding in her head. His girl. Wow! She stole a quick glance at him. And he is looking at her! What happens now? How she wished she could add two years to her age. Then she could do as she wanted. Go with Richard. He wants that, doesn't he? He has plenty of money and she gets two thousand a month when she becomes eighteen. We could go anywhere we want, do as we please. No more hounding by her mother. She had an okay dad, but her mother—so proper. When her dad wanted to dress groovy, unbutton his shirts and all, boy did her mom ever put a stop to that. All in one day. Whatever she said made him stop trying to look better, more fun. Course he was sad for weeks and he had only wanted to look younger. But no, not with demanding mother. Even grandma joined in on the fun at times. His girl. He had called her his girl.

"Okay, funny face. What are you thinking? Five minutes have gone by since you said super." Richard used his handkerchief to wipe a smudge from her nose. If his fingers lingered on her face, well then, it made her happy and making her happy was such an easy task. Go slowly and carefully, he cautioned himself.

"Just what a perfect day this has been. How cool it is to be with you." The passion and excitement he had tried to instill in her, showed naked on her face. She's like an overripe peach, ready to be devoured, mused Richard.

He turned to her, put his hands on her shoulders, "Yes, a perfect day." Their eyes held. Hers offering all sorts of promises, his, as always, calculating what great benefits lie ahead.

Richard started the car and followed the line of automobiles out of the parking lot. After traveling several miles he pulled into a parking lot at Red Lobster.

"Hope you like seafood. The dinners here are terrific."

"I guess today it wouldn't matter where we ate as long as we are...."

"Don't say it," he interrupted, "just feel it."

"Okay," she gave a long sigh. "A perfect day."

"I'll call your grandmother to tell her we will be late. No telling what kind of a line there will be at the restaurant or how the traffic will be." Richard once more appreciated Florida's casual dress codes. His jeans and short-sleeved shirt and Carolyn in her cut-offs and tee shirt were approved garb almost anywhere.

"Tomorrow night I'll take both my girls out to a fancy restaurant. You bring dressy clothes or is a shopping trip in the cards?"

Both his girls—both his girls, not just my girl. Carolyn felt disappointed. He called her grandmother his girl as well. Well, she supposed her grandmother had to be included but, if only she and Richard could spend her remaining two days with just each other. And, yes, it definitely sounded better for him to call grandma his girl rather than his wife. Wife seems so permanent. Carolyn wolfed down the cheese biscuits. Richard smiled and ordered another basket of the delicious specialties. Then Carolyn began tearing bites off the biscuits with her fingers, playing with her food, making little designs on her plate. Still a little kid, he realized. And no real money for nine years. Too long for him, even though she had a young and enticing body.

"I have a skirt and top that will be okay, course shopping is always cool."

"Marian and I will take you to the mall. Get something special to help you remember your time with us."

Carolyn sobered. All of a sudden her grandmother is in the picture. No more "us" meaning just her and Richard. Still... Two more days. Anything can happen.

"I'll remember. Nothing will stop that."

"So will I, Carolyn. We have something special between us. We definitely will stay in touch and you can call me whenever you want."

"Can we fix a time so that I can talk to just you without anyone else around?" '

"Sure we will, and I'll tell you something else, if you were older, I would be pushing to change my life."

"I'm old enough."

"No, you aren't and I know that. But you are in my life and we'll see what the next few years bring."

A few miles away from the restaurant, Carolyn moved closer to Richard. "When are we putting on our new tee shirts." She would show him she is old enough. Just wait. Her arm brushed his.

God, this kid. Have sixteen-year-olds always been this aggressive? She was really asking for it. He knew better, no way.

"Tomorrow. We can wear them when we go shopping. Think Marian will like the one we got for her?"

"Sure. We can change in the car," her face turned to his, he was aware of her and what would be so easy to do.

"Believe me Carolyn, it is tempting but I'm thinking of you. Right now our emotions are wrapped up with each other. It would be so easy to follow our desires, damn easy, but we both have other obligations and we need to let some time go by. You need to finish school and I..." He certainly couldn't tell her what he needed to do, what he planned to do, " I will be here."

"I'm not a child," she stated with a pout to her lips.

"Believe me, I know that." And Richard will chalk up this decision to another virtuous act on his part. Not hard to remember these acts. There weren't many. And if she thought it was to protect her from harm, or from doing something she may regret, then she was wrong. This virtuous act protected him as well, and from considerbly more harm. Still he planned to keep her emotions at a high peak. Keep doing a little touching, or hugging., and kissing. He wanted her to remember him and desire him. And doing that, always a piece of cake for him. Didi had taught him so much! More than she knew. If he could twist Didi into such a frenzy, certainly Carolyn could be manipulated as well.

Marian used her time alone to finish a novel. Another one by Edna Buchanan who had now become Marian's favorite author. This one, "Miami it's Murder," just as exciting as

Buchanan's others, and just as hard to put down. Marian had never read mysteries or for that matter many novels, until the move to Florida. Now it seemed so relaxing to sit around the pool and read something besides committee reports. Where once she poured over budgets and compared funding from one year to another, she now found time for herself and reading became enjoyable once again. And since Edna Buchanan's books were set in Florida they quickly became favorites. Marian had been tempted to contact her and suggest she write more prolifically.

Ah, the dryer buzzed. And since she now did the laundry herself, she hurried to unload the machine and smooth out the clothing. No ironing if she acted quickly, although Richard insisted his shirts be ironed. She did his tee shirts as well. She found it a little like playing house as they had on Kauai. Not so much work that it became a chore, just kind of nice to do things for her man and Richard always looked immaculate. She decided to put his clothes away. She knew exactly where they belonged. The first drawer in the chest held handkerchiefs, and he had so many with the monogrammed R, and socks. Not many pairs of those in this Florida heat. Still he did wear them when he went out-of-town for his job. No wearing comfortable sandals for this work he had told her, whatever it was.

The tee shirts went into the second drawer and that's all she took care of. His papers, a few traveling flyers, photographs, three pairs of shoes, and in Marian's opinion junk, filled the two bottom drawers. Maybe she could straighten them out. They looked a mess . She casually opened the third drawer. No way should she rearrange those papers, and she reasoned this drawer looked okay. Lots of blank paper and envelopes, tape and scissors. Well, she knew where to find supplies if she needed them.

Opening the bottom drawer, she thumbed through a pamphlet on living in Costa Rica. Looks nice. A photo of a small quite pretty girl with red hair, black roots though, Marian smiled. She didn't know her. A sister, perhaps? A small paperback on legal and illegal drugs and effects they have on..... what? Let's look at that more carefully.

She turned to a section on poisons and noticed several phrases underlined. A section on cyanide had two lines marked. She read the entire chapter on drugs which are undetectable in one's system. So, he has a book on this. Who knows why he's interested in such things? She put the book back as she had found it and closed the drawer. If she asked, he would readily tell her why. Thoughtful, she remained sitting on the floor for a few moments.

She opened the drawer again and began a thorough search of the contents. Yes, there it is, the same one. The little bottle she had had tested that day. She held it up to the window. About a teaspoon is gone from the time she had placed it back in his chest of drawers while still in Chicago. So he had brought it with him and he has used some of it. She pondered his reasons. Rats? Just a drop on a piece of food and rats would scurry in search of water only to die before finding any, no matter how nearby it may be. Perhaps rats in the parking garage. Except the maintenance men handle such situations. Marian knew it hadn't been used for rats. She meditated his reasoning.

She arranged items in the drawer exactly as they had been, thinking a few times was this on top of that or the other way around. She had to be sure. Richard noticed every little change. No problem remembering where she had found the bottle. In the toe of a shoe. One had to look very carefully to find it. Another one of Richard's funny little secrets. Or maybe not funny.

Marian made cupcakes and chocolate chip cookies, then a chicken casserole she knew Carolyn liked. She didn't expect them home in time for dinner, but just in case. Carolyn is such a sweetheart and Richard a real gem for taking her to Walt Disney World. Hope they aren't too bored with each other. Then Marian sat at the table, put her head in her hands and cried. Oh, Peter. Did we do the right thing? This is the very table where we sat and decided your fate. Did we hear it correctly? What did Nate actually say? Nothing! Nothing incriminating. He hadn't said a thing, all insinuation. Oh, Peter, what have I done? Marian sobbed. Richard, Richard so sure, so convincing. What is the truth? Will she ever know. Did we rule correctly?

She finally dried her tears. She showered, feeling the cold water tingle against her skin. She put on a flowered patio dress, that in Hawaii were called short muumuus, stirred a glass of instant iced tea, and picked up a new mystery novel, "Kiss the Girls," by James Patterson. She went to the deck to wile away the rest of the day. Her mind did not stray from the book until the call from Richard, telling her he and Carolyn would be late. Traffic and dinner. "I think our little girl is hungry." He sounds tired and probably is anxious for this day to end, she wrongly predicted.

Shopping with Carolyn or perhaps any teenager, can be wearing, decided Marian. Carolyn only chose pricey clothes, looking at the brand name and price tag before considering the article. Price made no difference to Marian, nor to Richard. But it did occur to Marian that Carolyn had no idea that money should be earned. Not that Marian had ever earned any. Still, she had an appreciation of work that Carolyn lacked. Course, Marian reflected, how could it be different? Didn't she and Nancy, as well, shop in boutiques? Carolyn grew up knowing only affluence.

Marian said no to the thong swim suit. Carolyn pouted. Richard said let her get it, she's only young once. She can't go out in public in that or even by the pool and certainly can't take it home to Illinois, insisted Marian. Well, Richard said, she's just a kid, let her wear it. But only if one of us is with her and she wears a cover-up. Oh, she would, she would, a cover-up, and probably never take it off, but this is the latest thing and she wants it so much. Please, it's so cool.

Richard and Carolyn persevered on the swim suit as well as on the short, tight black dress with an over-the-shoulder side strap. Special going out to dinner dress, Richard told Marian.

"Her mother will not allow her to wear those clothes and I'm not sure I will either," Marian protested.

"Oh, Grandma, I don't wear little taffeta dresses with ruffles anymore. I'm not a child," Carolyn disgustedly said.

"Not a child," mocked Richard, whose speculative expression announced a completely different meaning.

Purchasing sophisticated makeup (Carolyn had used only light lip gloss) and sultry perfume, ended the shopping spree. Carolyn beaming, Richard anticipating, and Marian thoughtful.

Carolyn could use a few makeup pointers from Jaki, Richard contemplated while knowing that would never happen. Jaki would see his intention in a heartbeat. Carolyn wore her heart on her face for all to see. In a couple of years Carolyn may even rival Jaki's beautifully endowed body. Jaki definitely was not blind. Richard knew he must make a supreme effort to keep Marian unaware of his interest in Carolyn as well.

Carolyn pranced out in her silk shorty p.j.'s. "I'm taking a run on the beach after breakfast. Does anyone want to come?"

"You're not going out like that!" Marian stated.

"Course not Grandma, I just came out for some orange juice and toast. I'll wear shorts and a very sedate top."

"I'll go with you," said Richard. "I go for a run every morning, usually before this, but such a terrific dinner last night as well as fantastic company made me sleep like a baby." In truth, Richard hadn't slept much. He lay awake planning Carolyn's last day before returning to Chicago, and pondered his actions. Several scenarios kept cropping up in his mind, though he knew strong discipline must prevail. And if he was smart, he knew he would keep Marian close by. Intelligence doesn't always win, as he heard himself tell Carolyn, he would run the beach with her. And he knew they would run to an area out of Marian's line of vision and he knew very well that Carolyn would be wearing the thong suit under her shorts and "sedate" top. His mind wandered. Such a ripe untouched body. No, he wouldn't. Get a grip, he told himself, something like that could mean jail time. Not worth it. Jaki was less than a half hour away. Still.....

"Oh, super," replied Carolyn. Do you want to come with us, Grandma?" Such an innocent question, course she wouldn't. Marian could hardly walk after all that trouncing around the shopping center she told Carolyn.

"You two wore me completely out and look at my feet, I do believe they're swollen," Marian remarked.

Carolyn had decided she would make another attempt to (should she call it seduce?) Richard, Richard wondering would he seduce (he definitely called it that) Carolyn, and Marian thinking isn't he great, he's going far and beyond what she should expect in entertaining Carolyn. The little disappointments long forgotten. Their life seemed back on track. Yet, an uneasy feeling crept in.

To the chagrin of both Richard and Carolyn, other joggers filled the beach and had even discovered Richard's little, he thought, private cove. They hung around the cove hoping the others would leave. They didn't. Richard told Carolyn they must return to the condo.

Finding the cove occupied was not the only discovery of the morning. Marian, straightening Carolyn's room, noticed the thong swim suit missing. She wasn't snooping, Carolyn's clothes lay on the bed. The new purchases at one end, laundry in a little pile at the other end, and, scattered in between, were her other clothes---shorts, a tank top, the flowered swim suit, several tees, the shorty p.j.'s and that was it. Marian searched the new purchases once again. That thong suit is gone. She wore it.

Fear immediately filled Marian's heart. She remembered seeing Richard watching Carolyn when she tried on that swim suit. At that time, Marian felt a small jab of fear as she saw the look in Richard's eyes and then later at dinner as he watched Carolyn's movements in the tight dress. Marian dismissed Richard expression, not calling it lust, telling herself that he thought Carolyn such a cute young grandchild. Now, though she remembered Carolyn brushing close to Richard several times and him smiling at her. And Richard insisting that Carolyn have that thong suit. Human. They are human. Carolyn on the brink of womanhood and Richard ---- she looked down at her legs, the bulging varicose veins that covered much of her legs and her swollen ankles. She can't be that attractive to him she reasoned. And they hadn't shared a bed in weeks. Carolyn had looked at Richard as if he were God. Carolyn! She must find Carolyn. Marian began the slow descent from the condo to the beach. There were so many places they could be, but, if she could only get them in sight, if they could see her then..... then Carolyn would be safe. But how could she see them, or they her. Which way did they go? Right or left? Finding them seemed hopeless. Her walk slow and labored took minutes to even cross the wooden walkway that led to the beach and they planned to run. Marian observed the joggers, the walkers, the strollers, but no Richard nor Carolyn. Chills ran down her spine. It was no use to expose her legs to this pain any longer. She slowly and with foreboding returned to the condo.

She filled a mug with left-over breakfast coffee and zapped it in the micro. She remembered unfinished orange juice . Half a glass left. She might as well drink it. As she raised the glass to her lips, did she detect a slight odor of almonds? Something clicked in the back of her mind. A day months ago when Richard took a drink from her hands, poured it down the drain and furiously washed the glass. She put the glass of orange juice on the table and rushed to the bedroom, opened the bottom drawer of Richard's chest and pulled out the shoes. There, the bottle. Once again she held it to the window. Yes, more of the liquid was gone. Such a small bottle. She could easily tell about a teaspoon had disappeared since she last examined it. She carefully replaced the bottle, covered the shoe exactly as she had found it, closed the drawer, and sat on the floor as she had two days before, trying to determine what to do with her life. David and Nancy well into their own lives, rich, very rich by most standards; Jason and Carolyn to be wealthy in their own right in a few years. What did she contribute to their lives? And Richard, what could she provide that he actually needed or wanted for that matter? Her life had been full and basically happy with a few highs and lows along the way. The low pendulum more pronounced lately. She had overlooked so much. Little nagging suspicions about Jaki, about Nate, and Peter. She never mentioned money and Richard not contributing to their joint accounts or loans not being paid back. She tired more easily now, smiled less, pained more. Is it all worth the struggle she pondered.

She retraced her steps to the dining room table, picked up the glass of tangy orange juice, and drank.

Richard and Carolyn returned to find Marian bathing her eyes with a cold damp cloth.

"What's wrong dear?" Richard asked solicitously. "You look pale. Aren't you feeling well?"

"Can't seem to get a handle on this headache," Marian bravely smiled.

"I didn't know you had a headache, Grandma," Carolyn said. And Marian noted Carolyn seemed a trifle unhappy, not the smiling jubilant teenager she generally showed when returning from the beach.

"I only got it, sweetheart. Maybe not enough breakfast. I wasn't hungry so had only juice and coffee. I'll make some toast and tea and I'll feel fine."

"I'll make it for you, dear, why don't you lie down." Richard's words sounded caring yet his eyes were bright, excited.

Am I reading more into his eyes than is actually there? wondered Marian. "All right, if you don't mind. I'll sit here and watch the water."

Carolyn drummed on the table. Restlessness showing in her actions and voice. "I'll put my clothes in the wash if someone can show me how to work the machine."

Richard exchanged a can-you-believe-she-doesn't-know-how-to-wash-clothes look with Marian. Actually Marian could believe it. Carolyn had been raised with household help. Nancy didn't do much either.

"It's pretty simple. I'll show you," volunteered Richard. "Do you want to see a movie this afternoon or do you have some other desires?"

"A movie, I guess, only I don't want to go alone."

"We couldn't let you go alone. If your grandma doesn't feel like going I'll take you."

Marian pondered this a few moments. A theater should be fine. People around and why is she thinking that way anyway. She must get rid of these suspicions.

"I'll stay here and perhaps nap if that's okay. Richard, you're wonderful to take such good care of Carolyn. Isn't he wonderful, Carolyn?"

"Oh, yes, " Carolyn gazed at Richard, "wonderful."

Poor Carolyn, Marian mused. The young always survive a first love. And early tomorrow morning Carolyn will be on her way home.

After Richard and Carolyn left for the movies, Marian glanced in Carolyn's room. As she had surmised, the thong swim suit was back and lay on top of the newly purchased clothes. Regretfully, Marian realized she had guessed right.

"Ah, the headache is gone," Richard announced as he and Carolyn returned from the movies.

"Yes, it was excruciating for awhile." Marian was busy in the kitchen preparing dinner. Carolyn's favorite chicken casserole. The evening spent at home watching television (what color will she wear tonight?) or working a Wyland puzzle, one featuring his ever-popular whales and colorful fish, another purchase from Kauai. Carolyn kept trying to catch Richard's eye, but to his credit, he treated her as he would a loved grandchild and caught Marian's eyes several times in mock exasperation of Carolyn's antics. Marian only smiled and waited for the day to end. A day of puzzlement for her.

After Carolyn's flight Richard had "catching up to do." "She took a lot of time, and I was glad to help you, but now it's back to work for me."

"You're such a gem," remarked Marian.

For Carolyn, the flight home was filled with bitter-sweet thoughts of "almosts." Almost changing shirts in the car, almost finding that private cove on the beach unoccupied, almost being alone in a row of seats in the theater, his hands almost touching her---almost. Of course, they held hands, of course his hand rested on her leg, at times creeping higher---almost reaching between her legs---almost. Of course they arranged telephone calls. He promised to rent a post office box so she could write letters to him without her grandmother noticing. He couldn't write to her, he said. A chance they couldn't take. How would Carolyn know he never put anything in writing, at least anything incriminating. How would she know that he already received private letters in a post office box? How could she guess that in the dark theater when he nibbled at her ear and told her he loved her he was manipulating her very thoughts? In two years he had told her, if she still felt the same, then they would run away together.

"What about Grandma?" Carolyn asked.

"She would be the first to want us to be with the one we love, our true love. But, we need to keep our plans secret not even telling best friends. If word gets out then, Richard's eyes bore into hers, "we are through."

Carolyn gasped.

"It has to be that way. Until you are eighteen I have to treat you as a child. Unless, " he smiled, "we are completely alone." Smooth lies coming from Richard's lips that sounded like a life full of promise and joy for Carolyn.

If only she could share her secret with her friend, Michelle. Wow! Michelle would just die if she knew about Richard. An older man. True love! The heart-tugging sweetness of keeping their love a secret for two years. Living their passion through letters and furtive telephone calls. And in their dreams. Oh, yes, the dreams. Michelle would just die!

Carolyn once again opened her bag and caressed the diamond ring Richard had given to her. A real diamond but, he said, if anyone discovered it then tell them it is fake, that you bought it for yourself. Real gold, as well Richard bragged, and cautioned her to keep that a secret. More lies, but how could she know?

And wouldn't it be great to tell Katie about Richard? Katie who thought she knew and had everything. Always putting Carolyn down for the curfew Carolyn had to obey, the nearly colorless makeup that Carolyn's parents allowed. Katie who had her own car and already had two speeding tickets which her lawyer dad got her out of, and who told everyone that she had vodka in a little silver bottle in the car's glove box. No one had seen it, but Katie could get away with anything. Carolyn would love to tell Katie about Richard. Maybe she would. Katie would just die. And Carolyn would love,oh, love to see the envy in Katie's eyes when she saw the ring. A real diamond. Carolyn caressed it once again. Would she ever love to show it to Katie. She would just die!.

Marian met a new friend at a bridge party, an event she rarely attended anymore since her legs pained her so. Richard out of town for the day. Marian took a cab, and accepted the ride home from Irene. The two talked constantly about mutual interests, including the love of cooking. This new interest of Marian's amused Richard and he encouraged her to attend the various classes. Irene introduced Marian to more of Florida's exotic fruit, and gave her a small thin unbound book depicting fruit drinks for every special occasion along with "weekend" specials.

Marian was delighted to try the special drinks and Richard smiled and tried to guess which fruit she would use at any given time. She seems to be her old self again he mused and bought a second car so she could attend bridge and cooking classes again. What had he been thinking he asked himself, to keep her inside the condo so much. Gave her too much time to think, and he admitted, she is an intelligent lady. Now that she had functions of her own to attend he had even more free time. More time to spend with Jaki and since Marian knew nothing of his activities, there was no way she could ever find him during the day or even nighttime.

Even though Marian used the car infrequently, it was there for her and that gave her a sense of freedom and inde-pendence. Both Marian and Richard appeared to be happier than either of them had a few weeks earlier. A new friend and an automobile had worked wonders, guessed Richard.

CHAPTER TWENTY

"Mother," Nancy's telephone call woke Marian from an afternoon nap, a new habit to help Marian fight off the fatigue she seemed to suffer and to keep her awake longer in the evenings when Richard needed her, she thought. "I have some bad news..."

Marian interrupted, " Carolyn, did something happen to Carolyn, or David or what Nancy?"

"Just listen, Mother, and try to stay calm. Peter killed himself last night and..."

"Oh, no, oh God, no," Marian screamed. She sobbed, huge gulps of air fighting to reach her lungs. She pounded her head against the bed, hit the night stand with her fists. "How, why?" Her words incoherent, she barely was able to say them. Nancy's words nearly drove Marian into shock. She moaned, cried, screamed.

Not Peter, not her very best friend. Not the little boy who grew up to be the kind, intelligent, and considerate man. Not Peter. What had she done?

"Oh, Sybil, Peter forgive me. I always loved you and love Sybil and oh, God, not Peter," sobbed Marian, nearly out of control.

Nancy remained silent, waiting for her mother to control her intense grief. Nancy understood. Peter had been part of her and David's life as well. The two families had shared special times forever, it seemed to Nancy. Peter and Sybil, childless, treated Nancy and David as their own. Nancy was devastated when Marian explained Peter's "problem," and like Marian found it hard to believe. But, now, had it been true and Peter couldn't face public knowledge? And Sybil, what must she be feeling and thinking?

"Mother, can you talk now? Can you understand what I'm saying?" asked Nancy.

After a huge sob Marian responded, "Yes, please tell me what happened."

"All I know is that Peter shot himself. Sybil called me an hour or so ago. He left her a note, but she didn't read it to me, only that he said, he said..." Nancy began crying. It was several minutes before she could continue.

"He said he couldn't face the humiliation of the lies, couldn't put Sybil through it. If, and Mother please control yourself, if his best friend didn't believe him, how could he convince anybody."

"Oh, God," Marian began crying again. She couldn't utter more than "Oh, God."

"Sybil asked me to call you since they were not allowed your telephone number." Nancy's voice held a note of censure. Nancy had always felt the telephone number change to one unlisted had isolated her mother from long-time friends.

Finally Marian managed to control her crying and asked, "Will there be services? I must see Sybil."

"Nothing is set yet. Sybil is calling me again tonight and I'll let you know."

"I could call her. Where is she staying?"

"She didn't say." Nancy's voice sounded flat, sad, and her words a monotone.

"When she calls, please give her my number and get hers so I get in contact," pleaded Marian.

"Open the gate now, Mother?"

"Don't be cruel to me Nancy. I'm terribly, terribly upset about this. I can hardly stand it."

"I'll ask her Mother, only I'm not sure what she may say. I know you are upset. We all are. Is Richard with you or are you all alone?"

"He's doing a small favor for Vinnie, but will be home soon. I'll be all right. I just want to get all these tears out. Then I can think straight."

"I'll call you tonight after I hear from Sybil."

The call didn't come. Marian paced the floor, drank innumerable cups of hot tea, picked up the telephone to call Nancy, only to put it down again. And Richard had not arrived. Marian knew there would be a fresh set of tears when she related the day's events to him. Her guilt lay heavy in her heart. Had she caused Peter's suicide? The question would never be answered. She would never know. Was there something else in his life she knew nothing about? The owner's decision to fire Peter was unanimous, not just hers, wasn't it? Oh, God, how long before this pain goes away?

"Richard come home and tell me I'm not to blame," Marian sobbed to the empty walls. Her mind went over and over Nate's remarks and her call to Peter. Was it true? This question would haunt her the rest of her life. Could she have been so wrong in reading Peter's personality? When Peter was young, did she miss a big problem that she should have seen? Was Sybil aware of a problem, keeping it to herself? And Richard, where are you?

Richard arrived home shortly before ten. She had expected him at two in the afternoon. Eight hours of agony for Marian. Her tears had exhausted her emotions. She felt drained of all feeling and sat looking at the ocean, not seeing and trying not to think.

"Marian, I'm sorry I'm late. There was more to do than I thought. Hope you didn't hold dinner for me." Richard contrite, reached her side and put his arm around her shoulders. He hoped the smell of Jaki had vanished in the slight warm breeze through the open car window.

"Oh, Richard, " Marian sobbed. "Something terrible has happened." She could not utter another word. She moaned and for once Richard felt a twinge of anxiety.

What had she heard? Did someone tell her about Jaki? His dealings? His ultimate plan. No, no one knew about that, so he felt safe in that regard. But still, she looked as if she might go into shock. She shivered.

"Marian, calm down. I can't help you if you don't tell me what's wrong," Richard more apprehensive about his actions than sympathetic towards Marian. Nothing new. He always thought of himself first.

"Peter...Peter," Marian began. Then a new set of tears took control.

"Peter what?" Is he suing for defamation of character? Had he finally realized it was all a lie? "What, Marian?" Richard shook her and slapped her across the face. "Come out of it, Marian. Get control for God's sake."

She did. The crying stopped and she clung to him. He stroked her hair and waited, pondering what in the world set her off like that.

"Peter killed himself last night. I'm waiting for Nancy to tell me more," gulped Marian.

"My, God!" Richard felt a sense of elation that he hadn't caused the outburst. "Where, how?"

"A gun. That's all I know." She slumped against him, too exhausted to say more.

"You're shivering. I'll make some tea."

"No, I've been drinking tea all evening."

"Have you eaten anything at all?" Richard kept his arms around her trying to calm her nerves.

"I can't." Marian clung to him as if she couldn't bear to let go. Afraid, he too, may vanish.

"When is Nancy calling?"

"When she hears from Sybil. She called me around two this afternoon. She didn't know anything else then."

"Why didn't you call her back?"

"I don't know," answered Marian in a flat, emotionless tone.

"I'll call her now. It's earlier there. Do you want to talk to her or are you too drained?"

"If you reach her I'll talk to her."

Richard talked to Nancy only a few moments before returning to Marian announcing that Nancy had learned nothing new.

"There was no reason for you to talk to her. We'll know in the morning. Right now you need sleep." And Richard wanted to alert Nate to the unexpected situation. Not that it mattered to Richard. So what if Peter killed himself, just one more person out of his way. But, as his mother used to say, "Forewarned is Forearmed." Not an original expression, but one she used frequently.

Sybil scheduled a memorial service for Peter in the chapel of a mortuary. Suicide is a sin in their religion and she didn't ask their long-time friend and minister to do the service. In fact, she could not even, in good faith, ask that it be performed in a church. His body had been cremated and later his ashes would be scattered in the ocean he loved so much. Of course Nancy and her family were welcome to attend the memorial. If Marian and Richard wanted to attend, well, then, the mortuary is open.

Marian and Richard did attend the memorial service. Marian needed to speak with Sybil, to be assured, somewhat, that Sybil did not blame her for Peter's death. If Sybil could give some sign that Marian did not cause the death then, perhaps, Marian could sleep through the nights, could stow away the guilt, could face herself in the mirror.

The young man handling the service had a low modulated voice. Dressed in a black suit, black shoes and black socks, he looked and acted the part he was expected to play. The chapel had a strong muggy odor. Even the scent of flowers could not hide what everyone knew-that only funerals were held here. A woman dressed in a choir robe played hymns preceding the service. The organ music, soft and very low, brought tears to Marian's eyes as she recalled singing those very songs to Peter when he was a child.

"Family and friends of Peter William Jacobson, " the young man began, "we are gathered here today not to mourn his death but to celebrate his life. A life lived all too briefly, but one that made a positive impact on those with whom he came in contact. A life that will be remembered for kind and thoughtful deeds. Left to grieve Peter's unexpected departure from his life on earth is his beloved wife, Sybil, to whom he had been married for thirty-six years; a brother Christopher Jacobson; two nephews, Daniel and David Jacobson, and one niece, Rebecca Marian Jacobson; a sister-in-law, Sonja Harvey and her husband, Bruce Harvey; a large contingent of loyal co-workers and many, many friends."

Marian nearly lost it when the young man named Peter's niece. Rebecca's middle name was chosen because of her. As Marian had before the service began, she counted the number of flowers in the sprays, anything to keep her mind busy and keep from remembering why she was here. Thirty-six large purple orchids surrounded by white pikaki was the backdrop for the small silver urn holding Peter's ashes. Flowers from Hawaii--in remembrance of the cruising days in the islands. The orchids depicting the number of years the Jacobson's had been married, Marian counted fifty red and white carnations in a large anchor shaped spray. Then she counted them again in case she was wrong. A game she played with herself---counting, instead of thinking. Once again. Yes, fifty. Twenty-five red, twenty-five white. She and Richard had sent red roses as did several others. She listened once again to the young man standing at the pulpit.

"Peter Jacobson loved the sea, he devoted his entire working years to his chosen occupation. Retiring just this month as captain of the Golden Sea, a cruise ship operating between the west coast and the Hawaiian Islands. His beloved wife made the journeys with him. During their married years they also traveled in many parts of the world and their home, the captain's quarters on the ship and a small farm in western Illinois testified to their joy in acquiring works of art from foreign lands as well as throughout the United States."

Marian remembered a small marlin carved from obsidian, hard shiny black volcanic glass, with such intricate detail that the Jacobsons received offers from various art experts to purchase the piece. The carving had been done by Virgil Keltz, an well-known artisan who did his work in Anacortes, a northwest Washington state city. The Jacobsons carried the carving with them always. They named it Ebony, or Ebb for short. They loved the smooth shiny marlin and subsequently purchased another piece of art work from Keltz. Marian brushed a tear from her eye.

"When a young lad, Peter built model sailing ships and his favorite books were those depicting life on the sea. Peter Jacobson was a loving and dutiful son who brought great pride to his parents with academic achievements as well as in sports. He participated in many school activities both in high school where he graduated fourth in his class, and in college where he was outstanding in crew, becoming the captain in his senior year. A further testimony to his love of the sea.
"Peter and Sybil Olson were married September 14, 1959 and though they were not blessed with children, they gave generously of their time and money to help less fortunate youngsters. Sybil will carry on their work with the establishment of a five thousand dollar scholarship to be given annually to a deserving graduate of Peter's high school here in Chicago."

Marian remembered Peter had received a scholarship and, with the support of his parents, chose to give it to a student who could not have furthered his education without it. The student attended a trade school which Peter stated was just as important as a four-year school. Marian recalled the two had remained friends and she casually looked about her wondering if the man was here today.

"We do not know, we cannot guess what is in someone's mind. The mind is such a complicated machine. Yes," the young man paused, "machine. Always moving, always thinking. We may try to guess at one's thoughts, but we do not really know what those thoughts actually are. Peter Jacobson had many thoughts. Some he shared. Some he did not. Let us not dwell on Peter Jacobson's final thoughts. Let us not try to second guess what may have led him to this action. Instead let us remember the ideas, the stories, the joyous times he shared with us. Let us be grateful he shared a portion of his life with us and that he let us into his life for a short time. Turn our energies to those in need, whatever the reason. And remember we are not the judge. Only God will judge and we pray that He will judge Peter Jacobson for his lifetime of being a kind and just man."

Oh, yes, please God, remember Peter as the young boy playing on a swing, the young man hesitant, but still turning out for high school football; remember the honor society student; the chairman of the debate team; Sir Lancelot in the high school play, his voice strong as he sang the love song to his leading lady, forever giving him a love of music; and his college years snow-mobiling and ice skating during the cold Minnesota winters; oh, yes, God, and more, remember the good and fine things Peter accomplished and forgive his final act, Marian pleaded.

"Let us pray. Our Father, we pray for the soul of Peter William Jacobson, that you will in your wisdom take his soul to Heaven where he may dwell with Jesus for eternity. We pray you will put your hand on Peter's beloved wife, Sybil, and comfort her in this time of sorrow. Help her to understand that we never know what life holds for us and that we must take one day at a time. Give her and Peter's family and friends strength to face each day and to thank you for all you have given to all of us who knew Peter in this lifetime. We pray that you will take his soul and you will prepare a place for us to join him in eternal life. Amen."

The young man read scriptures from the Bible and closed the service by asking the audience to join him in repeating The Lord's Prayer. Marian felt a calmness in her heart from the service. She knew she would see her friend again and now she wanted to comfort Sybil.

That was not to be.

"Friends, the family of Peter wishes to announce that they will not be available for visitation at this time. We wish to sincerely thank you for coming." The voice of Bruce Harvey was strong and adamant. He left through the back of the chapel as did the other family members.

Marian tried to join them but was rebuffed by the young man who had conducted the service. "Please respect the family's wishes. They are completely devastated."

"I want to help, I've known Sybil for years," Marian pleaded, but to no avail.

CHAPTER TWENTY-ONE

The weeks following Peter's death were weary for Marian. The sky didn't seem quite so blue, the sun not as brilliant, plumeria not as fragrant, the world took on a dull, colorless concept. Richard stayed away more and more, longer and longer. And when he did come home he often smelled of wine mixed with some other woman's perfume. Not that she blamed him for either as she gazed at her swollen feet and ankles. Her shoes didn't fit and lately she wore bedroom slippers and her robe around the condo most of the day. He wasn't home to see her anyway, so what did it matter? And the headaches came more frequently as well. Tension, she told herself. How could she not be tense, she questioned more than once. Richard seeing other women, money in large amounts disappeared from the joint accounts with no explanations. If she asked Richard about an expenditure, he gave an indifferent answer, if he responded at all. Nancy, who had visited with Sybil was now cool to Marian or maybe it had to do with Carolyn and her visit to Florida.

Well, they had agreed when they married that they would share everything jointly. She had willingly opened her savings, checking, and credit card accounts to him. And to be honest with herself, she still loved him. He excited her with a smile, a touch of his hand, a soft word. Younger than she, he needed space. She gave him that, no reproaches, no nagging. She must try harder to make his life as comfortable as possible so he would find home a pleasant place to be. She had been in this situation before. She waited it out then, she would wait it out now.

Richard believed life to be just dandy. While his goal had been (and still was) to be a rich widower he had all the perks of that. Money, lots of money to spend. And the safety of being married. It certainly didn't matter how he spent his time. Marian didn't question his activities or his "work." She gave him space, she didn't nag. He wished she would so he could smack her. He loved seeing the hurt questions in her eyes when he twisted her arms or "accidentally" tripped her. She was fun to punish. Oh, he didn't actually injure her and no one could see the bruises. He had learned his lesson after Nancy had made such a fuss that time when she discovered Marian's swollen thumb and bruised hand. Now he had found such a great place to poke. Her breasts bruised so easily. If only she gave him some reasons to push her around. Most of the time he had to pretend it was an accident.

Richard freely spent Marian's money. That horse of Jaki's and the bets she insisted on had cost plenty. The horse had never won a race. Never even finished most of the time. He must have lost over three hundred grand on bets alone. And he loved buying jewelry for his women. Now that he had ready access to endless cash, he never bothered switching gems. He bought gold bars for himself and stock. Several million dollars in various stocks. Just a hedge on the chance Marian's assets were frozen after her death. She never questioned what he spent and never knew he had purchased other condos for an investment. All in his name. Worth plenty in his own right now. Marian probably didn't know how much he spent anyway.

She did know though. Knew that he had spent eight million dollars in the seven months of marriage. And this not counting their condo which, of course, she had purchased. She knew, as well, that he had not put as much as a dollar in the joint accounts.

Richard's spending had slackened this past month. The other women had about all the jewelry he planned to buy and really, how much money can a person spend? Even a dedicated spender soon ran out of purchase material. It had been fun to trade the new cars in on a monthly basis but he wanted to keep this one.

Richard used Marian as a safety net against other women strongly hinting marriage.

"She's ill. My principles wouldn't allow me to divorce her right now no matter how badly I want to marry you," he told more than one hopeful. And his expression said I-have-such-high-moral-standards-and-deep-feelings-of-responsibility. It worked everytime. The women said they loved him even more because of his dedication to his bed-ridden wife. They would wait. Certainly anyone that ill must be on death's bed, they reasoned. Richard thanked them for understanding.

"I just feel obligated to do all I can for her. She has such a short time left to live," his eyes sad as he spoke those words.

If after a few weeks he cast his eyes in a new direction, then, so what? Variety fed his vanity. Only Jaki remained constant in his life and she certainly harbored no thoughts of marriage. Not to Richard anyway. She knew he would always be a cheat.

"Jaki, I'm taking a delivery to New York and I'm going to talk to Vinnie about you and I leaving," said Nate. He appeared to have lost weight and the exuberance of a happy young man was gone.

"Don't make waves, Nate. Think of the money we make."

"But at what cost, Jaki, what cost? Can you honestly say you want to stay here and do the things we have to do?"

"My job is better now, I just make arrangements, I don't perform."

"Still..... I thought you wanted out of here. Wanted to make a new life with me."

"I thought so, too, and I like you a lot, but," she waved her hand around her luxurious condo, "this is a beautiful place to live."

"It must have cost you a fortune. How did you manage to buy it? The payments alone must be huge!" Nate gazed around the room with its wall of windows looking out to the azure water.

"No payments," Jaki brightly said. " Richard bought it for me."

How would Jaki know that the title to the luxury condominium remained in Richard's name along with ownership of the race horse? And many of Jaki's jewels were indeed fake. Richard wanted to control her even more than any other person. Perhaps she was strong and as manipulative as Richard himself. He had to be the winner in whatever game they were playing. And of course, cheating came easily to both of them.

"Richard! I thought you and I...I didn't think you saw Richard anymore."

"Nate, I have to and well, he isn't so bad. Kind of fun really." Jaki studied her fingernails, rubbing her thumb back and forth over the ends of the nails.

"I see. At least I guess I see." Nate was wounded. The life of happiness with Jaki gone. He saw that now. Had she ever loved him? He wondered. Is Richard the reason why she so often couldn't be reached? Why the pieces of unexplained jewelry? And her interest in racing? Has Richard been in the picture all along? Sending Nate on long trips so Richard could be with Jaki?

"I think, Nate, you and I want different things out of life. I don't like everything I do, but this has been my work all of my life and now I'm making real money."

"So, you're staying. Even if Vinnie says we can go, you're staying?" Nate, his eyes brimming with tears, pleaded with Jaki.

"Vinnie won't say that. And well, just how much money could we make somewhere else? I'd be back walking the streets or you would be my pimp. I don't want that. I've been there."

"We had some great plans, or at least I thought we had," Nate sadly said.

"I'm sorry," Jaki remarked. "I just like my life the way it is right now."

"And the little Black and Cuban kids. You like that too?" asked Nate.

"I only make arrangements, I don't watch." Jaki looked straight into Nate's eyes a defiant expression on her face.

"I see. I guess you're right. We do want different things. I still have to go to New York and I still want to talk to Vinnie If you change your mind." Nate hesitated. "But, I guess you won't."

"I won't." Jaki paused. "Uh, Nate, Richard doesn't want me to see you anymore. I told him we were only friends but he said for you and I to stay apart."

"You said okay didn't you?"

"Well, what else could I do? Besides, he..."

"That's okay, Jaki. I understand. I finally do understand."

"It's been fun. No hard feelings?"

"No hard feelings." Nate looked at her for a long time. Beautiful, ruthless Jaki. It will take awhile, but he knew he would get over her, he told himself. Richard may have found his match. Or Jaki may have found hers.

Nate did talk to Vinnie. He told him that he wanted Jaki. Only she wanted Richard, so Nate thought it best to leave the area and find another job.

"Just as I thought. Richard wasn't satisfied very long with an old woman for a wife," remarked Vinnie. "I see your point. Richard's hard to compete with."

"He has lots of money and can buy Jaki whatever she wants."

"Tell you what, kid. I'll send you to Los Angeles to work with my cousin Dino. He can set you up, okay?"

"I kind of thought I'd like out of the organization," said Nate.

"No way, kid. Told you that when you came. Once you're in you're in. Los Angeles is the best I can do for you, and Dino's a nice guy. Do what he says and you'll be okay. Nothing like here. Different kind of work. Not as many deliveries. Otherwise..."

Nate knew the "otherwise." He said Los Angeles sounded fine, that he had always liked the west coast.

"Dino's a fine man. You'll like him and he'll like you. Find a nice Italian girl. They make good wives. Jaki, well, I know you like her now, but I knew the first time I saw her well, let's say, she is the only person I know that can handle Richard. Serve him right. He already got a nice wife, a real nice wife. Doesn't deserve Marian, but that's Richard. I known him all our lives. Best friends. Always best friends. Always will be."

Nate understood completely.

"I have something you have to drop off to Richard and then you can leave for L.A. Even give you a car to drive. The one you have out there. Only have a couple of stops to make on the way. One in Houston and in Denver. Little stops. Okay?"

"Sounds great to me." It had to sound great to Nate. He knew the alternative.

"Like I tol ya, I take care of my kids." And Vinnie believed he had done Nate a supreme favor. Maybe he had.

CHAPTER TWENTY-TWO

"Mrs. Snider, I have a small package for Richard. From Vinnie. Is he home?" asked Nate through the intercom.

"He isn't, but come on up, Nate. He should be home soon and you can leave it here." Marian pressed the button allowing Nate to enter the condominium building. Once in, he could either climb the three flights of stairs to the Snider's, or take the elevator. He opted for the stairs. Nate had a slight fear of small enclosed places.

"Come in, Nate. I just made some iced tea and you look as if you could use a cold drink." Marian handed Nate a tall Tervis glass decorated with sea birds, one of her favorites.

"Out of shape," Nate puffed, "I need to get more exercise."

Marian silently agreed with him. She observed his waistline had grown thicker and his stomach was showing the beginning of a pouch.

"Join the club, Nate. These hot days are easier to endure inside with AC and iced tea. I can't understand how Richard can run in this heat."

"Vinnie wanted me to deliver this personally to Richard." Nate placed a small package about the size of two boxes of blank checks on the white-tiled kitchen counter.

"It's okay. I'll make sure he gets it when he comes home."

"Do you know when that will be? Vinnie wanted him to call."

"I don't know for sure. But if he isn't here by eight, I'll call Vinnie. I know him very well so don't worry. Sometimes something unexpected comes up that Richard has to do."

Nate knew very well where Richard could be found. It still hurt. Jaki so lovely, so soft, so out of his life. Nate gulped the cold tea. He breathed easier now. My, God, that was only three flights of stairs. Maybe in L.A. he wouldn't be too frightened to get out of his apartment and he could run along the beach or workout in a gym. Lately he felt like he was being followed, though when he rationalized his thinking, he knew his paranoia stemmed from guilt of his "job" and the deliveries he had to make.

"Richard has a lot of stamina and dedication," responded Nate.

"Ah, yes, he has that," remarked Marian.

"Mrs. Snider, I'm real sorry about the captain. I know he was your real good friend and I'm sorry." Nate stumbled on his words and Marian noticed tears brimming his eyes.

"Thank you, Nate. I knew him all of his life, but not as well as I thought it seems," Marian sadly responded. "It's hard for me to acknowledge that he was hiding such a dark side to his personality."

"Well, uh," Nate grasped the glass tightly in his hands and stared out the window. Goodness, Marian thought to herself, lucky the glass is unbreakable, he's squeezing so tightly it's making his knuckles white. He seems upset. Maybe he needs someone to talk to, like a mother or close friend. He's so young and seems so vulnerable.

"What's wrong, Nate," Marian gently asked, guiding him to a chair near the windows. She sat on the nearby sofa.

"Well, I didn't think he would kill himself over it," Nate's lower lip quivered. "I only......."

"Nate you only did what you had to," Marian softly responded.

"No, I, no I lied, Mrs. Snider. The captain didn't do any of those things. And now he's dead and I can't sleep at night, and..." Tears flowed from Nate's eyes. He put the glass on the small elephant-shaped end table and held his hands tightly together. He sobbed.

"What do you mean, Nate?" Marian was shocked, still she remained calm wanting to hear more from this young man.

"I had to do it. He made me say it. I didn't really say it but I didn't say it wasn't true either." Nate's eyes pleaded with her to understand.

"Who made you say it, Nate?" Marian felt a cold chill travel from the back of her neck to her heels. She was afraid she already knew. "Richard made you, is that it?" she asked in a quiet voice. Marian knew she must remain calm and in control even though her heart pounded so loudly she was sure Nate could hear it.

"He will kill me. I better go." Nate rose from the chair and made a move toward the door.

"Wait, Nate. I understand. You aren't to blame. Please sit down. I'm not angry. You didn't cause his death." Marian reached deep into her soul to remain calm. She wanted to scream and pound her fists into the wall. "Tell me about it and you'll feel better."

"You're a nice lady." Nate wiped his hand across his eyes, picked up the glass and finished the iced tea. Marian refilled his glass, dropped in a couple of ice cubes, added a wedge of lemon, and returned to her seat on the sofa.

"I can help you, so don't be afraid." Gently Marian urged Nate to continue. She wanted to hear this.

"I told Jaki you would help us. She said you wouldn't cause she knew you from before."

"Are you in love with Jaki?" Maybe Richard isn't seeing her. Maybe she's seeing Nate.

"I was, I still am, but she loves someone else. Maybe not love him but sees him. She doesn't want me."

"I'm sorry." So it is Richard. Marian knew from the moment they had met in that restaurant, the day she and Richard found the yacht.

"Let's go back to the captain. Tell me who made you say what you did. Tell me the whole story. I promise I won't mention it to anybody. I know most of it anyway and I can help you. I know it, but please tell me your side."

"For some reason Richard hated the captain. I don't know why. He wanted him to lose his job. That's all, just lose his job."

"How did you and Richard become friends?" Marian remembered the story Richard had told but as she had painfully learned these past months, his stories didn't always follow the truth.

"On the ship and I'm ashamed of my part in this."

"When you say 'this', do you mean more than just the captain?"

"Kind of. Richard caught me cheating and sort of." Nate paused.

"Sort of what?" Marian probed.

241

"Sort of blackmailed me into some things."

"What things, Nate." Marian's voice, soft and kind. Nate felt a big relief that he had found someone to confide in, someone who was on his side, that he could count on.

"I don't know if you want to hear this."

"I know it already. If you say it you'll feel relieved, I know. Just say it." Marian smiled at Nate using all of her will power to bring a smile to her lips.

"Richard had me point out the rich women to him. The captain told us you owned most of the ship, so I told Richard about you and you guys fell in love and got married. We were all happy and....."

Marian stopped breathing. Richard knew. He had known all along about her money. It was all a sham. The casual meeting by the ship's rail was a setup. And oh, how easily she had fallen under his spell. How cunning to make her believe he had found his true love.

"He asked you to point out wealthy women? How can you tell?"

"Can't always. A couple we knew from before and you."

"When you say 'we' who are you talking about?"

"Other crew members. We talk a lot."

"I see. So the crew knew he was looking for a rich woman?"

"Not everyone. Only a few of us." Nate seemed eager to reveal this to Marian. Perhaps thinking she would find it amusing.

"How many did you point out to him. How many did he consider?"

"I think either five or six." Nate actually smiled remembering .

"So, he met them by accident or how?" Marian thought again about her "accidental" meeting with Richard.

"Yes, one he spilled a drink on. It was really funny. Really looked like an accident and one he pretended he had met before and, but, when he met you, Mrs. Snider, he really fell in love. I could tell. He never left your side." Nate seemed happy to relay this information.

Marian kept her composure carefully enunciating each word so there would be no quivering in her voice. Stay in control she told herself. No tears.

"Why do you suppose Richard did not like Peter. Do you have any ideas?" she asked.

"I don't know for sure, but one time after he met you he was talking to one of the other rich women and he watched her walk away and I saw the captain watching Richard with a strange expression on his face. Maybe the captain knew Richard. Well, I don't want to say anymore. I really don't know."

"Of course not. You did right by telling me and it's really okay. Richard and I did fall in love so it worked out just fine. We understand each other and our needs." Marian, though wondered if, indeed, she had been his choice or if the other woman had turned him down.

"Only please don't mention I told you. He wouldn't like it and...." Nate trembled.

"Oh, I won't. Never would I do that. And don't worry any more about the captain. There were other things in his life that he hid. You didn't harm him in any way."

Nate was visibly relieved. "I'm going to Los Angeles. Vinnie is getting me a job out there. I need to get out of here." Nate explained to his, he thought, new-found friend. "I'll work with his cousin. I wish I could get out of the organization altogether, but I guess I can't."

"Tell me what you've been doing, Nate. What the organization is about," asked Marian, smiling all the while hoping to put Nate at ease.

It worked. Nate told her all about Jaki, the young children where Jaki worked and what they were forced to do, the man in the Georgia woods and the body they buried, Goldie, the man's dog and the pleading eyes Nate couldn't forget, the little boy who watched his father being killed and then proceeding to do what was expected, no, demanded of him. Nate, to coin a phrase, poured out his heart and soul.

Marian quietly listened. She knew that later her emotions would go haywire, but for now she put on a friendly, sympathetic face. She absorbed all that Nate told her and knew she would never forget any part of it.

Marian watched the waves lap the shore and reviewed her months of marriage with Richard. "He knew, he knew." These words kept pounding in her head. He calculated his every move and it had been so easy for him. The loving words, she believed so earnestly, were only lies. But she had been so eager to hear someone say them again, and Richard such a master of deceit. Oh, Nancy, you saw it right away and I let him drive a wedge between us. And David, Richard forced him to choose a visit with me or keep his wonderful Kira from Richard's racial slurs. Had any of Richard's words, such wonderful words, been true?

She placed her hand on her stomach. No, no lump protruding, although it seemed as if a hard knot kept growing and growing, trying to burst through her skin. And she touched her heart. No blood even though it felt as if a sharp knife had sliced it in half.

Marian had believed tears would explode from her eyes as soon as Nate left. But perhaps the pain went too deep. There were no tears. Sadness permeated her body. Sadness! Because of Richard so many lives had fallen apart. And she had gone into the relationship willingly, having no qualms about opening her saving and checking accounts, giving access to her credit cards. But most of all, opening her heart to him. Believing in him. Insisting on not having a pre-nuptial agreement. Why need to do something so worthless, she insisted. We'll be together forever he had said. Forever she said.

So now what? Where do they go from here? What does the future hold? Richard had manipulated her life so completely could she now live without him? She asked herself the question, yet she was afraid to know the answer. Did she still love him? Can love die that quickly? Less than an hour. Nate at the condo less than one hour and her world fell apart. She thought, too, of the good times and there had been many. The private jokes, little touches, happy days and nights that make up a marriage. Could she salvage it?

Marian pondered had anything actually changed? Couldn't things go on as before? So he had chosen her because of her money. Did that matter? Wouldn't she have shied away if she had known that he knew of her money? Of course she would have. She knew that. She had before when she had seen the look of greed in a man's eyes when he discovered who she was.

Richard had handled the situation perfectly. Couldn't she now handle it just as perfectly?

The ringing of the telephone interrupted her reminiscing. She picked it up on the fourth ring.

"Hello." Marian's mind still focusing on Richard and what the future may hold, answered in a flat monotone.

"Hello, yourself," Richard responded on the other end of the line.

244

"I was just thinking about you."

Richard instantly became apprehensive. She sounded different. Has she heard about Jaki or discovered his "work?" His constant worry.

"You sound unhappy. Something happen?" Richard hoped for a clue so he could determine how to react.

"Oh, no. Nate came by and left a package for you. From Vinnie. He wants you to call him. Vinnie I mean. Will you be home soon?"

Nate being alone with Marian was not good news, thought Richard. No telling what Nate may say, although he knew very well what he should not reveal. "Right away. I just talked to Vinnie about fifteen minutes ago, so I know about the package."

"I'd like to go to Rico's for dinner. That okay with you?" asked Marian.

What a relief. Richard immediately agreed. She sounded happier. Dinner out would take away the need for explanations of his activities. His apprehension abated. This is getting to be a chore. This marriage is taking too much work, wondering each day if someone would reveal some incriminating information about him and Marian would cut off his money. And he didn't exactly trust Jaki to keep their relationship a secret either. It would be just like Jaki to let something slip and blow his whole plan. He must make changes. Immediate changes. Tonight!

As Richard came in the door Marian handed him a tall glass of her fresh fruit concoction which was now becoming a daily ritual.

"Umm, this is good," said Richard, elated that Marian seemed her old self again. He took a long drink. He gave her his you-are-so-wonderful smile. It worked everytime. She made life easy for him. Too bad she isn't young and great looking like Jaki.

Marian smiled. "The mango gives it a special twang doesn't it?"

"Yeah, hon. Will you get my other wallet from the den? I think it's in my gray pant's pocket. Or maybe the brown ones. Or in the top drawer of the phone stand. Richard took her glass and set it on the counter.

"Sure." She hurried from the room.

Richard hurried from the room as well, picking up Marian's glass and taking it with him. Now, he told himself, this

245

may be the time for the big dose. It took him only a few seconds. He placed the glass in the same location just as if it had never been moved.

"I couldn't find your wallet," said Marian as she returned to the kitchen. She took a big swallow from her glass and then stirred it with a swizzle stick. Did Richard have enough time to have gone into the bedroom, she wondered. Yes, she determined, she had been in the den several minutes ostensibly to look for the wallet which she knew was only a ploy to get her out of the room. She had seen this happen too many times not to recognize his maneuver.

"I just remembered. I left it in the car, I hope." He smiled as if to say dumb me. "Did you make reservations?"

"Yes, for," she glanced at her watch. The watch with the fake diamonds which had replaced the brilliant ones so many months ago, "we have to leave now."

"Let's finish our drinks first. They're too delicious to leave."

"Mine has kiwi, your favorite. Do you want to trade?" Marian asked, toying with him since she knew he would never take a sip of her drink. Not since the trip to the bedroom anyway.

"No, I like this. Drink up," he said, urging Marian to hurry. When the glasses were empty, Richard scrubbed them with hot water and detergent, dried them with a clean towel he took from a drawer, and put them away. Marian observed this ritual, remembering an earlier time which mirrored this action. What does it matter she said, but only to herself.

As they left their building, Richard smiled and waved a greeting to a neighbor. "Taking my lovely wife out to dinner," he said and put his arm around Marian's shoulders.

"Lucky me," added Marian. And she thought that Richard could be so sweet. He must have had a very productive day. He opened the car door for her, an action he mostly ignored, unless someone happened to be observing. Nice when he does those little things, she mused. Was it for show? Oh, well, for whatever reason tonight he is acting the perfect gentleman and while not quite feeling treasured, she did feel content.

"I chose Rico's because we had our first dinner in Florida there. And it's one of your favorites. I like it as well." Marian gushed. "It's so private and they seem to do everything right."

"Close by, too," agreed Richard. He glanced at his watch. Real diamonds surrounding the face. No switching those gems. A Rolex. He has a Rolex for every day of the week, reflected Marian. Rico's offered valet parking and Marian noticed Richard tipped the attendant twenty dollars. And there was always another twenty when he brought the car back. Richard tipped very generously. The Sniders were welcome patrons.

"Ah, Mr. and Mrs. Snider, how nice to see you again. Your special booth is ready." Another twenty. The maitre d' knew if Cecily had been on duty in her long black dress and her red hair piled atop her head, the bill would have been a fifty. Mr. Snider tipped more freely to the ladies. All the employees laughed about that.

"My lovely wife and I are celebrating eight months of an extremely happy marriage." Richard beamed at Marian while thinking it seems like eight years. Not quite eight months, Marian murmured to herself. Another week to go, but who's counting anymore.

"Congratulations. You look lovely Mrs. Snider," the maitre d' remarked.

"Doesn't she though. Wearing one of my favorite dresses and I love the color. Melon isn't it called, dear?"

The shirtwaist dress with white buttons down the front and a belt of the same melon color was Marian's favorite as well. The color accented her bronzed skin and brought out the highlights of her light brown hair that now had gold streaks because of the chlorine in the pool water. She knew she looked as good as she could. She still turned heads when she made the effort and tonight she had made a supreme effort.

"Your waiter will be Alberto. Have a nice evening." Yes, Marian surmised it would be a nice evening. She would do her best. Richard, as well, anticipated a memorable evening. And if his thoughts were on the opposite side of a scale to Marian's, well then this evening and the results were long over- due. Both Marian and Richard agreed to that.

The maitre d' brought a bottle of champagne to the table and with great formality presented it to the Sniders.

"To a lovely couple for a great celebration with our com- pliments."

Marian and Richard smiled and vowed undying love and expressed appreciation for such thoughtfulness.

This whole atmosphere is terrific, Richard reflected to himself. Here we are a very much in love couple celebrating an anniversary. How shattered he would be when Marian suddenly collapsed of a heart attack. His frantic efforts to save her life would be observed by dozens. She would die in his arms while he called her name over and over, begging her to speak to him. He would become inconsolable. People would try to pry his arms from her body. Someone would call 911, but it would be too late.

"You look as if you just won the lottery," remarked Marian. "Penny for your thoughts."

Richard jumped as if awaking suddenly from a deep sleep when Marian spoke. Alas, it was a dream. But not to worry, it would soon be coming true. His long awaited dream of becoming a wealthy widower. He looked at his watch. In fifteen minutes she should feel a fierce headache beginning.

"Just very happy at this moment," answered Richard. "Did I tell you that you look terrific tonight as usual?" He added the last remark as Alberto approached the table.

Marian had been deep in thought as well, recalling experiences of the past eight months and pondering about the future. Her thoughts did not parallel Richard's, although she did exude joy. The evening was going so well. Just as she planned.

Alberto, as well as others, offered congratulations on the anniversary celebration making Richard and Marian even more pleased to have chosen Rico's. They smiled at each other. Marian reached across the table and took Richard's hand. "Did anyone ever tell you you have hair like Robert Redford's?"

"You're kidding. No, no one ever did. That's your very own observation." Richard lied, giving her his aren't-you-great smile.

"Ummm, well you do," she added.

"Thank you dear." Richard smiled. Marian smiled. Alberto smiled. What a happy couple, thought Alberto. And what a great tip he will leave.

"I watched the waves again today trying to decide which is the bigger wave," remarked Marian. "Remember when we first met and we did that?"

"The luckiest day of my life," remarked Richard.

"Oh, maybe not. I'm sure you've had some great days in your life."

"Not as terrific as that," insisted Richard. "Did you decide which is the bigger wave?"

"No. I got sidetracked by watching the windsurfers. They do such exciting things with those boards." She didn't mention that her thoughts had centered on other things.

Marian ordered linguine with chunks of lobster in alfredo sauce. Richard chose the seven-cheese lasagna and reminded himself that the meal probably would not be eaten. He had "doctored" Marian's juice with enough of his special potion to kill her in about twenty minutes. First the headache and then she would feel a sudden tightening around her heart. And that would be it. Away she would go. Very little pain——just one savage piercing jab to her heart. So violent that she couldn't cry out. Then total collapse. His goal! So close that it made him hyper. Richard glanced at his watch.

Marian looked at hers as well.

Alberto served the salad. Fresh garden greens, lush Ruskin tomatoes, Vadalia onions, herb-seasoned croutons, and then tantalized with Rico's honey-mustard dressing. Richard savored the salad. Marian picked at hers, her mind far away. Nancy, David, Carolyn, Kira, Jason, Kenneth. Her family, how she loved them and they loved her, but they had lives of their own to lead and this really is the end, she believed.

"If you aren't going to eat your salad, I'll take it." Richard reached across the table, exchanging his empty salad plate for Marian's nearly full one.

They were silent while Richard finished the salad. Alberto served a basket of hot cheese rolls. Richard poured Marian another glass of champagne and held the bottle up once again ostensibly to read the year. He had already done that, remembered Marian.

"A very good year," he remarked as he filled his own glass. "They must like us around here." Another glance at his watch. Her headache should be starting. He grew apprehensive, after all, this is a stressful situation. No wonder his head twanged. Sympathy pains? He chuckled. This is a perfect opportunity for his plan.

"Richard." Marian once again reached for his hand. "You've given me some very happy times."

"Oh, Marian, let's not get sentimental," his eyes were not warm and loving. There was no one around to see or hear, so no need to put on a show.

"No, not sentimental, only truthful. There are a few things you need to hear and, " she checked the time, "you have exactly twelve minutes to listen."

"What are you talking about?" He glanced around the room. Don't raise your voice, he cautioned himself. Not yet. Timing is everything.

"First of all, I never minded about the money. You've spent over eight million dollars from our joint accounts and never contributed a penny."

"You said the magic words, joint accounts," he sneered.

"Like I said, I didn't mind. It made you happy and there is a lot of money. Then the Jaki thing. I figured out that you turned on the mic that day and made sure I heard all your wonderful talk."

"Come on get real, Marian. You aren't making sense. As you recall your daughter arranged the whole thing and only to make trouble for me. You even agreed to that. You're dreaming a lot of things that simply aren't true."

"I didn't dream it, Richard. And I didn't dream the racial slurs you gave Kira, hurting her, so she and David stayed away. And you know what?"

"I have a feeling you will tell me."

"Kira is on the brink of a discovery that cures AIDS. She could earn more money from that than I ever had. But the wonderful thing, she is more interested in the fact that she will cure so many people who have suffered for years than the income. All she earns will go to the University Medical Research program. Millions. I know you could never understand that."

"She's stupid, that's all." Richard made no pretense of a happy husband. His goal at this point was to endure the final minutes of Marian's life. Take it easy. He chided himself on his blunt statement. He didn't want Marian to become angry and stomp out. No, she won't do that, he told himself. Too well bred to show anger in public.

"No. She isn't stupid. She is a very caring person. David is lucky to have her as his wife. But, to go on," she looked at the time again. She must hurry. "I overlooked your, what should I call it, your fascination with Carolyn."

"This too?" Richard curled his upper lip.

"I thought at first you were being kind. I had some qualms about the bathing suit, the look in your eyes and Carolyn trying to come on to you. But I made excuses for you. I didn't believe you would have harmed her. I still don't...."

"My, how generous."

"No, I call it self-preservation. Nancy would have been relentless. I would have as well. I love my granddaughter."

"How touching."

"Carolyn will get over you. This only served to give her status among her friends."

"We'll see. Are you done now?"

"Oh, no, the best is yet to come."

"I can hardly wait." Richard's sarcasm came spilling from his lips. "You are just full of venom tonight aren't you? And on our anniversary. For shame."

"You won't have to wait long." The watch again. "There are only a couple of more things. We will wait, though. Until Alberto removes our salad plates."

Marian smiled as Alberto approached the table. Richard smiled as well and reached across the table to pat Marian's hand. Alberto tried to guess will it be twenty, maybe forty dollars? He had eighty so far and the arrival of the dinner crowd was just beginning. A great night for tips, he judged.

"Ah, thank you. The salad was delicious." Richard gave his you-will-get-a-big-tip smile.

"Your dinners will be ready in just a few moments," responded Alberto.

Marian and Richard were silent as they watched Alberto walk away.

"Now let's hear the rest of it. You must have spent hours compiling these wonderful observations," snarled Richard.

"Ah, yes, I found out about the gem switching. She looked at her watch, touching the fake diamonds. "It bothered me at first and then, and you will find this amusing, I believed you must have had a poor childhood and couldn't abide such luxury. Isn't that a joke?"

"Should I laugh? Ha, ha."

"I did wonder how Jaki managed to show up in Florida and how Nate happened to meet her. But I believed your explanation. Maybe," Marian gazed at a spot above Richard's head, "I wanted to. And no pre-nup. That was handled ingeniously. I give you a great deal of credit for that."

"Your decision as well as mine. Don't forget that. You agreed with everything. You were so eager to get a man," remarked Richard.

Marian ignored his remark. "Do you remember that little bottle of liquid you keep in the toe of your brown shoes?"

Richard's face lost all color. How did she know about that? What does she know about that? Think man, think. Say something.

"The shoe brightener you mean?"

"No, the extremely potent poison. That one teaspoon kills in a half an hour or less."

"You're nuts."

"No, I'm not. I saw it in Chicago. Found it quite by accident. I put some things of yours away, to save you time." Marian found that spot above his head once again. "At any rate, I took it to my doctor who analyzed it and informed me that it was illegal to even have it in this country. He demanded that I destroy it. Instead, I put the bottle back in the shoe exactly as I found it." Marian saw Richard emit a long breath. He relaxed. All is okay he breathed a sigh of relief. She kept her gaze level on his face watching his every expression.

"So, your doctor apparently doesn't know everything. I used it to cover worn spots on my shoes."

"Sure you did. Here in Florida?"

"You are a snoop. My opinion of you just went down to zero."

"As I said. So many things I excused, but one I cannot and one I have to blame myself for as much as you."

"Are we leading up to a big surprise? I never dreamed anniversaries could be so exciting." Richard opened his eyes wide and waved his hands around.

"Maybe it will be a surprise to you. It certainly was to me." Marian continued. "When Nate was here today he told me about the rich woman search on the ship."

"That little stoolie. He's history." Richard couldn't hide his anger.

"That's what I have to blame myself for. I made it easy for you because I honestly fell in love with you. You played the part so well. You should have gone into the theater. You're a pro."

Richard smirked.

"The one thing I cannot forgive is what you did to Peter. To a very fine man who did you no harm, never did anyone harm in his whole life." Marian's eyes never left Richard's face. "Because of your lie, you took Peter's life and sentenced Sybil to a lifetime of loneliness and guilt. Always wondering if she contributed to his death, even when she was told it was all a lie, she will always wonder if she should have been stronger or if she could have foreseen Peter's action."

Marian stopped talking and took several deep breaths. She rubbed her head. Richard anticipated the heart attack coming close. His eyes brightened. Soon, he thought.

"I do not believe I can forgive myself for my part of the deception. I do not feel I could ever face Sybil again knowing what I do."

"Too bad. Poor Marian. Well, you won't have to face her." Richard felt hyper. So she put the bottle back. Her honesty will be the very thing that kills her. He must have been born under a lucky star or maybe there's a guardian angel hanging around. He could listen to her triads several minutes more. It won't be long now. He gazed at the ceiling.

"No, I won't have to." Marian looked into Richard's eyes several moments. Yes, she could see how easy it had been to manipulate her. He's very handsome and extremely charming when he wants to be and it's to his advantage. She had been vulnerable and ready for attention. Perhaps she had been his conquest.

"The thing I haven't told you yet," she raised her eyes once again to his, "is that while I did return the bottle to its original place, I put the contents into one of my empty prescription bottles. I'm not sure why I kept it. I never intended to use it. But, I guess since it didn't belong to me, I felt I had no right to throw it away. So you see, my husband of nearly eight months, you have been dropping only clear water in my drinks. It looked the same. Clear liquid, with only a slight almond taste. Hardly noticeable."

"But the headaches. You had headaches." Richard seemed dumbfounded by Marian's revelation.

"I faked those. Yes, clear liquid. Like this." She picked up her water glass and twirled the liquid around. She drank.

Richard could only stare at her. Is she mad? What has she done? What did she do with the poison? Did she put it in her drink? It sounds as if she is saying good-bye.

"You had such a great hiding place. I decided to use one of my shoes as well to keep, what turns out to be, my little secret, out of sight." Marian took another drink of water, seeming to stare at the clear liquid.

"Today I decided to kill you. As you know very well, if you have been looking at the time and you have, I watched you check your watch several times, and if you remembered our delicious fruit drink, you have less than five minutes to live. You already have the headache. You probably blamed it on the things I have been telling you." Marian fixed her eyes on his.

"You won't get away with it. An autopsy will show that you poisoned me. You, you...."

"Oh, my love. Do you think I will let anyone cut into your beautiful body? Or touch the hair that looks like Robert Redford's. Would I let that happen?" Marian's expression did not change.

"You. I'll kill you. I hate you." But Richard could not say anymore. His throat began to constrict. He tried to swallow, but it seemed he had no feeling in his mouth. He could not move it. He frantically looked around . He met no ones eyes except Marian's. She had asked for a private booth. Oh, what cunning, thought Richard. The bitch.

"And guess what?" remarked Marian. "It was such a great idea to forego the pre-nup. All you own goes to me. Think of it. Jaki's condo. The race horse. Oh, yes, I know about it. The other two condominiums you bought that you thought I knew nothing about. But, you know, your agent called and said the papers were ready to sign. All I had to ask was for which transaction. Of course he told me. I asked him to call back in the evening to tell you. He did. You may remember the phone call you answered in one word sentences."

Pure hatred glared from Richard's eyes. He tried to move from the booth. His legs were paralyzed. Marian only watched. She had read all about the effects of the poison and could predict to the moment the consequences. In fifteen seconds she would scream and the attendants would come scurrying to help.

Fifteen seconds.

Marian opened her little white leather bag. She removed a small prescription bottle and focused her eyes on the clear liquid. She poured it into the glass containing the champagne. Such an excellent year. She twirled the contents around and stirred it with her finger. She gazed into Richard's now sightless eyes.

Marian raised the glass to her lips and drank.

She waited. There was nothing more to do.

About the Author

Mary Syreen is a Pacific Northwest native and considers herself an island person. She lives on an island in Puget Sound, spends time on Kauai, and vacations on pretty Anna Maria Island in Florida.

She is currently working on a book of poetry especially for her daughter Marilyn.

Kevin Cox is an Air Traffic Control Chief Petty Officer in the United States Navy. He edits manuscripts and provides photo-ready copy for book production. He lives in San Diego with his wife and two daughters.